MY FAVORITE MISTAKE

**Available from Chelsea M. Cameron
and Harlequin HQN**

My Favorite Mistake

Coming soon

My Sweetest Escape

MY FAVORITE MISTAKE

CHELSEA M. CAMERON

Refreshed version of MY FAVORITE MISTAKE,
newly revised by the author

East Baton Rouge Parish Library
Baton Rouge, Louisiana
38786212

HARLEQUIN® HQN™

If you purchased this book without a cover you should be aware that this book is stolen property. It was reported as "unsold and destroyed" to the publisher, and neither the author nor the publisher has received any payment for this "stripped book."

Recycling programs for this product may not exist in your area.

ISBN-13: 978-0-373-77829-4

MY FAVORITE MISTAKE

Copyright © 2012 by Chelsea M. Cameron

This is the revised text of the work, which was first published by Chelsea M. Cameron in 2012.

Revised Text Copyright © 2013 by Chelsea M. Cameron

All rights reserved. Except for use in any review, the reproduction or utilization of this work in whole or in part in any form by any electronic, mechanical or other means, now known or hereafter invented, including xerography, photocopying and recording, or in any information storage or retrieval system, is forbidden without the written permission of the publisher, Harlequin HQN, 225 Duncan Mill Road, Don Mills, Ontario M3B 3K9, Canada.

This is a work of fiction. Names, characters, places and incidents are either the product of the author's imagination or are used fictitiously, and any resemblance to actual persons, living or dead, business establishments, events or locales is entirely coincidental.

This edition published by arrangement with Harlequin Books S.A.

For questions and comments about the quality of this book, please contact us at CustomerService@Harlequin.com.

® and TM are trademarks of Harlequin Enterprises Limited or its corporate affiliates. Trademarks indicated with ® are registered in the United States Patent and Trademark Office, the Canadian Trade Marks Office and in other countries.

Printed in U.S.A.

For anyone who has ever made a mistake in their life....
Maybe it wasn't a mistake after all.

CHAPTER 1

The first time I met Hunter Zaccadelli, I punched him in the face. Granted, he completely and totally deserved it. He also asked for it, in so many ways.

When our fourth roommate bailed on us three days before school, Darah, Renee and I assumed housing would take care of it and shove some poor unfortunate in with us. Probably some poor girl who had decided to switch colleges at the last minute to follow a boyfriend, or someone who had their apartment plans fall through. We weren't sure what to expect, but come move-in day, I did not expect who was waiting outside when I opened the door. I knew the upperclass housing was coed, but never in my wildest and craziest dreams did I think it would actually happen to us.

Instead of a desperate and frazzled girl, he showed up with a footlocker, a backpack and a guitar. It was so beyond cliché that I didn't say anything for the full three seconds it took for me to assess him. Dark hair buzzed so short his head was almost shaved, purposeful five o'clock shadow, piercing blue eyes and at least a foot on my five feet. And a cocky smile to top it all off. He might as well have had *Trouble* tattooed on his forehead. Speaking of ink, I could just make out some on his arm, but I couldn't see what it said. His thin T-shirt hugged his chest in a way that didn't leave much to the imagination. Maybe he'd borrowed it from his little brother.

"Are you Darah, Renee or Taylor? You look like a Taylor to me," he said, looking me up and down.

I wasn't at my best, considering I was dressed for moving heavy objects in a blue UMaine T-shirt and black soccer shorts, and I had my light brown hair in a haphazard bun against the back of my neck. His eyes raked up and down twice, and for some reason the way he assessed me made me blush and want to kick him in the balls at the same time.

"There must be a mistake," I said.

He adjusted his bag on his shoulder. "That's a creative name. What do you shorten it to? Missy?"

"That's not what I meant."

His grin somehow got wider. Either his dad was a dentist, or he was really into flossing because those teeth were pretty perfect. I noticed things like that, having gone through my own dental saga between three years of braces and night headgear. I still had to wear a retainer every night.

"Is that her?" Darah called from her room, where she was arranging her photo frames so they were exactly level. She was neurotic like that.

"I'm Hunter, by the way. Hunter Zaccadelli."

Of course his name was Hunter. The only Hunter I'd ever known had been a complete douche. Looked like this guy was going to carry on the tradition.

He pointed to his footlocker. "So, should I bring my stuff in or...?"

My brain wouldn't stop misfiring.

"Who's that?" Darah finally emerged. Our other roommate, Renee, was still unloading stuff from her car.

"New roommate, hey," he said.

"You're the new roommate?" Her eyebrows migrated so they were nearly hidden under her dark bangs. She gave him the same up and down as I did, but he didn't do the same to her. He was still looking at me.

"Yeah, my housing plans fell through at the last minute. My cousin was going to let me live at his place, but that didn't work out, so here I am. Do you mind if I come in now?"

"You can't live here," I said, crossing my arms.

"Why? This is a coed living facility, last time I checked." He flashed his grin again and shouldered his way into the room, completely ignoring me as his chest brushed mine, and I got a whiff of cologne. It wasn't that cheap crap that punches you in the nose. It was spicier, almost like cinnamon. I stood my ground, but he had height and weight on me. But I had surprise on my side.

"Well, it's better than sleeping on my cousin's couch," he said, plunking his bag on the floor and surveying the room. The suites were small, with a kitchen and tiny nook for a dining table on one side and a tiny living room for an apartment-size couch and a recliner on the other. The bedrooms were the worst, with two lofted beds crammed perpendicular to each other along the wall, the desks crammed underneath, and room for only two small closets.

"Can I see some identification?" Darah said, propping her hands on her hips. "How do we know you're not some random creep?"

"Do I look like some random creep?" He spread his arms out, and I finally saw what the tattoo on his left biceps was.

A number seven in curling intricate script. My eyes moved up to his face.

"How are we supposed to know?" Darah moved closer to him, using her stature. They were almost the same height.

"Look, all I know is that I submitted an application and they sent me an email with a room number and your names. Here, I printed it out. Do you treat all your guests like criminals?" He drew out a many-times-folded sheet of paper and handed it to Darah. She glanced at it, sighed and handed it to me.

"Why wouldn't they have notified us?" I said once I'd read it. There it was in black-and-white.

"Who knows?" Darah said, still eyeing him warily.

"Oh my God, I swear I'm never moving again," Renee said from the top of the stairs, her arms full of boxes and two bags dangling from her arms. "Who left their crap in the hallway?" She stepped over the footlocker and guitar case, giving them a look of disgust. "Has our new roommate showed up—oh, hello." Her voice changed from irritated and dry to sweet and sugary the second she saw Hunter. "I'm guessing that's your guitar in the hallway." She dropped her stuff and proceeded to pop her hip out and lean to one side. Oh, please.

"This," I said, pointing to Hunter, "is our new roommate, according to housing."

"No way." Renee's eyes got wide in her tiny face. Renee looked like a blond-haired, blue-eyed china doll you plucked off a shelf and put in a Victoria's Secret tank top. "Are you shitting me?"

"What a reception," Hunter said.

"Shut up," I said. He just smiled again. God, I wanted to smack that smile right off his face.

"I should probably get my junk out of the hall," he said,

going and picking up the footlocker as if it weighed nothing more than a shoebox. Show-off.

Hunter had to navigate boxes and random pillows and crap that littered the rooms, which he did with grace. He found a spot and set the footlocker down, looking at us.

"So, who am I sleeping with?" he said, leaning against the door to my bedroom.

The agreement had been that since Darah and Renee had already been roommates last year, and I was joining their little group, that the new girl would live with me. But that was so not happening now that the new girl wasn't a girl.

"Did you seriously just say that?" I said.

At the same time Darah said, "The only free bed is in Taylor's room."

"There is no way he's staying with me," I snapped, readjusting my arms so they covered my boobs better. He'd been staring at my chest since he'd made the sleeping-with comment. Not that I had much of one to speak of, but that didn't stop his eyes from traveling there.

"No, we're calling housing right now and straightening this out," I said, pulling out my cell phone.

"Tay, they're not open on Monday," Renee said.

"I don't care. There must be someone there. It's move-in day."

I grabbed the campus phone book that had been on the doormat when we'd gotten there that morning and thumbed through it until I found the number for housing.

"Aw, c'mon, Missy, you don't want to live with me?" Who did this guy think he was? I'd known him all of ten minutes and he'd already given me a nickname and propositioned me.

"Call me that one more time…" I didn't finish as I furiously typed in the number. Darah and Renee whispered to Hunter, but not quiet enough so I couldn't hear them.

"It's best to let her go when she gets like this," Renee hissed.

"I wouldn't mess with her," he said as I listened to another ring.

Finally, a message picked up, telling me what the hours were and giving me some extensions I could try. I punched in the first one. No answer, but a message machine picked up. I left a short message, explaining the situation in the most urgent of terms, and then called back the original number. I didn't stop until I'd left messages for all five of the contacts on the housing voice mail list. I slammed my phone down on the counter.

"Feel better?" Hunter said.

"No." I chucked the phone book on the couch. Darah and Renee were looking at me like they were worried I was going to explode. I was on the verge. "If you were a gentleman, you'd offer to sleep on the couch," I snapped.

"Well, Missy, you'll come to find out that I'm not a gentleman. I plan to take full advantage of this situation." My mouth dropped open in shock. No guy had ever talked to me that way.

"Is it hot in here? I think I'll open the window," Renee said, scurrying over to our one window, located at one end of the couch.

Darah looked at me and then Hunter and back. "Well, there's nothing we can do right now. Let's get his stuff in, and then maybe we can go down and see if anyone is at housing," she said. Darah was always the peacemaker.

"Sounds good to me," Hunter said, walking right into my bedroom as if he owned the place.

"I can't believe this is happening," I said, closing my eyes.

I heard "Back in Black" by AC/DC coming from my room. Hunter's ringtone.

"Hey, man. No, I just got here. Room 203. Yeah, that would be great…" He nudged the door shut, and I glanced at Renee and Darah.

"I didn't think we were going to have to do this so early, but I think we need a roommate meeting," I said. We'd agreed that we would have weekly roommate meetings to air our grievances. I was all for getting that shit out in the open so we didn't end up hating each other. I'd had a horrible roommate last year, and I didn't want to deal with that again.

I listened, but it sounded like Hunter was still on the phone. I could hear him rummaging and prayed he wouldn't break anything. Then I would kill him.

"I don't see what the big deal is," Renee said. "I mean, it would be the same if one of us had a boyfriend staying over. Paul stayed over all the time when Darah and I lived here last year."

"But that was because you were sleeping with him," I said.

"Maybe I'll sleep with Hunter," she shot back. Renee had broken up with Paul extremely recently and was on the prowl for a rebound. We all knew she and Paul were meant to be and that they would eventually realize that, but Renee was still in the anger stage.

"Are you uncomfortable with staying with him, Taylor? It's okay if you are," Darah said.

"I can't imagine why I would be uncomfortable about sharing an extremely small room with a guy I've known all of a half hour who keeps making creepy comments. Can't *imagine* why I'd have a problem with that."

"If you want, Renee and I can switch. I'll stay with him, and Renee can stay with you," Darah said.

"Why can't he stay with me?" Renee whined.

"Because you'll rape him in his sleep," I said.

"You can't rape the willing, Tay," she said, winking.

"You're disgusting."

"How about we draw straws?" Darah said.

"Do we even have straws?" Renee said. "How about we do numbers or something? Here," she said, grabbing a UMaine notepad that someone had left on the kitchen counter, along with a pen. "I'll write our names down and we'll put it in…" She grabbed the baseball cap I'd discarded earlier. "And Hunter will pick. There you go. Problem solved."

My door opened and Hunter emerged, another grin on his face.

"You weren't talking about me, were you?"

Like he didn't know. I rolled my eyes as Renee wrote each of our names on little bits of paper and tossed them in my hat. She put her hand over the top and shook it up.

"Pick one," she said, shoving the hat in his face.

"Okay," he said, sticking his hand in and pulling out a folded slip of paper. Renee slowly unfolded it. We all waited as she paused dramatically.

"Taylor," she said, turning it around so we could all read my name in black-and-white.

"Shit," I said.

CHAPTER 2

"What's with all the peacock stuff?"

It was an hour later, and I was just as stuck with Hunter as I was when he'd walked in the door. I'd even gone down to housing, which was right down the hill from our dorm, but no one was there. Too busy making sure the freshmen didn't collapse under the weight of their massive electronics when they carried them down the hall, no doubt.

I was doing my best to ignore Hunter, but he wouldn't shut up. Clearly, he was one of those guys who liked to chat.

"Don't you know peacock feathers are bad luck?" Out of the corner of my eye, his biceps with the seven tattoo flexed as he pulled a couple of shirts out of his footlocker.

Yes, I did know they were bad luck for most people. It was none of his business why I had them everywhere, including on my comforter, hung in frames on the wall and strung on a dream catcher my sister had given me. It was none of his goddamn business.

I wished Tawny was here. My sister would have known exactly what to say to Hunter to get him to leave. She couldn't get out of her work as a paralegal, and Mom couldn't get off work, either. I guess they figured since I was a sophomore, moving wasn't such a big deal. Still, I missed Tawny.

"You pissed at me, Missy?"

The nickname was the last straw. I whirled around and glared at him. "Look, I don't know you. You don't know me. As soon as humanly possible, I'm getting you out of here, got it? I'm not your baby. I'm not one of those girls you can smile at and crawl into bed with. Got it? Stay the fuck away from me."

Those blue eyes seared into me. He was the kind of guy who could see things that other people couldn't—things that I'd spent my entire life covering up and hiding from the masses. I'd only met a few people who could see past my carefully cultivated facade. I'd dropped most of them like a bad habit, with the exception of one. I'd have to squash this ASAP before he decided he might want to see what the world had done to piss me off so much.

"It's kinda hard to stay away from you when we're living in the same place," he said.

"I. Know. That," I said through gritted teeth.

He held up his hands. "Don't be mad at me. Fate picked your name."

"I don't believe in fate."

He laughed. "Me neither. I just believe in luck." He pointed to the seven on his arm. "Never can be too careful."

"I don't believe in luck, either."

"Clearly."

We were interrupted by a booming voice. Hunter stepped over the chaos that still covered the floor and poked his head out the door.

"Mase, man, what took you so long? You get lost?"

A male voice answered, "Nah, I just got held up. This your place?" Sure, just come on in everyone.

"No, I just walked into a random room and started putting my shit in it. Yes, this is my place."

He walked into the living room and I followed. Darah and Renee emerged from their room. I'd heard lots of banging and yelling, so they'd probably been hanging Darah's picture frames to her exacting specifications.

Standing in our doorway was a guy who looked like he could have been Hunter's brother. His hair was a little lighter, his build a little stockier and his eyes a little darker, but there was no mistaking the resemblance.

"And who are these lovely ladies?" the new guy said.

"This is Taylor, Darah and Renee, my roommates," Hunter answered.

"Dude, are you serious? How the hell do you get so lucky all the time?"

"Born under the right star," Hunter said. "This is my cousin, Mase."

"Nice to meet *you*, Mase," Renee said, diving forward to shake his hand. Mase took it and shook her hand, looking a little dazed. "I'm Renee."

"Nice to meet you, Renee. I'm guessing you must be Darah," he said, pointing to Darah, who waved. "And *you* must be Taylor. I've heard so much about you." How could he? I glared at Hunter, who made an innocent face. "That was so nice of you to take in my poor, unfortunate cousin in his time of need. I thought he was going to be able to crash on my couch, but one of my roommates gave it to another guy who was willing to pay to stay, and I was overruled. Sorry, man."

"It's okay," Hunter said.

For the first time since I'd met him, I could see something

other than a cocky douche. Someone real. But that person was gone behind a cocky face before I could study him closer.

"I can see that. Do you need any help?"

"I think I'm good," Hunter said.

Renee piped right up. "I could use some muscle. My bed's a little askew, and I can't seem to get it in the right spot. Want to give me a hand?" She twisted from side to side, as if she was showing him what could be his if he complied. Jesus, she was so obvious.

"Sure, no problem."

With that, we let another strange guy into our apartment. I turned my back and returned to my room, hoping no one else was going to pop in. Hunter followed me.

"Are you hungry? I was thinking of getting some Pat's. Their delivery guys are probably swamped, so I could go get it. My treat," he said as he grabbed some more shirts to put in his dresser.

Was he trying to be nice to me? Did he feel sorry for me? I stared at him, trying to figure him out.

"Do you like pepperoni?" His voice had lost that cocky edge. It was softer, and...No. He was the same. He was still trying to play me. I knew how those guys were. They were only nice until they got what they wanted, and if they didn't get what they wanted, they took it.

"I'm a vegetarian," I said and went to the bathroom, just so I could get away from him.

As I passed Darah and Renee's room, I heard Mase saying something that made them both laugh. Great. Just great. I shut the door of the tiny bathroom and braced myself on the sink. I was losing control. I looked at myself in the mirror. The horrible lighting didn't do much for my complexion, but it really didn't do much for anyone. I splashed some water on my face and then hopped up on the sink, setting my back against the mirror. In a matter of a few minutes, my sophomore year had turned completely upside down.

What was I going to do? This strange guy had just invaded my life. Not only my life, but my space. Our bedroom was smaller than a double-size dorm room. We'd be stepping over each other all the time. He'd see me when I woke up in the morning. He'd be the last voice I heard when I went to bed. I was going to see that damn tattoo and that smile all the time.

Hunter Zaccadelli would be the last thing I saw when I went to bed and the first thing I'd see when I woke up. That was not going to fly.

A knock at the door made me jump, and I banged the back of my head against the mirror.

"You okay in there?" It was Hunter.

"Jesus Christ, can't you leave me alone?" I got down off the sink and yanked the door open.

"I'll make you a deal, Missy."

"Why would I want to make a deal with you?"

He smirked as if he was waiting for me to say that.

"Just hear me out. If you can prove to me that you hate me, absolutely hate me, then I'll leave. Find a couch to crash on."

I snorted. "That should be easy. You can go pack your stuff now."

"You haven't heard the rest of the deal. If you can prove to me that you love me, absolutely love me, I'll leave." For the first time his face was serious.

"Are you fucking kidding me? I would never, ever love a guy like you." I would never, ever love anyone, but that was beside the point.

"Prove it. If you can prove either of those things by the end of the semester, I'll go."

"You're going to be out on your ass before then."

His smile was easy. He was playing with me.

"Maybe, maybe not. But you look like the kind of girl who likes a challenge."

The small bathroom space contracted around me, the walls pushing us closer. He took a step toward me, and then another. I backed up until my legs hit the toilet.

"Prove it to me. Show me you hate me." His voice was soft, and his eyes were demanding. My breathing became desperate, and my vision narrowed to those blue eyes. Something snapped, and my fight instinct took over.

Before he could move closer, I pulled back and slammed my fist into his jaw and my knee into his groin. He doubled over, clutching his face and his balls.

"I fucking hate you. Never corner me again, you son of a bitch." In his compromised position, I was able to shove around him and get the door open to find three stunned faces.

"What did you do to him?" Renee said.

"Nothing," I said, pushing past them and running down the hall, down the stairs and out of the building. My lungs heaved as if I'd been running for miles in Gym and had just been allowed to rest. I put my hands on my knees and gasped, feeling like my lungs would never be full again.

People gave me strange looks as they unloaded lampshades and pillows and under-bed boxes from their cars. I ignored them and started walking down the sidewalk toward the parking lot. I pulled out my phone and hit Tawny's number, hoping she was on her lunch break.

"Hey, Kid, how's the moving going?" Tawny's voice brought instant calm, as did her use of my nickname. Everyone in my family had always called me Kid.

"You would not believe the day I've had."

"Tell me," she said without hesitation.

I proceeded to give my version of the day's events, including punching Hunter. I had to hold the phone with my left hand because my right had started to swell from its encounter with Hunter's jaw. I was going to need some ice soon.

I was surprised no one chased after me, but Darah and Renee knew about my freak-outs. They knew to leave me alone and give me my space. It hadn't been the first time they'd seen me like that. I tried to keep most of it under control, but Hunter had pushed my buttons. No one ever cornered me in a tiny space and got away unscathed.

"Aw, Kid, why did you do that?"

"He cornered me, what was I supposed to do?" My hand was red and starting to turn a lovely purple shade.

"You could have told him to back off. That would have been the logical thing to do."

"You know I'm not a logical person."

"No shit." She sighed, and I could hear her munching on something. "Don't you think you should talk to someone again?" She'd asked me the same thing at least a thousand times.

"Because that worked so well before. No, thank you."

Tawny sighed again. I finally found my car, Sassy, a red Dodge Charger, in the lot and hit the unlock button. I sat in the driver's seat with the door open, chatting with Tawny about moving in and stupid stuff. Anything but Hunter.

I could talk to her for hours every day and still find something to say. We were six years apart, and we were as close as two people could be without being twins. Not that our personalities were similar, because they weren't. Tawny was prettier, smarter, more well liked. I was shorter, not as pretty and angry. I didn't try to be so angry, and I wasn't most of the time, but sometimes it just happened. Hunter had made it happen today.

"When are you coming up to see me?" I asked.

"Probably this weekend. Lunch date at Margaritas?" It was one of our favorite semi-chain Mexican restaurants.

"You're on. Hey, I completely forgot to bring that cute pair of pj pants and the top that goes with it. Can you stop by the house and get them for me?"

"I *guess* so. You gonna buy my lunch?"

"I *guess* so," I said.

"Hey, I have to go, but call me tonight. Call me before you punch someone again, okay? You're going to have to rein it in if you're going to live with this guy. Also, you should probably ice your hand."

"I'm not living with him."

"Yeah, babe, you kinda are. Unless you win that bet. How the hell are you going to get out of that one?"

"I have no fucking clue. I didn't technically agree to it."

"I think you punching and kicking him in the balls was sort of a handshake."

"Whatever. I'll call you later. Text me if you want."

"Bye, Kid."

"Bye, Tawn." I clicked my phone off and rested my head on my steering wheel. What the fuck was I going to do?

CHAPTER 3

I didn't go back inside until my hand hurt so much that I desperately needed ice. The living room was quiet when I snuck in. Most of the boxes were gone, and Darah was unpacking her pots and pans in the kitchen.

"Hey, are you okay? We were kinda worried about you. Hunter, Renee and Mase went to get pizza."

"I'm fine. Just need some ice," I said, holding up my hand, which was purpling all over my knuckles.

"Oh my God," she said, running to the freezer. Luckily, someone had left an ice pack in the freezer that maintenance had forgotten to clean out. She wrapped it in a dish towel she took out of one of the boxes and handed it to me.

"How's his face?" I kind of wished I'd messed it up, just a little.

"You got him pretty good. He's already getting a bruise." Score.

"Did his nuts recover?"

"I think he'll be able to have children someday," she said, studying me as if I was going to freak and do it again. She leaned on the counter, her organizing abandoned for now. "What happened? All he'd tell us is that he said something that pissed you off and that he deserved it."

"He said that?" I winced as the cold ice met my burning hand. I was surprised. I thought he'd blame everything on me and call me a psycho bitch. In the back of my mind I'd had a tiny ray of hope that my display of violence had freaked him out so much his stuff would be gone when I got back. No such luck.

"Yeah, he did."

"Huh."

Voices drifted down the hall. Familiar voices. I turned around, and they stopped when they saw me. Hunter had two pizza boxes, and Renee carried two bags with chips and soda. Mase had what probably was some beer, cleverly concealed in two layers of shopping bags.

"Hey," I said to all of them.

They entered cautiously, in a way that was almost funny. I was both the shortest and youngest person in the room, but they were wary of me.

"How's your hand?" Renee said, setting the bags down on the dining table.

"Fine," I said. She started examining it anyway, and I looked at Hunter. "How's your face? And your balls?" I cracked a smile, hoping it wasn't too crazy-looking.

Hunter grinned back at me.

"Both will recover, I think. You've got a hell of a hook, Missy," he said, touching his jaw. There was an impressive-looking bluish mark starting. Nice.

"I misjudged you, I think. Respect," Mase said, coming over and holding his hand up for a fist bump. I gave him one with my left hand, and he gave me a wink. Guess the cocky behavior was genetic.

"I got this one with all the veggies. Wasn't sure what you liked," Hunter said, holding out one of the pizza boxes toward me. Everyone held their breath as I took the box from Hunter. Hell, it was more delicious than an olive branch.

"Olives," I said. "I hate olives. Everything else is fair game."

"Shall we?" Renee said, now that the tension was broken.

"Sure," I said, cracking open the box.

The heavenly scent of Pat's pizza filled my nose. It had been the same recipe for however many years it had been open, serving hungry, hungover or stoned college students for decades. Somehow they had found the perfect ratio of cheese to sauce to thin crust to toppings. A perfect ratio, which was why they'd survived for so long in a town that had at least twelve pizza places per college student.

"Have you unpacked the plates yet?" Renee said to Darah.

Rummaging for plates, napkins and cups ensued, and somehow we all ended up on the living room floor with paper plates, paper towels and Solo cups with soda or beer. I wasn't a big beer fan, so I stuck with soda. Darah, Renee and Mase were all twenty-one and joked about me and Hunter being underage. Hunter was only a few months older than me at twenty, while I was the baby at nineteen.

Turned out Hunter was also a business major; what a surprise. The only other major I would have picked for him would have been broadcasting so he could be a sports reporter and watch as many games while getting paid to do it. Mase was the biggest surprise. His major was international relations. Apparently he wanted to go work overseas as a diplomat or something. His real name was Johnathan Mason III, which explained the nickname.

"What's your major?" Mase asked, winding some cheese around his finger.

"How about we guess?" Hunter said.

Didn't I just punch him in the face? Was he asking for it again? I gave him a look, but he just picked up another piece of pepperoni and chewed thoughtfully.

"Education? No, that can't be it. Not advertising. Boxing? Nursing? How about electrical engineering?"

I just rolled my eyes.

"Tell me what it is then." The cocky smile returned as if it had never left his face.

"Women's studies," I said, picking off another offensive olive and setting it on my plate.

"Huh," Hunter said.

"No smart comments? Not gonna ask me if I'm a lesbian?" Mase snorted. Renee rolled her eyes. I should really tone it down.

"Are you?" Hunter raised one eyebrow. There were always jokes about the Women's Studies Department being a bunch of men-hating lesbians. I'd chosen the major for a different reason, but he was never going to know about that.

"What if I was?" I said it slow.

Mase snorted his beer through his nose and choked. Darah banged him on the back. Yes, I still wanted Hunter gone, but I wanted to torture him a little as payback first.

"That would be one of the sexiest things you've said to me. Even if it isn't true." He leaned forward, a predatory look on his face. The room started to get hot, and I took a sip of my soda so I could stop looking at him.

"What is it with men and lesbians? I've never understood the attraction."

"Are you kidding? Two women together is superhot, unless they're butch. Then not so much," Mase said.

"But lesbians generally don't want men, so why would you be attracted to them?" Darah said.

"Doesn't matter to me. I'd be happy to watch," Mase said, bumping shoulders with Darah. She rolled her eyes.

"It's because the female body is beautiful. It's a work of art. All curves and softness. You double it, and you just have double the beauty." Hunter looked right at me as he said it.

"Double your pleasure, double your fun," Mase said and we all laughed.

"So, what are your plans for the rest of the night? Hooking up the Xbox?" Mase said to Hunter.

"You have an Xbox?" Renee said. She was a closet gamer and had been searching for a used one on the campus message board forever.

"Yeah, I have a Kinect, too."

"Please tell me you have Skyrim. Please, please," Renee said, clasping her hands. I blamed Paul for her gaming addiction.

Hunter proceeded to produce the device, and they spent the next hour hooking it up and playing Skyrim.

Mase said he had stuff to do, so he left, saying he'd be back again. Lovely.

I went to unpack the rest of my room and text Tawny.

The rest of the afternoon was spent getting everything into drawers and making my bed and figuring out where to fit everything, including the massive amount of books I'd brought. I wished I could have moved off campus, but I had a scholarship that was specifically for on-campus housing, so I was stuck. With Hunter, apparently. He stayed out with Renee and Darah, which was great. I kept shoving his stuff out of my way, irritated, but at the same time curious as to what else was in the footlocker. Maybe it was a body.

Darah knocked on the door and asked if I wanted to go to the grocery store with her to get some provisions. I was itching to get out of the tiny space, so I grabbed my keys and got some cash from everyone and made a list.

"You need any help?" Hunter said.

"Do I look like I do?"

"Not really, but I figured I'd be an ass if I didn't ask."

"You're an ass anyway."

He nodded and went back the game. He was probably ready for another punch soon.

I came back loaded down and found the apartment in chaos.

"Hey, we're going out to Blue Lagoon, you want to come?" Darah was sliding long silver earrings into her ears and had changed into skinny jeans and a glittery silver top.

"I can't. Not twenty-one," I said, pointing to myself.

Blue Lagoon was the current name of the club right off campus. It kept getting shut down due to underage kids getting in or too many bloody fights. Sometimes both. It had a new owner, but I didn't hold out that this one would last any longer than the previous.

"Crap, I forgot. Sorry."

A blow-dryer sounded in the bathroom. Oh, this must be serious if Renee was straightening her hair.

"Where's Hunter?" I hated saying his name out loud.

"Hunter? Don't know. His cousin came back, and they went off somewhere. He said he'd be back before we left." She winced as she shoved one of her earrings in.

"He's not twenty-one either."

"You know he probably has a fake ID." Yeah, he probably did. "Maybe we can sneak you in."

"No, it's fine. I'll just hang out here. Maybe I'll call Megan and see if she wants to come over."

Megan was a friend from my women's studies classes I'd gotten close with last year and the only other person I'd actually call a friend. She lived with her boyfriend in an off-campus apartment, but his friends were always crashing there so she was always desperate for girl time.

Just then the door opened and Hunter and Mase came in with two other guys trailing behind.

"Hey," he said, nodding to me. "This is Dev and Sean. Guys, this is Taylor and that's Darah."

"Hi," I said, waving.

Darah said hello.

Dev had lovely dark skin the color of earthenware, and dark hair and eyes. He was also crazy tall and thin as a rail. Sean was blocky and built like a wrestler, with short blond hair and brown eyes. They both gave me and Darah the once-over. I'd never been checked out so much in my life.

"So, you coming out with us, Missy?" He was staring at my boobs again.

I crossed my arms. "Some of us aren't into breaking the law."

"You are now," he said, holding something out to me. It was a fake ID, complete with a picture of a girl who could almost be me, and a birth date that wasn't mine, but was at least twenty-one.

"Where the hell did you get this?"

He shared a look with the guys. "I have my sources. Go, get ready. You're not wearing that."

"What's wrong with this?" I would never go out clubbing in my current attire, but I wanted to push his buttons.

"I'd want to screw you no matter what you're wearing, but you might want to spruce up a little so everyone will want you," he said.

"Fuck you," I said, chucking the ID in his face and going to my room. I heard the guys ribbing Hunter as I shut the door.

I rifled through my dresser, coming up with a pair of black leggings, a red tunic and a pair of black boots. I yanked my hair out of the bun and brushed it furiously before drawing on a quick stroke of eyeliner around my bluish-greenish eyes and slicking on some lip gloss. I walked into a cloud of my favorite grapefruit body spray, and I was ready.

"Better?" I said, leaning against the wall.

"Fuckable. Let's go."

Darah and Renee were already chatting with the other guys like they'd known each other forever.

I wasn't going to admit that I was scared of getting caught. I was nervous, sure, but it was more than that. Being in the club would mean I'd be pressed up against a ton of sweaty strangers. That was the part I didn't like. But there was no way I was going to let Hunter call me a pussy. So I shoved the fake ID in my pants pocket, grabbed some cash and followed everyone outside.

The night was balmy, the summer not having loosened its grip on Maine yet. We all walked in a large blob, no one really in front. Luckily, the club was within stumbling distance of campus.

"You won't have to buy any drinks tonight," Hunter said, turning around and walking backward while simultaneously leering at me.

"And why is that?"

He shook his head. "Do you seriously not see it? Mase, man. Would you screw Taylor?"

"Hell, yeah," Mase said, giving me a thumbs-up. "I mean, if you wanted to."

"Dev?"

"Yeah, sure." Sean also agreed that he'd do me.

"Is that all you think about? Sex?"

"What else is there to think about? Everyone thinks about it. We're programmed to think about it. Even you, Missy." He stopped walking, and I nearly bumped into him. He grabbed my arms to steady me.

"Let me go."

"It's on you, Missy. I'll be gone in five seconds. Just prove to me that you love me or hate me."

"Love and hate are completely different."

"Not really. They're the two sides of the same coin. One flip and you can be on the other side before you know it. I'll take either one from you."

"I hate you right now. What do I have to do to prove that to you?"

He touched the bruise on his face that I couldn't see in the dark. "I'm sure you'll figure something out." He turned around and jumped on Mase's back, nearly taking him down.

The boys were acting like they were already drunk, pushing and laughing and being too loud. I stuck close to Darah and Renee because they had previous club experience. I didn't.

The closer we got to the club, the more nervous I got. I could practically feel the music pounding through the pavement out front. The building was small and had no windows. Several people smoked around the edges, and a few girls wearing clothes that hardly qualified as clothes stumbled outside, laughing and clutching on to each other.

I rubbed my arms, even though I wasn't cold. We made a line, and Hunter put himself in front of me. The bouncer looked like he was probably on the football team and greeted Mase like they were long-lost friends, doing that weird one-armed hug, back-pat thing dudes do when they don't want to hug. He waved the other guys in and gave the girls IDs a cursory check.

"Jay, man, how are you? Long time no see. This is my new friend, Taylor."

"Another friend, Z? You have more friends than I have socks. Nice to meet you. Be careful," he said, laughing and waving us in before I could say, "Nice to meet you, too."

The club was dark, loud and hot, just like I'd thought it would be. The ceiling was low; there were too many tables and too many people. Lights flashed, nearly blinding me.

"Let me get you a drink," Hunter said in my ear.

He had to yell because the music was so loud. I couldn't see a DJ anywhere. My eyes searched and finally found Darah, Renee and the guys at a corner table. They all had drinks.

"Come on. Let me buy you a drink."

"Whatever," I said and went to stand next to Darah.

"You made it through," she said, cupping her hand over her mouth so I could hear her.

"Yeah, he didn't even look at it," I said, shrugging. No wonder this place was always getting busted.

"Lucky you," she yelled back, sipping on her drink.

Hunter came back moments later, shouldering his way through the crowd. He had this amazing way of walking, like he had all the time in the world.

"You look like a rum and Coke kind of girl," he said, handing me a glass. There was a lime wedge on top that I squeezed into the glass and then stirred it around before I took a sip. Hunter had a Coors Light. Typical.

I sipped my drink warily. I definitely didn't trust him.

"I didn't drug it, I swear. I wouldn't need drugs to get you into bed," he yelled in my ear. His hand brushed down my bare arm, and it took everything in me not to throw the drink in his face.

"Go ahead, throw it at me. You know you want to," he said.

Bodies swarmed on the dance floor, gyrating and bumping together. Some had better moves than others. Some were practically having sex.

Instead, I took a sip. The Coke fizzed on my tongue and the rum chased it, the taste dark, heady and warm. It was freaking delicious. How did Hunter know I would like it?

"Is it good? I had him use the spiced rum. I figured you'd like a little spice." *Oh, bite me.*

Darah and Renee sucked down their drinks and chatted with the guys, who were eyeing the dance floor. Mase caught Hunter's eye.

"Dude, these guys are amateurs. Want to show them how it's done?"

"I'm in. Dev?"

"It's on like Donkey Kong," Dev said, and they all headed toward the crowded floor.

"What are they up to?" Renee said.

"I have no idea," I said.

"You'll see," Sean said, leaning back in his chair.

Mase went toward the back, where I finally noticed the DJ. They had a word and the song flipped to "Party Rock Anthem" by LMFAO. Dear Christ, what were we in for?

Hunter and Dev somehow cleared a space, and as soon as

the song got going, they started dancing. Not just dancing, they were breaking. Mase joined in, and they *rocked* it.

The space around them got bigger, and people started clapping. Mase and Hunter had this routine worked out that was perfectly synchronized, complete with the worm and all these spins and moves that I'd only seen in music videos. Dev was doing the moonwalk in front of them and doing these smooth spins on his heels and toes.

For a white guy, Hunter could move. Like, *really* move. If I didn't loathe him with every fiber of my being, I'd say it was damn sexy. There was nothing like a guy who could dance, in my opinion.

He did a turn and stopped, looking right at me. I couldn't tell in the swirling lights, but I swore he winked at me. Douche bag.

The club was going nuts. Everyone was clapping and egging them on. Then Hunter grabbed Mase's foot and flipped him backward. The club exploded with cheering and hollering. They finished out the song and everyone applauded. They all high-fived and made their way back to our table, getting clapped on the back the whole way.

"That. Was. Amazing!" Renee said as the guys grabbed their drinks and gulped. They were all a little winded and had a light sheen of sweat on their skin.

"What did you think?" Hunter asked me.

"Meh," I said, shrugging one shoulder. "I've seen better." I sipped my drink, savoring the rich taste.

He just grinned at me and lifted his beer to his lips. "Sure you have, baby."

Now he was calling me baby? I ignored it and finished my drink.

"You want to dance?" Renee asked me. The alcohol had

started making its way through my system, making my cheeks heat and my head floaty.

"Sure, why not?" I said, even though I was apprehensive about throwing myself into the chaos of strangers' bodies.

Renee grabbed my hand in one of hers and Darah's in the other, and we headed to the crowded space. I had to tell myself a few times that I was okay, no one was out to get me and I was going to have a good time. The alcohol also helped. I wouldn't normally have waded into a mosh pit full of strangers, but when in Rome.

I didn't have many talents, but dancing was one of them. I let the music take me over and didn't care who was watching me.

There was one set of eyes I knew was on me. Hunter's. At one point, I turned, swiveling my hips and dipping down to the floor and slowly coming back up. It might have been my imagination that he swallowed and his eyes widened a little. I'd classify the brief look that crossed his face as stunned. *Take that, asshole.* I smiled and grabbed Darah's arm, twirling her around and then giving her a hip bump. We danced for three more songs before we got too sweaty and had to get some air. I was relieved to get out of the crush of bodies. I'd had a few moments where the panic threatened to attack me, but I'd managed to slam the door in its face and keep dancing.

The guys followed us outside, probably to protect us from drunken gropers. I'd read last year there were several episodes of unwanted sexual touching reported in the campus newspaper. Hunter put his hand on my back, but I let him because it was his hand or a strange guy's, and I'd take the hand I knew over the hand I didn't. Not that I knew Hunter. Christ, I'd only met him that morning.

Outside we stood in a cloud of smoke, but the air felt nice on my heated skin.

"I've seen better," Hunter said in my ear. His warm breath tickled my neck, and I moved my hair to hide my shiver.

My phone vibrated in my pocket, and I pulled it out. Mom. She always texted me at the oddest hours.

How are you, Kid? Haven't talked today :(

Good. All moved in. Drama city. Out with friends. TTYL?

Sounds good. Luv u, Kid.

Mwah.

"Was that your boyfriend? He worried about you being out late with strange men?" Hunter said, trying to read the messages over my shoulder

"Nope." I wasn't going to satisfy his curiosity. I checked my phone. It was nearly midnight, and I was toasted from getting up early and driving from my mom's house in Waterville all the way to Orono and unpacking my stuff. And dealing with jerks.

"You guys ready to go? I have to be up early for macro tomorrow," Darah said, miming shooting herself in the head. She was an accounting major, but hated economics with the burning passion of a thousand suns.

"You with Wesley in DPC 100?" Mase said.

"Yeah."

"Me, too. Guess I'll see you there," he said, stretching his arms over his head. It might have been my imagination, but I thought I saw her smile at the prospect of seeing him again so soon.

We all walked back to Mase's car and said good-night to Sean and Dev. Mase said an extra good-night to Darah. Oh, dear, there was definitely something there.

When we got back into the apartment I realized two things. One, I really needed a shower, and two, Hunter and I were going to be sleeping in the same room.

Darah and Renee said good-night and shuffled off to their room.

"Well, here we are," Hunter said.

"I'm going to take a shower," I said and prepared for the comment I knew was coming.

"You know what they say, conserve water and shower with a friend."

I walked past him to gather my pj's, not answering. I made sure to lock the door before I stripped and got into the shower. I wouldn't put it past him to try to get me naked. Guys like that were all the same. They took what they wanted and left you with nothing.

CHAPTER 4

When I came back from the shower, Hunter was in bed, shirtless and in just boxers, sitting with his back against the wall, guitar in his lap. It was a scene most girls would have swooned over. Between the dancing skills and the guitar, he could rack up plenty of attractiveness points. He plucked a few strings before realizing I was in the room. For a split second, I saw a dreamy look on his face. He quickly hid it behind a smirk.

"You're all wet."

I didn't miss the double entendre. I tossed my balled-up clothes in the hamper and twisted my hair in my towel to squeeze some of the water out.

"Not the kind of nightwear I was picturing, but it'll do."

I looked down at my oversize T-shirt and shorts. I'd thought twice about wearing a tank top and boy shorts, which normally I would have, given the temperature. I'd left my bra on so my nipples wouldn't show through the thin jersey material.

"Are you one of those douches with a guitar, or can you really play?" I tried to keep my eyes on the guitar and not on his bare chest. There was another tattoo on his left pectoral. A four-leaf clover.

"I only play if you're a paying customer. Although I'd take a trade instead of money."

Why had I even asked? I'd been trying to break the ice, but he didn't seem to want to. I went to my dresser and found a quarter that I chucked at him.

"There. Now play, music boy." I sat down on my bed and faced him.

"What do you want?"

I thought about it. I wanted to pick a song there was no way he would know. I threw out anything hard rockish or folksy. He seemed like one of those guys who would be into Bob Dylan.

"'C'est la Mort' by The Civil Wars."

He gave me a look like that wasn't what he was expecting.

"What? Don't know it? Not hip enough for you?" He looked away from me and down at the guitar. He plucked a few notes. I waited.

Then the song emerged from his fingers, slow and haunting. I sat back against my pillows, getting lost in the music. I hated to admit it; he played very well. He hadn't had just a few lessons last week. He'd been playing for years. He finished the song with a flourish and looked up at me. The dreamy look was there again, and it took longer for him to put it away.

"Singing is extra," he said.

"You can dance, you can play the guitar. Jesus, Hunter, what can't you do?"

"I'm very good at a lot of things. If you want to come over here, I can show you a few more," he said, laying the guitar back in the case. My throat suddenly went dry, and I had to swallow. His comments had been different when we were fully clothed and with a group of people. In this dark, quiet room they took on a heavier meaning, or at least they did to me. I was making too much of it.

I sat up. There was something about lying down that made me feel more vulnerable.

"I'm not sorry for punching you," I said for no reason in particular. My hand was still swollen and sore, and I hoped his face hurt for a long time.

"I know you're not. I'm not sorry you did either. Most girls bore me. You, Taylor, do not bore me."

"Thank God, I can die a happy woman."

"I'm not going to make a move on you, if that's what you're thinking."

I had been, but I didn't want him to know that.

"I never screw girls I like."

"That doesn't make any sense." Wait, he liked me?

"Of course it does. All relationships end eventually, right? So why not end it before it begins and save yourself the trouble?"

"That's pretty fucked up thinking, Hunter. What did your parents do to you?" In my experience, guys like Hunter usually had deep-rooted Mommy issues. It was why they could never have close relationships with women.

"Wouldn't you like to know?"

I got up and put my phone in the charger, mostly so I could stop making eye contact with him. Normally, my nightly routine would involve putting in my retainer, slathering my face with moisturizer and putting on an eye mask, but there was no way in hell I was letting Hunter see any of that.

It was too intimate, too personal. Maybe tomorrow housing would be open to finding him another place. I would simply tell them that I was uncomfortable living with Hunter. I wanted to believe that I would have the balls to tell him to get out. It would have been so much easier if we could have taken care of this hours ago. Also if he hadn't played that stupid song. Why had I picked that? I should have picked something stupid like "I Am the Walrus."

He clicked his lamp off, and we were left in almost total darkness. The only light came from the small lamp on my dresser that I hadn't turned off yet.

"Just to let you know, I talk in my sleep." He shifted on his bed and chucked something on the floor. It could only be one thing. "Also, I sleep naked."

I made a sound of disgust. I was definitely sleeping with my bra on, even though I'd have uncomfortable marks in the morning. I climbed into bed and pulled the comforter up. I was the one who felt naked. I swore I could hear his sheets rubbing against his skin. Damn, I should have gotten some earplugs.

I wasn't going to sleep at all.

I also talked in my sleep, but I wasn't going to tell him that.

"Well, good night. Feel free to dream about me naked and scream all you want. I'll sleep right through it."

I wished I had a pillow, or perhaps something heavier, to chuck at him. I quietly grabbed my retainer and put it in, hiding the case under my mattress. I wanted to pretend like I didn't give a shit what he thought of me, but honestly, I did.

It felt rude not saying good-night, so I did. I got a mumble in response. I lay on my back and looked at the ceiling. Even with the memory foam mattress pad the dorm bed was as comfortable as a sack of hay.

Hunter was breathing quietly, but his disturbance in the room was unmistakable. I didn't know why, but guys breathed differently than girls. Deeper somehow. I heard every single time he shifted or moved or twitched at all. I knew the exact moment he was asleep when his breathing became slow and he stopped moving so much. I tried closing my eyes, but it didn't work.

I grabbed my MP3 player and put it on Shuffle. I had tons of fast songs on there, so I had to keep skipping things. Usually, alcohol made me tired, but the soda had been a bad idea. It was too late to take my sleep medication, so I was stuck. I only had two classes the next day, and they didn't start until eleven. I hoped Darah and Renee weren't too loud in the morning. I hoped Hunter wouldn't be too loud in the morning.

I hit repeat when "C'est la Mort" came on, and I finally faded off.

"Taylor, Taylor!"

A hand grabbed my shoulder, shaking it.

"What the fuck?" I said, flailing against it, trying to get it to let me go. "Don't touch me!" I whipped my arms around and made contact with something warm and fleshy. A chest.

"Jesus Christ, stop it!"

I finally opened my eyes and assessed the situation. I was in bed, and there was a shirtless boy holding my arm. I froze, and he let go of me.

"What are you doing?" I snapped at him, but it came out slurred because of the retainer. I spit it out in my hand.

"You were screaming in your sleep and freaking out. It woke me up." *Shit.* Usually when I took my sleep medication, I didn't have the night terrors, but I hadn't been able to tonight. Great, just great.

"I'm sorry. Go back to bed. I'm fine."

"Do you, uh, need anything?"

He stood there, as if he didn't know what to say. My eyes

drifted down his chest and saw that he had a towel wrapped around his waist. At least it covered everything it needed to cover.

"No, I'm fine. Good night." I flipped over, hoping that would be the end of it. He sighed, and I heard him crawl back into bed.

"Good night," he said and flipped over as well.

CHAPTER 5

Hunter was gone the next morning when I woke up at nine. So was Renee, but Darah was at the dining table eating a bowl of cereal.

"How was your night with the boy?"

"Fantastic," I said, stretching my arms over my head and listening to my spine pop. I shuffled to the coffeepot and found that there was just enough for one more cup. I had no idea how long it had been sitting there, but I didn't care. Coffee only got really nasty if it was past four hours. I poured myself a cup and sat down with Darah. She looked about as bad as I felt.

"You're okay with him here, really?" she said.

"No, I'm really not." I sipped the sweet elixir, wrapping my hand around my cup. "But what can I do?" I still hadn't told them about the bet, and Hunter hadn't either. I wasn't sure if I was going to go there. If housing could settle things, then they never had to know. I just hoped if housing found him another place, he would go quietly. I really had no idea what kind of a fight he would put up.

"Not much. Just give housing hell. I don't know what they were thinking." She shook her head.

"And they didn't even notify us! It's just crazy. This damn school." I got up and slammed two pieces of bread into the toaster. There was something else that was bothering me, but I wasn't going to tell Darah about it. Unless...maybe she had heard me last night. I glanced over my shoulder to find her watching me. Yup, she'd heard. "You probably heard me last night, didn't you?"

"The walls are like paper, so yeah. I didn't want to bring it up unless you were uncomfortable. Do you want to talk about it?"

"Not really. I forgot to take my meds. Sorry if I kept you up."

"It's no big deal—we were just worried about you. It's been a while since you had one."

"Renee woke up, too?"

Darah nodded. Great, just great.

"I'm really sorry." It had only been twenty-four hours and I was already a bad roommate.

"Don't worry about it. Did Hunter wake up?"

"Yeah, he actually woke me up. He sleeps naked, by the way."

She snorted milk through her nose and had a coughing fit before she could answer.

"You're kidding me," she said, her eyes the size of dinner plates.

"I didn't see Hunter Junior, if that's what you're thinking. He didn't take his shorts off until he was under the covers. What a gentleman, right?"

"Listen, if he makes you uncomfortable, we can switch

rooms. Although, we might have to pull Renee off him in the middle of the night."

"He'd probably screw her. He seems like that kind of guy." My toast popped up, and I spread some butter and drizzled some honey on it.

"Hey, I've gotta go to macro, but I'll see you later, okay? Let me know if you hear from housing."

"Will do," I said, saluting her and munching on my toast.

She grabbed her bag, and, for the first time since moving in, I had the place to myself. I should spend that time on skimming the first chapter in my textbook, but I wasn't that ambitious. Instead I plunked down on the sofa with a crappy reality show marathon and dazed out. I was just about to start getting ready when the door opened.

"Hey," Hunter said, setting his messenger bag by the door. "You recovered from last night?"

"Yeah, I'm fine."

"Sure you are."

I was not going to put up with him today so I went to get dressed and brush my teeth. He grabbed the remote and changed the channel. Of course.

"Don't you have class?" I asked.

"I don't have another until two-fifteen. You?" He didn't take his eyes from the television.

"I have Feminism in Cinema at eleven-fifteen."

"Sounds thrilling," he said, finally settling on the History Channel. Looked like a marathon about Hitler.

"See you later," I said and went to get ready. He didn't even say goodbye when I walked out the door a few minutes later. I'd never met someone who ran so hot and cold. He was worse than Maine weather, which changed with alarming frequency.

My walk down to class was relatively quiet. Our building

was on the outer edge of campus, like a spoke on a wheel. UMaine centered on a grassy mall that had the library at one end and the memorial gym at the other. Most of the important buildings were near the mall, and the less important were behind them. The English building where I had my class was one of the less important and happened to be just down the hill from my dorm.

The class was relatively small, so it was easy to find Megan's flaming red hair. Women's Studies was a small department, so everyone pretty much knew everyone else and took the same classes.

"Hey," I said, sliding into the seat next to her and pulling the retractable desk up with a horrible grinding noise.

"We meet again," she said. "How was move-in?"

"You wouldn't believe me if I told you." We had a few minutes before class started, so I gave her the quick and very dirty version of the previous day.

"You are kidding," she said, sitting back.

"I wish I were."

"I didn't think housing could *do* that."

"I know, right? No notice, nothing."

We were interrupted by the arrival of our teacher, Jennie, who I'd had a previous class with. She was young, only about twenty-eight, and was so obsessed with movies, she made even the most boring topic interesting. She also wouldn't let us call her by her last name.

Class started with the usual handing out of syllabi and going over rules and policies. I tuned out most of it and let my mind wander. Of course it wandered to my most recent irritation. Hunter Zaccadelli.

There was something seriously wrong with Hunter. One minute he was talking about going to bed with me, the next he said he didn't want to have sex with me because he liked me and then he was colder than a Maine winter. Maybe that was something I could bring up with housing. I'd had to turn my phone off during class, but couldn't wait to check it and see if I had a message. I also planned on stopping there after lunch, before my last class.

We finished early, and Megan and I decided to get lunch at the Union. She went for a cheeseburger from the grill, and I got a tomato wrap filled with hummus and veggies. Somehow we found two empty seats and set everything down.

"So you need to give me some more details on this guy."

"I don't really know much, actually. Except he's a douche and he's sleeping in my room."

She covered her burger with ketchup and smashed the bun. "Is he cute?"

I had to think about my answer. There was no denying that Hunter was gorgeous. He had everything the typical female would want. Good body, perfect teeth, great hair and everything (that I could see) in proportion. Given a personality transplant, I would have been seriously crushing on him. He also had this fabulous jawline. Not that I'd noticed.

"Oh, he's a hottie all right, but it's his personality that could use some help."

"Still, better a good-looking jerk than an ugly nice guy."

"What category is Jake in?"

"He's a little bit of both," she said, munching a fry. "I like to think he combines the right amount of hotness and niceness."

Megan's boyfriend was a nice guy. It was just his friends that needed some work. They weren't jerks; they were just gross. Megan often walked into her bathroom to find one of them had forgotten to flush, another had left hair and floss on the sink and another had left hair in the shower drain. She only stayed for love, she said. I would have been out of there faster than you could say Clorox.

"Well, Hunter is all asshat."

"But a good-looking one. You can overlook a lot if he's hot."

"Trust me—it's not going to happen."

I finished my wrap, and when we went to chuck our trays I said goodbye to Megan, who had calculus.

I had some time to kill before I had my next class and didn't want to walk all the way up the hill to our apartment, so I went to one of the computers in the Union and checked the jobs board. Last year I'd worked at one of the dining commons. It hadn't been horrible, and I'd made some good friends, but I'd had more than enough of chopping salads and making endless grilled cheese sandwiches. I wanted something new that might offer some intellectual stimulation. The library was my first choice.

I scrolled through the listings for student workers. Most of them were in the dining commons, but there was one that caught my eye for a library aide in the government publications department, whatever that was.

I clicked on the link and filled out the application, trying to make myself sound as academic and smart as possible. I clicked Send and hoped I'd get a return email for an interview. I scrolled through the rest of the jobs, but nothing jumped out at me. I quickly checked my email for anything from housing. I had nothing on my phone. I'd checked at least twelve times.

I decided that housing hadn't gotten back to me, so I was going to them. Their office was on the third floor of the Union, so I took the stairs, composing myself before I walked into the office. The receptionist looked up when I walked in. There were two other students, a guy and a girl, waiting already. They both looked surly and unhappy, and the girl had clearly been crying.

"Can I help you?" the woman said, looking up from her computer.

"Yeah, I'm having a housing issue and I really need to talk to someone right away. I called and left messages, but you weren't open yesterday."

"Okay, let me check. You hold tight."

She got to her feet and shuffled off to one of the offices, knocking softly on the door before going in. She closed the door so I couldn't hear what she said. *Damn.* I grabbed a hard candy from the jar and unwrapped it, earning glares from the other two people waiting. A few seconds later the secretary came back. I tried to judge from her face whether it was good or bad news.

"I've talked with Marissa, the head of housing, and she's aware of your situation. If you want to sit and wait, she'll be with you as soon as she can. These people were ahead of you, and it's first come, first served," she said with a tight smile.

"Do you know how long it's going to be? I have class soon."

"Would you like to set up an appointment?"

"When is the soonest you'd be able to do it?"

"Let me check," she said with a barely audible sigh. I wasn't trying to be difficult. "This is a very busy week. Hmm…" She scrolled through her computer, her eyes looking for an empty space. "The earliest we can do it is Friday afternoon at two."

"Friday?" *Seriously?* "Isn't there anyone else I can talk to?"

"Let me check Roger's schedule. He's the assistant director." She scrolled again, and I crossed my fingers. Not that I believed in luck. "The earliest he can do is next Monday at four."

Great, just great. I tried not to scream in frustration.

"Okay, I'll take Friday. What am I supposed to do before then?"

"You should contact your resident director and he can help you work through any issues you may have, okay?"

She wrote out my date on a card and took my name, typing it slowly into the computer. Yeah, our resident director. I'd seen the guy all of once when I'd moved in. He'd introduced himself and given some speech about how his door was always open. Yeah, I was going to go to some complete stranger with my problems. Not likely.

I thanked the woman and tried not to stomp out of the office. My phone buzzed, and I looked down to find a text from "Sexy Roommate." I opened it, wondering what the hell.

Sitting in class, thinking about you. You thinking about me?

I had an idea who it was. More than an idea. I just didn't know when he'd gotten hold of my phone to put his number in.

Who is this?

The guy u slept with last night. One of them at least.

Bite me.

Saw u walking across campus today.

U stalking me now?

I was minding my own business and u crossed MY path. Who's stalking who now?

This is harassment. I'm going to report you.

Do whatever you want, Missy. You still haven't given me an answer on our bet.

Me kicking u in the nuts wasn't enough of an answer?

In most societies, a handshake usually symbolizes the making of a contract.

Whatever. I'm shutting my phone off.

I waited for a reply, but it didn't come. I shook my head and turned the phone off. I still had some time to kill before class, but nothing better to do so I went to get a good seat. Somehow I'd managed to weasel my way into Human Sexuality. It was the most popular class on campus, and most people couldn't get in until their senior year. Maybe I'd just gotten lucky. Ha-ha.

The class was located in what people called DPC 100. The DPC stood for David P. Corbett Hall. It was the largest classroom on campus and could hold up to 350 people. It was this crazy dome shape, with the seats stacked like a 3-D movie theater. It was always a thousand degrees in there from all the people, and you never knew if you were going to trip on a half-empty Starbucks cup.

Despite being nearly a half hour early, there were already at least a hundred people in the room. I walked down the sloped side, trying not to trip and also trying to find a seat that wasn't close to anyone else. I liked my personal space, thank you very much.

Most of the seats on the outer edges were taken, but I found one near the front that had a buffer. The desk next to me was broken, so I was pretty sure no one else was going to sit there. I pulled out my e-reader so I could finish the story that had made me late driving up yesterday. It was the latest in a paranormal series I'd gotten addicted to this summer. I was fully engrossed when someone tapped me on the shoulder.

"Is this seat taken?"

I had to blink a few times before my brain registered that Hunter was standing next to me and he was asking if he could sit next to me.

"What are you doing here?"

"Learning about human sexuality. Isn't that what you're here for?"

I glanced down and then back up at him. Maybe he was a mirage. He smirked, clearly delighted.

Nope.

"You have got to be kidding me."

"Granted, I don't have much to learn, but I figured I could use my knowledge and get an easy A." He slid by me and took the seat with the broken desk, setting his bag down by my feet.

"You are not in this class."

"I am. You want to see my schedule? I'll prove it."

"Whatever," I said, going back to my book and turning so that my back was as much toward him as I could make it in the small space.

"You know, if you ever want to practice any of the techniques we're going to discuss, I'd be happy to be your study partner," he said in a low voice. For some reason, his quiet voice made the proposition even more seductive. Not that I fell for it.

"Screw you," I said before I realized I'd walked right into that one.

"I'd like to."

"I thought you didn't screw people you like." I looked at

him out of the corner of my eye. He stretched his arms over his head, his shirt riding up and showing just the tiniest bit of lean stomach. I snapped my eyes away quickly. It wasn't like I hadn't seen it the night before.

"For you, Missy, I'd make an exception."

I glanced at my phone, but we still had at least fifteen more minutes until class started. The room was nearly full, and the chatter echoed in the acoustically tuned space.

"I was thinking about making dinner tonight. You in?"

What was wrong with him? Seriously, he had to be bipolar. Or he just really, really liked messing with me. Or maybe it was a little of both. I shouldn't respond.

"What are you making?"

"You tell me what you like and I'll make it." His face was set in a smile, but it was different than his cocky smirk. This was more genuine. The smile you'd give a friend if you hadn't seen them in a while. Open, honest.

"You'd really make what I wanted?"

"Why not?"

There had to be a catch.

"You made me pay for a song, what do I have to do for dinner?"

"Sit next to me while we eat."

"That's it?" That couldn't be it.

"That's it," he said, opening his hands.

I narrowed my eyes, trying to root out the catch I knew was there. He just looked at me innocently, which made me want to laugh. I was interrupted by a teaching assistant shoving a stack of syllabi in my hands and telling me to pass them down. I took one and handed the stack to Hunter. Our hands brushed briefly, and I pulled away as fast as I could, grabbing my notebook and writing the date neatly in the corner.

to tell them to shut up but didn't want to start anything. The room buzzed with the hum of chatter the entire hour and a half. Granted, it would have been impossible to keep that many college students quiet for that long.

Hunter was fidgety the entire class. Whether it was pen tapping or knee jiggling or stretching or twitching. He was like a five-year-old high on cotton candy. I hadn't noticed him twitching so much the day before, but maybe I just hadn't been paying attention. But I thought I would have seen him vibrating like he'd had twelve cups of coffee. It was very distracting.

"Are you on speed?" I whispered as Marjorie was going through the grading scale for our homework assignments.

"Huh?"

"Are you on speed? Your knee is going a mile a minute."

"I'm fine," he said, leaning over and putting his ankle on his jiggling knee.

He started pen tapping again, and I reached out so he'd stop. My hand connected with his. It was the first time I'd really touched him. My fingers closed over his fist and the tapping stopped. I removed my hand without looking at him.

"Thank you," I said.

He didn't respond, but his hand stayed still the rest of the class. When it was time to leave, I was hoping he'd just get up and go, but that didn't happen, of course. He packed up his things slowly, as if he was waiting for me. I took my sweet time.

"Do you have another class, or is this it for you?"

"I'm done for the day," I said, standing up.

He followed suit and walked behind me as we left the room. I hated the fact that he was behind me because he had a full

MY FAVORITE MISTAKE

Our teacher was a woman with gray hair who wore a purple gauzy top and matching purple pants. She remi[nded] me of someone who had been a hippie and had never [for]gotten over it. There were a lot of those at UMaine.

She called us to order as the TAs collected the last o[f] extra syllabi. There were four TAs for such a large class.

Marjorie, she introduced herself as, got her PowerPoin[t] and running, and took us through her extensive lesson p[lan] including her personal history and educational credentials, papers she'd published and the degrees she held. For some[one] who looked airy-fairy, she certainly had a lot of degrees [and] accolades. I'd heard nothing but amazing things from ot[her] people who had taken the class, and I had to admit the sub[ject] matter interested me. How could it not? Sex was interesti[ng.]

"I'll bet you already cracked the textbook open and to[ok] copious notes."

So sue me, I'd skimmed it before class. I was curious abo[ut] how graphic the diagrams would be. Turned out, pret[ty] graphic.

"I'll bet you're going to rip the pages out and plaster the[m] on the ceiling," I whispered back as Marjorie walked back an[d] forth, using one arm to gesture and the other to click throug[h] the PowerPoint slides.

"It's all up here," he said, tapping his head.

I was facing forward, pretending to be engrossed in th[e] slides. He grinned at me and pulled out a pen, tapping it on his knee one, two, three, four, five times before he paused and started again.

I stole the quickest of quick glances and noticed something else behind his left ear when he moved his head. Looked like another tattoo, but it was so small I couldn't tell what it was.

The girls behind me yapped the entire class, and I wanted

view of my ass as I walked up the stairs. I half expected him to grab it, but he didn't.

We walked side by side out into the bright sunshine. It was blinding after being in the dark lecture hall.

"Mind if I walk back with you? I don't have class again until four, so I figured I'd crash for a little while."

"It's not like I can stop you. It's a free sidewalk," I said, looking left and right before crossing the road. He walked beside me, shortening his stride so he could match my stubby legs.

"True, but if I ask it makes me seem like a nice person."

"You're not a nice person," I said.

He laughed. "You're right. I'm not."

He shook his head as if it was the funniest thing ever. It wasn't, really. Most people wanted other people to like them so they tried and were overly nice. Hunter wasn't like that. He was what he was and didn't give a shit if people liked it or not. No matter how crazy he drove me, I had to admire that about him. Sometimes I cared too much what other people thought of me. It must have been freeing to go through life like that.

We didn't talk much as we walked. At first it was strange, but the more we walked, the easier it was. It was the longest I'd heard Hunter go without a sarcastic comment or sexual innuendo. It was kind of nice.

"So, about dinner," he said when we walked into the apartment. "What do you want me to make?"

The room was quiet; the other girls must still have been at class.

"You're serious?"

"As a heart attack."

I set my bag down and leaned on the counter. *Okay, Hunter Zaccadelli, you can make me dinner.*

"Stuffed French toast, sweet potato hash and strawberries and cream."

"Breakfast for dinner? You rebel, you."

I shrugged. "What can I say? I live on the edge. So, think you're up to the challenge, Z?" I said, using the ridiculous nickname the bouncer had used last night.

"Piece of cake. Or toast, in your case. I'll stuff your toast, baby."

I rolled my eyes. Soon I would be desensitized to his comments, but I hadn't quite gotten there yet.

"Whatever. I'm going to take a shower. No, you can't come with me," I said, cutting off whatever comment he was going to make.

"Anytime you change your mind, you know where to find me."

Unfortunately, I did.

CHAPTER 6

"How the hell did you do that?" I said, looking at the dining room table. It was spread with mounds of my favorite French toast that was stuffed with oozing Nutella; sweet potato hash that he'd made exactly how I did, despite my vague and confusing-on-purpose instructions; and strawberries that he'd somehow cut and stuffed with the hand-whipped cream. He'd even found champagne and made mimosas.

"I'm a man of many talents. Some of them are hidden. Some are not. Maybe sometime you'll let me show you some of the hidden ones." I was too dazzled by the meal to make a snappy comment.

"Holy crap, dude. I didn't know you could cook," Renee said, coming out of her room.

Darah had already picked up her job as a desk attendant at the Union and wouldn't be back until late.

"We should probably eat it before it gets cold. Dig in, ladies," he said, handing me a plate. There was definitely enough food for about twelve people. "I hope you don't mind, but I invited Mase over. Dev and Sean might come, too."

So that was why he'd made so much. I couldn't really stop him from having his friends over, but I didn't want our apartment turning into a frat house with beer cans everywhere and strange girls sneaking out in the morning from one-night stands on our couch. Yuck and ew.

"Fine with me," Renee said, piling her plate with strawberries and cream and only one piece of French toast.

What was it with girls being afraid to eat in front of guys? I'd never had that fear, so I loaded my plate up. Just as I was about to plunge my fork into the French toast and unleash the Nutella-y goodness, there was a knock at the door. I had to hand it to them, at least they hadn't just barged in.

Hunter opened the door and Mase and Dev came in.

"What are you making? It smells fantastic," Mase said, going right for the table full of food.

"I made this on Taylor's request. She doubted my cooking skills, so I had to show her what I've got."

"You should never doubt Hunter when he brags about something. Most of the time if he's bad at something, he just won't talk about it. If he's bragging, it means he's telling the truth," Mase said, grabbing a fork and shoveling French toast onto a napkin.

"Do you want a plate?" I said.

"Nah, I'm good like this. Then you don't have to wash an extra."

How considerate. Dev was more cautious, asking me where the plates were and waiting until everyone else had gotten their fill before taking what was left, which wasn't much. Sean followed suit. There weren't enough chairs, so we crashed on the couch and the living room floor like we had the night before with the pizza.

Choruses of "oh my God," "mmm" and "dear sweet Jesus"

were interspersed with loud chewing and swallowing. Other than that, the conversation was nonexistent.

Okay, okay, I had to admit it. Hunter hit it out of the park. French toast was one of those foods that seemed easy to make, but was crazy easy to screw up. He'd overstuffed the middle with so much Nutella that it oozed out when I cut it with my fork and dripped down my chin when I bit it. I wiped it off and licked my finger. Hunter was watching me, as if waiting for my reaction.

"It's okay, I guess," I said, cutting up another piece and shoving it into my mouth. He raised his eyebrows and took a bite of his own, chewing slowly.

Sweet Christ it was like I'd died and gone to breakfast heaven. I really hoped he wouldn't use his cooking skills as leverage for sexual favors. For this, I might have to give in.

"I think we need to have a toast," Renee said, raising her glass. Well, it was really a plastic cup. None of us had brought champagne glasses with us when we moved in. "To hidden talents," she said.

We all clinked our glasses. Hunter winked when ours met. I wrinkled my nose at him.

"If you guys are going to eat like this every night, I might have to move in," Mase said. "All we have is microwave popcorn, beer and week-old fried chicken that no one remembers buying."

I shuddered, as did Renee.

"My ex-boyfriend never stocked his fridge. I always had to bring my own groceries when I stayed over," Renee said, emphasizing the word *ex*. As if everyone hadn't caught it.

"I think it's a guy thing," I said.

"Not every guy," Hunter said.

"Apparently not," I responded.

My phone vibrated with a text from my mother, and I excused myself to chat with her. Hunter gave me a questioning look, but I hit Call, put the phone to my ear and ignored him.

"Hey, Kid, long time no talk! I thought you were lying in a ditch somewhere," she said as I settled onto my bed to chat.

"Nope, sorry to disappoint. I'm alive and well. Sorry I haven't called you. Things have been a little nuts."

"How did moving in go?"

I gave her a quick rundown. I felt like I needed to record myself telling the story so I could just hit Play when someone asked. I left out a lot when I gave her the mom-version. I didn't want to worry her. She always worried about me more than Tawny. I wasn't sure if it was because I was the baby or because of my issues. Perhaps both.

"Oh, no." She proceeded to urge me to go right down to housing and give them hell. I told her that was what I had done, but I hadn't gotten anywhere.

"Well, I'm going to call and give them a piece of my mind. That's ridiculous that they won't do anything. They're just being lazy. Hang on," she said, and I could tell she was putting me on speaker so she could look up the number.

"Mom, it's okay. I'll deal. You don't have to fight the bullies for me."

"But I'm your mother. I'll always want to beat the crap out of people who are mean to you."

"No one was mean to me. It's fine." I was beginning to regret telling her. Mom was always trying to make up for not protecting me that one time. She'd been making up for it since I was twelve, and I didn't know when it was going to end, or at least lower in intensity. I loved her more than I could say, but I didn't need her to fight my battles for me.

"Are you sure? You know I can make things happen."

It was true. That woman could talk her way in or out of anything. She had this way of making people believe what she wanted them to. In another life I thought she would have been a lawyer.

"I know you can, and I love you for it. I've just gotta deal with it, okay? How about we talk about something else. How's work?"

She was reluctant to leave the topic but switched for my sake. We chatted for a few more minutes while she told me funny stories about her coworkers at the bank and silly customers who couldn't understand how to use a debit card. She'd worked her way up at a local bank from teller to manager. I chatted a bit about my classes and told her about my job search. Nothing heavy, nothing serious.

"Your father called today," Mom said, casting a dark cloud over our chat.

"What did he have to say?"

"Not much. He said he wanted to see you soon."

He said that every time he called. My parents had gotten divorced when I was thirteen and he lived in Connecticut now, which wasn't far enough, in my opinion. He called me every now and then, but I always deleted his voice mails.

"I'm sure he does."

"You should go and see him. I know he misses you."

"If he missed me, he'd come to see me."

"I know, Kid. I know." She sighed, and I twisted my hair around one finger.

"Listen, I'll call you this weekend and we can talk more, okay?"

"Okay, Kid. Love you."

"Love you, too."

I hung up and sat back on my pillows, closing my eyes. A

soft knock made me sit up. "What do you want?" I knew it would be Hunter. The door cracked open, and he poked his head in.

"Just wanted to let you know the guys are gone, and Renee went to the library to get some reading done, so if you wanted some privacy you didn't have to hide in here."

Renee already had massive amounts of reading since she was a nursing major. She also had a sick obsession with gory descriptions of diseases.

"Where are you going to be?" I said.

"Where do you want me to be?" His smirk was back.

"Wherever I'm not," I said, getting off my bed and pushing past him into the living room. I really didn't have any homework that had to get done tonight, so I decided to finish the book he'd so rudely distracted me from reading that morning.

I got out my e-reader and folded myself on the couch. I had to use my left hand to hold it because my right was still recovering from the encounter with Hunter's face. I should probably have put some more ice on it, but I didn't want to give him the satisfaction.

The kitchen was spotless, the dishes already in the drainer and all other evidence of the breakfast buffet was gone. Guess cleaning was a hidden talent as well. Darah hadn't had a chance to make our chore chart yet, but I was sure she was on it.

"Do you mind if I play?"

"No, go ahead," I said, not looking up from my book.

He went to our room and came back with his guitar. I hadn't really looked at it the day before, but it had definitely been through the ringer. It was black and dinged and scratched all over. He sat in the chair across from the couch and settled the strap around his neck. I kept reading but waited for him to start.

"Requests?"

"I thought I had to pay for them," I said.

"I'm feeling generous. I'll give you a few freebies."

"How generous." He strummed a chord. I thought about it for a second. "'Smooth Criminal.' Either version."

He looked surprised for a second, and then he started to play. I couldn't help but groove to the familiar tune. Against my will, my head bopped and my feet twitched. He didn't sing, but he played the song and that was enough. He was very talented. When the song ended, he continued to strum a transitional tune.

"Next?"

"'On My Own.'" There was no way he'd know that one. I'd had a brief obsession with musicals in high school and had a minor part in the community theater production of *Les Misérables*. I'd wanted more than anything to play Eponine, but there were too many other girls who tried out and had been in theater since they were born, so I didn't get the part. I'd been mildly crushed for at least a month.

"You think you're going to stump me, but I assure you, I can play pretty much anything," he said before he launched into a guitar version of the song.

Honestly, I'd thought even if he knew it, he wouldn't be able to play it on a guitar. I had been proved wrong again. I was still holding my e-reader, but the book wasn't captivating me as much as Hunter.

He got lost in the music, throwing his whole body into the song. It was like he wasn't even aware of what he was doing; he was just getting lost in the music. It was beautiful to watch. Hunter played with everything he had and he was good. No, he wasn't good. He was amazing. Hypnotic. Could this be the same boy who'd said I was fuckable last night?

He abruptly ended the song, placing his hand on the strings so they'd stop vibrating.

"Free request time over. If you want to pay, I'll continue."

I could only imagine what he'd take in payment, so I just picked up my book again. After a few minutes, he started again, just picking out random notes and tunes. He'd play a few lines of a song, enough for me to recognize it, and then it would melt into something else.

"Can I ask you something?" I said a half hour later.

"You can ask whatever you want, doesn't mean I'm going to answer." He quickly plucked one string.

"Why are you a business major? I'd rather eat glass than admit it, but you have talent."

"This?" he said, pointing to the guitar. I nodded. "So I can be a starving artist? There are ten thousand guys with guitars who can play."

"But if you love doing it, then why wouldn't you?"

"I am doing it. Right now."

I just wanted a real answer from him. If I was going to be stuck with him for the rest of the week we might as well get to know each other. He may have been a jerk, but he was an intriguing one. I wanted to know how he'd become the guy he was. You know, before I tossed him out on his ass.

"You know what I mean." He shrugged and went back to strumming. "Oh, so you shut down when you don't want to talk. I see how it is," I said.

"You don't want to know about me, Taylor. You really don't. Trust me when I say those things are not worth knowing."

"I could be the judge of that, I think."

He gave me a smile, but it was twisted.

"That's what they all say. Everyone says they want to know you, but they don't. They want to know the nice things, the pretty things. No one wants to know the ugly parts, the parts that keep you up at night. They say they're okay with it, but then they drift away and you never see them again. I've seen it happen way too many times. Girls don't want to know that shit."

"Maybe this one does."

His smile appeared again. "That's what they all say," he repeated.

I decided to give up and went back to my book. He went back to strumming, and we stayed like that until Darah got back at ten-thirty. She seemed shocked to find us in our current positions, but she recovered quickly.

Renee got back a little while later when the library closed, her eyes glazed over from all the medical terminology she'd tried to cram into her brain in just a few hours. I was exhausted from the previous night, so I wanted to turn in early. I made sure to take my damn pill so I wouldn't wake everyone up with my night terrors. I was already in bed and had my eyes closed when Hunter came in after his shower.

The smell of his clean skin overwhelmed the room, and I tried to pinpoint what it was. It was something similar to wood or cinnamon. Something warm.

I heard him get into bed and slip his boxers off.

"I don't know if you're awake or not, but good night, Taylor."

I decided to pretend I was asleep. He waited for a response, but when I didn't give one he rolled over and sighed.

"Damn you," I heard him say under his breath.

Right back atcha.

CHAPTER 7

I was the first to wake up the next morning. Somehow our blackout curtain had gotten pushed aside, and a crack of sunlight was poking under my eyelids. I opened them and moaned. Stupid sun. I rolled over and checked the clock. It wasn't even seven yet. Why had I woken up? Then I heard a voice.

Hunter was talking in his sleep, just like he'd said he would.

"No, I don't think so," he said. It was hard to make out what he was saying because his back was to me and he was mumbling. Figuring I probably wasn't going to get back to sleep, I turned so I could see him.

"Don't. Stop it. Put it down." His voice was calm, but his words were not. He seemed to be having a nightmare. Guess I wasn't the only one.

"Please don't." His voice had a hint of tears in it. I wondered if I should wake him up. He tossed in his sleep, throwing his covers about. I didn't have time to shut my eyes, but luckily his blanket covered strategic places. It was also still pretty dark.

Even still, it showed enough. His back was to me, and I saw yet another tattoo in the middle of his back.

"Stop!" he said louder.

I got out of bed and stumbled over. Maybe I could poke him and get back into bed quick enough so he wouldn't notice. I shoved his shoulder, but he moved so fast that I stumbled and nearly fell on top of him. A hand lashed out at me, and I had to duck to avoid it.

"Hunter! Wake up!" It was déjà vu. I hoped this wouldn't become a pattern.

A strong, warm hand grabbed my shoulder, and his eyes flew open. He gasped, as if he didn't know where he was. His grip relaxed.

"Hey, it's okay. You just seemed upset."

He glanced at his hand on my shoulder as if it didn't belong to him. He let go and pushed away from me.

"Go back to bed," he said.

"Are you okay?"

"Go. Back. To. Bed." His teeth were gritted, and he looked like he was angry that I'd woken him. My bad.

"Sorry," I said before stepping away and crawling back into bed.

He breathed heavily and rolled back over. I didn't go back to sleep, and I could tell he didn't either. A half hour later I heard him get up and put his boxers and a T-shirt on. I pretended I was asleep. A little while later I heard low voices in the kitchen. Deciding it was about time, I got up and went to find some breakfast.

Hunter was hunched over a plate of eggs and toast when I came out of our room. Renee was on the couch with the television on and a bowl of cereal. I heard the noise of the shower and made the deduction that Darah was in there.

"Good morning," I said to whoever would answer.

Hunter grunted and Renee made a similar noise. It was only the second day of classes, but everyone was still on summer time.

I grabbed a bowl of cereal and went to sit with Renee. I was getting bad vibes from Hunter. That boy and I were going to have to have a chat sooner or later. I had the feeling he was going to avoid it as long as he possibly could. I'd have to be the one pushing.

One by one, my roommates went to their various morning classes until it was just me and Hunter. Surprise, surprise.

"We need to talk," I said, "and you can't do that thing where you shut down or don't answer or make some sort of innuendo so I'll get distracted or off topic. If we're going to live together, we've got to be able to talk to one another. Got it?"

He put his plate in the sink and turned around, bracing his back against it. His eyes told me I was in for a battle.

"Don't make me punch you again, because I swear to God, I will." That elicited a smirk. His face still had a slight shadow where I'd gotten him. "I also have no qualms about going for your man bits again."

"I don't doubt you for a second, Missy."

"I've talked with housing about you. I have a meeting on Friday with the head of housing."

"Still trying to get rid of me?"

"I just don't see how this can work out. You're…you." I couldn't come up with a better way of saying it.

"Yes, I am." He seemed to get it. "But I fail to see that as a reason for kicking me out. If I came home drunk or had sex with strange girls or made you uncomfortable, that would be a reason."

"You do make me uncomfortable."

"But not in that way. I make you uncomfortable because I shake up what you thought about people. I make you nervous. You want me, but you don't know why and you can't stop fighting it."

I sputtered for a second, shocked. "You are so..." My hands shook with anger. I really, really wanted to punch him again.

"I've hit a nerve, I see. Means I'm right."

"You are the cockiest, douchebaggy asshat I've ever met, and I can't wait to get rid of you."

He laughed for the first time. On anyone else, it would have been sexy as hell. On him, it just made me more enraged.

"Fuck you, Hunter. Fuck. You."

"You want to, that's part of your problem."

Before I could react, he crossed the room and stood right in front of me.

"Tell me you don't want me. Look me in the eye and tell me if I kissed you right now, you wouldn't kiss me back. Tell me."

"I don't want you," I said, grinding my teeth around every word. Breathing became difficult. He was so close. I couldn't see anything beyond him. My eye level was at his chest, where the ink from his tattoos showed through the thin cotton. His smell surrounded me, and I caught a tiny whiff of sweat. My mouth went dry, and I kept my eyes on his chest because I knew I couldn't look up.

Two days ago, I hadn't known Hunter Zaccadelli existed. Today, I couldn't look him in the eyes for fear I'd lose myself. No, I had to shut this down.

I closed my eyes and stepped away.

"I don't want you," I said, looking at his eyes and not blinking. "Now get away from me." He didn't move, so I walked away.

One thing was sure: I had to get Hunter out of my life.

I wanted him. I wanted him to kiss me and touch my face and put his fingers in my hair. I wanted him to pick me up and hold me and be with me. I was losing it. Absolutely losing it. I had to get out of this space. He took up too much of it. He made my brain do funny things and not think clearly.

I had to get away.

I got dressed as quickly as I could and threw my books for the day into my bag. I dashed to the bathroom, hoping I wouldn't run into Hunter. I could hear his guitar in the living room. I didn't look at him as I rushed out the door. As soon as I was in the hallway, I was able to breathe.

What was it about him? Was it the tattoos? The way he called me Missy? The way he was so open about his sexuality? Maybe it was a combination.

It was a combination I couldn't say no to, but I would have to. I was never going to fall in love. I was never going to be with someone like that. People only hurt you when you loved them that way. They took what they wanted and used you up. My mother still missed my dad, even though it had been so many years. She still looked at their wedding pictures and smiled, thinking about times when they were happy. But it hadn't lasted. Nothing like that lasted.

Boys like Hunter burned everything they touched. Boys like that were dangerous. I knew that without a doubt. If I let him, Hunter would drag me down. I would not let it happen.

I spent the rest of the day looking for Hunter around every corner. I turned my phone off so I wouldn't see his texts, if he sent any. I made sure to keep a lookout in the Union. I kept thinking I saw him, but it turned out to just be a look-alike. There were a lot of guys who sort of looked like him, but no one quite close enough.

I did everything I could to avoid going back to the apartment and ended up finishing all my homework before the end of the day. I had my last class of the day with Megan and offered to have dinner with her so she could avoid eating with the "cannibals," as she called her boyfriend's buddies. It wasn't completely to avoid Hunter, because I really did want to spend time with Megan.

"Have you figured out your roommate issue?"

"I wish," I said, biting into my chocolate croissant. Hunter was the kind of person who made me need chocolate therapy. "It's really complicated."

"Things with the opposite sex usually are."

"How's everything working out for you?"

She lifted one shoulder. "Jake's my soul mate. I know that. Sounds cheesy, but I know that we're not complete without each other. So I put up with his disgusting friends and their endless *Family Guy* marathons because I love him. Someday we'll move in with just the two of us, and I'll be able to have a clean bathroom. Someday..."

We finished eating, and I walked Megan to her car.

"Girls' night this weekend? I think the guys are going to a party, so the house will be free. I'll make margaritas," she said in a singsong voice. "Come on, please? I'm inviting Haley and Robin, too." They were two other girls from our major that we'd formed a little group with. They'd be the perfect antidote to too much Hunter.

"Sure, it's on. Just text me when would be a good time. You want me to bring anything?"

"Every single girlie movie you own."

"Done," I said.

She squealed and gave me a hug before hopping in her car. It was still light out, so I didn't have to worry too much about walking by myself. I said goodbye to her and reluctantly walked back to the apartment. I kept my fingers crossed the entire way that Hunter would be gone or at least one of the girls would be there as a buffer.

I took a deep breath before I opened the door.

"Hey, where have you been?" Renee said, looking up from one of her massive nursing textbooks. The television was blaring; I didn't know how she could focus.

"Had dinner with Megan. Where's everyone else?"

"Hunter went somewhere, and Miss Darah is on a date with Mase, if you can believe it."

"No way," I said, joining her on the couch. "I thought I saw something there, but I didn't know he'd move that fast." College was a strange situation. Things always seemed to happen at warp speed.

"Me neither, but it was really cute. I think she really likes him."

"I have a really hard time picturing them together, but if he makes her happy, then that's what matters."

"Well, she hasn't even come home yet, so we can reserve judgment until then."

"If she does come home," I said, raising my eyebrows.

"You know she's not that kind of girl."

I did, but I never underestimated anyone when it came to that.

"I'm bored. I don't think I can do any more reading. You want to do something?" She closed her book.

"Like what?"

"I don't know. Mall?"

I wasn't much for shopping, but if we got to go to the bookstore, I was in. Also, it would get us out of the apartment in case Hunter came back from whatever he was doing. I only had a tiny temptation to text him, but quickly squashed it. I was staying away from him until I could get rid of him.

"Sounds good, just let me grab some cash." I ran into my room to grab some money from the jar I kept in my desk. I had to leave my debit card at home when I went into a bookstore or else I would drain my account. I was about to leave when I saw something on my pillow. Curious, I picked it up.

This is me giving you space. See? We can live together without living together. You still haven't given me an answer about that bet. All you have to do is prove one way or another and I'm gone. The ball's in your court, Missy.

I crumpled the note in my fist. He knew what I was trying to do, and that infuriated me. I didn't like him knowing what I was thinking, since I almost never knew what was running through his head. I shoved the note in my desk and slammed it shut.

"So what is with you and Hunter? I know you've got this weird I-hate-you-but-I'm-really-attracted-to-you thing going on, but could you, like, tone it down?"

"What are you talking about?"

"Oh, please. You guys eye-fuck each other every second you can. It's disgusting, really."

I hopped into the passenger's seat of Renee's Mazda.

"We don't do that." We totally did, but it was Hunter's fault. "I don't *mean* to anyway. He definitely does."

"That's what attraction is. That uncontrollable urge to jump someone's bones, even in mixed company. You guys haven't..." She didn't need to finish.

"Oh, God, no! I'm not that kind of girl, either."

I had never told Darah or Renee that I was a virgin. The only person who knew about that was Megan, and that was because we were so close, and I knew I could trust her with something like that. I'd trusted her with a much bigger secret.

"Never say never, doll. Did I ever tell you how Paul and I met?" I knew they'd only met about a year ago, but had gotten serious, fast. "I was wasted at a party, and this guy was trying to take me home. I don't really remember this, but Paul shoved him off me and asked me where I lived. I somehow managed to tell him, and he got me into a cab and helped me back to my room. Darah was gone for the weekend, so I was all alone. He stayed with me the whole night and took care of me. I puked my guts out, and he held my hair and everything. You'd think he'd never want to see me after that, but he ended up staying the whole day. When I sobered up I realized that he was pretty damn special. And I think you can figure the rest out. So, never knock sex early in a relationship. I mean, it didn't work out with us, but it was great while it lasted."

Her voice was filled with longing. I knew she missed him, but she refused to take his calls or answer his texts. I didn't even know why they had broken up, but she insinuated it was something he had done. I'd asked her if he'd cheated on her, but she said it wasn't that. Darah and I had racked our brains, but we hadn't figured it out. We'd been tempted to ask Paul but didn't want to go behind Renee's back.

I'd never really had a boyfriend. I'd had too many public angry episodes for the boys I'd grown up with to even consider wanting to date me. In eighth grade when the other girls were having their first boyfriends and getting kissed, I had a mouthful of metal braces and a bad attitude. When I got older and other girls were getting serious and hooking up and so forth, I spent my time reading and glaring at any boy who gave me the once-over. Soon my reputation as an ice queen became well-known enough that the boys left me alone, which was how I wanted it.

I'd never been around anyone who challenged me and fought me on everything until I'd met Hunter. He scared me in a way, and I'd never been scared of a boy before. That was why I had to get rid of him.

Maybe I could take his bet. I hadn't been able to make him see that I hated him, because I didn't. I hated him at times, but my other feelings for him seeped through, clouding the hate into a murky substance that I couldn't define.

The other part of the bet? The making him believe I loved him? I couldn't do that either. I'd shut off that part of myself when I was twelve, and there was no turning it on now after so many years. Hunter would see right through me if I tried to fake it.

I was between a rock and a hard place. I was going to have to wait and see what Friday brought.

CHAPTER 8

Hunter and I barely saw each other for the rest of the week. I assumed he went and hung out at Mase's, but I didn't know for sure because he barely said twenty words to me. When he did come and sleep at the apartment he always arrived after I was out and left before I woke. I didn't know how he did it, but he was like a shadow, sneaking in and out.

When I did see him, he pretended not to see me. Darah and Renee noticed, but after making inquiries, which Hunter and I both shot down, they stopped asking.

Friday afternoon finally came, as did my meeting with Marissa.

I had to wait ten full minutes before Marissa finally opened her door and called me in. Her office was nasty-neat and could have been a stock image for what an administrative office should look like with the generic watercolor print and motivational poster. Gag.

She adjusted her glasses on her nose before sitting behind her desk, absentmindedly straightening her wrist rest. Everything about her was orderly: her short hair, crisp shirt and flat expression.

"So, what can I do for you, Taylor? You said you were having an issue with one of your roommates." She leaned forward and braced her arms on the desk.

I gave her the rundown, leaving out a lot of what Hunter had done. I wasn't repeating what he said, word for word.

"So he makes you uncomfortable? Have you tried talking with him about it?"

"Yes, I have," I said. Her face had been blank when I'd told my sob story, and I could tell this was going to be a dead end. I could just feel it. But maybe I was being pessimistic.

"Have you gone to your resident director? They are always available to talk or discuss disputes, and they have training on how to help with those situations." It was like banging my head against a brick wall.

"I was really hoping that this could just be resolved, seeing as how it was a mistake to begin with."

"Well, there isn't really anything we can do right now. Unless there is an emergency, we have to keep places available for those who really need them. It sounds like it's more of a personality conflict. I'm going to recommend that you have some mediation with your RD, and you can come and see me in a few weeks, okay?"

I wanted so, so much to say, "Are you fucking serious?" but that wouldn't have helped my case.

"So there's nothing you can do?"

"Not unless there is a direct threat. Has he threatened you? Don't be afraid to speak up."

I thought about it for half a second, but I knew if I told her Hunter had threatened me, then he would get in trouble and could get kicked out of school. Campus security would get involved, and he could even get arrested. As much as the image of Hunter in jail amused me, I couldn't be the one to put him there if he didn't deserve it. Seeing as how I was the one who technically assaulted him.

I was stuck.

"No, he hasn't."

"Okay. Here's my card. Never hesitate to call us if it's an emergency. Sounds like you two just need to have a chat. I'll have your RD contact you about setting up some mediation." She stood and held out her hand, effectively ending the meeting. I had no choice but to stand, shake her hand and leave with her card clutched in my hand.

What a fucking waste of time.

I didn't know why I had expected anything more. In a university with around twelve thousand undergraduate students, I was a number. That was why I'd chosen UMaine instead of a smaller college. Now I was paying for it.

I stormed back to the apartment. Darah had gone home for the weekend to celebrate her mom's birthday, so she was already gone. Renee had a nursing group meeting, so I knew if anyone was going to be there, it would be Hunter.

I tried not to slam the door but failed.

"Rough day?" a male voice said.

I glanced at the couch to find him sitting there with his guitar. I held my composure for a second. "You're on," I said, walking over to him and sticking my hand in his face. "The bet, you're on."

He stared at my hand for a second, and a slow smile spread across his face. "Once we shake hands there is no going back."

I nodded, but I pulled my hand back before he could touch me. "There have to be some parameters. This whole thing about loving and hating can't be proved. I told you I hated you and punched you, but you didn't believe it. If I said I loved you right now, you wouldn't believe me. So how do we measure this?"

"It's harder to say you love someone than to say you hate them. So you have to say the words. And they have to be real."

"How will you know they're real?"

He shrugged. "I'll know. You'll know."

"And the hate part?"

"I'll know you hate me when I see that look in your eyes. I've seen it before, and I'll know."

"So you're going to determine this. I have no say?" I balled my hands at my sides, wanting to hit him.

"I'm not forcing you to accept this. You can call housing and tell them that I'm sexually harassing you. They'll drag me to a disciplinary hearing and probably kick me out of school. You could say the word right now. But you aren't going to do that."

"I can't," I said. As much as it would get him out of my life. "You're a jerk, but you're not that. If you were, I would have gotten rid of you so fast, your head would have spun around."

"Exactly. You're not a girl who puts up with anything. You can take care of yourself—you showed me that on the first night. You'll let me know when I've gone too far."

"I will."

"Okay then."

"Okay," I said, and we shook hands. I tried to let go, but he took my hand and pulled me so I crashed into his chest.

"So, here we are. You're stuck with me until Christmas," he breathed.

He let go of my hand, and I stepped back. It was not an easy thing to do. My body was drawn to his like the opposite pole of a magnet.

"You think you're the one who makes my life difficult. I can make it so much worse for you," I said, smiling sweetly. His blue eyes were skeptical.

"How so?"

"You really want to know? I'm going to invite a bunch of girls over, and we're going to watch girlie movies and talk about our periods and burn all kinds of scented candles and we'll probably stay up all night giggling."

"When do the naked pillow fights and making out start?"

I smacked his shoulder. "You pig, that's not what happens at sleepovers unless they're in the movies. But Darah and Renee and I can gang up on you. You have no idea how bad it could be."

"What makes you think any of that would make me uncomfortable?" he said, throwing a wrench in my spur-of-the-moment plan to get him back.

"Because all guys run away when girls start talking about their menstrual cycles. You're supposed to run away now."

He stepped closer to me. "Doesn't bother me."

"Tampon," I said.

He took another step.

"Cramps. Bloating. Heavy flow."

His chest was almost touching my nose. I tipped my head back to meet his eyes. He didn't blink. I could almost feel the cotton of his shirt against my skin. He slowly reached up and put his thumbs on either side of my face.

"Keep going," he said, pulling my face up, so I had to go up on my toes. Oh, my.

At that precise moment, my brain stopped working. It stopped thinking and even trying to think.

"Out of words, Missy?" he said, one side of his mouth tipping up.

That smirk snapped me back into reality. I glared at him and pulled away from his hands. He chuckled.

"You're going to have to work really hard to prove you hate me. The other thing, maybe not so hard."

"You're full of it," I said, crossing my arms.

"And you have no idea how sexy you look right now, so pissed at me."

My mouth dropped open. I didn't have anything to say, so I pulled my knee back like I was going to get him in the balls, but stopped short of hitting them. It was awesome to watch him flinch.

"Watch it there," he said.

I just grinned at him. "Don't forget you have something you value very much more that I can damage. Just remember that."

"How could I forget?"

"Don't you have somewhere to be? Some other girls to objectify?" I asked.

"Why would I go anywhere when I have all I need right here?"

I was going to make a snappy comment, but couldn't come up with one. It surprised me that a twenty-year-old, good-looking guy wouldn't have plans on a Friday night. But hey, what did I know?

Hunter treated me with the same cocky manner he'd used the first two days I'd met him, which was quite a change from the cold indifference. He made comments that would have made me blush a few years ago. Renee came back from her meeting and kept giving me a look when he did it. The I-told-you-so look.

I wasn't going to sleep with Hunter. I wasn't going to sleep with anyone, at least not right now. I couldn't even think of having sex without my hands shaking and my stomach turning.

I had no problem with other consenting adults doing it, but I knew that sex was messy. It was complicated, and some people used it as a weapon. I was never going to let that happen to me. If I did it, it would be because I wanted to. And I hadn't met anyone who made me want to.

Yet.

He stayed up late on Friday night playing the guitar. I was exhausted from my failed meeting, so I went to bed. He asked me if I minded if he stayed up and played.

"Knock yourself out."

"You wish," he said and played a little tune from a commercial. Ha-ha. I rolled my eyes and put the covers over my head, as if I was blocking him out. "You know you like it."

Yes, I did. More than I would ever admit.

I fell asleep to the sounds of guitar strumming. When I woke up, he was mumbling again. It would have been downright adorable if he wasn't so upset. I considered waking him again, but I didn't want to lose my face. So I let him go and listened.

"Mommy, wake up. Please wake up." His voice was scared.

I looked around and found a pair of socks that I balled up and chucked as hard as I could at him. They bopped his shoulder, but he didn't wake up. I tried to find something else. I looked around and found a metal coat hanger on my closet door. I unfolded it and used it as a poking stick to jab him. It took a few tries, but he finally grabbed at the spot where I was poking.

"What the fuck?" his half-awake voice said.

I quickly threw my poking tool down and pretended I was asleep. I heard him turn over, and I could feel his eyes on me.

"Did you just poke me?"

I decided to play dumb. "What?" I said, attempting a sleepy voice.

"You just poked me with something."

"No, I didn't. I was sleeping until a moment ago."

"No, you weren't. You were poking me with that piece of wire that's sitting on the floor. Very sly, Missy, but I'm not a moron." He got up, and I heard him picking up my poking device. "I was talking again, wasn't I?"

"Yeah," I said.

"Don't tell me what I said. I already know."

"How?"

"Because I shared a room with my cousin growing up, and at one point he told me what I said."

"You lived with Mase?" I asked, turning over. This was the first time he'd talked about his family. It was crazy early to be up on a Saturday, but this was worth getting up for. This was the first time Hunter had initiated talk about himself without me having to attack him for it. "What happened to your parents?" I said quietly. I didn't want to scare him off.

He got back into bed. I rolled over so I faced him. He was sitting up, his back against the wall and his legs over the edge.

"They're dead." The air left the room, and I found it impossible to breathe. I couldn't find words to say to him. Nothing I said would mean anything. "Yeah, that's what I thought," he said after a few moments of my silence.

"I'm sorry. I just didn't know what to say, so I didn't want to say something stupid. I was trying to think of something to say that wasn't stupid. Guess I failed."

To my surprise, he laughed.

"You don't have a filter. It's one of the things I like about you. Don't start now. Say whatever you want."

"I'd say that's one of the saddest things I've ever heard, and it explains a lot."

"Yes, it does," he said, looking down at his hands. "And you're one of the only people who has said they were sorry and I really believe you. People say things they don't mean all the time. It's easy to spot the bullshit."

"Yeah, it is." I was a professional bullshit spotter. It was one of my hidden talents.

"What happened to them?"

"Someday I'll tell you," he said, rubbing the top of his head with his hand, as if he was rubbing a lucky spot. I decided to change tactics and ask another burning question I had.

"Okay, then tell me about your tattoos."

"I told you I didn't believe in fate. I believe in luck. So I figured, why not have all the luck I can with me?"

"How many do you have?"

He turned his arm and showed me the seven. "One," he said, and then pulled his left ear so I could see the ink behind it. "Two." He turned his back and pointed to the one between his shoulder blades. "Three." He pulled his foot up and showed me another that I hadn't seen before, which was a star. "Four." He pointed to the one on his chest. "Five. I want to have seven when I'm done, but I only do one when I get the urge, so I haven't gotten one in a few months."

"What are they? I can't really see from here," I said. It wasn't a ploy to get him to come closer in his shirtless state, I swear.

He got off his bed slowly and walked toward me. The look on his face wasn't confident. It was open, as if he was showing me a piece of himself that he rarely shared. I knew this moment was precious, easily broken, like a finger through a soap bubble.

"This one you can see is a seven. It's a lucky number in

many cultures. This," he said, pulling his ear forward, "is your standard horseshoe. Sailors used to nail them to the masts of their ships to help them stay out of the path of storms."

He turned his back, and I finally saw what the one on his back was. If I hadn't done a project in sixth grade on Egyptian mythology, I might not have known it was a scarab beetle. The beetles would shed their outer skins, carapaces, and the Egyptians saw that as a symbol for rebirth and thus thought the beetles were immortal.

"You're really mixing up your mythologies there, Z."

He glanced at me over his shoulder, rolling his eyes at the nickname. "I'm all for diversity," he said drily.

I got out of bed and went to study it closer. It was beautiful, the colors nearly shimmering on his skin. Whoever he had gotten this from was a real artist. I resisted the urge to reach out and touch it to see if it was real.

"So, there you have it," he said, turning around. "And then I just have a little star on my foot. Now you have my ink history. Show me yours." His mouth turned up at the side, and Mr. Cocky was back. What a shock.

"Sorry, dude, none to show," I said, hopping back in bed.

"I wasn't asking about your tattoos, Missy." He leaned forward and braced his hands on either side of my legs, almost, but not quite touching my skin. Even though he wasn't touching me, my skin tingled as if he was.

"Why, Hunter, are you asking to see my lady parts?"

"Asking is putting it mildly," he said, and there was the tiniest growl in his voice.

The want to push myself forward and mesh his body with mine was so strong, I had to grab on to the sheets to stop myself from doing it.

"You're just messing with me," I said, my voice a little

breathy, like I'd just run up the stairs. "You said you didn't screw girls you liked."

"Oh, Missy, if you only knew," he said. He slowly moved forward until his face was right in front of mine before pulling back and walking out the door.

Damn him. Damn him and his blue eyes and his interesting tattoos and his take-what-I-want attitude. The fact that he had a tragic past just added to the mystery of Hunter Zaccadelli.

"Hey, Kid!" Tawny said, hopping out of her Volvo convertible. I ran to smash her in a hug. I had seen her only a week ago, but I'd missed her.

"Whoa, you okay?"

I'd hugged her a bit too enthusiastically. She also must have read the tension on my face.

"Let's get you a drink and I'll tell you about it."

We walked into Margaritas, the only decent Mexican place in downtown Orono. It was crammed between a clothing store that sold fashions for larger women and a real estate office. It was ridiculously narrow, but it had two floors so there were plenty of cozy nooks and private places. The tables were hand painted, and there were tons of sombreros and chili lights strung on the wall. Soft music played in the background.

Tawny and I went upstairs and found a table for two in a corner behind a large beam. I ordered a Coke, and Tawny got a margarita.

"I'll give you a sip when no one is looking," she said.

I filled her in on the whole Hunter saga while we waited for the waitress to come back so we could order.

"He sounds like an ass" was her assessment.

"He is," I said, laughing

Tawny paused with her drink midway to her lips. "Oh no."

"What?" I said, looking around.

"You like him."

"What? No, I don't."

She put her drink down, her mouth dropping open in surprise. "Yes, you totally do! Jesus, Kid, what are you thinking?"

"I do *not* like him," I said, lying through my teeth.

"Don't insult my intelligence. I know your face better than anyone else. I also know every single tone of your voice. You can lie to yourself all you want, but you're not lying to me. So, tell me about him."

"He's..." I said, struggling to find words to describe him. "He's a jerk, and he says whatever is in his head and he is always pushing my buttons and pushing his luck. He says he doesn't sleep with girls he likes, but then he's always coming after me. He's complicated."

"He sounds complicated. Good-looking?"

"Yeah, you could say that."

"Well, then, what's the problem?" she said as the waitress came to take our order.

We paused the conversation. I ordered nachos with extra guac, and Tawny went for the steak quesadillas. I tried to think about my answer to Tawny's question.

"You know what the problem is."

"Kid, that was so long ago. I got over it."

"You never get over something like that," I said softly.

"No, you're right, you don't. But you learn to live with it. Like a scar. You need to stop hating everyone."

"I don't hate everyone," I said.

"Close, Tay, close."

I changed the subject, and Tawny let me. We didn't come

back to Hunter until we were sharing our fried ice cream, which was ice cream covered in a crunchy topping with honey drizzled on one side and chocolate on the other. I had the chocolate side.

"What's the worst that could happen?"

"You know what the worst is," I said.

"You can't let one bad apple ruin the whole barrel. There were a lot of signs that I chose to ignore. Does Hunter make you feel unsafe? Is he controlling?"

"No," I said. Hunter had never made me feel like he was going to hurt me physically. Kiss me, yes. But those were two different kinds of fear.

"You know the signs. You know the red flags. Have you seen any of them?"

"No."

"Then why not stop being so hostile?"

"He likes me hostile, I think."

"Okay, I've gotta meet this guy. I also want to see your new place."

I hadn't planned on taking Tawny to the apartment. In fact, it hadn't even occurred to me to do so.

"I guess. I can't promise he's going to be there."

"Text him. I didn't come all the way up here from Belfast *and* bring your clothes to not see this guy."

I sighed and pulled out my phone.

U home?

Maybe. Y?

Bringing my sister by.

If she looks like you, she's welcome.

And if not?

I'll vacate the premises.

U ass.

He didn't answer, so I shut my phone.

"He said he'll be there as long as I said you looked like me."

She laughed. "Yeah, that guy totally wants you, Kid."

"He's just pushing my buttons."

"That's not all he wants to push," she said, pointing her fork at me. Ugh. Maybe Hunter and Tawny would get along. That would be the worst.

We left Tawny's car downtown and took mine back to campus.

"Stop freaking out."

"I'm not freaking out," I snapped.

I was freaking out, and I couldn't exactly say why. Maybe it was because Tawny's was the opinion I trusted the most. I trusted her judgment more than my own. If she didn't like Hunter, really didn't like him, that was it.

"Aw, this is so cute," she said when I opened the door. "Not nearly as scuzzy as I was expecting."

I glanced around, but I didn't see Hunter. Guess he'd decided not to be home after all. I heaved a sigh of relief, and then the bathroom door opened and he emerged in a cloud of steam, wearing only a small towel around his hips.

He saw us, and his face spread into a grin.

"Hello there, you must be Tawny. I'm glad I stuck around. I figured if you shared the same genes you would be just as hot."

I glanced at Tawny to see her reaction.

"And you must be Hunter," Tawny said, her eyes raking

him up and down. I had a hard time not doing the same thing, even though I'd seen him shirtless before. "Yup, you were right," she said to me.

"Right about what?" Hunter said, shifting the towel so it didn't fall. Sweet Christ.

"You think?" I said. It was fun having a secret that Hunter didn't know. How do you like me now?

"Yup," she said, walking closer to Hunter and slowly circling him and taking him in. "Just as you said."

I nodded. "Red flags?" I asked.

"Not yet," she said, making another circle. In all fairness, Hunter stood still and let her assess him.

"You look like you're enjoying yourself," I said, because he did.

"I have two beautiful women undressing me with their eyes. What's not to enjoy?"

Tawny tipped her head to the side and squinted. I saw his eyes flick down to her forearm, which was covered in a peacock feather tattoo she'd gotten as soon as she turned eighteen.

"So, what are your intentions toward my sister?"

Hunter met her eyes without blinking. "Well, at first I wanted her for the best one-night stand of my life."

"And now?"

"I don't just want her for a one-night stand," he said, his eyes lasering into me. My skin went cold and then hot in waves.

"Are you aware that I am in the position to grab your dick and break it off if I wanted to?"

"Very aware," he said, tearing his eyes away from me. Was it getting hot in here? I needed to open the window.

"Good," she said, patting him on the shoulder and sitting

on the couch and grabbing the remote. "Why don't you put some clothes on before you and my sister eye-fuck each other to death?"

Hunter laughed and shook his head. "You're not single, are you?" he said.

"In your dreams, towel boy. Run along and put some clothes on," she said, motioning with her hands.

"Yes, ma'am." He winked at me before shutting our bedroom door. It must have been my imagination that I heard a hint of a southern accent when he said it.

"Well?" I said.

Tawny grabbed the remote and clicked the television on. "He's one of those guys. But there's something about him I like. I can't really put my finger on it. If I was a few years younger, I would have totally gone for him."

"Really?"

"Hell, yeah. What girl doesn't want a guy who isn't ashamed to say he wants her? Everyone wants to be wanted." I sat down next to her, and she put her arm around me. "Just be careful. A boy like that can be the greatest thing to happen to you or the worst."

"What do you think Hunter will be?"

"That's up to you. You've got him totally whipped already. Despite what he says, if you told him to jump off a bridge, he'd do it."

"Yeah, right." I put my head on her shoulder and pulled my feet up on the couch.

"Just wait, Kid." Tawny didn't mess around, and she called things like she saw them. But I couldn't believe that about Hunter. To him, I was just another conquest. A shiny toy that was out of reach. While he didn't know I was a virgin, I was sure he suspected. Guys like that had virgin radar.

"Just wrap it before you tap it, Kid."

"Tap what?" Hunter came around the corner wearing a Radiohead T-shirt and black workout pants. Even that made me stare at him. He was really good-looking. How had I not seen that? He really did have a fabulous jawline. He'd shaved, but I preferred the nonshaved look on him.

"Wouldn't you like to know?" Tawny said, grinning at him.

"I think I do," he said, taking the crappy chair because Tawny and I had taken over the couch.

"God, it's hot in here," she said, fanning herself.

"You want some water?" I said.

"I'll get it," Hunter said before I could get up.

"With ice," Tawny called as Hunter went to the kitchen. *What the what?*

"Told you so," she whispered in my ear.

"You're crazy."

"No, I'm right," she said as Hunter came back with a sweating glass, complete with ice.

"Thank you, towel boy. Now fetch me a piece of cheesecake." I nudged her with my shoulder. "So, what's your story? Did you win the room assignment lottery?"

"Looks like it. I was supposed to live with my cousin, but that fell through. I contacted housing, and they sent me an email and I showed up. Your sister answered the door, and that was it."

"I also heard she punched you in the face."

He rubbed his jaw, which was now bruise-free. "And kicked me in the balls, yes." Hunter looked down and smiled, as if it was a fond memory.

"What did you do to deserve that?"

I was staying quiet through Tawny's interrogation. I wanted to watch Hunter flounder under her scrutiny.

"I may or may not have offered her a proposition," he said.

"I heard, and that's the most ridiculous thing I've ever heard, that my sister would agree to something like that. And *you*," she said, pointing at Hunter, "you are an ass, plain and simple."

"I am aware of that fact," he said calmly. "I thought it would give her a way out."

"Yeah, but only when you decide. That's an asshole move, and you know it. How dare you take advantage of my sweet baby sister."

"Tawny," I said. "I think I can take care of myself." This had been a bad idea. I'd thought she'd simmered down about the bet, but apparently not.

"No, don't you do that thing. I'm your sister, and I get to be pissed if someone is taking advantage of you."

"He's not taking advantage of me." Hunter sat back and watched, but I could tell he was taking everything in. "Maybe he is, but I'm not unaware, and he knows that if he does anything I don't like, I'll punch him again. I'm not a damsel in distress. I'm not a baby, and you can't fight my battles for me." I stopped talking, embarrassed that Hunter had seen that.

"She takes good care of herself," he said.

"Don't you dare tell me about my sister. You've known her for five seconds. You probably don't even know her middle name."

"Elizabeth," he said. How did he know that? I couldn't recall ever telling him. "It was listed on your Mainecard. You left it on the table one day."

"Oh," I said. That was way less creepy than I thought it would be.

"Prove to me that I can trust you with her. I'm not leaving until you do." Tawny pulled me closer and angled her body so she was in front of me. Oh, please. Now it was going to turn into a pissing contest.

Hunter stood up.

"Hit me," he said, looking at me.

"What?" I said.

"Go ahead, hit me. I know you want to. You always want to hit me, so get it out of your system. It's been almost a week since the last time."

"I'm not going to hit you." Given other circumstances, I'd love to, but I didn't want to do it just because he told me to.

"Come on, Missy. Go ahead," he said, putting his hands behind his back and looking at the ceiling.

I glanced at Tawny, who was studying Hunter.

"Well, what are you waiting for? Give him a good one."

Tawny tried to pull me upright. What the hell was she doing?

"I am not going to hit him just for the hell of it. You're both crazy."

"Why not?" Tawny said. Hunter started whistling the *Jeopardy* tune. That was it; they were both psychotic.

"Yeah, I'm going to go to the bathroom. Don't kill each other until I get back."

I got up and blew past them, not breathing until I'd shut the bathroom door and locked it. It was still filled with steam from Hunter's shower. I couldn't escape him. He was *everywhere*. In my head, in my room, in my face. I sat on the sink after wiping it off with a towel. I had to hand it to Hunter; at least he wasn't a slob. In fact, he was one of the cleanest guys I'd ever met. He didn't leave his clothes on the floor or hair in the sink when he shaved. He showered regularly and cooked. So what was the problem?

I put my head on my knees and let out a sound of frustration.

I waited for a knock at the door and a voice to ask me if I was okay, but it didn't come. I took a deep breath and hoped that Hunter and Tawny weren't strangling each other in the living room.

I peeped out the door, and laughter met my ears. *What the what?*

"No way, she did not do that."

"I swear, she did," Hunter said.

I came around the corner and saw that he was sitting down again and Tawny was back on the couch. There wasn't any blood and no one was missing a limb, which shocked me.

"Hey, guys…" I said hesitantly.

"We were just talking about that night at Blue Lagoon," Hunter said. "I was filling in your sister on your dance skills."

"You hussy," Tawny said. "I didn't think you had it in you."

"Why not? I went to plenty of dances."

"There's a difference between high school prom dancing and club dancing and you know it."

"Is there? Because I saw plenty of girls at prom who should have been attached to a pole."

They both laughed at me.

"Has she always been like this?" Hunter said.

"Not always. She changed a lot after our parents' divorce."

I glared at Tawny. Hunter didn't need to know about Dad.

"So your father isn't in the picture?" *Great, thanks a lot, Tawny.*

"You could say that," Tawny said.

I struggled to find some way to change the subject. "Why don't I give you a tour of campus?" I blurted out. It was the first thing that came to mind.

"That would be fun. I've never really seen the whole thing.

You want to come?" Tawny directed the last part toward Hunter. "Unless you have somewhere else to be?"

"Not right now," he said. "You okay with me tagging along, Missy?" His eyes teased me, knowing that my plan had been to get him away from Tawny.

"Fine," I said, smiling brightly. *Suck on that, Hunter.*

"Let me just find some shoes," he said.

I glared at Tawny when he left.

"Oh, Kid, you've got it so bad, but so does he." She just shook her head. "I'll give it a week before he's tattooing your name on the other side of his chest."

"I thought you didn't like him. What happened to being pissed at him about the bet?"

Tawny shrugged. "I was overreacting. Typical big sister move. He explained why he did it, and it makes sense, in a slightly twisted way. He's not a bad guy. He's just a jerk. But a nice one."

"That doesn't make any sense."

"Men rarely do."

CHAPTER 9

After the longest tour of the UMaine campus *ever,* Tawny decided it was time for her to get back to Belfast.

"Remember what I said. He could be the greatest or the worst thing to happen to you. It's up to you to choose," she said as she hugged me. "Don't let my past dictate your future, okay? I want you to be happy."

"You sound like a Hallmark card," I said when she let go.

"I know what I'm talking about, Kid." She pressed her thumb in the middle of my forehead, as if to impart her wisdom into my brain. "I'll call you when I get back. When are you coming home next?"

"Not sure, might do a weekend in October, but if I don't, it'll be Thanksgiving."

"Well, I'll try to get up again before then. Love you, little sister."

"Love you, big sister," I said as she put the top of the Volvo down and cranked the radio. She honked as she drove away. I just shook my head.

★ ★ ★

When I got back home, Hunter was gone, but there was another note on my bed.

Went out to objectify some women. May have sex with some of them. Be back later. By the way, your sister is welcome back anytime. He signed it with just the letter *Z*.

I crammed that one in my desk with the other. For all I knew, he was having sex with a bunch of different girls. I hated to admit it, but I'd snagged his phone one night when he was in the shower and scrolled through his contacts. He'd messed with mine, so I had to return the favor.

I recognized a few of his contacts, including his cousin and his guy friends. The others, not so much. He had six contacts named Ashley alone. Ashley B, D, H, F, R and T. The theme continued for the other common names like Heather, Sarah and Liz. I couldn't even count how many names there were. Really, though, was I surprised? Not so much.

I rarely ever saw him talk on his phone, but he texted a fair amount. Every time he did, I wondered which one of the Ashleys it was.

I didn't see him until I came back that night from Megan's, where I'd had my fill of chocolate, girl talk and objectifying Richard Gere and Channing Tatum.

"Did you have a good time talking about your periods?" he said, not glancing up from something in his lap.

"Yeah, we even started discussing Pap smears. Hey, is that my e-reader?" It totally was.

"Maybe. You left it on your desk."

"So you thought you'd just use it? How much of my other things have you used?"

"Just your underwear," he said, his eyes still on the screen.

"Hand it over," I said, holding out my hand.

"No way, I have to find out who she ends up with." He held his arm up so it was out of my reach.

"Give it back," I said, hopping on the bed and grabbing at his arm. He kept moving it out of my reach. I grabbed his arm with both of mine and yanked, but he chose that moment to poke his fingers into that ticklish spot right under my ribs.

"Hunter, stop it," I said, trying not to curl up in the fetal position as he continued to tickle me. I tried reaching for the e-reader, but it was no use. He tossed it on my bed and came at me with both hands, flipping me onto my back and attacking me. I was laughing so hard I couldn't breathe. He was laughing at me, but there was nothing I could do about that.

"You want it back? You really want it back?"

"Yes," I gasped.

"Then tell me if I kissed you right now, you wouldn't kiss me back."

His hands didn't leave my ribs, but the tickling stopped. I tried to catch my breath and tipped my head so I could look at him. He was serious. His body hovered over mine, and I realized I was lying in his bed. His sheets were soaked in his scent, and I wanted to turn my head so I could inhale it better.

"You have a great laugh, by the way. Low and sexy."

"I wouldn't kiss you back," I said slowly, because it took a lot of time to find the words. Most of my brain was distracted by his face and his body and how warm he was and how good he smelled and other thoughts about him.

His face came so close that his breath moved the hair on my forehead. "Liar," he said and slowly got off me.

I stayed where I was, unsure if I could actually move.

"Here you go, Missy." My e-reader came into my line of vision. He had been reading the first book in the series I'd also been reading. "I'm rooting for the vampire," he said before leaving the room and shutting the door.

It took several minutes for me to peel myself off his bed. Most of the blood seemed to have left my brain and gone to other places. It was a good thing I wasn't a guy, because I would have needed a cold shower and a few minutes alone.

Hunter was right; I was a liar. I would have kissed him back. I would have done a lot more than that. I would have wanted him to do anything and everything and then asked for more. Yeah, I needed a cold shower.

Things cooled off for a few days after that. Hunter backed off. Again. Not from his comments about wanting to sleep with me or telling me that I looked hot or any of that, but he stopped invading my personal space. Well, he stopped invading it so much.

He started a new routine every night when we went to bed. "Love me?" I'd answer no. "Hate me?" I'd answer that with sarcastic comments, listing the things that he'd done that day that pissed me off. The list was usually pretty long. I'd end that with saying no again. Then we'd both turn over and go to sleep. It was a strange thing to do, but it turned out we were both strange people.

I stopped caring if he saw me put in my retainer. He started taking more of my stuff and caring less when I got pissed.

Darah came back from another date with Mase with her eyes glowing. Somehow he had completely won her over, and he became a fixture at our place, as did Dev and Sean. They were both a little smitten with Renee, and she flirted back with them but never took it further than that.

Classes ramped up in intensity, and I spent more and more time reading and writing papers and doing other busywork.

Hunter and I spent our first mediation meeting with the RD trading quips back and forth.

The RD, Chris, tried to steer us back on track, but he wasn't a very good mediator. I just ended the session wanting to punch Hunter, and he ended it with a smile on his face. So, we'd made zero progress. We still had to meet the next week, and I didn't have any hope things were going to change anytime soon. Besides, I'd agreed to the bet, so I couldn't really go and throw him out without backing out, and I wasn't going to do that. I'd given my word, and I was going to stick to it.

On Wednesday, I finally got an email about the library job, and they wanted me for an interview the next afternoon. It was short notice, but I agreed to it. The money I'd made at my summer job at a local lobster shack was quickly disappearing.

I found the department in the back of the library tucked into a corner. There were a lot of pipes and ugly green paint, and it was clear this was a neglected part of the building.

I met with Tom, the head of the department, and he asked me about my work ethic and all those questions about hours and so forth. Standard stuff. I'd practiced before I went and was grateful. I'd thought about asking Hunter to let me practice with him, but he just would have asked me ridiculous questions and would have been no help. So I'd asked Renee to help when Hunter was at class.

All in all, I thought it went well, and when I shook Tom's hand and left, I felt fully confident I had it.

I made a detour to the gym before I went back to the apartment. It had been forever since I'd worked out, and I was really missing my kickboxing class. Luckily, there was a sign-up sheet for a Saturday afternoon class, and I immediately put my name down. I hit the elliptical for a while and then did some weight training, but I wished I had something to punch.

I was still riding the high of my interview and my workout that night when Hunter decided to make another crazy delicious meal and have everyone over. It had somehow turned into a ritual, and we'd even picked up a few more people in our complex that had smelled the food and wandered over.

That night we ended up feeding no less than fourteen people. We'd turned our apartment into a mess hall, of sorts, and had actually started to leave the door open. People would walk by and say hello, and I found that I liked a lot of them.

"What are you making for the crew tonight?" I said. Hunter was surrounded by shopping bags. I had no idea where he got his money, seeing as how he'd never mentioned a job.

"Well, since we're feeding about half of campus, I thought we'd go with pizza. Then everyone can do their own and bake them in their own ovens."

"Sounds like a plan. You need any help?"

"Yeah, if you could start chopping those peppers, that would be great."

I pulled out a cutting board and started chopping. Renee came home and helped me, and Darah arrived shortly with Mase, her fingers entwined with his. They were an odd couple, but somehow they worked. Mase was so laid-back and chill, and Darah was so uptight and orderly. Maybe they'd even each other out. Time would tell. God, if they broke up, it was going to be really awkward.

Everyone pitched in, and we got an assembly line going. Greg and Todd, two of the guys who lived next door, offered their oven and started putting in pies as soon as we could finish them. It was complete chaos, but somehow out of that emerged a group of people all intent on one goal: delicious pizza. I refused to go near the pepperonis, so Hunter dealt with that, washing his hands after and helping me assemble my veggie pizza and shoving it into the oven with the plain cheese pizza.

Our pizza party spilled out into the hallway as people either stood or brought chairs from their own rooms. We put on some music, and it was loud and crazy and fun. Sophie, Heather and Gabby also offered the use of their oven, putting in the done pizzas so they could stay warm.

We broke out the Solo cups and everyone pitched in with what alcohol they had. Hunter found some spiced rum somewhere and made me a rum and Coke. The alcohol flowed, and everyone told stories and laughed.

"Thirsty Thursday!" someone yelled every now and then, and we were all required to drink. I hoped that no one would call any of the resident assistants to come check IDs. We would definitely be screwed.

At some point Hunter pulled out his guitar and started playing.

"'Free Bird'!" someone yelled. Hunter rolled his eyes and played it, and we all sang along. Then someone yelled another song and another. We turned our pizza night into an impromptu sing-along. I joined in and caught Hunter watching me. He played, but didn't sing. We ended with a rousing rendition of "Billie Jean."

Everyone shuffled back to their rooms after disposing of their plates and cups and napkins. We all agreed to do it again next Thursday, and everyone started voting for taco night. I was fine with that, as long as I could make my own in a separate pan.

Dev and Sean wanted Hunter to come over and play video games, but he declined. After only one drink, Renee said she had to head to the library, and I decided to go with her after finishing mine. I had a paper to write for my medieval history class that was going to take a lot of concentration. I'd taken to escaping to the library frequently. Trying to do work with Hunter around was too distracting.

It started drizzling as we walked down, so by the time we got there, we were both damp and irritated. Luckily our bags were waterproof, so our books and my laptop were not harmed.

Renee got right to work, pulling out one of her anatomy textbooks—the kind with graphic pictures of nasty diseases. Yuck. I booted up my laptop and tried to resist the urge to click on the internet icon. I opened a blank Word doc and got out the research I'd done the other day. Ugh, this was going to be horrible.

Two hours later, I had ten pages, aching wrists and burning eyes. Renee had gotten through twenty-five pages of reading, which was a lot considering the print was absolutely microscopic and she had to take copious notes. We both stretched and blinked our eyes multiple times to make sure they still worked.

"I'm beat. You ready?" Renee said, shoving her book back in her bag as I packed up my laptop.

"Wonder what Hunter's gotten up to while we were gone."

"Who knows? I really wonder what he does when we're not around."

"Probably jacking off. He can't really do that when you're sleeping in the same room."

"Oh, God, I don't even want to think about that."

"You know he does it," Renee said, pushing open the library door. It was fully dark, the security lamps fully illuminated.

"I really, really don't want to know." Yes, I knew that guys had to do that, but that didn't mean I wanted to think about it, especially thinking about Hunter doing it.

"Oh, grow up," Renee said, shoving my shoulder. I changed the subject, and that carried us up the horrendous hill and up the stairs.

I was still trying to get the image of Hunter jacking off out of my head when we walked into the apartment.

"What is that?" Renee said, sniffing the air. It smelled like someone had lit about a million chocolate-scented candles.

"Surprise," Hunter said, pointing to an absolutely gorgeous-looking cake with peanut butter frosting and chocolate dripping off the sides.

"You made that?" It looked professional, like he'd gone out and bought it.

"I did." If I hadn't seen demonstrations of his cooking skills before, I would have thought he was full of shit.

"What for?"

"Just because," he said, shrugging. His face was serious, and I could tell something was on his mind.

"I don't trust you," I said, eyeing the cake.

He chuckled. "You shouldn't."

"Can we eat it now?" Renee said, tapping her foot.

Hunter handed her a cake cutter I'd never seen before. "Be my guest."

Renee grabbed it and sliced into the beautiful cake. We should have taken a picture of it beforehand. I wasn't sure how often we were going to be seeing things like that. She pulled the piece out with her hands and then seemed to realize that she didn't have a plate. Hunter handed her one from a stack he had waiting. He'd thought of everything.

"I wanted to make this, but I didn't want the masses

devouring it. Nothing sinister, I swear," he said, holding up his hands.

I still didn't trust him, but I cut myself a piece anyway. It had three layers, with a thick layer of frosting in between. I knew before I tasted a bite it would be heaven.

It was.

"I'm not going to sleep with you in exchange for this cake," I said.

"I don't need to use cake to get you to sleep with me," he said, handing Renee a fork so she'd stop using her fingers.

"Can we stop with the sexy talk? I'm eating over here," Renee said, her mouth full.

I crossed my eyes at her, finished my slice of cake and licked my fingers. Hunter swiped some frosting from his cake and smeared it on my cheek.

"Hey!"

"That's it," Renee said, taking her plate and going into the living room. "When the frosting starts to fly, I get out of the way. If you two want to have sex on the counter, can you just clean it up after? Oh, and please don't screw each other on the cake? I'd like to have another piece."

I really, really wanted to retaliate, but instead I swiped the frosting off my face and stuck my finger in my mouth.

"Tease," he said.

"Takes one to know one. What kind of guy makes a girl an amazing cake without expecting something in return?"

"A guy who doesn't exist!" Renee yelled from the couch, her mouth still full of cake. I hoped she didn't choke.

"Me," he says.

"Whatever. You do owe me for the e-reader incident."

"You enjoyed that as much as I did."

"Whatever."

"Like I said, Missy, I wouldn't need cake to get you into bed." He looked at me in a way that made me go bright red. Ugh. I looked away as quickly as I could and grabbed the cake cutter.

"I will stab you with this. Don't think I won't."

"Threatening violence, interesting. You know you do that when you're uncomfortable." His voice lowered until only I could hear it. Renee was licking her plate to get the last of the cake crumbs.

"Bite me," I said.

"You also say that when you're uncomfortable. Why, Missy? Are you sexually frustrated?" That was none of his damn business. "You're not ever lying in bed, thinking of me in the next one, sleeping naked right across the room and my hands and—"

I turned and snapped my elbow toward his stomach. His flinch was satisfying.

"Nope," I said, flipping the cake cutter in my hand and catching the handle again. I'd taken baton for like a month when I was five and my wrists were still good at flipping and catching things like that.

"Liar."

I ignored him and went to sit with Renee. I needed her as a buffer. Darah came in a few minutes later, so I had at least two people. Not that it made Hunter have any more of a filter. I was pretty sure he was born without one. Well, I didn't have an anger filter. When those two things combined, it was anyone's guess.

CHAPTER 10

Monday morning I woke up a little excited. It was my first day at the library in the afternoon, and I was nervous but happy to be having some money coming in. I would cut off my hand before asking my mother to spot me some. She had enough worries without me being a mooch.

I took out my retainer and glanced over at Hunter. He was on his back, one arm thrown over his eyes, as if he was blocking them from the sun. His other arm was slung over the side of his bed. Somehow his sheets always managed to cover what they needed to cover. Except...

I shoved my face under the covers. I did *not* just see that. I peeked out again. Yup. Hunter Junior was awake and standing at attention. Oh. My. God. I faced the wall, unable to look at it anymore. He moaned, rolling over. I stayed as still as I could, but suddenly I got a fit of the giggles. I stuffed my blanket in my mouth, but it didn't help. Hunter sighed and moved again. I really, really didn't want him to wake up.

The giggling continued. I was in deep, and there was no end in sight.

"What's so funny?" His voice made me jump, killing all hope I had of pretending I was asleep. I froze anyway, hoping he'd think I was having a nightmare or something.

"I can still hear you laughing," he said, and I heard him grabbing his boxers. How could he get them on over...

"Why don't you come over here and give me a hand instead of giggling like a twelve-year-old," he said, somehow getting the boxers on.

"Why don't you just take care of it yourself? That's probably what you usually do."

"That's what you think."

He walked out of the room and shut the door. The giggles finally took over, and I was lost. Something about man bits was just hilarious. My fit continued until I had tears on my face. I lay in bed after it was over, gasping and trying to regain my composure.

It was only seven, but there was no way I was going to be able to sleep. I might as well get up and do some homework. I needed to wash my face and brush my teeth, but I wasn't going near the bathroom once I knew Hunter was out of it.

I parked myself in the living room with my textbooks, a bowl of cereal and a cup of black coffee. I heard the shower turn off and glued my eyes to my book.

"Shower's free," he said behind me.

I made a noncommittal sound and pretended I was absolutely fascinated with my French textbook. I heard him walking closer, and I kept my head facing away. "You come any closer with that and I'll break it off. Got it?"

"You're feisty this early in the morning. I like it. Whatcha reading?" He leaned over my shoulder, his damp skin inches from my face.

"Go away, Hunter. Seriously."

"Fine, fine." He shuffled back to the bedroom, and I went back to my homework.

An hour later Darah stumbled toward the coffeepot.

"What are you doing up so early?" she said.

"Couldn't sleep."

"Was that you laughing like a psycho earlier?"

"Yeah, sorry. I didn't wake you up, did I?"

"Meh," she said, gripping the coffee cup and taking a deep sip. "I wake up if Renee breathes too loudly. Not your fault. So," she said, shoving some of my books aside so she could sit next to me, "what was all the giggling about?"

"It's nothing," I said, the giggles threatening to come up again. "Just something I was thinking about."

"Or someone?" She poked my shoulder.

"No."

"Yeah, that was very convincing, Taylor. There is something going on between you and Hunter. Everyone else seems to see it but you."

"The only thing that's going on is that he drives me up a wall and I want him to get hit by a bus."

"Right, sure."

"I'm serious!"

"Okay, Taylor. Whatever you say." She gave me a look and went back to her coffee, and I went back to whatever the hell I was working on and *not* thinking about Hunter.

I headed for my first day at the library with nerves and excitement. I punched my old-fashioned time card and walked back to the office.

"Hello, Taylor, it's nice to see you again," Tom said, shaking my hand. There were a few other people who worked in the department, and I was introduced to Nancy, Mary and Jeff.

"And this is the student worker section. We usually only have two workers at a time. The other student who shares your shift should be here any moment."

I was a little early. He showed me to a desk that was split into two workstations facing each other with two ancient desktops, lots of stamp pads and pens.

"Oh, here he is," Tom said, turning around. I turned my head and saw my coworker.

"Fancy seeing you here, Missy. Small world."

Hunter Zaccadelli, we meet again.

"You have got to be kidding."

"Do you two know each other?" Tom looked both confused and uncomfortable.

"We're roommates," I said.

"Well, it is a small world. That's not going to be a problem, is it?"

"No, not at all," I said. There was no way I was giving up this job.

"Agreed," Hunter said.

Tom gave us a look but took our word for it. "Okay then. For today I just need you to complete a few workplace safety tests. It's a pain you have to do them, but they're required for all new employees."

Hunter sat down directly across from me and booted up the computer. I did the same as Tom told us how to log in to the website and what the test would entail. Didn't seem too difficult.

"You sure this is okay? I know how hard it can be to work with someone you live with. My wife used to work in this department." He smiled, and we both reiterated that it would be fine. At least for now. We'd only been there for a few minutes, and I was still reeling. I didn't believe in luck, but I seemed to be having a lot of the bad kind lately.

Hunter and I got to work on a stupid safety multiple-choice test. I had to keep moving my feet because he kept invading my space.

"Will you stop that?" I said after he stretched his feet out under my chair for the millionth time.

"Why? I like pissing you off. It's the best part of my day."

I wanted to tell him to go fuck himself, but instead I turned my attention back to my computer screen. Seconds later, my email made a pinging sound to tell me I had a new message. I'd pulled it up in case any of my professors sent a message that I needed to read right away. I didn't need more than one guess to know who the ping was from.

Subject: You're totally picturing me naked right now
Missy,
So how about you and I head up to the stacks to do some "shelving"?

I glared at the message before hitting Reply.

Subject: This is a work environment and this is harassment
Mr. Zaccadelli,
I am writing to inform you that your proposition has been rejected. Due to both the fact that we are coworkers, as well as roommates, I would find it inappropriate to "visit the stacks" with you. I will reject all further offers at this time. If, in the future, I decide to entertain such an offer, I will inform you via correspondence.
Respectfully (not) yours,
Miss Taylor Caldwell
P.S. Stop fucking emailing me.

I watched his eyes skim the message and a smirk cross his face. He looked straight into my eyes as he typed away, never glancing at the keyboard.

He banged the enter key with a little nod.

Ping.

Subject: Not a chance
Missy,
I accept your challenge, and may I remind you that if you want me to leave you alone, there is that little bet we have going. Win it, and I'm gone.
Impatiently (and nakedly) yours,
Mr. Hunter Aaron Zaccadelli, Esquire
P.S. Bring it on.

Oh, he was not getting the last word. I turned the volume down on my computer and did a quick visual sweep of the room to make sure we weren't going to get busted. Everyone else was absorbed in what they were doing.

Subject: Challenge accepted
Mr. Zaccadelli,
If you keep this up, I'm going to report you to the workplace hotline for harassment. They don't take kindly to tattooed, guitar-playing dudes making advances toward sweet, innocent girls. Game ON.
Sincerely,
The Girl You Will Never Have
P.S. Esquire? You are so full of shit.

I heard a muffled laugh from Hunter's side of the desk, but I kept my eyes glued to the computer screen. Ladders. Safety precautions when working with ladders...

Ping.

I glared at the computer in irritation. Guess you couldn't turn the sound off.

Subject: Get back to work

Missy,

You're distracting me from the very important topic of workplace safety. How would you feel if I improperly climbed a ladder due to not learning the proper procedure and then fell to my death?

Always,

The Boy You Dream About

P.S. I'm also a lost prince from a faraway land. Want to do me now?

"How are we doing?" Tom was back.

I closed my email window and went back to the test. I wasn't as far as I should be with the test, but that wasn't completely my fault.

"Done," Hunter said with one last mouse click. Asshat.

"I have a few left," I admitted.

"Okay, well come find me when you're done, and we'll do a little tour and get you started on some shelving."

Hunter leaned back in his chair, and from the look on his face I could tell he was pleased with himself. God, I wanted to punch him again, but then I'd get fired and I really needed this job.

I finished my test with Hunter looking on, and I didn't get any further emails. I wanted to text him that if he fell from a ladder it would save me from having to try to win the bet, but I wasn't going to give him the satisfaction.

The rest of our few hours of work was uneventful, if you could call Hunter "accidentally" brushing his hand on my ass several times as Tom showed us the closed stacks on the third floor of the library where most of the documents were kept and taught us the rudiments of the call number system uneventful.

"One more time and those fingers will be gone," I hissed

when Hunter brushed my backside a third time as we got back in the elevator to go down to the first floor.

Tom went over our schedules and wrote them on a whiteboard. I was relieved to find that Hunter and I only had two shifts the same, so at least I'd have the rest of the time Hunter-free.

"Well, we're very happy to have you on board and we'll see you tomorrow," Tom said as Hunter and I gathered up our bags.

"Thank you again. I really appreciate it," I said.

"See you tomorrow," Hunter said, gesturing for me to exit first. "Ladies first."

I walked through, and I could feel his eyes on my butt. I didn't say a word until we were outside. I turned around and gave him a sweet smile, stepping close and biting my lip.

"So, um, I was thinking…" Hunter's eyes went wide for half a second before he started to smile. Ha-ha. I grabbed his hand and dragged him into a nook behind the library where people wouldn't see us. I laughed and moved closer to him. He reached for me.…

And I slammed him with my bag.

"You asshole! Are you seriously stalking me? Of all the places for you to get a job, you choose the same office as me? *Seriously?*" I went for another hit, but he was ready this time.

"Hey, hey! I didn't know, okay?" We fought for control of the bag, but since he had more leverage he won. "Jesus, stop hitting me. Has anyone ever told you that you have an anger problem?"

"More than one therapist," I said, lunging for my bag.

He pulled his arm back and up so it was securely out of my reach. "Whoa, there. Calm down."

"Don't tell me what to do."

"Okay, fine. Freak out."

He held the bag out to me, and I waited a second before I ripped it away from him. For only the third time I saw a look other than cocky assurance on Hunter's face. I hated the look of concern even more than the confident one.

"Screw you," I said, storming away. I hated him. I hated how he got under my skin. I hated how, for a second, I thought about pushing him up against the library and making out with him. I hated him. I *hated* him. How could I prove it before it was too late and I actually followed through with kissing him? I couldn't fall for Hunter. I couldn't fall for anyone.

CHAPTER 11

"So he showed up at your work? Kid, that's weird. You sure he's not stalking you?" Tawny said.

I was in my bedroom, my homework spread on my bed. Hunter was off with Mase getting pizza, so I took my Hunter-free chance to call Tawny and hash out the recent developments.

"He says he isn't, but I can't understand how he keeps showing up everywhere. It's just weird. Renee says it's the universe telling us we should be together."

Tawny snorted. "Yeah, Renee would say that. Isn't she the same girl who tried to set you up with that guy, what was his name?"

"Robbie."

Most. Awkward. Experience. Ever. Renee had ambushed me one night last year and told me to "get pretty" so I could meet someone. I said hell no, but she wouldn't take no for an answer. So, I put on some mascara and put on a T-shirt that made my boobs look decent. She'd hauled me out for pizza with her and Paul and Robbie. Turned out Robbie was Paul's only single friend, and of course I was Renee's single friend so we were perfect for one another. Needless to say, Robbie turned out to be a mega-creep, and it was no secret why he was single.

"That's it. I still don't understand why he thought you'd want to know about how to properly perform a blow job. I mean, it's not rocket science."

"He was just trying to spread his knowledge to the world and enlighten us uneducated virgins in the ways of the BJ." Because we needed to be educated, according to Robbie. He'd gone through every girl he'd ever had in graphic detail while I died a little inside and Renee tried to change the subject.

"Gag me," she said.

"Literally."

"Blow jobs aside, you can say you hate him all you want, but I'm pretty sure he's not going to believe you, even if you do. Because you definitely don't. I think there's only one person you really hate in this world and his name isn't Hunter." No, his name wasn't Hunter. "I don't know if it's possible for you to hate more than one person at a time."

"Can you love more than one person at a time?" I said.

"I think you can love multiple people, but in different ways."

"So why can't you hate more than one person, but in different ways?"

"Because."

I sighed. "That's not a reason."

"I'm your big sister. It's true because I said so, Kid." She'd used this reason when we were younger, and it hadn't worked then, either. I wasn't a because-I-said-so kind of person.

"Whatever. I'm not giving up."

"I wouldn't expect you to. Still, I don't think it's a fight you're gonna win. You're not going to get rid of that boy."

"Maybe I can pretend that I love him." That was my last resort.

"Kid, pretending and the real thing aren't that far away. Just be careful." I heard the commotion in the living room that meant the boys were back.

"Gotta go, he's back."

"Spit, don't swallow!" Tawny yelled as I ended the call. I stifled a laugh as Hunter popped his head in the door.

"You hungry?"

"Maybe."

"Aw, come on, Missy. Don't be pissed at me. You were the one who pretended you were going to seduce me and then hit me with your bag. By the way, do you carry bricks in there? I think I've got a bruise. You want to kiss it and make it better?" He started to lift his shirt up, revealing a few inches of flat stomach. That was just what I needed.

"Why don't you go fall off a ladder?"

"Can't. I completed the safety test and now can properly use a ladder without incident."

"Damn." He crossed his arms and gave me a satisfied look. Why was his face so...perfect? "Why don't you be a gentleman and fetch me some pizza. I'm a little busy," I said, pointing to the mountains of notes and textbooks.

"I said I was a prince. I never said a charming one," he said as he went out the door. He came back a moment later with two plates of pizza, two sodas and a roll of paper towels under his arm.

"I thought we could celebrate our first day of work. If you're not going to throw this drink at me. That's considered assault in the state of Maine, FYI."

"How do you know that?"

"Oh, the vast stores of things I know could fill many volumes, Missy girl," he said, handing me a plate and a cup and dumping the paper towels in my lap. I should throw the drink at him. Assaulting Hunter would be quite satisfying.

"I can *imagine*," I said, rolling my eyes. He chuckled and seated himself on the floor.

"Come on, floor picnic." He patted a spot beside him that was free of clothes. I hadn't had a chance to do laundry in a while, and a few of my clothes hadn't made it to the hamper yet. Hunter didn't seem to care, even though he was an obsessive neat freak, for a guy.

"Are you bipolar?" I asked. He stared at me for a second and threw his head back and laughed. "No, seriously."

"Says the girl who has been to more than one therapist."

"So what? It wasn't my choice." I didn't want to talk about me. I got down from the bed and moved a sweatshirt out of the way so I could sit far enough away from him.

"Parents make you go?" he said, taking a bite.

I picked up my piece of pizza and studied it. He'd gotten all my favorite vegetables on it, and he was eating a piece of it, too. "Sort of. It's complicated." I did not want to discuss my dark and twisty past.

"I had to go, too," he said, wiping his mouth and balling up the paper towel in his hand.

"What for?"

"It's a long story. Complicated." His hand went to his seven tattoo and rubbed it three times before he picked up his pizza again.

"Huh," I said.

"What?"

"Well, I just never thought we'd have something like that

in common. Guess we're both a little fucked up." I was a lot fucked up, but I didn't say that.

"A girl like you? No way."

I laughed. "Oh, Hunter. You have no idea." I hadn't showed him even a fraction of the crazy in my head. True, I probably hadn't seen a fraction of his, either.

"Well, we can just be fucked up together."

"No, thanks." I munched my pizza and scooted away from him. Hunter was always too close for comfort.

"You talk to your sister lately?"

"Why are you so concerned about my personal business?"

"Because I'm a gentleman. And your roommate."

"Bite me."

"Deflecting, I see. You seem to do that a lot. I bet it's because your sister likes me. Admit it. I've never been with sisters before, but for you I'd make an exception."

I reached behind me for the closest thing I could throw. Turned out to be a kitten heel. For the first time in my life, I wished I wore spiked heels. Really sharp ones.

He ducked my shoe assault.

"Shoes don't count under the assault category, do they?" I asked.

"Not sure, I'll have to check my law books."

"You do not have law books."

He nodded and picked up his pizza, totally blasé. "My uncle does. A whole room full of 'em. I used to read them when I was a kid."

"Law books. You," I said, pointing to the smirking dude across from me, "read law books? Did you get punished a lot as a kid?"

"Why, you wanna punish me, Missy?" His eyes sparkled, and he smiled wickedly.

I closed my eyes and shook my head to rid myself of the mental image of doing just that. It wouldn't be as fun for him as it would for me in my version.

"Nah, I just liked reading them. I don't know. There's something comforting about the law. Most of it's written down, and there are rules to follow. It's equal for everyone."

"Yeah, the law is great." We were veering into uncomfortable territory, but I didn't want Hunter to know that. "Works every time."

"How would you know?" His playful tone was gone, and his face was serious again. *Shit.*

"I watch a lot of crime shows," I said, rolling my eyes and shoving my pizza into my mouth so I wouldn't have to talk.

"Uh-huh," Hunter said, but he dropped the subject.

We both looked up when there was a knock at the door. Mase slowly poked his head in, as if he was expecting to surprise us in a compromising position.

"Hey, guys," he said, taking in our floor picnic. He seemed relieved that neither of us was naked. "I just wanted to see if you were coming to the house this weekend?"

"Yeah, I gotta meet with Joe, so I'll be over for dinner."

Mase's eyes flicked from me to Hunter and back. "Cool, I'll tell Dad. See you later, man."

Hunter nodded good-night, and Mase closed the door softly.

"Who's Joe?"

He got up and tossed his pizza plate and chugged some of his soda. "Family friend."

"You have to 'meet' with him? Doesn't sound friendly." *Well, hello, secret that Hunter didn't want me to know. Nice to meet you.*

He drained the rest of the can. "I'm gonna go shower. Care

to join me?" The flirty smile was back, but it didn't reach his eyes. *Gotcha.*

"Hmm, that sounds a lot like deflecting, Hunter." He slung his towel over his shoulder as I sauntered over to him. I tipped my face up and smiled. "Now who has a secret?"

"You know, for a girl who claims to hate me, you're doing a really good job of trying to get into my pants. We could fix that, right here, right now."

"What about the bet?"

"Missy, if you slept with me, I'd say screw the bet. Whatever you wanted, I'd do."

"So if I sleep with you and told you to get the fuck out, you'd do it?"

"Scout's honor," he said, putting up his fingers.

"Bullshit." I was calling his bluff. Also, I was not sleeping with him. Still, if I had one more chance of getting rid of him, I'd take it. Maybe more opportunities would come my way.

He stuck his hand right in my face. "Shake on it?"

"Deal," I said.

"Why, Missy, if you wanted to get rid of me, you chose the most fun way of doing it."

"Oh, Hunter, I'm not going to sleep with you. Dream on," I said, brushing my hand on the front of his jeans, just near a very important area. He made a little groaning noise and tore himself away from me, slamming the door.

Who was in the driver's seat now?

"So who's Joe?" I said when Hunter came back after his very long shower. He looked distinctly grumpy.

"I told you, a family friend. Don't stick your pretty nose in places it doesn't belong, Missy. You might find something you don't want to find." He had no idea.

"How do you know that I don't have secrets?"

"Oh, I know you do. I'm just not as overt as you are about finding them out. The best way to get what you want is to pretend you don't want it."

"So are you telling me you don't want me?" Could have fooled me. I was pretty sure you didn't proposition people you *didn't* want to sleep with every five seconds.

He pointed to me. "You're my exception, Missy. I don't make exceptions very often. It's bad luck. I can want you without liking you, so don't take that as a confirmation that I like you."

"Am I bad luck?"

He laughed. "No, Missy, you're a jackpot. Best lucky break ever."

"So you're saying you do want to sleep with me?"

"Given the fact that I just took my millionth cold shower since I've moved in here and I have to constantly recite the Gettysburg Address and the Bill of Rights in my head when I'm around you? Yeah, I'd say so. Why, you want me, too?"

"No. I hate you." I gave it a shot.

"Not a chance, Missy. But if you wanted to get this over with, I could be out of here in an hour." He hopped up on his bed and started pulling his shirt over his head. *Oh, God.*

"No."

"No?" He stopped with half of his stomach exposed.

"No." My voice was firm. It was not going to happen. Joking aside, if he *ever* tried to force himself on me, they would have to drag me off his dead body because I would have beaten him to death. He must have seen my anger rising or sensed that I was about ready to do something crazy again, because he pulled his shirt back down and put his hands up in a peace-making gesture.

"Message received. Shirt is staying on. Well, until we go to bed, but that's nothing new." He rubbed his tattoo again. I'd seen him doing that more than once.

There were other little things I'd noticed about him. Like the fact that he was really into the numbers three, five and seven. Well, the seven was obvious. Five was more subtle. I'd heard him counting under his breath once, like it was a way to calm himself or something. When we walked, sometimes he counted his steps, one, two, three, four, five, one, two, three, four, five. I'd never said anything about it because I knew he wasn't aware of it, or he didn't think I was aware of it. I didn't want him knowing I noticed things like that.

When we'd had our pizza night with our neighbors, he'd freaked out when we had thirteen people.

"It's uneven. We have to have fourteen." So he'd stuck his head out the hall and yelled, "Free pizza!" and some dude we'd never seen before joined us. Hunter had seemed relieved. He was always giving my peacock stuff a wide berth.

Hunter was quiet as we both finished our homework and prepared for bed.

"I wrote something for you," he said, grabbing his guitar for our nightly "music sex," as he called it. The first time I'd heard his singing voice, I'd been blown away. His talking voice was amazing, but his singing was like honey and smoke had hooked up in the back of a van at a rock concert and had a love child. Smooth and rough at the same time.

"Awesome. I can't *wait* to hear it."

He strummed a chord and grinned. "Oh, believe me. This is Billboard material. Top ten. Platinum record." He started a little meandering tune.

I'm gonna tell you a story 'bout a girl I know,
Her name is Missy, and wants to do me so,

I wanna tell you about my Missy girl,
Her hair is brown and her lips are pink,
Her eyes are greenish or bluish I think,
She fights and flirts with me all day long,
Which is why I decided to write this song,
She may think that I've crossed the line,
But she tells me she hates me all the time,
So I don't really believe anything she says,
I like the way she glares when she's mad at me,
I like the way she smiles when she thinks no one sees,
She may think this song means I like her,
But she'd be very wrong,
I was bored in macro, so I decided to write a song,
There are two more things about Missy I like,
Could someone please hand me a mic?
The way she flips her retainer when she reads vampire smut,
And I really, really like her—he winked at me—*ass.*

I threw a pillow at him, but that didn't stop the song. It was all about me.

My silly, cute and sexy Missy girl…Missy girl…Missy girl…

He strummed the last chord and then quieted the guitar. "So?"

I bit my lip so I wouldn't laugh. What a ridiculous song. "Is it possible to be both impressed and insulted?"

"Sure, why not? What do you think of my songwriting?"

"Not much." I couldn't hide my smile. No one had ever written a song about me, let alone all the weird things about me that I thought other people would hate or find unattractive. The weird part was, I had no idea about the retainer thing. That was news. "So you like the retainer, huh?" I said.

"Nothing like a girl who has good oral health." I rolled my eyes at that, and he plucked a string. "And a cute ass."

"I never knew it was song-worthy," I said, getting up and craning my neck to look at it.

"You need to stop doing that."

"Why?"

"Because you shouldn't focus my attention there right now."

"Oh, I'm *soooo* sorry. Does this bother you?" I shimmied my hips a little and struck a pose.

"You're an evil, evil girl, Missy."

"Don't you forget it." I hopped back in bed and popped my retainer in, giving it a little flip and putting my arms up like a gymnast completing a vault.

"Ten!" Hunter said, holding up ten fingers.

It was times like this when I thought that Hunter and I could be something. That *we* could be something. That maybe...he could be the person I would break all my rules for. I hadn't had a lot of luck. Maybe I was getting it all at once in the form of Hunter Zaccadelli.

"So, can I get some payment for that song? It took me a whole hour to write it," he said, moving his guitar and raising one eyebrow up and down. I'd never been able to do that. "Why don't you bring that fine ass over here and take care of it? Or do you want me to put it on your tab?" And just like that, the lucky feeling was gone.

"I have a tab? Please, tell me what's on it."

"How much time do you have?"

"Whatever." I grabbed my pajamas and prepared to head to the bathroom to change. It was a pain to have to do that, but there was no way I was getting naked in the same room with Hunter Zaccadelli. I was sure he would tell me he was completely turned around, but I wouldn't believe that for a second. He'd been trying to catch me sans clothes since day one. I'd somehow managed to evade him thus far.

I had my fingers crossed.

When I got back Hunter was naked, under his covers, and the light was off.

"Why, Hunter, are you tired?"

"Yes. Being with you is exhausting, Missy."

I crawled into my bed and grabbed my e-reader and clicked on the book light.

"Who's she with now?"

"The vampire."

"Which one?"

"The one you don't like."

"What is she doing with him? She knows he's going to break her heart. He can never love her because his heart belongs to another." For a second I thought he was making fun, but then I realized he was actually serious. "And don't get me started on that werewolf," he said, propping his head on his arm. "He's just trouble."

"Aren't all werewolves?" I said.

"Hairy trouble." He shook his head.

I started giggling again. Seemed I'd had a bad case of them today.

"You may laugh, but when the full moon hits, you'll wish you had some silver bullets."

"Good night, Hunter."

"Love me?"

"Nope."

"Hate me?"

"More than the DMV."

"Ooh, burn."

I went back to my book, and Hunter went back to his sleeping. Well, he wasn't exactly sleeping. I could tell he was awake. Hunter was only very still when he was pretending to sleep. The actual thing was pretty restless.

I read until my eyes begged me to shut them. I spent most of the night thinking about Hunter and how the hell I was going to get rid of him. The hate thing wasn't working. Unless he did something to seriously piss me off, which was pretty likely, or I had sex with him, or I made him believe that I loved him.

Three options. Three paths to take. As long as they led me away from him, I'd take whichever one would do that. I was drawing the line at turning in my V card. I'd only said yes to that bet to mess with him. Hunter was insane if he thought I would go to those lengths to get rid of him. I mean, really, who would do that?

I went over and over my options as Hunter mumbled in his sleep. The stupid tune he'd made up was also stuck in my head. If he wasn't so much of a dick, things would be so much easier. I watched him throw his hand over his face and frown.

Easy wasn't my style.

CHAPTER 12

I saw Hunter when I woke up. I saw Hunter as I ate a bowl of cereal. I saw him in Human Sexuality, where he seemed to be trying to break a record for most innuendos in one hour. I saw him at work, where he assaulted my email. I saw him every night at dinner. I saw him go to and from the bathroom. I saw him at our stupid mediations, which were as pointless as socks with sandals.

I. Saw. Him. *Everywhere.*

I'd never spent so much time with someone I wasn't related to, ever. I escaped to Megan's every chance I could get, even with the smelly boys that were always there. We were too broke to go out, but sometimes we went for walks around campus or near her apartment.

"My couch is open anytime," she said when I told her about the newest bet. "I'm sure if you told housing about it that they'd do something."

"Been there, done that." I'd tried again with housing, but they just told me to continue with mediations. They were still dealing with all the freshmen playing musical roommates, so maybe around the end of October I'd be able to do something.

"Are you sure you want him gone?"

"Yes. The more time I spend with him, the more I want him gone. I just…I can't." I kicked at a pinecone, and, a few steps later, crushed it with my foot to a satisfying crunch.

"I know, I know."

We took a few more steps. Megan paused. I knew she wanted to say something else, but she was doing that waiting thing she did when she wanted to pretend she had moved on to another topic.

"I know you've been through a lot, and no one would blame you for giving up on men, but have you ever thought that you can't let one guy ruin all guys?"

"Sure, I've thought about it. I don't know, Meg. I think about it and then I remember that night, and it all comes back to me. I can't see someone like that without it reminding me of that night." It wasn't chilly, but I wrapped my arms around myself and pulled my sleeves over my hands.

"Therapy didn't help?" She knew the answer, but she had to do the friend thing and ask anyway.

"I had a string of interesting therapists who didn't really know what to do with me. They tried, but I guess I just couldn't be helped. Haven't you heard? I'm a lost cause."

"No one's a lost cause, not even you."

"I don't know, Meg, I'm pretty fucked up."

"Have you met my boyfriend? He thinks running around in the middle of the night pretending he's an elf is a good time. If that's not fucked up, I don't know what is."

"You love him, though."

She sighs, a little smile on her face. "Yeah, I do love him. I just don't love his stinky friends. You have no idea how much

I spend on room spray and air fresheners. I should buy stock in that stuff."

"Now I know what to give you for Christmas."

"Please, the strongest you can find. I don't care if my house smells like a pumpkin threw up in it."

"Pumpkin Barf. Got it. Not sure if that's an official Yankee Candle scent, but I'll check."

We laughed and moved on to talk about other things. Megan never harped on things I didn't want to talk about, which was one of the reasons I liked her so much. She wasn't pushy or in-your-face. She was sweet and loyal, and she'd do anything for her friends. Even her boyfriend's friends, who liked to take advantage. One of these days they were going to push her too far. I'd seen Megan snap, and it wasn't pretty.

Actually, one of my therapists had found a way for me to deal with some of my issues. All I needed was some watercolor paint, straws and paper. I decided to treat myself and went down to the art section of the school bookstore and splurged on the real deal.

That evening I had the place to myself. Darah was on a date with Mase, and Renee was at the library again. I didn't know where Hunter was until he walked in on me blowing my brains out through a straw.

"So *this* is what you do when I'm not around."

I blew out the rest of the paint drops to the edge of the paper. I was working on a calming blue piece, blending in some green so it looked like the ocean. Some people actually tried to make a picture, but I just liked to mess with the colors to see what I could make and then try to find images in the mess. Like clouds.

"It's called blow painting," I said, taking the straw out of my mouth. At the word *blow* his eyebrows migrated farther up his forehead.

"Is that so?" He dropped his bag and came to examine my work. He turned his head from side to side, as if he was trying to figure out what it was.

"It's not supposed to be anything," I said.

"Oh."

"I just do it sometimes." Suddenly, I wanted to hide my picture. It wasn't like it was anything special. Picasso, I was not, but it was a personal thing I did, and I didn't share it with a lot of people.

Hunter looked at it again after rubbing his tattoo. One, two, three. Someday he was going to rub it off.

"Got another straw?" I handed him one, and he paused over the paint. "You don't mind, do you?"

"No, go ahead." At least he'd asked.

He dipped the straw in the dark blue paint, making sure he had a decent amount before dropping it on the page and puffing up his cheeks and blowing the drop of paint as far as it would go. The drop split out into several drops, and he separated each one with a blast of air, making the paint look like it was exploding. He took the straw out of his mouth and examined it.

"I think you need a little more of the dark blue here," he said, pointing to a corner I hadn't gotten to yet. He turned his head, and our noses almost touched. He laughed a little, his breath moving the little wisps of hair that had escaped my ponytail.

"Go ahead," I said. He looked shocked for a second. "The paint. Go ahead." My brain seemed to be only capable of firing a few words at a time.

His mouth opened just a little, and my eyes zoned in on his

lips. They were very nice lips. Full, for a guy, but they looked like he slathered them with ChapStick. For all I knew, he kept it in his pocket and only applied it when he was by himself. It seemed like something he'd do.

He slowly drew the straw to his lips. Funny, he didn't seem to have a snappy comeback, but then again, neither did I.

He was the first to break eye contact, and I felt like all my air had been sucked out when he did. I grabbed my straw and stuck it in the green paint. I did one corner and he did the other, and somehow our paints met. Without hesitation, we put our heads together and went crazy on the paint until we couldn't get it to go any farther. Our heads knocked together, and we both dropped our straws.

"Ow," I said, rubbing the spot.

"Sorry, Missy. You okay?" Jesus, it was just a little bump.

"Yeah, no big," I said, looking back down at our masterpiece.

"You sure?" He raised his hands, as if he wanted to check and make sure, but didn't want to touch me for fear I might freak out. He knew me too well.

"Yeah."

"More blue?"

"You can never have enough blue," I said, picking up my straw again.

By the time Renee got back from the library, we'd done another painting, this one in autumn tones.

"I think that one's a keeper. That should go on the back of the door. I can get a frame if you want."

"It's not that great, Hunter."

"What's not great?" she called after coming back from the kitchen with a banana, a spoon and a jar of peanut butter. Ugh. I hated bananas with the fiery passion of a thousand suns.

"We made you a picture," I said in pretend-kid voice.

"Here's me and here's you, and that's Darah and Mase and Hunter."

"It's beautiful, darling. That one's going on the fridge right next to the A you got on your spelling test," she said, playing along.

Hunter was looking at me like I'd grown an extra head. "What?" I said.

"You are so odd sometimes."

"Says the boy who has a vendetta against werewolves."

"Hey, they can't control themselves during the full moon. They're completely unpredictable."

"Hey, they look way better shirtless. Also, they still have beating hearts. Having sex with a vamp is like having sex with a corpse. I'm not into that," Renee said, wiping a glob of peanut butter on the end of the banana. She saw me watching her. "Want some? Oh, right, I forgot."

"Forgot what?"

"Tay hates bananas."

"Oh, really?" Here we go. The boy I'd done a blow painting with a second before was gone, and the boy who was always trying to get in my pants was back.

I didn't respond, but started picking up the painting stuff. I didn't like doing it with a lot of people around. It was a personal thing. Hunter was the first person I'd actually done one with, but he didn't know that.

"I'm sorry, but you walked right into that one," he said.

"You don't have to make everything into an innuendo, Hunter. Not everything is about sex."

"Okay, well, I'm going to go eat this somewhere else. See ya," Renee said, skittering away to her room.

She must have sensed that I was close to another blowup.

I hadn't had one for at least a week. That must be some kind of record.

I gathered the brushes and water cup and threw them in the sink. I didn't want him to know I was hurt, but it was too late. I turned on the water and started vigorously washing the brushes. I could feel Hunter leaning against the counter. I hated how aware of him I was. If he was in a room, it was like I had radar that went off and tracked his every movement.

"Taylor, I'm sorry. You should know by now that I'm an ass most of the time."

"You don't have to be an ass *all* of the time." It wasn't true. He could be sweet and funny and charming, and…He could be so much more than a guy who was always talking about getting laid.

"You're right. I'll try. For you, I'll try."

I nodded and wiped the brushes on a paper towel and threw them in the sink drainer to dry. The counter was covered in our breakfast dishes.

"It's my turn," Hunter said, pointing to the chore chart on the fridge. It was my turn for dishes the next day.

"Many hands make light work," I said, handing him a sponge. "If you promise to not make a pass at me for the rest of today, I will help you do the dishes. If you do, you have to do them tomorrow. Deal?"

"For real? God, Missy, you drive a hard bargain."

"All I'm asking you to do is not be an ass for—" I looked at the clock "—less than eight hours. You can do it. I believe in you."

He looked at the dishes, including the several that were crusted with oatmeal. "Deal."

We shook on it and got started. The sink was small, and

the counter made an L, so we were squished in close. Hunter started humming a tune as I handed him a cup.

"What are you singing?"

"Well, to distract myself from being an ass, I'm writing another song. It's called 'Doin' Dirty...Dishes.'"

"Clever."

He started beating out a rhythm with his foot, and I joined.

Soap and water and a pretty girl,
We turn on the water and watch it swirl,
We're...doin' dishes, we're...doin' dishes,
Oooh, oooh, ooohhh,
Scrub, scrub, scrub, yeah,
Scrub, scrub, scrub, yeah,
Scrubby, scrubby, scrubby, scrub, scrub, scruuubbb.

He ended the song with a little flourish and a bow. I clapped my wet hands, spraying both of us with soapy water. He was such a dork sometimes. The song was pretty terrible.

"See what you can accomplish when you're not being an ass?"

"I had more suggestive lyrics, but I decided not to use them. You know, because I'm not being an ass."

"Right."

"But I'll save them and sing them to you at a later point when I'm allowed assery again."

"Okay."

That stupid little song got stuck in my head, and Hunter sang it again, with me providing sound effects with pots and a wooden spoon.

"What are you doing out here?" Renee said, emerging from her room with her "study" look: dazed expression, hair in a clip and her ratty old UMaine sweatpants.

"Hunter has decided he's not going to be an ass today. Isn't that nice?" I said.

"Is that even possible? No offense, dude."

"None taken. I am fully aware of my asshattery."

"Oooh, I like that. Asshattery. I'm gonna use that now," Renee said, going to the fridge for an energy drink.

"Late night?"

"I have a test on autoimmune diseases. Want to see a picture of dermatitis herpetiformis?"

She was always trying to get me to look at gross disease pictures.

"Yeah, I think I'll pass. I don't know how you can eat and do that stuff," I said.

Renee shrugged.

Darah came home a minute later, towing Mase by the hand.

"Oh look, it's the fearsome twosome." Renee got a little bitter whenever she saw happy couples. I wished she'd just call Paul, forgive him, have some awesome makeup sex and be done with it. I'd much rather have Paul around and have Renee happy than not have him around and have to deal with crabby Renee.

"Are you doing dishes?" Mase said, gaping at Hunter.

"Why, yes, I am."

Mase looked at me as if it was my fault.

"Hey, his name is on the chore chart," I said.

"You have a chore chart?" Mase said.

"It was Darah's idea," I pointed out.

"So that no one gets stuck with doing everything, and we're held accountable," Darah said.

"Hey, anything that can get this guy to do dishes is okay by me. Good job, Dare," he said, giving her a peck on the cheek. She smiled in satisfaction.

"What is it with you people and nicknames? Do you have one for me?" Renee said. Sometimes we called her Nene, because we'd heard her mom call her that once when she visited, but Paul was the only one allowed to use it without getting a glare from Renee.

"How about Re? As in, ray of sunshine?" Hunter said. Smooth. "Or Ne? That's cute, too."

She thought about it for a second.

"I'll take it."

"So I'm bringing Darah home with me this weekend to meet Mom and Dad, so we're gonna go together."

Darah looked at him with a giddy-nervous smile. Wow, meeting the family was big.

"Wow, meeting the Masons. Big step, Mase," Hunter said.

"I know," Mase said, winking at Darah. "She's going to do great."

I was painfully curious about Hunter's family, especially how he hadn't grown up with his parents. He'd said they were dead, but when had they died? How old was he? Did he miss them? The questions had been running through my mind since he'd first told me they were dead. Any way you sliced it, he didn't want to talk about it. I could respect that, seeing as how I had plenty of things I didn't want to talk about.

"Got any advice for me, Hunter?" Darah said.

"Just talk to John about technology stocks, the *New York Times* crossword, real estate or World War II and you're good."

"Uhh," Darah said, the panic clear in her eyes.

"I'm kidding. Although, you could talk to him about the real estate market. He loves British comedies, the Pats, Asian cooking and classic cars."

"Oh thank God. Cooking and cars. Got it. Although I could have held my own with stocks."

"You're gonna do great. Don't worry so much," Mase said, flipping her hair.

Hunter's eyes flicked over me before he lowered his voice. "Have you told her about Harper?" Like I couldn't hear him. He was standing two feet away.

"Of course."

Darah, Mase and Hunter all looked at me. Seemed I was the odd one out.

"Who's Harper?" I said, asking the obvious question.

"My sister. She has cerebral palsy from a fall she had as a baby. It's not a big deal, but our house is filled with ramps and equipment and stuff, so it's better to prepare people ahead of time," Mase said.

"How old is she?"

"Seven," Mase said. I could feel Hunter watching my face, as if he was anticipating my reaction. How did he think I would react?

"So, anyway, that's where we're going to be this weekend. I'll see you tomorrow?" Mase said.

"Okay," Darah said, giving him a kiss.

I could hear Renee rolling her eyes.

"Bye, Dare."

"Night, John."

Mase nodded to the rest of us and left.

Darah sighed and leaned on the counter.

"John? Wow, I think you're the first girl he's ever let use the first name. You must be doing something right," he said with a wink.

"Hunter," I said in a warning tone.

"What? That wasn't ass-y. It was playful."

I pointed at him and narrowed my eyes. "You are on thin ice, mister."

"What are you talking about?" Darah said.

"Hunter is not supposed to be an ass for the rest of the day." She gaped at Hunter. "For real? Is that even possible?"

"Am I that much of a douche?" he asked us all.

"Yes," we said in unison.

"So, can I be an ass now?" he said at ten-thirty.

"Nope. You have to finish out the night. When you wake up tomorrow morning, go back to your asshat self. Until then, you have to be nice."

He'd been surprisingly nice, letting me go first for the shower, and he'd put up our blow paintings on the back of the door. He'd even made me a cup of tea and brought it to me. It was like he was buttering me up, but I couldn't figure out why.

"Nice is boring."

"Nice is nice," I said, not looking up from my e-reader. Hunter was busy with his guitar, just plucking random strings.

"That doesn't make any sense."

"So, what's your meeting with Joe about?" I tried again. I'd been trying to squeeze it in, hoping to catch him off guard.

"Nice try, Missy. Just because I'm supposed to be nice doesn't mean I'm going to be a doormat."

"It's not being a doormat. It's telling the truth."

"Sometimes people don't want the truth. Sometimes the truth is worse than a lie." He set his guitar aside and climbed under his covers. Any moment now the boxers were coming off.

I had to agree with him on that. We'd been doing this dance around our separate secrets, getting close and then moving away. I didn't know which one of us was going to slip up first.

CHAPTER 13

I was disturbed from my Saturday morning solitary cartoon-watching by Hunter ripping the door open, looking frantic and carrying his guitar case. That was a first.

"Can I borrow your car?"

"What's wrong with yours?" It was early, and I hadn't had my coffee yet. I'd been planning on vegging out for a few hours, since I had the place to myself. Renee was home for the weekend, and Darah and Hunter were supposed to be visiting the Masons.

Or so I had thought.

"It won't start, and I have to get home. Can I have your keys, please?" he said, holding his hand out as if I was just going to pass them to him, no questions asked.

Oh no. There was no way I was letting this guy drive Sassy, my red Charger. No effing way.

"I'm not letting you drive my car," I said, crossing my arms. "No one drives Sassy but me."

"Your car is named Sassy?" he said and then shook his head.

"Never mind, I'll ask about that later. Will you please let me borrow your car? I have to get to Bar Harbor."

"You're not driving my car." That was one line no one crossed. Not even Tawny.

Hunter looked like he was going to blow up and yell. Instead he dropped the guitar case, reached down, grabbed my hand and pulled me to my feet. "Fine, you drive."

I tried to pull away from him, but it was early, and he was strong and determined and I didn't have my wits about me yet.

"No way, I'm not driving you to Bar Harbor."

"Then I'm taking your car. It's your choice, Missy. Either take me or I take the car."

"You're not going to steal my car," I said.

"Missy, I can hot-wire it if I have to."

"You're bluffing."

"Want to test it out?"

We glared at one another, neither willing to blink. Finally, I realized that I'd be a horrible bitch if I said no. It wasn't like he was asking me to drive him to a bar to get wasted.

"Fine. Let me get dressed."

"Hurry up—we have to go," he said, pointing at a non-existent watch.

"Why, you going to be late for your appointment with Joe?" I said through the bedroom door.

He was enough of a non-ass today to not follow me. He must really be in a hurry, because this would be a prime opportunity to catch me naked. I tore through my closet. Damn, did he expect me to come in with him and, like, meet them?

"Are you decent yet?"

"Don't rush me. If I'm meeting your family, I have to look at least presentable."

"You're going to meet them, not try to sleep with them. Whatever you wear will be fine. You'd look gorgeous in one of those hospital gowns."

"Well, I'd like to look like I at least tried to make an effort." I ripped through my closet, looking for my favorite baby blue gauzy shirt.

"Oh, for the love of—" He banged the door open.

"I swear to God, if I was naked, I would have torn your eyeballs out of your head," I said, with my head in the closet.

"I don't doubt it. Now, what are we searching for?"

"Top. Baby blue. Kind of ruffly on the sleeves." Why was my closet so freaking dark? It didn't occur to anyone that I might need a light in there?

"Like this one?" He held up the exact shirt he'd somehow extracted from my dresser drawer.

"Yes! Now I need jeans," I said, glancing at the mess I'd made. I had a pair of dark skinny jeans that would look great with a pair of silver sandals I knew were under my bed.

"Here," Hunter said, finding the exact jeans I was thinking of.

"Are you sure you're not gay? Because you can put an outfit together."

"Can you just get ready?"

Hunter was not in a playful mood. If I didn't know better, I'd say he was stressed. Hmm. That was a new emotion for him. What was he so stressed about, and what did this Joe guy have to do with it? Looked like I was going to get to find out.

"Okay, keep your shirt on. I'll be right back."

I grabbed a new set of underwear when he wasn't looking and dashed to the bathroom. I brushed my teeth with one hand and finger-combed my hair with the other. I was going to leave it down, but it was doing this weird poofy thing on one side, so I whirled it into a messy bun and called it good. I usually didn't wear much makeup, and today didn't seem like the time to mess around with my new mascara.

"If you aren't done in thirty seconds, I'm going to break the door down, whether you kick me in the balls or not."

I waited until he got down to ten before I opened the door. He stopped counting.

"Better than a hospital gown?"

"You could say that." He blinked a couple more times and rubbed his tattoo. I tried not to smirk in satisfaction.

"Don't we need to go?" I said when he hadn't moved.

"Right. Here," he said, tossing me my keys.

"These were in my purse."

"And?"

"And you would have had to go into my purse to get them."

"We're in a hurry," he said.

"We will discuss this in the car," I said, pointing my keys in his face. "And we're listening to my music. No arguments. Also, we're stopping for breakfast and you're buying."

His eyes narrowed, but when I didn't move, he sighed.

"Fine. Let's go." He picked up his guitar, and we were off.

"What do you need that for?"

"Harper," he said, as if that explained it. He was still grumpy so I didn't push the issue.

We trooped out to the student lot, and it took me a second to remember where I'd parked Sassy.

"Sassy, this is Hunter. Hunter, Sassy," I said, pointing from car to boy and back.

"Am I supposed to shake her hubcap?"

"No mocking my love for my car. I can leave you by the side of the road, Mr. Zaccadelli."

"Yes, Miss Caldwell," he said, opening my door for me.

"Thank you."

I got in and cranked my Florence and the Machine CD as he stowed his guitar in the backseat. If he made any cracks about Florence, he was going *down*.

"God help us," Hunter mumbled when he heard the music.

"What was that?"

"I love this song," he said, bopping his head and tapping his hand on his knee. One, two, three, four, five. Pause. One, two, three, four, five. Pause.

"You are so full of shit." I turned the radio up louder and yawned.

We stopped at a drive-through, and I made Hunter get me an iced coffee and cheese Danish. He got black coffee and a bagel and seemed to be okay with my musical selections. I'd switched to The Band Perry, and I even caught him humming along.

"So where does your family live?" I said.

"Bar Harbor."

"Yeah, I got that part when you said we were going to Bar Harbor. Can you be a little more specific?"

"I'll let you know when we get there. You've been there before, right?"

"Sure." A few times. Bar Harbor was actually part of an island known as Mount Desert Island and was home to Acadia National Park, the only national park in Maine. It also had a lot of rich people.

I finished my Danish as we passed through Bangor.

"So, aren't you going to give me a pep talk? Like, things to avoid, what to be prepared for? I know about Harper, but is there anything else?"

"Not really. Hope is my aunt. John is my uncle. You don't have to call them Mr. and Mrs. Mason. They kind of hate that.

The only other person of importance is Harper, and you'll get to meet her, too."

"So they aren't your legal guardians?"

"I'm over eighteen. I don't have a guardian." Ugh, he wouldn't stop shutting me down as I fished for information. So frustrating.

"But when you did need a guardian, were they your guardians?" I glanced over to find him watching me intently.

"Has anyone ever told you that you ask way too many questions?"

"Nearly every teacher I've ever had. They used to call my mom in for parent-teacher conferences and they'd always write that in my evaluation." True story.

"It's a long story, and one we don't have time for."

"When will you have time? I'm really not trying to be nosy. I'm just curious." He was my roommate, and I guessed maybe he was a friend...sort of. I wanted to know about his life. I wanted to know how he became the gorgeous douche who wrote a song about doing the dishes one minute and grabbed my ass the next.

He shifted in his seat, clearly uptight with the direction our conversation had taken.

"Do you mind if I change it?" he said.

"Sure, CDs are on the visor." If he was going to answer my questions, he could play whatever he wanted.

He flipped through my eclectic selection and finally settled on Parachute. Huh. Not what I would have picked for him.

"I can hear you judging me," he said as I merged onto I-395.

"I just didn't think you were a Parachute kind of guy."

"Why not?"

"No reason. So, you were talking about your aunt and uncle."

"Right," he said, but I knew he remembered. He let out a deep breath that seemed to go on forever. "They took me in when I was eleven. My parents died, and there was nowhere else for me to go." He stopped, and I waited a few seconds before asking my next question.

"So Hope is your mother's sister?" I had no idea, so thought I'd take a stab at it.

"Right. My mother's younger sister, but they were only two years apart. My mother's brother lives in Texas. He's an ass."

"So it runs in the family?"

"It's genetic, what can I say?" Well, he was okay enough to joke, so that was good.

"That explains why you and Mase are like brothers."

"We are, more or less. We grew up together, we beat the shit out of each other to solve our issues and we'd take a bullet for the other one."

It was like me and Tawny. If I had to stand in front of a moving truck to prevent it from hitting her, I would. She'd saved my life once, and I could never pay her back.

"I know what that's like," I said.

"So do I get to ask you about your family situation now?"

I shrugged. There wasn't much to tell. "My parents split up when I was thirteen. Dad's an ass who just pretends like he cares. My mom's amazing, and then there's my sister. I have a few aunts and cousins and such, but they all live in different states."

"So that's why you have anger issues with men."

It took a second for the comment to penetrate my brain. He was getting very close to pushing a button he most certainly did not want to push. If he'd thought I was nuts before, it was nothing to how I could be. He hadn't seen the worst. Not by a long shot.

"Walk away, Hunter. You have stuff you don't want to talk about, and I respect that. So I'm asking you to walk away."

"Okay," he said, turning the volume of the CD up and staring out the window. "Pie."

"What?" Not that it wasn't great, but I didn't see what that had to do with anything relevant.

"Hope loves making pie. She'll probably send you home with one. There's a tiny apple orchard in the back of the house, and she always goes nuts in the fall, making as many pies as she can. She made so many one year, she walked around downtown handing them out to the local businesses. They started calling her 'the pie lady.' So, I hope you like pie."

"What kind of a question is that? Who doesn't like pie?"

"A very fucked up person."

"I guess I'm not *that* fucked up then."

"Not even close," he said, pushing his seat back.

I kept driving until we got to Bar Harbor. I rolled the window down to catch the salty air. There was nothing like the smell of the ocean. We'd switched the CD to Coldplay by mutual consent.

"Turn here," he said, pointing to a road on the left. I put my turn signal on and made the turn. "Turn here," he said a minute later, and we made another turn and then another.

We were off the main road, and all I could see were quaint houses with little porches and cute lighthouse mailboxes and wind chimes. It looked like a really nice place. I kept going until he pointed out one last turn onto Mason Drive. I should have seen that coming.

"Here we are," he said as I stopped the car. *Oh, Jesus.*

The house was effing huge. The little cottages along the rest of the road had not prepared me for this. It was at least twice, if not three times the size of my house. My eyes traveled up to count three floors. It was white, sort of Victorian looking with a huge wraparound porch that had a handicap ramp leading up to it on one side. There was a huge red barn as well. Somehow I didn't think there was a tractor in it. I recognized Darah's Camry nestled between a BMW and a brand new Impala, with an Escalade on the other side.

"Shit, Hunter. You never said your family was loaded."

He shrugged one shoulder. "You never asked."

CHAPTER 14

The house was even more gi-huge-ic when I got out of the car and stood in front of it.

"Well, I assumed since you drive a crappy car and couldn't find housing that you were poor," I said.

"Never assume, Missy. Never assume," he said, walking toward the house, swinging the guitar case. My feet seemed to be glued to the ground. I was overtaken with a hard-to-breathe-can't-think feeling. I was panicking.

"I love how you can punch me in the face and not bat an eyelash, but a large house makes you want to run away. It can't hurt you, you know?" He nodded toward the front door. "Come on."

Somehow, my feet unstuck themselves from the driveway, and I moved forward.

"Jesus, you'd think we were leading you to the guillotine."

"Bite me," I snapped as we stood at the front door. It had fancy swirling glass in it, and I could definitely see a chandelier. A fucking chandelier. Where there was a chandelier, there was a foyer, and a den, and spiral staircases, and taking your shoes off and other fancy things. Not that I didn't like fancy things, I just didn't really belong in a house full of them.

Hunter just opened the door, calling out as he walked through. "Anyone home?"

"Hunter? Is that you?" called out a female voice that I assumed belonged to Hope. It had a thick southern twang to it.

"Yeah, I'm here. I brought a guest."

"Is it Taylor?"

What? I stared at Hunter.

"I may have mentioned your name. Once or twice."

As I tried to keep myself from craning my neck to check out the chandelier in more detail, a tall blonde woman came around the corner, wiping her hands on a dish towel and beaming perfect white teeth. So that was where he got them from. She gave Hunter a hug, kissing him on the cheek before turning her attention to me.

"Oh my goodness, you're as pretty as a picture."

Her southern accent only added to the intimidation factor. Not to mention she was wearing heels as if she were born with them, and her hair and makeup looked like they'd been done by a team of professionals. She was the after picture of the before and after.

"I'm Hope. I've heard so much about you."

She came at me with a hug that I had no choice but to return. Hunter must not have told her I wasn't a hugger. Or maybe she didn't care.

"It's nice to meet you, Mrs. Mason."

"Come now, didn't Hunter tell you to call me Hope?"

"He did. I just…I don't know," I stuttered. Grace was not my middle name. Also, I felt the overwhelming urge to call her ma'am.

"Taylor was a little intimidated by the house," Hunter said

as I tried to give him a pinch, but he ducked out of the way and blocked me with his guitar case. *Thanks a lot, dude.*

"Oh, don't worry about that. You come right in," Hope said.

I guessed I didn't have to take off my shoes, since she was wearing hers, but the floors were so shiny, I was scared to place my unworthy feet on them.

"Hunter?" a little girl's voice called.

"Hey, Seven!" Hunter's face lit up as a little red-haired girl in a motorized wheelchair came down the hall. The chair was pink and had glittery stickers all over it. Nice.

"Seven, this is my friend, Taylor." Her eyes got huge as she heard my name.

"Your name is *Taylor?* That's my favorite name in the whole world."

"Thank you," I said, startled by both her sincerity and her wide gold-green eyes. She reminded me of Anne from *Anne of Green Gables.* I'd always wanted red hair. "I like your name too, and seven is my favorite number."

"She's my good luck charm. Born on December seventh. I tried to get Hope to name her Seven, but she didn't go for it," Hunter said, flipping Harper's ponytail, making her giggle.

"Harper's favorite musician is Taylor Swift." A girl after my own heart.

"I'm going to her concert soon," she said.

"You are? I'm so jealous," I said. Hunter gave me a look.

Seriously, I was. I'd just never found anyone who would go with me.

"Maybe if you're really nice, Taylor will sing with us," Hunter said, giving Harper a wink. She giggled, and he put his guitar down to give her a hug and a kiss on her forehead, crouching down so he was at her level.

"Would you?" Her little voice was so cute, how could I say no to her? God, she'd make Hitler melt.

"Of course. I'm not a very good singer, but I'll try."

"Don't listen to her. She has a beautiful voice." How the hell would he know?

"Joe's waiting for you in the study," Hope said to Hunter.

"Right."

I wondered where the study was. Maybe I could somehow excuse myself to go to the bathroom and somehow find myself there.

"Why don't we go sit down?" Hope said, leading us into what must be the den. It had leather couches, flowers in painted vases and a bright cheerful feel.

"I've heard you in the shower," Hunter whispered in my ear as he walked beside me. His hand brushed my back, and I experienced a bad case of the goose bumps. "If you ever want to duet, you know where to find me."

I wanted to sputter with outrage, but the thought of Hunter, in the shower...*Get your mind out of the gutter, Taylor. You're meeting his family, for Christ's sake.*

"I'll be back," Hunter said, winking at me before he left the room.

"Can I get you anything? How about some iced tea?" Hope said as we seated ourselves and Harper parked her wheelchair. Hope sat down on a floral-patterned chair. No, she didn't sit. She floated down until she was sitting. Was that something they taught in the South? If so, could I get lessons?

"That would be lovely, thank you."

She left and it was just me and Harper. I wasn't very good with meeting new people, but she leaned over and motioned me closer, even though we were the only two people in the room.

"Do you wanna hear a secret?" she whispered rather loudly

after she'd looked around to make sure we were absolutely alone.

"I'd love to hear a secret," I whispered back, cupping my hand over her ear. She giggled and did the same.

"Hunter likes you." Aw. She was adorable.

"He does?" I said, playing along.

"A lot. A lot."

"Like Eric loves Ariel?" There was no doubt this was a Disney girl. There was more than one *The Little Mermaid* sticker on her chair.

"Uh-huh."

"Whoa."

I wondered how long I could wait before I could somehow escape and find out what Hunter was up to.

Hope came back with a tray of sweating glasses, complete with sliced lemons perched on the side.

"Momma, Taylor likes *The Little Mermaid*," Harper said as her mother handed her a glass and a napkin.

"She does? Well, imagine that." Hope gave me a wink as she handed me a glass. I took a sip so I wouldn't laugh. Delicious. Damn, this woman should have her own lifestyle show. I fiddled with my napkin and set my glass down.

"Um, where's your bathroom?"

"Oh, of course. It's down the hall on the left. There's a sign on the door that says powder room."

"Thanks," I said, escaping from the room as Harper dropped her glass and brown liquid pooled everywhere.

"Oh, Harper," Hope said with a sigh.

I found the powder room but kept going. Crap, this house was big. I tiptoed down the hall and ducked into what turned out to be a closet when I heard voices above. I heard Darah giggle. Mase must be giving her a tour of the house or something. I emerged from my hiding place and turned on my hearing, walking slowly and quietly. I paused at each door, listening to see if anyone was inside. Finally, I got to the last door on the right. This had to be it. I paused outside. *Bingo.*

"I just don't think it's a good idea," said a voice that must belong to Joe.

"I figured you wouldn't. But it's not really up to you, is it?"

"Hunter, I've known you your whole life. It's time for you to grow up and take responsibility for your life. For this."

"I. Don't. Want. It."

I heard a chair scrape back. Shit. I did the most awkward tiptoe run back to the powder room and shut the door, breathing heavily. I turned the water on but stayed by the door, waiting to hear Hunter's footsteps. They didn't come, and I had to go back into the den or else Hope would think I'd fallen in. I washed my hands just for the heck of it and left the powder room, which, ironically, was decorated in powder blue.

My mind was reeling with what I'd heard from Hunter and Joe. What wasn't a good idea? What didn't Hunter want?

"See? I told you she'd come back," Hope said when I walked back in the room.

"Where did you think I was going?" I couldn't wait to hear the answer.

"I don't know."

"Maybe later you can show Taylor the apples?"

"Do you wanna see my apple trees?"

"Absolutely."

I caught Hope giving me a weird look. I must have had an unnatural expression on my face, so I did my best to try to look normal again.

I heard voices from upstairs, and then Mase and Darah

came around the corner with a man who must have been John Mason the second. He looked just how I'd thought he would: tall, dark hair, bronze-rimmed glasses and a sensible shirt and tie. I felt like I might as well be wearing a hospital gown compared to these people. Except Harper. She had a T-shirt that said Princess in glitter. We were soul mates.

I was going to beat Hunter senseless when I got the chance for not preparing me for this. Also, I was going to beat him so he would tell me about Joe and what he was hiding from me.

If it was any consolation, Darah was also looking a little starstruck.

Hope got up to introduce me. "John, this is Taylor. She decided to come up and give us a visit. Isn't that nice?" She could make a root canal sound nice with that voice. Mr. Mason's eyebrows went up when she said my name. It was official. I was infamous.

"Oh, yes, Taylor. How nice to finally meet you," he said, holding out his hand as Hunter came back in the room. For a moment, I saw an angry expression on his face, but he wiped it away and turned on the charm. How did he do that? I was still freaking out.

Where was Joe?

I wanted to trip him, but it would have been obvious. He'd probably just dodge me and make another comment, and then where would I be? Also, I couldn't do it in front of Harper. I had to set a good example, so I shook Mr. Mason's hand and said I was pleased to meet him.

"Well, I should get back to the kitchen. That chicken salad isn't going to make itself. You'll stay for lunch, won't you, Taylor?" Hope said.

"Hope," Hunter said, as if reminding her of something.

"Oh! Of course. I'll make you a salad. Hunter told me you didn't eat meat, and it slipped my mind."

"That's fine. You don't have to make a big production. I don't want to be a bother."

She waved the dish towel at me as she left the room. "Never you mind—it's no bother at all. No wonder you keep that pretty figure. I should try that." Like she needed it. God, if most women looked like her, they'd be walking around naked.

"So, what made you decide to come and see us, Taylor?" John asked.

"My car wouldn't start," Hunter said for me.

"Again?" Mase said, pulling Darah down onto the sofa. He definitely didn't fit in this pristine environment. His jeans were torn on the bottoms, and his shirt had been through the wash more than a few times. I wondered what Hope thought of that. "I keep telling you to get rid of that thing. I told you that Bob Karrigan has an old Audi he doesn't use anymore that he'd be happy to let you have for a couple thousand."

Hunter shook his head. "It's fine. I'll get it fixed," Hunter said.

"Daddy, Daddy! Taylor said she would sing with me," Harper said, using the joystick on her wheelchair to come closer to me.

"Yes, Angel. You should say excuse me when other people are having a conversation if you want to say something."

She thought about that for a second.

"Okay. Excuse me, Daddy. Taylor said she would sing with me."

I caught Darah's eye, and we had to press our lips together so we wouldn't laugh.

"That's great. Did you ask her nicely?"

"Yes."

"Good girl."

"Give me some skin, Harp," Mase said, holding up his hand for a high five. She reeled back and smacked as hard as she could, and he pretended to recoil in agony, rolling over on the couch. Her laughter filled the room like bubbles, and we all joined in. Thank God for Harper, because otherwise this might have been a very uncomfortable situation.

"Hunter, why don't you give Taylor a tour of the house?" John said. It would probably take a few years, at least.

"Sure," Hunter said.

"Want to come, Seven?"

"May I?" Harper looked at her father with big pleading eyes.

"Why don't we let Taylor and Hunter do the tour and then you can show her your room."

"Okay," Harper said, clearly bummed.

"We'll be back soon," I said.

"Promise?"

"Pinkie swear," I said, holding mine out. We linked, and she smiled again.

"Hunter," John said. Hunter nodded in understanding. *Wait, what?*

"Shall we?" Hunter said, holding his arm out for me to go first, bowing slightly.

I gave Harper a little wave before we rounded the corner and stood in a long hallway with a set of glorious stairs. I stared at the study door, hoping Joe would come out, but nothing happened.

"I am going to rip your arms off and then strangle you with them," I hissed at Hunter when I was sure we were out of hearing range.

"So this is the hallway," Hunter said, ignoring me. "Elevator, if you ever need it."

"You're not even listening to me. How could you not tell me?" He started walking down the hallway.

"There's a music room back here—"

I yanked on his arm to make him stop. "How could you not tell me?"

He still wouldn't look at me. I reached up and grabbed his chin, turning his stubborn face so I could meet his eyes.

"Come on," he said.

"No, I want to talk about this."

"We will, just not here."

He took my hand and pulled me behind him up the stairs. I caught lots of fancy paintings and furniture that didn't come from IKEA. Down another hall we went, and he pulled me into a room, shutting the door quickly.

"This is my room," he said.

I was momentarily distracted from screaming at him. It looked very much like our room at school, only twelve times the size. Clean and neat and with dark colors. Slate, black, blue. There were a few band posters, including the Goo Goo Dolls and Matchbox Twenty.

"I didn't tell you because I know you and I knew you'd freak."

"So springing it on me was a better idea?" I hoped I wouldn't get so mad that I would spill that I'd spied on him.

"It seemed so at the time," he said, pulling a chair out from behind a huge desk. It looked like something an old crusty writer would use to compose masterpieces on his typewriter. "Now I'm not so sure. You're freaking anyway."

I threw up my hands in frustration. "How else was I supposed to react? It's not just that you sprung this," I said, gesturing to the general situation of the house being effing enormous. "It's that I feel like I don't know you. There's this whole huge part of your life, and I had no idea. And you're meeting with some guy named Joe about some mysterious thing, and if I didn't know better, I'd say you were involved with the mob."

"Why do you care?" That was the million-dollar question. Why did it bother me so much?

"Because you're my roommate," I said, floundering.

"That's not enough of a reason. You wouldn't throw a hissy fit if you found out Darah or Renee lived here or had secret meetings with a guy named Joe. So why me?"

"Because."

"That's not a reason." He got up from his chair and stood right in front of me, our chests only inches apart. He tipped his head down to look in my eyes. "I think it's because you like me. As much as you would rather choke to death than admit it. And you want to know things about the people you like. You want to know what they do when no one is watching, what movie makes them feel better when they're sick, what they really want to be when they grow up. Am I right?"

He was so close, every time I breathed, I could smell him. You'd think after sharing a room with him for several weeks, I'd be used to his smell, but it seemed it had gotten even more potent. I had to close my eyes for a moment to gain some composure.

"No, Hunter. I don't like you."

"Good. I don't like you, either."

We breathed in unison for a moment, and for that moment, the world stood still and we were the only two people in it. I opened my eyes and let myself get lost in his blue ones. Most of the time I avoided them. They were hypnotic, and I didn't like being caught staring.

"I. Don't. Like. You," he said, bringing his face a fraction closer with each word. I couldn't speak or breathe or think.

Our lips were so close that I could feel how warm they were. He exhaled once and pulled away. It was like someone had snapped a rubber band in my brain. He stepped back from me.

"I don't like you," he said again. I wasn't sure if he was trying to convince me or himself.

"You said that," I was finally able to say.

"Well, it's true."

"I know."

"So, let's go see the rest of the house."

"Okay." I robotically followed him out of his bedroom.

I don't like you.

I don't like you.

I don't like you.

Well, I didn't like him, either. There wasn't a word for what I felt about Hunter.

CHAPTER 15

I had one thing to say for Hope Mason. She had damn good decorating sense. The house was absolutely gorgeous, and everything seemed to fit together, even if it didn't look like it went together. There were subtle touches that I noticed. Things that looked like they might have come from yard sales, like a wooden rocking horse and old silver tins and glass perfume bottles.

There were also accommodations for Harper everywhere, from ramps to the elevator to a special sink in her bathroom. There were also strange things hanging from the ceiling in her bedroom.

"So she can get herself in and out of her chair without help," Hunter had said. "When she gets older, they'll get more stuff so she can do a lot more, but since she's still so little, it's easier to carry her."

I couldn't imagine. Harper didn't seem bothered by it at all. She maneuvered her chair like she was born with a joystick in her hand.

When we'd gotten back from the massive tour, Joe was

apparently gone, seeing as there was one less car in the driveway when I caught a glimpse out of a huge picture window in the den. I was no closer to solving the Joe mystery.

Harper insisted on sitting next to me at lunch, and I had Hunter on my other side.

Everyone dug into the chicken while I devoured an avocado, mozzarella, spinach and tomato salad.

"This is amazing. Thank you so much," I said, taking another forkful. I'd had one panicked moment when she'd called us for lunch, envisioning multiple forks and picking the wrong one.

Thankfully, it was a nice day so we ate out on the back porch, which was much more like a terrace that looked out on the apple trees. The smell of the sweet leaves washed over me and made me think of fall and pies and hayrides and pumpkin carving. I loved fall.

"Remind me to give you the recipe for that dressing," Hope said, returning my attention to the present moment.

"I will."

"Momma, can I have some more watermelon, please?" Harper asked.

"Yes, Harper, you may. Thank you for asking so nicely."

"You want some, Dare?" Mase said.

"Sure, thanks." Darah seemed to be as nervous as I was. She'd already dropped her fork twice and had knocked over her water glass.

"So, Taylor, Hunter told us you're a women's studies major. That must be interesting," she said, dishing some watermelon cubes onto Harper's plate.

"I want to work at a crisis center or somewhere that helps women recover from trauma," I said, wondering if that was

TMI. I didn't want to seem like the damaged girl, but it was hard not to.

"That's very admirable. What made you choose that as a career path?" I'd been asked that a million times, so I had an answer.

"I want to help people, and that seemed like a good way to do it."

"Well, aren't you just the sweetest? I'm glad you brought her, Hunter. She's much better than that other one. What was her name?"

"Chastity," he said, not looking at me. I remembered seeing her name in his phone.

"What an awful name. It's been my experience that when you name a girl like that, she's more likely to embrace the opposing virtue," Hope said, giving me a knowing look. I'd also had that experience with a girl named Charity, who had been anything but charitable.

I was in the perfect position to kick Hunter under the table, so I did. Who the hell was Chastity? I knew next to nothing about his dating history, except that it was long and there were a lot of names in that little black book. To be totally honest, I didn't really want to know much. Ignorance was bliss in this situation.

Hope brought out strawberry shortcake, and we all stuffed our faces. The conversation lulled as we chewed. The sun was high in the sky, and it was turning out to be a warm, lazy Saturday.

"So, JJ, I was thinking you and Hunter could give me a hand with that tractor after we're done here." I assumed JJ stood for John Junior.

"Excuse me, Daddy, but we're going to sing," Harper said while Hope wiped whipped cream from her face.

"Yes, Angel, we'll do that first."

"Okay," Harper said, nodding her head.

We finished lunch, and Hunter grabbed his guitar. Darah and Mase went to help Hope with the dishes. I offered, but Hope refused, so John, Hunter and I sat with Harper.

"'Our Song'!" Harper chanted.

Oh, there was no way that Hunter knew that. He seemed to read my mind as he gave me a wink and started the song without further ado. It was clear within three seconds that he had played this song more than a few times. His normally rough voice blended with Harper's in the most adorable way. He knew *all* the words. I hummed along, tapping my foot.

He finished the song and Harper clapped.

"Can we do 'Love Story'?"

"Sure, Seven. Why don't you ask Taylor to sing with us?"

"Will you sing, please?" Her little voice, combined with her clasped hands, was irresistible. This child was the key to world peace. All she'd have to do was bat those eyelashes and smile that dimpled smile and world leaders would be falling over themselves to sign a peace treaty.

"Sure." Hunter started the song, and I was a little nervous about singing in public, but this wasn't really public.

I joined in, my voice blending with the other two. My voice was a little too deep to be like Taylor Swift's, but I did love singing her songs. I hated the fact that Hunter knew I sang in the shower. I should probably put a lid on that.

John got a call on his cell phone midway through the song and excused himself.

Hunter ended the song, and our voices faded out.

"You have a pretty voice," Harper said.

"Thank you, Harper." She was just the sweetest.

"Do you wanna see the apple trees?"

"Lead the way," I said, getting to my feet. Ugh, I'd eaten too much.

She zoomed down the little ramp that was attached to the porch as Hunter and I followed.

"Joe didn't want to join us?"

"He had other things to attend to."

"He's not a hit man, is he?"

Hunter laughed. "No."

"Then why all the secrecy? Unless you're doing something illegal?"

Harper was singing as she tooled along ahead of us.

"It's just personal business. Once again, I ask you, why do you care?"

I pressed my lips together and walked ahead of him, threading my way through the fragrant trees. Hunter was watching me. I always knew when he was watching me. As if he were calling my name inside my head.

"This is my favorite," Harper called from two rows over. The trees all had little green pre-apples on them. "I call him Monty."

"Harper names all the trees," Hunter said with a straight face. "That's Walter and that's Shirley and that's Cinderella..." He kept going, naming at least ten more trees.

"Do you have their names in your phone?" I said without thinking.

"What?"

"Nothing."

He shook his head and turned me around so we weren't facing Harper, who was talking to Monty the tree.

"The only way you would know what numbers I have in my phone would be if you looked in my phone, which would be an invasion of my privacy."

"Oh, like going in my purse and finding my keys isn't? Like taking my e-reader isn't? Like trying to catch me naked isn't? You filthy hypocrite," I hissed at him, glancing to make sure that Harper was still chatting with the tree.

"Don't touch my phone," he said, stepping close to me.

"Don't touch my ass then."

"The problem with that, Missy, is that you want me to touch your ass. If Harper wasn't here right now, you'd want to be pushed up against one of those trees with the leaves in your hair and my hands all over you. I do *not* want you to touch my phone."

"You are such an asshole."

"Watch your language in front of Harper. She's very impressionable." He stepped away and crouched next to Harper's chair.

Normally, Hunter was a douche, but a nice one—if there was such a thing. But it seemed like something had flipped a switch. Hunter had never been mean to me before. Not like that. I had the distinct feeling that it had something to do with Joe and the mysterious meeting.

"Will you come back and help me pick them?" Harper said after she'd introduced me to several more trees.

"Of course I will," I said, leaning down next to her chair. She held her arms out for a hug, and I gave her one.

"You promise?"

"Pinkie swear."

While Hunter and Mase worked on the tractor—I very much doubted the existence of said tractor—and Darah played with Harper, Hope and I had a little chat. I'd heard from Darah that she'd already had the Hope interrogation that morning and it wasn't that bad.

"You are such a pretty little thing. What are you doing with a boy like Hunter?"

I nearly choked on my third glass of iced tea. That stuff was good. "I honestly don't know."

She gave me a look. "He can be a sweet boy when he wants, but sometimes I worry about him. I don't even want to know what he gets up to."

No good, that was what. Lots and lots of no good. I bit my tongue.

"He does have that bad boy charm about him though," she said with a smile. Damn that woman could win the World Smiling Championships. "John was like that, too. Trouble written all over him." Darah and Harper were playing Go Fish, and, from what I could tell, Harper was kicking ass.

"I wasn't very happy when he started inking up his body, I'll tell you that much. If his mother, God rest her soul, knew she would have had a litter of kittens."

I really, really wanted to ask about the mother, but I didn't want to seem like I was trying to pry. I also wasn't going to tell her that I thought his tattoos were beyond sexy.

"As long as he doesn't get a motorcycle, I think my heart will be able to take it. Thank the stars that John Junior never got into that sort of thing. I would have had his hide." I laughed. "You have a great laugh. Has anyone ever told you that?"

"Hunter," I said without thinking.

"He would." She turned away from watching Harper and stared at me. Like really stared. Like she was trying to see deep down into my soul. I tried not to flinch while she completed her examination.

"I think of Hunter as my son, and as his mother it is my

job to vet any potential females he may be interested in. This is nothing personal—it's my job."

"And?" I asked hesitantly. This woman clearly had a set of fangs behind those pearly whites. Noted.

"I don't want him to hurt you. I don't want you to hurt him."

"Me neither. We're not involved...that way anyway." I didn't know what way we were involved. I was pretty sure there wasn't a definition for it yet.

Hope gave me another once-over with her laser eyes. It was worse than airport security.

"Yet. You're not involved yet. But, honey, I've never seen that boy as smitten with anyone as he is with you. You'd have to be blind not to see it."

Yeah, yeah. I fought the urge to roll my eyes. She didn't understand how complicated it was.

"Love is simple. You fall, and that's it. You'll work the other stuff out. You just gotta let yourself fall and have faith that someone will be there to catch you."

I didn't want to do any falling. Falling usually led to meeting a hard surface in an unpleasant way.

"All right, that's enough of the third degree. Now tell me some more about yourself. That top is just darling on you."

I didn't tell her that Hunter had found it for me. We continued our small talk, but I could tell that she was watching me.

CHAPTER 16

"They're great. Your family," I said later that afternoon as Hunter and I drove back to campus. He'd been mostly silent since we'd left. Hope had given me a huge hug and told me to come back soon, and Harper had made me promise I'd sing again with her. John had shaken my hand again and said I was a lovely young lady. Mase and Darah were staying another night, so I'd said I'd see her the next day.

"They are."

"You're being weird."

"How?"

"I've never seen you so quiet. You'd think someone had died." I instantly realized my mistake. "Sorry, that was mean."

"No, I deserved it. I'm not very nice, Taylor." He almost never called me by my real name. I found I didn't like it much.

"I know. But that doesn't give you license to be a jerk."

"I am what I am. If you don't like it, there's a simple way out of it. You have three options. Hate me, love me, do me. Pick your poison."

"Fuck you."

"That's one of the options."

"I am never giving you a ride again."

"That's fine. Now I know where you keep your keys. Sassy and I would have a good time," he said, patting the dashboard.

"I swear to God, Hunter, if you steal this car, I will stab you in your sleep."

"Fine. Go ahead."

What was wrong with him? I turned on an old Avril Lavigne CD just to piss him off. He stared out the window and tapped his leg. *One, two, three, four, five.* I wanted to break each one of his five fingers so he couldn't tap them anymore.

I didn't speak to him again until we were back on campus. Hunter carried his guitar, and I carried a plastic container with leftovers from Hope that she had forced on me as I walked out the door. How could I say no?

I immediately went to our room and shut the door.

I stayed in there for several hours, munching on the leftovers from the Masons and reading. I thought about calling Tawny, but I didn't really want to know what she'd have to say about this situation. I didn't want advice, which would be what she would give me, however unsolicited it might be.

I was deep in the throes of *Gone with the Wind* when I heard voices in the living room. Must be Dev and Sean. There was a soft knock on the door. Hunter never knocked on our door.

"Hey, we're going to Blue. You want to come? I'll buy you a drink."

I shook my head, not looking up from my book.

"Come on, Missy."

"You've been saying that a lot to me lately."

"Thank God, she speaks."

"Bite me."

"You're insulting me. Must mean you're back to normal. Come out with us. It'll be fun. You can dance and tease me again."

"Will you let me smash a beer bottle over your head? Because I'd totally sign up for that."

"Let's get you out and see how things go. I might let you get a punch in, depending on how drunk I get."

I'd never seen Hunter drunk. He had a few beers, but I'd never seen him out of control like most people got. Since I was small, alcohol affected me like a hammer. I just needed one or two drinks and I was in happy land. I'd never really seen the appeal of getting drunk. Until tonight.

"I'm in," I said, swinging my legs over my bed and hopping down. I'd cleaned up the clothing disaster from that morning, but finding the right shirt was going to take another trip through the mire.

Hunter stared at the closet. He knew where my mind had gone.

"Wear that pink one on the left." He pointed, and I saw a scrap of pink. It was a shirt I had but never wore. It just wasn't really me. Tawny had given it to me a few years ago, and I couldn't part with it because I didn't want to make her mad. It had a little fabric flower on the neck and was kind of drapey.

"And those dark black skinny pants."

"Who are you, my fashion consultant?"

"If it'll get you ready faster, sure. I'll be your fashion consultant."

I grabbed the shirt and held it up. Actually, it didn't look that bad.

"We're ready when you are," he said before he left me to change. It was going to be interesting to go out with just me and three boys. If I was a guy, I'd be a pimp. There really wasn't a good equivalent for a girl.

I decided to leave my hair down. It was looking better than it had that morning, which was unusual, so I decided to embrace it.

"Fuckable?" I said when I came around the corner into the living room.

"Definitely," Hunter said. I enjoyed the semi-stunned look on his face. God, he saw me every day, but still, when I put on something nice he couldn't speak. I enjoyed it very much. You didn't do that with someone you didn't like.

The other boys smiled politely. I hadn't seen much of them lately.

"Okay, let's go, boys. Who wants to carry my purse, and who wants to be my drink bitch for the night?"

They all looked at each other.

"Joke. That was a joke. I wouldn't emasculate you like that."

"Carrying a purse wouldn't emasculate me," Hunter said. *Yeah, I bet.*

"I'd carry it, but it doesn't go with my outfit," Dev said. We all burst out laughing.

"Ditto," Sean said as we left.

I took each of their arms.

"Shall we? To the bar!" I said, raising a fist.

We all walked in unison, Hunter trailing behind.

"You got a third arm for me?" he said.

"No, sorry. You can have my purse." I tossed my black clutch at him, and he caught it. "Well done. You may fetch my drinks this evening."

"And what are they going to do?" he asked.

"Fan me and make sure I'm comfortable. Right?"

"My fanning skills are at your service," Dev said, squeezing my arm.

"I guess that means I'm on comfortable duty," Sean said.

"Man, are you always this easy?" I said to them.

"That's what she said," Hunter mumbled behind me.

"I heard that," I said over my shoulder.

"You walked right into it, what was I supposed to do?"

"Control yourself, purse man."

The slight chill in the air made my skin pimple, and I wished I'd brought a jacket.

"You cold?" Sean said.

"I'm fine. We're almost there."

Blue Lagoon was hopping again. It seemed that everyone had been bitten by the fall bug, or maybe it was a holdout from summer. There was already a girl puking her guts out next to a car in the parking lot.

"It is your job tonight, all of you, to make sure I don't turn out like that," I said, pointing to the girl, whose hair was being held by an equally drunk girl who could barely stand.

"Hold on a second," Hunter said.

"What's he doing?" Dev said.

We all watched as he went over to the girl, who was making sure she steered clear of the vomit stream coming from her friend's mouth.

"I have no idea," I said.

He talked to the girl who wasn't vomiting. She shook her head, and he motioned to me.

"You got your phone? My battery died. I'm going to call them a cab. They don't live on campus."

"Of course," I said, fishing out my phone and searching for the number for one of the local cab companies that frequented the campus.

"I don't know where my purse went," the non-vomiting one said. "Purse" came out "pursh." The other girl was slumped on the pavement, moaning.

"It's okay—you'll find it tomorrow. We're gonna call you a cab, okay? Do you know where you live?" he said.

She gave him the address, and I relayed that to the cab company in case they forgot.

Dev and Sean got in on the action, helping vomit girl up and running inside to get a wet paper towel and a cup of water so she could try to clean herself up.

The cab came a few minutes later, and we got them both in. The cabbie assured us he would get them home safe and refused payment when Hunter pulled out some cash.

"No need. One good turn deserves another," he said, waving to us and taking the drunken girls home. They probably weren't going to remember the kindness Hunter showed them, but I would.

"Everyone ready to go in?" I really wanted to get away from the vomit smell, and my teeth were starting to chatter.

"What is it with girls and not having coats?" Hunter said.

"Well, I didn't plan for this random moment of Good Samaritan–ship."

"You never do," he said, walking to the door.

We saw a different bouncer this time, but he also knew Hunter. He was certainly a popular fellow. My fake ID was barely scrutinized before I was let in.

"One girl, three men. Damn," he said.

"These are my toys," I said, feeling bold. God, I hadn't even had a drink yet.

"Need one more?"

"Maybe. I'll let you know," I said with a wink as I sashayed away.

"Are you sure you're not drunk already?" Hunter said, his face a little stunned by my sassiness.

"Drunk on life, Hunter. Drunk on life."

An hour later I was a drink and a half in and having a good time with the guys. We'd seated ourselves at one end of the bar and were busy watching the mayhem around us. Hunter was next to me, and it wasn't my imagination that his hand kept finding itself somewhere on my body. My back, my shoulder, my waist. I was too blissed out on rum and Cokes to bother slapping it away. Besides, I was feeling nice since he had been so concerned about those drunken girls.

He'd been a jerk today, but he'd also been sweet and adorable with Harper. They were like two peas in a pod. She was an odd little girl, but he *got* her.

"Do you want to dance?" he said in my ear.

I knew my face was red from the alcohol, but it got redder and hotter with him standing behind me.

"Sure."

I was a tiny bit unsteady when I got down from my stool, but I could walk fine. Dev and Sean were busy chatting up two girls who had spotted them from across the room and were on the prowl. I didn't think they'd be going back to their own apartments tonight.

"I'm going to get you drunk more often. You're very compliant tonight," Hunter said.

"I'm not that drunk, Hunter." I really wasn't. Just pleasantly buzzed. I'd never really been drunk before. It didn't seem like a thing I'd want to do.

"Not yet. I just need to get a few more drinks in you and then you'll be swooning in my arms."

"Whatever."

I took his hand and led him to the dance floor, which, big

surprise, was crowded. I shoved and pushed until I found a little bit of room. Hunter came with me, making his own room. I started to groove, but Hunter stopped me.

"Oh no, I didn't bring you here to dance like that, as much as I love watching you do that thing with your hips." He yanked me close, wrapping his hands around my waist, and creeping down my back to my ass. *Watch it, mister.*

"I want to dance," he said, starting to move, "like this. I want to dance like we're the same person."

"I thought you didn't like me."

"I don't," he mouthed, and then he closed his eyes for a moment. Before opening them and meeting my eyes. "Dance with me. Just dance with me."

So I did.

We danced for what seemed like hours. Hunter left for a moment and returned with another drink that I somehow balanced while we danced. My body felt liquid, heavy and smooth. Hunter had another drink, and he seemed to be lost. Like that moment in his room when we'd been the only two people on a planet that was standing still.

His hands were on me, mine were on him, we were both sweating and breathing heavily and the music hurt my head and pounded in my skull and it was all too much and not enough.

Eventually I got too hot and I started to walk away to take a break. Hunter followed me, and it was like the dance bubble we'd been in had burst.

"Do you want another drink?"

"Some water would be good," I said, fanning myself.

Dev and Sean had come to find us earlier to say that they were headed to a house party with the two lovely ladies whose names I couldn't remember at the moment. Abandoned in my time of need, I was.

Hunter came back with a glass of water for me, complete with a lime wedge and another beer for himself.

"How you feeling?"

"Fine," I said.

"You gonna be ready to go soon?" It was still relatively early.

"Why, do you want to go?"

He shrugged. Yup, the dance moment was broken. We each sipped our drinks in silence.

"I still don't like you," he said suddenly. "Despite all of that." He waved his hand. I supposed he was indicating the vertical expression of the horizontal desire we'd been doing only minutes before. We were back to walking that fine line between roommates and...whatever else.

Hunter drank his beer, and I sipped my water. We were sitting at the same bar, but it was like we were sitting across from each other with the Grand Canyon between us.

Hunter finished his beer and got another. He was on his fifth or sixth, I couldn't remember. I'd never seen him drink so freely. I sat and fiddled with my phone and sipped my water and watched the other dancers. Hunter wouldn't talk to me, even though I tried a few times.

After he finished his most recent drink, I said I was ready to go. It hadn't turned out to be the fun night I'd expected. The memories of Hunter and I dancing sizzled in my mind, setting me on fire.

We walked back to our place slowly, trying to avoid tripping on unsteady feet. He was just as bad as I was. When we got back to our apartment, Hunter crashed onto the couch. I sat down in the recliner, pulling my feet up and resting my chin on my knees.

"Are you mad at me?"

"What?" It was like he'd just remembered I was there. Like he'd been in a trance.

"Are you mad at me? You've barely talked to me all night."

"Not everything is about you, Taylor," he snapped.

"I know that, you jerk. Why won't you just talk to me? Something is obviously bothering you. I have some idea that it has to do with your secret meeting with the mysterious Joe. Am I getting warmer?"

"You have no idea what you're talking about," he said, his eyes cold as steel.

"Then enlighten me. You don't have to keep everything to yourself."

"Maybe I do. I've told you that you don't want to know the truth, so I'm not going to tell you."

"Don't tell me what I will and will not do, Hunter Zaccadelli. You don't know anything about me."

He closed his eyes, as if he was trying to compose himself or praying for patience. "You only play Pistol Annies when you're pissed, usually at me. I know your fake laugh from your real one. You have a great laugh, by the way. I know which shirts are your favorites, because they're the first ones you wear after you've done your laundry. You lick your bottom lip when you're trying to concentrate on your textbook reading. You cry during those commercials with the abused animals when you think no one is looking. No, I don't know you at all."

"That doesn't mean anything," I whispered.

"It means something."

"I thought you didn't like me."

"I don't want to." He got up and crouched in front of my

chair so fast I almost jumped. "What is it about you? Is it the eyes? Your smile? That sexy laugh? The way you call me out on my shit? I don't know. All I know is that I don't like it. I don't like it." He moved his face close to mine. His breath smelled faintly of beer but more like him. That spicy smell that clung to him. "I don't like it," he whispered against my lips. They were almost touching. Almost...He pulled back.

I'd had enough. If I didn't kiss this boy right here, right now, I was going to die. I slammed my hand on the back of his head and pulled his head toward mine. Enough talking. Time for kissing.

Our lips met, and that was it. All our resistance crumbled, and, suddenly, I was being thrown backward as Hunter tried to devour me none too gently. We landed on the floor as the recliner flipped up.

"Ow," I said into his mouth.

"Hmm," he said, ignoring the fact that the recliner was bottom-up and we were on the floor. He grabbed me and rolled me, so we were free of the chair that had sabotaged our kiss.

"I don't like that chair," he said as he kissed up and down my face and down to my neck. I rubbed my hands up and down his head, feeling his short hair prickle against my palms. He had just a little bit of stubble on his face, and I could just feel it scraping my hypersensitive skin.

He bit my earlobe, and I laughed because it tickled.

"What are you laughing about?"

"Tickles" was the only word I could form before his lips were back on mine again and then his tongue was in my mouth. Kissing Hunter was like nothing I'd ever experienced. It was both awful and wonderful at the same time. He was too much, too close; his mouth was too demanding. I'd never been kissed like that before, with pure unadulterated need.

No guy had ever kissed me as if his salvation depended on it. Hunter kissed like he was going to hell, and he had this one kiss left and he was going to make the most of it.

"You're so beautiful," he said when he pulled back to breathe for a second. I was having trouble with it myself.

Instead of answering, I reached up for his lips again. I wanted them more than I wanted oxygen.

The sound of the door closing sounded like it was miles away, but then a voice said, "Well, hello there."

Hunter and I both looked up to meet Renee's irritated face.

"It's about time."

CHAPTER 17

So apparently Renee had had a fight with her mother and had decided to come back to the apartment rather than stay home. She'd texted both of us to let us know so we didn't freak out if she was there, but neither of us had been paying attention to our phones. We hadn't been paying attention to much of anything other than the other one's lips.

Hunter and I had rolled away from one another, breathless and still buzzing with the energy of the kiss. I wasn't sure if I was ever going to recover from such an explosive kiss.

"What happened to the recliner?" Renee asked.

For some reason, I looked over at Hunter, who was on his back on the floor, looking up at the ceiling. He met my eyes and grinned. We both started laughing, and once we started, we couldn't stop.

"Okay then. I'm going to bed. You can, um…Yeah. Just don't be too loud. I really don't want to hear anything. You know what? I'll put in earplugs. Carry on." She scurried to her room and slammed the door.

Hunter and I both lay on our backs, wondering what the hell had just happened.

"Just because I kissed you doesn't mean I like you. I still don't."

"Yeah, because I make out with guys I don't like *all* the time."

"I told you that I didn't make out with girls I liked. So there you go. I don't like you."

"You have a weird way of showing it, Mr. Zaccadelli."

"You have delicious lips, Miss Caldwell."

So did he. So delicious I couldn't remember why we had stopped kissing. Oh, right. Renee had walked in on us. Oops.

Somehow I was able to peel myself off the floor and right the recliner. Hunter was still on the floor, his eyes closed and his hand rubbing circles on his tattoo.

"I'm going to bed," I blurted out. It was late, and I was tired. Granted, if he wanted to keep making out, I'd find the energy somewhere.

Oh my God. I'd kissed Hunter.

The reality crashed down on me, and I ran to the bathroom. I wasn't going to get sick, but I felt like it. I wasn't supposed to be kissing Hunter. I wasn't supposed to be kissing anyone. I braced my hands on the sink and looked at my face in the mirror, surprised to find that my lips weren't bruised. They felt like they'd been ravaged by him. My hair had somehow gotten all over the place. It looked like I'd had a rough night.

I had.

I ran the cold water and washed my face. I wanted to take a shower, but I didn't know if I'd have the energy. Suddenly I was very, very tired.

I went back across the hall to our bedroom. Hunter was in the living room, the Xbox going. Once I was alone in our room, I put my pj's on and crawled into bed. The cool sheets weren't enough to soothe my fevered skin. I was burning up but not with sickness. I was burning with something else. I shoved my retainer in my mouth and grabbed a book.

My brain wouldn't focus on the words. My brain wouldn't focus on anything but remembering how Hunter had kissed me like we were the last two people on earth and it was time for our last kiss. My brain wouldn't focus on how he said my lips were delicious and how he'd said I was beautiful. It wouldn't focus on anything but the feel of his hands on my body, as if he wanted to touch every single inch of me.

I shook my head, but that didn't help. I shut off the light and put my iPod on, turning up the music loud so maybe my brain would be distracted. It sort of helped, and the pain in my eardrums was at least a little distracting.

I heard Hunter come to bed an hour later. He stumbled around, removing his clothes with less grace than normal. I had the feeling he was still slightly intoxicated. He sighed loudly as he got into bed.

"What have you done to me, Missy?" he whispered, thinking I was asleep.

What had he done to me? That was the question.

Shattered. He broke me apart in a million pieces. I hoped I'd be able to put them back together.

"No! No!"

A yell woke me up later that night. Hunter was having another nightmare, this time a violent one. He was thrashing, and I was afraid he was going to fall out of bed and hurt himself.

"Hunter, Hunter!" I slapped his shoulder. He wasn't an easy one to wake when he was having a nightmare. It took three more slaps before his eyes opened and he blinked at me, his chest heaving.

"You were having another nightmare," I said as he struggled to bring himself back under control. "Are you okay? Do you want to talk about it?"

"No."

"No, you're not okay, or no, you don't want to talk about it?"

"No to both." He took several slow breaths. I felt stupid standing there.

"Okay then. I'm going back to bed." I turned, but he grabbed on to my arm to stop me.

"Don't. Will you stay with me? I just…please."

"You want me to sleep with you? Hell no."

"I'm not talking about that, Missy. I just want you to lie with me. Just shut up and hand me my boxers." I did so and averted my eyes as he slid them over his hips. "Forget it. Just go to bed."

"No, no. It's fine." The thought of having Hunter's arms around me was both something I wanted and something I was scared of. His eyes found mine in the dark.

"Will you stay with me? I think I'll sleep better. I swear I won't hurt you." He lifted the covers up, and I climbed in. The bed was small, but Hunter moved so his back was against the wall, so I had enough room to turn on my side, my back to his front. He pulled the covers back up.

"Good night."

"Night," I whispered.

He was trying to touch me as little as possible, which was nearly impossible in the small bed. I took a deep breath and moved closer to him. I heard a sharp intake of breath before my back met his skin. His arm came around and cradled me.

We were in the bubble again. The world could end and we would still be here, like this.

"Good night, Missy," he whispered into my hair.

Good night, Hunter.

I woke in the morning with my face pressed into Hunter's chest. Somehow in the night I'd turned so we were face-to-face. His chin was on top of my head and his arm was around my back, holding me close. One of us had kicked off the blanket, and our legs were wrapped around one another, like we'd somehow twined and become one person during the night.

I knew I should move. I knew my legs shouldn't be wrapped around his. That his arms shouldn't be around me, and that it shouldn't feel like I was exactly where I was supposed to be for the first time in my life.

Hunter shifted just a little so I knew he was waking up.

"Hi," he said.

"Hey."

"How did that happen?"

I gathered he was referring to our present position. "I don't know."

Neither of us made a move. His hand started making lazy circles on my back.

"I like waking up with you in my arms," he whispered, inhaling the scent of my hair. He looked so vulnerable. So sweet. He smiled, and it felt like my heart was going to explode. This couldn't be.

I moved away from him.

"Well, this is the first and last time. My bed is more comfortable." I rolled as far as I could while still being in the bed. He held on for a moment but then let me go. Bubble burst.

"But it doesn't have me in it."

"Exactly. Which means I sleep much better." I hadn't gotten the best night of sleep with Hunter, but waking up wrapped up with him had been more than worth it. If only we'd had a bigger bed.

No. I was not letting myself go there. This was not going to continue. I couldn't let it. Kissing and such led to other things.

I climbed out of Hunter's bed and stretched my arms, feeling like a little piece of happiness had broken off and fallen to the floor. I left it there among my clothes and books and went to the bathroom to take a shower.

Hunter and I skirted around one another for the rest of the day. He went out to play ultimate Frisbee with Dev and Sean in the afternoon, and I decided I needed a little shopping therapy and called Megan.

"Girl time? Do you even need to ask?" she said.

I picked her up at her apartment, which had a ton of trash in the yard and empty plastic cups littering the porch.

"Guys had a blowout last night. I'm tired of cleaning."

"Sounds awesome."

She glanced at my face. "Okay, what happened? You've got the weirdest look on your face."

"Hunter kissed me."

"What? Did you kiss him back?"

"You could say that."

"I knew it!" she shrieked as I pulled onto the main street. "How was it? Was it good? I bet he knew what he was doing."

Oh, did he ever.

"There's more."

"You didn't…"

"No. But I met his family and we kind of slept together last night. Like, in the same bed. With no sex."

She shook her head side to side. "Damn. You move quick."

"It's not like that, Meg."

She rolled her eyes. "Then what is it like? Because usually when you kiss someone, meet his parents and sleep in his bed, it means you like him."

"I don't like him."

"But you don't not like him."

"That's a double negative."

"You're deflecting." Hunter would have said the same thing.

"You know I can't get close with someone like that."

"It's not that you can't. It's that you won't. Those are two different things, Taylor."

"Not to me. I just...I just can't. Every time I think about it, all I remember is that night and what happened."

"You shouldn't let that one night define the rest of your life. You're not going to get over it. No one would. But you can't let it dictate who you are and if you can love someone. That's just letting him win."

Megan didn't understand. She hadn't been there that night. She hadn't seen his face. She hadn't watched while he...She hadn't heard him say he was going to kill me if I ever told. She didn't have dark memories that affected every single day of her life. So who was she to tell me how to deal with them?

"He didn't win. He's in jail."

"For how long?"

"A while." Another two years, to be exact. By the time he got out, I'd be ready for him if he came for me. I wasn't going to be a victim twice. That reminded me, I really should go to kickboxing more than once a week. You never knew.

"What are you going to do when he gets out?"

"Be ready. If he comes for me, then so be it. He won't get out of it alive."

"You wouldn't really kill him."

"Yeah, I would." I could say this without fear or reservation. He didn't deserve to live. He was never going to hurt anyone else again if I had anything to say about it. I'd been too young when it happened, but I wasn't a child anymore.

"That scares me, Tay."

I shrugged. I never said I was a saint.

I changed the subject as quickly as I could, but I kept seeing Meg watching me. As if I was going to suggest going to a sporting goods store and purchasing a gun right then and there. Oh, I had plans for that. I was going to ask for shooting lessons for Christmas from Tawny. I had a pellet gun, but I wanted to learn how to use a proper gun. You could never be too careful.

The day wasn't a total loss. We flitted from store to store, looking for deals and trying on earrings and testing lotions.

"What do you think of this one?" She held out her wrist for me to smell. It was spicy and sweet, like pumpkin pie. Yum.

"Pumpkin barf?"

"Damn close." She got three bottles.

"So what was the family like?"

"Well, his parents are dead, so he lives with his aunt and uncle in this huger than huge house. It makes a mansion look like a double-wide."

"You're kidding."

"Wish I was. That chandelier must be a bitch to dust."

"There was a chandelier?"

"And a grand staircase and a den, and an apple orchard in the back. It had the works."

"Were there maids?"

"Not that I saw, but it could have just been their day off. I'm telling you, it was massive. I was afraid to breathe."

"Why didn't you take any pictures?"

"It didn't cross my mind," I said as we lined up at the smoothie stand.

"So who else was there?"

I told her about Harper and Mase and Darah's budding relationship. I didn't mention Joe or the spying. For some reason, I couldn't share that with anyone. Not even Megan.

"You should marry him. Then you can be a trophy wife and have your own reality show," she said as she ordered her smoothie.

"I am a trophy for no man," I said, ordering a mango pineapple.

"You know that's not what I meant," Megan said.

"I know. I guess I'm still reeling from everything."

"And rightfully so."

We wandered with our smoothies a little more. I popped into the bookstore to see if they had the new book I was waiting for. They had one copy left, and I did a little happy dance in the aisle as I snatched it up, giddy.

"Thanks for the girlie time. We need to do a beauty day soon," I said, giving her a hug. I was still on a book-buying high, so I didn't mind a little affection.

"Call me. You know, if you need to talk. Anytime."

"Thanks, Meg. I'll see you later."

"Bye."

Darah and Renee were deep in conversation when I got back.

"You, spill," Renee said. "I've been *dying* to talk to you all day, but I had that stupid study session."

Crap. I was not getting out of this. Renee had that crazed look in her eyes like when she'd been studying for ten hours straight and was hopped up on too much coffee, or she'd been playing too much Skyrim. I did not like that look.

"We kissed," I said, sitting down on the recliner. Oh, that recliner...I got up and sat at the end of the couch, beside Darah.

"It's about time. You two have been dancing around each other since day one. So, how was it?" Renee put her head in her hands, as if she was expecting a juicy play-by-play. Wasn't going to happen.

"We didn't."

"You didn't? So I slept with my earplugs for nothing? Then what was the yelling I thought I heard?"

"That was nothing. Well, nothing sexual."

"You didn't do anything?"

"No."

"Nothing?" Renee looked really disappointed.

Darah was studying my face in a way I didn't like. "You seemed like you were having a good time yesterday," Darah said.

"For the most part. Harper was adorable."

"I know. She's just the sweetest. Mase and I are thinking of taking her to Funtown before it closes. Her parents don't want her to go, you know, because she can't do most of the rides, but Mase already called and they can make accommodations for some of them. He's so thoughtful." She smiled.

"He is." That reminded me of Hunter taking care of the drunken girls last night. I hoped they got home safe.

"So you're telling me you didn't have sex?" Renee didn't want to let it go. She was starved for romance since she didn't have one of her own currently.

"Nope."

"I'm sure you will soon. You can't deny chemistry like that for long. Sooner or later. Boom."

The kissing had been quite boom. I couldn't imagine anything being more intense than that.

"It's not like that."

"Uh, yes it is."

"I hate to say she's right, but Renee is right," Darah said.

"Why do you hate to say I'm right?"

"Because you're usually wrong when it comes to things like this."

"Things like what?"

"Relationships. It's not a bad thing. You just seem to think more with your head than your heart sometimes. It's not a bad thing," she said again, trying to sound like it was a compliment instead of an insult.

"Whatever," Renee said, waving off the thinly veiled insult. "So have you guys talked about it yet?"

"No. I'm going to avoid talking as much as humanly possible. I can't get involved with him. If we did, and then it ended, one of us would have to move out."

"Isn't that what you want?"

Was it? I'd been so sure that the solution to my problems was Hunter moving out. If he wasn't there, I wouldn't see him all the time. I wouldn't think about him all the time. I wouldn't want him all the time.

"Honey, if he moves out, that's not going to change your feelings. You're still going to want to jump his bones if he lives here or in Istanbul," Renee said.

"What about Istanbul?" Hunter said as he opened the door.

"We were just talking about how awesome it would be to visit," Renee said, not missing a beat. "I've always wanted to go there."

"Uh-huh," Hunter said. I saw that he had grocery bags on his arms.

"You get your car fixed?" I asked.

"Yeah, it was a belt issue. I got taco stuff if anyone wants some."

"But we don't have sombreros or margaritas," Renee said.

"Uh, no," I said.

"We can't have taco night without those things. They are essential." Renee got up and grabbed her purse. "Who's coming with me on a hat and marg mission?" She gave a pointed look to Darah, who also got to her feet.

"I'm in," Darah said.

Renee was trying to give me a subtle look, but it didn't really work. She just looked like she was in pain.

"I'll help you with the tacos," I said, sighing and getting up from the couch. I guessed Hunter and I were going to have to talk sooner rather than later, thanks to my roommates' interference.

"I got that fake meat stuff for you," he said, pulling it out of the shopping bag.

"Thanks." He'd also gotten me some bottles of cranberry-lime seltzer water, which I was addicted to.

We both were silent as we unpacked the bags, setting the stuff out on the counter. I took the initiative and started working on the vegetables while Hunter got two pans going with the meat and the fake stuff cooking.

"So are we going to talk about last night?" he said as he stirred each pan with two different wooden spoons. He was so considerate about keeping my food separate.

"I don't know," I said, washing a pepper in the sink. We were standing so close I bumped into him a few times. "Do you want to?"

"How about we talk about the fact that you say you don't like me, but you kiss me and then you sleep with me?"

"First of all," I said, wiping the pepper off vigorously with a paper towel and moving on to a second, "you were going to kiss me. I just made it happen faster. And second, you asked me to sleep with you. I was worried if you had another nightmare you were going to fall out of bed. I was looking out for your safety." I moved to the cutting board and started chopping.

He snorted as he stirred the meat and nonmeat.

"Yeah, that was why I woke up with your legs and arms and body wrapped around mine like an octopus."

"You didn't seem to mind."

He didn't answer for a second, so I looked up.

"I didn't," he said quietly.

"Me neither." We both thought about that for a second.

"So what now?" he said.

"What do you mean?"

"What do we do now? We can't just be roommates."

"You said you didn't like me."

"I don't like you. I don't like how your hair smells and how I can't stop thinking about waking up and seeing your face. I hate how my bed felt empty when you left. I don't like how good you were with my family, especially Harper, and how I wanted to see you with them again, but not just as a guest. As a member. You're right. I don't like you at all."

"When did you change your mind?"

"My mind never changed. I've wanted you since the moment you opened the door and had that stunned look on your face. It just took me a while to admit it. Why deny it now? It is what it is, and it's not going to change."

"Oh."

"This doesn't mean I'm going to be nice. I'm still going

to be an ass. I'll just be an ass who apologizes and brings you flowers to say he's been a dick."

"Chocolate," I said.

"What?"

"I'd rather have chocolate when you apologize."

"Chocolate it is." He smiled. "So does that mean what I think it means?"

"No. It just means that you get to bring me chocolate when you've been an ass. I'm going to weigh three hundred pounds." I focused my attention back on the peppers. I couldn't think about Hunter's declaration of...whatever it was.

Footsteps didn't make me look up.

"Taylor, look at me. Please." *Damn.* If only he didn't say please. "I can't promise not to make you mad. I can't promise that I won't hurt you. All I can promise is that I want you in my life, and I'll do anything to keep you there."

"What about the bet?"

"It still stands. A bet is a bet. The stakes are just a little bit higher, that's all."

"So if I asked you to leave, would you?"

"No. This is my apartment just as much as it is yours. I'll only leave under three conditions. The ball is in your court. I stick to my word. And I don't want to leave. Leaving means I don't get to see you all the time, and I don't want that."

I swallowed and tried to sort my scattered mind. Yes, I did like waking up with Hunter. Much, much more than I should. On the other hand, I couldn't get closer to him. That would only lead to things I couldn't deal with. I wasn't a carefree girl who could just jump into a relationship. I had too much baggage. I couldn't carry it myself, let alone foist it off on someone else.

I was fucked up. Much more so than he could imagine.

While it was true Hunter had his own secret, it didn't seem to burden him like mine did. He wore it like one of his tattoos, a part of him but not a dominant part. Megan was right; that one night did define me. It had since I was twelve. It wasn't going to change overnight.

If he got close, he was going to get burned. Or worse, he wouldn't like what he found. I couldn't let that happen.

"I wish you'd never moved in," I said, stepping back and looking at the peppers. It took all my effort not to throw myself on him, to kiss him, to tell him that I wanted him. Because to say that I didn't was the biggest lie I'd ever tell myself. I wanted Hunter Zaccadelli more than I'd ever wanted anything.

My hands were shaking so bad that the knife slipped.

"Shit!"

"Here, run it under the water." Hunter dragged me to the sink, putting my bleeding finger under the water. The cut wasn't bad, so I ripped my hand away as quick as I could.

"Thanks, I think I can manage. I've somehow survived nearly twenty years of life without your help, thank you very much."

"If that's the way you want it."

"Yes."

No, no, no.

He went back to the taco meat and nonmeat, and I went back to the veggies. We didn't speak again until Darah and Renee returned with sombreros and margarita mix and Mase and Dev and Sean and a few others from around the dorm.

I was relieved Hunter and I had a buffer of people to keep us apart. I didn't know what I was going to do tonight. In our dark, quiet room with just the two of us, I was vulnerable. I was much more likely to change my mind under the influence of large pieces of Hunter's exposed skin and the ease of sliding under the covers and sleeping with him again.

It would have been so easy.

Hunter went to bed early, and by the time I was ready myself, he had his back turned to me and the light off. He didn't even say good-night.

CHAPTER 18

He avoided me the next day, even at work. We had three carts of documents and things to reshelf on the closed stacks, which meant we were going to be alone up there for hours. Luckily, I brought the radio and turned it on as soon as we wheeled the carts, Dolly and Daisy and Dulcie, off the elevators. One of the other student workers had named all the carts and put little cow faces on them. I understood the obsession with naming inanimate objects. Exhibit A: Sassy, my car.

He took Dolly, which had the beginning of the alphabet, so I grabbed Dulcie, which was at the end. We'd have to work together when we got to Daisy, but maybe we wouldn't get to it today and then one of the other student workers would deal with it.

I finished my first cart faster than I would have liked. There were a lot of big books on it that were right in a row call number wise, so I sat there with the empty cart. I'd heard Hunter quietly working, but I didn't know if he was finished. God, what a baby. Suck it up.

I reached the cart just as Hunter did. Of course.

"Come on," I said, dragging the cart to the right aisle. I started grabbing things and shoving them on the shelf. They were in relatively the right place. A hand reached out to stop me.

"I know you said you didn't want this, but here's the thing. I don't believe you." He held my wrist gently, but I couldn't seem to move. He put his hand on my waist and slowly turned me around, as if we were dancing. We faced each other, and I couldn't escape his intense gaze. His eyes were locked on mine and they weren't going to let go. I was trapped.

"Look at me and tell me you don't want me to kiss you. Tell me you don't like it when I do this," he said, running his hand down my arm. "Tell me you don't like it when I touch your hair…." He did so, brushing it behind my ear. "Tell me you don't like it when I touch your face." He brushed his hands on both of my cheeks, moving up to my forehead and then back down. He rubbed both thumbs over my lips.

"Tell me you don't like it when I do this." He leaned his head closer, stopping just short of my lips. "Tell me to stop and I will. You're in charge, Missy."

Oh, but I wasn't. I'd never been so out of charge in my life. I hated being so out of control with him. This was only the second time it had happened, the first being Saturday night and the recliner incident. I closed my eyes and prayed to whoever would listen to give me some control so I could say no. I wasn't some horny teen girl with raging hormones. I was Taylor Caldwell, Ice Queen. That was what they had called me in high school. The boys had avoided me for fear of getting their balls frozen off. Or so they had said. I didn't mind. It made things easier. Any boys who had wanted to try to break through my exterior had been quickly squashed like bugs.

Hunter was different. He'd seen through my exterior, seen

through the wall of tangled thorns that guarded me. And here he was, asking me if I wanted to let him try to break through.

The answer was yes.

And no.

I was going to hell.

I leaned forward until our lips met. This time he waited for me. I pushed closer, and he responded, jamming me up against the shelf and devouring me once again. Were his kisses ever gentle? I hoped not.

My hands were trapped above my head so I couldn't touch him, but he was pressed against me, so I could feel him on every inch of my body, even through our clothes. I let my worries about control fade away, like letting go of a balloon string and watching it float away. Hunter demanded my attention.

I made a little moaning noise, and he laughed, slowing our kisses so they were sweeter. Also, I could breathe better. Not that breathing mattered a whole lot at the moment. It was secondary.

I pulled my head back, feeling dizzy.

"I don't like you," I whispered, giving him one last soft peck.

"Sure," Hunter said, reaching around me. I thought he was going to assault me, but he was just reaching for a book. "You just keep telling yourself that." He shelved the book above my head, looking down at me and smiling slowly. "Get back to work, Miss Caldwell."

I grabbed the nearest book and whacked him with it. "Dark. I like dark chocolate."

That night a bar of expensive dark chocolate found its way onto my pillow. Wonder how that got there. I picked it up and found something else. A black velvet box. What. The. Fuck.

With trembling hands, I picked it up, my brain telling me it must have fallen there by mistake. Maybe Renee had left it in my room, or thought it was mine, or maybe it was a gift from Mase to Darah and he decided to hide it in a place where she wouldn't find it or...

Just open the damn box.

Slowly, with a little creak, the box opened. *Fuckity, fuck, fuck,* fuck.

There was a ring inside. For like, fingers and such. It was gorgeous, with a clear blue stone in the middle, surrounded by what I thought might be diamonds (and I prayed were cubic zirconium) and then a double row of greenish stones of alternating sizes, all wrapped with silver. It made me think of a peacock feather.

"It's not what you think," Hunter said, scaring the bejeezus and daylights out of me all at once. I dropped the box.

"Must reassemble heart," I said, trying to remember how to breathe.

"Wow, I didn't know it would get quite that reaction." He picked it up and looked at it before holding it out to me.

"What? How? Why?" I couldn't form coherent words.

"It's a ring. It's for your finger. I bought it, and I thought you would like it. And it's to say sorry for all the douchey things I've ever done. Figured I'd cover my bases."

"Ring?"

"Yes. Ring. Hunter," he said, pointing to his chest. "Missy," he said, pointing to me.

I stared down at the sparkly thing. It was so pretty. It was the prettiest thing I'd ever seen in my life. Like someone had designed a ring just for me.

"It's not what you think it is. It's an apology ring. It's an I-saw-it-and-thought-of-you ring. It's not a commitment ring.

Promise rings are lame, and you know I'm not proposing. I'm not getting married, ever. So. This is a ring. Just a ring for your pretty finger. I had it sized."

"When?"

"I measured your finger while you were sleeping one night."

"What?"

He laughed at my still-stunned face. "Kidding! Damn, you're weird when you're surprised by jewelry. I'll have to do it more often. I stole one of the ones off your dresser I knew you wore a lot."

"You had this made for me?"

"Kind of. I saw the ring with the blue and the diamonds, and I just thought it could add a little more to make it something you'd love. Do you like it?"

My ears cringed at the word *diamond*. Maybe I'd heard him wrong. Diamonds were expensive.

"I don't *like* it. It's the most beautiful thing I've ever seen."

"I could say the same about you." I looked up to his face to find him smiling at me. "Would you put it on? For me?"

He plucked the ring out of the box and held it out to me. I slid it on my right ring finger. Too much symbolism with the left, at least in the United States. It fit as if it had been made for me. It was so shiny I could barely look away from it.

"How does it fit?" Hunter said, taking my hand and turning it so the ring glimmered.

"Perfect." I still didn't comprehend the fact that Hunter had bought me a ring with diamonds and God knew what else in it, as if it was nothing.

"How much?" I said.

"Price doesn't matter."

"I thought you didn't accept money from your family."

"I didn't. I bought it myself."

"With what money?" It had to be crazy expensive. He wouldn't meet my eyes when I looked up.

"Don't worry about it. Money is meaningless."

"No, it's not. Tell me how much it was."

"If I do, you're going to freak out like you did about the house, and then I'll be forced to kiss you again. Do you want me to kiss you again?"

"It's not my fault you keep trying to kiss me. How much did the ring cost?"

He grabbed my hands and tried to plant one on me, but I ducked away.

"Are you asking for me to kick your nuts again? Because I totally will."

"Why can't you react like a normal girl? Anyone else would be a puddle of goo at my feet."

"You didn't give this ring to another girl—you gave it to me. So deal with it."

"Do you want me to take it back? I'm sure they can cut it apart and use the stones for another ring."

"No!" It would be a crime to destroy such a lovely thing. Not that I was much for jewelry, but this was something different. This wasn't a ring. This was a work of art.

"Okay then. So I guess you like it."

"I love it."

"I have reservations about you wearing a peacock feather on your finger, but that's just a representation of one, so I guess it's okay. Just...be careful."

"Peacocks aren't bad luck for me," I said. He had no idea what they meant to me. Or maybe he did. "How much, Hunter?"

"It's not important, Miss. You're more important than money. Bottom line." I wanted to ask him again if he was bipolar. How could he say things like that and then make a comment about my ass the next? He was a conundrum. "So the only thing you have left to do is thank me. I know a really special way you could thank me, but it's really up to you." And there he was again.

"Okay," I said, having an idea.

I crooked my finger for him to come closer. I tipped my head up like I was going to give him a steamy kiss. I bit my lip, and his face went blank for a second. *Ha.* I went for his mouth slowly but moved at the last second, catching him on the cheek for a lightning-fast peck.

"Thanks," I said brightly before stepping away from him. I needed some space so I could breathe.

"Tease. You're a tease, Missy girl."

"You know you love me."

He shook his head.

"Nope, still don't like you," he said with a sigh.

"Liar," I countered.

"Hypocrite." He stepped closer to me.

"Douche."

He smiled slowly. "Gorgeous."

"Ass."

"Sexy." He was coming for me, and I couldn't stop him. Somehow I'd have to.

"Stop."

"Go."

"Red light."

"Green light."

"No."

"Yes," he whispered, reaching out to hold my shoulders. "Just say yes. Say you'll be with me."

"I can't."

"Why not?"

"I can't, Hunter. Don't ask me again."

"Aw, Missy. Why do you do this to me?"

"I'm sorry." My voice broke, and I was afraid I was going to cry. No, I was not going to cry. I promised myself no boy, no man, would ever make me cry again. And that was why. "I'm sorry," I said before I ran out of the room.

"What's wrong?" Renee said from the couch, where she was ensconced with her nursing books.

"Nothing. I'm going for a walk."

"But it's raining."

"So? I have an umbrella." I grabbed it from where I'd hung it by the door.

"Don't open it inside," Hunter said from the hallway. "It's bad luck."

I didn't respond as I got out of there as quickly as I could.

I walked around campus for two hours, just thinking and looking at the ring. It was still on my finger. He'd said it was just a ring, an apology ring, but it was so much more than that. Rings were symbolic. Rings were in circles. Circles never ended, which was why they were symbols of eternity. No beginning and no end.

God, it was so beautiful. How had he known? Granted, I did have a crap ton of peacock stuff, but the way he'd had it put together was just perfection. He'd been planning this for a while. How long? Yet another question I'd thought to ask him while out on my stroll. Campus was deserted, seeing as how it was too late for most classes and it was raining.

Rain didn't bother me. Hunter did. My feelings for Hunter bothered me the most.

I didn't end up crying, but I came pretty damn close. I couldn't remember the last time I'd cried. I'd never been much of a crier, and after everything that had happened, it was like someone had shut off the valve in my tear ducts.

I wanted to punch him again. I wanted to break things and scream, so instead I kept walking. I walked until I'd made it from one end of campus to the other twice, and my shoes were soaked through. I hadn't thought to wear my supercute rain boots I'd bought only a few weeks ago. What a waste.

The ring weighed a million pounds by the time I had made it back to the apartment. I looked down at it one more time. *Wow. Just wow.*

They were having dinner when I walked in.

"He's not here. He went to stay with Mase for the night," Renee said before I'd even closed the door. "What did he do to you?"

"This," I said, holding up my hand. There was a shattering noise as Renee dropped her plate.

"It's on her right hand," Darah pointed out.

"Oh," Renee said, leaning down to get the plate. "So I broke a plate for nothing."

"It's not exactly nothing," I said, shucking off my soaked sneakers and socks and laying my umbrella to dry beside the door.

"Lemme see," Renee said, grabbing for my hand.

"Shit. That is some rock. I'm pretty sure that was what sunk the *Titanic*."

"It's gorgeous, Tay," Darah said.

"I don't know what I'm supposed to do with it."

"Duh, wear it and make the rest of the female population jealous. Hunter Zaccadelli doesn't buy girls rings. That's just not a thing that happens," Renee said.

"How would you know?"

"No reason," she said, looking down at the ring again.

"What have you heard?"

"Oh, just that he's a playboy. One of the girls in my bio class had a friend that got a little burned by him. She was a little bitter."

"I bet that's an understatement." I wondered if she was one of the girls whose numbers was still in his phone. Maybe it was Chastity. "What was her name?"

"Briana? Britney? Something that began with a *B*. Damn, that is some ring."

It certainly was.

"Are you sure you don't want him? Because I'd be happy to take him off your hands."

"What about Paul?" Darah said.

"What about Paul?" Renee snapped.

"Don't play dumb, Ne. I know he called you and you talked. We sleep in the same room."

Yeah! The attention was on someone else for a change. I dived in, pestering Renee along with Darah until she spilled that Paul had called her and wanted to meet.

"I don't know."

"Why don't you have him over for one of our potluck nights? Then there won't be so much pressure," I said.

"I guess."

"Do it," Darah said. "Right now."

"Okay, okay. Hold your horses." She got out her phone and sent the text. "There. Happy?"

"Joyous," Darah said.

"So back to the ring," Renee said.

I sighed and showed it to them again.

I didn't see Hunter until the next night when he came back from classes. I was still wearing the ring. I'd gotten compli-

ments on it all day, and more than one of my female class-
mates had asked if I was engaged. I had to swallow hard and
tell them no.

Besides, Hunter had said he didn't believe in marriage.
I hadn't seen that it was so great either. My parents were
divorced, along with half of the married population. The
idea that there was one perfect person destined for each of us
sounded way too perfect. It was a fairy tale and not reality.
Not that I didn't like to indulge in the occasional delicious
fairy tale every now and then, I just knew that I had to come
back to reality.

"Should I assume that since you're still wearing it that you
like it and don't want it to go away?"

"Yes, I like it. It's just unnecessary. I only asked for chocolate."

"I had a lot of assery to make up for."

"That is true, but I don't think it was several thousand
dollars worth."

"You don't know how much the ring cost."

"No, but I'm not a moron. I can do internet research as
well as anyone else. I can figure out how much each of these
stones is worth, generally speaking, and then figure out the
setting and labor and so forth. What? You wouldn't tell me."

"You are one of the most curious girls I've ever met. You
just have to know everything."

"Curiosity isn't a sin."

"Too bad," he said. I fought the urge to stick my tongue out
at him, because that was juvenile, and I was an adult. "Don't
forget, we have mediation tonight at seven."

"Shit." I had forgotten. This should be fun.

"We could make a pact to go and just sit there and say nothing like in *Good Will Hunting*."

"I would pay good money to see you be silent for a whole hour. Just about as much as this ring is worth."

"I don't want the ring back. I'd lose that bet just so you wouldn't give it back to me."

"Why, Hunter? According to my research this ring is worth about as much as Sassy. If you couldn't find housing, where the hell did you get the money?"

"Well, Miss Caldwell, I prefer to discuss these issues at our mediation. I think that's a more fitting environment. Don't you think?" he said with a smirk. Oh, he was just infuriating. "I'm going to take a shower. Be sure to take off the ring before you join me."

"Never. It's never going to happen," I yelled as he walked into our room.

Oh, but it could. It could be a thing that could happen, if I let it. I stared down at the ring. I didn't know if it was my imagination that it seemed to get bigger the longer I wore it. Next week I was going to wake up and it would be the size of a football and all the bones in my finger would have been crushed by it. Then I'd have to get surgery and they'd probably never be able to get my finger back to normal and I'd have a funky finger for the rest of my life and a crazy story to tell.

I was thinking way too much about this.

Hunter was quiet during dinner, as if he was showing me that he could be silent. I wasn't very impressed. If he could do it for an entire day, that would be something impressive.

Renee was off at another study session and Darah was out with Mase, so it was just the two of us.

"Hey," he said as we were finishing, "it looks great on you. I'm glad you like it."

What wasn't to like?

"Thank you," I said again. It seemed to be the only normal response I could think of in regards to the ring.

"You have to stop saying that."

"Why?" I asked

"Because it makes me feel weird."

"Weird how?"

He'd said we weren't going to discuss the ring until our mediation, but here we were.

"It doesn't seem like enough. Seeing your face when you opened it makes me want to buy you a million things just so I can see that look every single day."

"I swear to God, if you buy me anything else, I will kill you."

"And that. I love that you get pissed about it but love it at the same time. It's adorable."

"Bite me."

"Such a charming girl. Didn't they teach you not to say things like that in finishing school?"

"I missed kickboxing last week, and right now I'd really like to kick some boxes. I think you'd like to protect yours."

"Is that what the kids are calling them these days?" he said, taking our plates and going to the sink. It was Darah's turn for dishes, which she would do as soon as she got back from her date. She stuck to the chore chart like it was her religion.

Hunter went into our room and grabbed his guitar.

"Got any requests?"

"*Rhapsody in Blue,*" I said, sort of being sarcastic.

"I gave you a beautiful ring and some chocolate and now you want *Rhapsody in Blue*? You're a demanding girl, Missy."

"Fine. Play whatever you want."

And then it happened. It was a simplified version, but it was *Rhapsody in Blue* nonetheless. He did Gershwin proud.

Granted, it wasn't the entire twenty-minute symphony, but it was decent. Hunter made the transitions from one section to the other flawlessly. He was a musical genius.

He ended the song and smirked at me. "Next."

"Why aren't you a music major?" I'd lost track of how many times I'd asked him that. He always made some comment about his uncle and having a good career and other stuff I could tell he was just spitting back to me. He sounded like a guidance counselor when he talked about it, which was why I knew it was total bullshit.

"I'd rather have a lucrative job as a lawyer instead of saying, 'Do you want fries with that?' Which is what I'd be doing as a music major."

"What about music education?" I'd seen him with Harper, trying to teach her a few chords. I'd also seen a pink guitar in her room that I had the suspicion he'd bought for her.

"Me with a roomful of kids? Are you serious?"

"You're great with Harper."

"She's one kid and she's different."

"How?"

"She just is. She's special."

"I think you'd be good at it."

He started strumming a random melody. Now who was deflecting?

"It's time for our mediation, Miss Caldwell."

"After you, Mr. Zaccadelli."

We trooped downstairs to Chris, our resident director's, room. Chris was about twenty-five and a grad student in some sort of engineering field I couldn't begin to understand. He was nice but awkward. You could tell he was only doing it for the free housing and the stipend they paid him.

"Hello, Hunter, Taylor. How are we doing?"

"Fine," we both said at the same time. I glared at Hunter. He winked back.

We seated ourselves on the couch, and Chris got his notebook out. Every now and then he'd make notes while we were talking, like he was a therapist or something. I was dying to know what he'd written about us, but all my attempts to steal said notebook had been futile. Maybe I could rope Hunter into helping me with a distraction.

"So let's get started. How has this week gone?"

"Fabulous," I said in a deadpan voice.

"It's been great for me," Hunter said.

"Okay," Chris said, looking down at his notes. "Do you have any issues you feel we should discuss?"

"How about that you won't stop kissing me?" Hunter said, turning toward me.

"How about the fact that you spent thousands of dollars on a custom-made ring and then just expect me to say thanks, and let's be together and live happily ever after? How about that? How about the fact that you had some strange meeting with a man named Joe that you won't tell me about?"

"Uh, let's, uh, stay on track," Chris said, floundering.

"How about the fact that you want me, I want you and for some reason, it's impossible for us to be together, according to you?"

"You still haven't answered me about Joe."

"You haven't told me why we can't be together." We were in each other's faces. His was getting redder, and I was pretty sure mine was as well.

"Because."

"That's not a fucking reason, Taylor." He spat out my name.

"Language," Chris said. "Let's cool off for a moment. Do I need to bring out the talking stick again?"

"No," we both said at the same time.

At our first session he'd had us hold this stupid stick, which was really a baton, so we could practice taking turns talking. It had ended with me hitting Hunter with the talking stick and him laughing. I really did want to hit him again, but I didn't want to get in trouble. Chris had looked the other way on the first talking stick assault, but I didn't think he'd be so forgiving for a second.

"I don't want to be assaulted again."

"I did not assault you."

"Missy, I really don't want to go through the legal definition of assault with you right now."

"Why don't we start with you, Hunter? What has been bothering you this week?"

Hunter ignored Chris.

"You're scared. You're scared about this big, dark secret you carry around. It's the reason you don't trust people, the reason you put up this huge flashing sign that says, 'Don't come near me or I'll kick you in the balls.' It's the reason you don't want to give this a shot. I want to know what it is."

"No." He could yell and kiss me and do whatever he wanted, but I wasn't discussing that with him. The only thing worse about him knowing and then running away would be him accepting it. What then? I'd have nothing left. No other reason to say no.

"See? This is what I have to put up with. She is content to try to root out my secret, but if anyone tries to get near hers, she's got more walls up than a maximum security prison."

"Taylor, why don't you respond?"

"It's none of his business."

"*You* are my business. I made you my business. I want you to be my business."

"I don't. That's all. He wants me, and I don't want to be with him and he can't take it. That's all."

"Is that true, Hunter?"

"Please, that's bullshit."

"Language."

"I'll talk how I like, thanks. It's bull because she keeps kissing me and flirting with me and dancing with me. Either you get a sick kick out of messing with me, or you like me but you're scared. I'm going with the second." He'd hit the nail on the head, but I wasn't going to tell him that.

"I like messing with you," I said.

"Prove it."

"Bite me."

"Okay, let's get more specific. Are there any things that Hunter does specifically that we can talk about to resolve?" He clearly hadn't been listening, or he was just reading from a script. Probably the second.

"He can stop trying to see me naked. That would be a start."

"Hunter, do you have a response?"

"If she would just have sex with me, then that problem would be solved. Also, it would get me to leave. Two birds, one stone, Missy."

"Fuck you."

"Please, let's keep this civil." Chris was trying to keep control, but he'd never had it in the first place. "Let's try a communication game." Not a game. I didn't know where he'd gotten these things from, but he made us play one at each of our sessions and they were always lame.

This one involved one of us being blindfolded and the other leading him or her from one side of the room to the other. It was supposed to build trust, but all it did was make me want to direct Hunter so he'd bump into things. It offered Hunter a chance to make me look like a moron, walking around in a circle with him making me do a crazy dance back and forth.

"You're an ass," I said as we walked back upstairs.

"Nothing I didn't already know, Miss."

"I hate you."

"Nice try."

"I love you?" Worth a shot.

"Not yet. But you will." I went to our room and shut the door in his face.

CHAPTER 19

The next week was strangely quiet. Hunter stopped his verbal assault about my secret, for which I was grateful, but it only meant that he was using other means to try to get it out of me. Lull me into a false sense of security or something like that. I knew he wasn't giving up. I'd just have to get him out first. Or at least find out what his was.

Something that distracted me from Hunter was Renee. She had been really weird and secretive. She'd be gone for abnormally long amounts of time to the library, and she'd come back with a goofy grin on her face. I asked her if she'd met a cute boy in the stacks, but she just smiled and said I'd understand someday.

Darah had even tried to get it out of her but had gotten zilch. One night when Mase was over and we were having dinner while Renee was out again, we discussed the possibilities.

"It's got to be Paul," Hunter said. I agreed, but I wasn't going to admit it.

"She's got to be hooking up with someone and not telling us about it," I said.

"Renee is terrible at keeping secrets. Why would she suddenly be good at it?" Darah said.

I shrugged. "I don't know, but the last thing she'd ever do is admit she's been wrong. You know she hates that more than anything else."

"True. But I saw Paul a couple of days ago and he didn't say anything about it."

"That's weird," I said.

The mystery of Renee was solved that night when I heard a crash in the living room and then loud giggling.

"Hey, wake up and put your pants on," I hissed at Hunter, grabbing his boxers and throwing them at him.

"It's got to be Renee," he said. "Sounds like her laugh." Then we heard a male voice.

"Looks like we're going to solve the mystery of her study dates." I stood behind him as he went to open the door and see what was going on.

He counted to five under his breath before he did it.

"Oh my God," I said, averting my eyes. Renee and Paul were all tangled up on the couch, both of them half-clothed and on their way to fully naked.

"Oh, hello," Renee said, laughing when she saw us. Drunk. She was drunk. "This is Paul."

"We've met," I said. Paul seemed to be a little more sober and at least had the sense to look mortified.

"Nice to, ah, meet you, Paul," Hunter said. "We're just going to, um, go back to bed. You two…you have a nice night."

We scurried back to our room as fast as we could.

"Oh my God," I said when we had closed the door.

"Well, I guess the mystery is solved." He looked at me, and we started laughing, resting our backs against the door. We heard one of them get up and bump against the coffee table and then Renee laughing like a nut.

"It's a good thing Darah's with Mase tonight."

"Ugh, I really don't want to think about what's going to happen in the room right next door. I'm gonna need my earplugs tonight."

"Why, does other people having sex make you uncomfortable?"

"No, it's just weird. Having them right over there," I said, pointing to the wall.

"That's college for you." He pushed off the door and got back into bed, flinging the boxers down on the floor and sighing.

I looked away and got back into my bed.

"You're not jealous, are you? That you're not the one getting lucky?"

"She's drunk. She probably won't even remember it."

"You are jealous. Well, Missy. I've told you we can fix these things."

"Why does everything come down to sex with you?"

"It's not just about the sex, Missy. Although, that part is a lot of fun. It's the other stuff. Waking up naked next to someone and knowing you've shared something. That you were connected, if only for a few minutes."

"Is that what it's like for you?" I couldn't imagine him having that kind of connection with Chastity or whoever else he'd had sex with.

"It would be with you."

"It isn't with everyone?"

"Well, do you connect with everyone you've been with?" *Oh shit.* I hadn't expected him to turn this around on me.

"No," I said too quickly. *Goddamn.*

"Jesus Christ," he said, sitting up and clutching the blanket so it wouldn't fall and uncover him.

"What?"

"You're a virgin."

"I am not," I said, sounding very much like someone who was lying.

"Shit. Oh, *shit*." He was acting like he'd just run over a puppy with his car.

"I'm going to bed," I said, because I didn't really have anything else to say.

"Is that it? Your big secret?"

Oh, if only it was that. I didn't answer.

"I feel like I've defiled you now. Why didn't you tell me?"

"Why does it matter? Great, now you know I'm a freak. Congratulations."

"That's not what I meant. Christ."

I was mortified, and I didn't know why it bothered me so much. It wasn't a secret I guarded that closely, but it ran very close to the one I did. This was why I hadn't wanted Hunter to get close. Because of this moment.

"You should have said something. I would have stopped."

"I'm not a child, Hunter."

"I know, but I wouldn't have said all those things if I had known."

"Really? *Really?*" I sat up, finally glaring at him.

"Maybe? I don't know. You just seemed so confident."

"You mean slutty."

"No. I definitely didn't mean that. You're not that kind of girl. I just meant that you seemed like you had experience, that you knew what you were doing. I guess…Wow."

He shook his head back and forth in disbelief. "Are you really a virgin?"

I took a deep breath before I answered. "Yes."

"But you've done other stuff? Like physically?"

"If you're asking if I've ever given or received oral sex or been fondled, the answer is no. I have been kissed, and my boob got grabbed once by a guy who I'm pretty sure will never have children after I was done with him."

For the first time ever, Hunter was speechless. Point for me.

"I don't know what to say," he said.

"Then here's a thought, don't say anything. Good night."

"No, no, no. We are talking about this."

I heard him reach for his boxers and then a shirt. Hmm. A minute later, the end of my bed dipped.

"Hey, talk to me. I just…it just seems unfathomable that it hasn't happened yet. If you were to yell out the window right now that you were a virgin, there would be at least a hundred guys lined up within five seconds."

"Whatever." I refused to turn over and look at him. I just wanted him to go to bed so I could continue to die inside in peace.

"No one's ever even tried?"

"No." Sure, I'd been asked out, but I'd never gone. And anyone who tried anything usually wound up with a very sore crotch.

"Then there must be something in the water where you live that alters logic. You should probably alert someone about that, because that's completely crazy."

"They called me the Ice Queen," I mumbled.

"What?"

"They called me the Ice Queen," I said, rolling over. Maybe if I satisfied his curiosity, he'd go away.

"They did not. You?"

"I guess I was chillier when I was in high school. Maybe you thawed me."

His hand touched my shoulder. "I'm sorry about everything."

"You don't have to be sorry. Just think before you speak next time. You don't want to go around insulting virgins. We can be fierce when we want to."

"I'll keep that in mind. Good night." He finally got up and went back to his bed. "Oh, and if you ever decide to turn in that V card, I'm here. Just so you know."

"I'm well aware."

"Good. Because we could be amazing. You and me."

"Good night," I said for what felt like the millionth time.

"Good night, Missy."

Hunter was ridiculously nice to me for the next two weeks as we passed from the last gasps of summer into fall.

Fall was my favorite season. Not only because my birthday was in November, but because of Halloween and crunchy leaves and pumpkin-scented things and hats and cute scarves. What wasn't to like about fall? I couldn't think of anything.

I usually got the baking bug in the fall as well, and one night I made pumpkin cookies with cream cheese frosting that made Renee propose to me, on one knee and everything.

"Thanks, babe," Paul said as he reached for another. Since Renee had brought him home, Paul had become a fixture in our apartment. He and Hunter had hit it off right away and had already had several extremely intense Halo tournaments and guitar jam sessions. Paul had a guitar as well and wasn't that bad. Renee would sit and watch, tapping her hand and bopping her head and yelling out requests.

I'd never seen her so happy. She was grinning from ear to

ear most of the time, and she was always touching him and laughing with him and kissing him. He was sweet and fun and kind of a dork. I liked him even more than I had when they'd dated last time. He seemed more settled. More mellow.

Between Paul, Hunter and Mase, we had quite a male presence in our place. Add Sean and Dev and we had quite a posse. I got used to having a million people around, all climbing over one another. Dinners were a production, so we made sure we had something for everyone. Somehow, even though I was the youngest, I'd become sort of a mom to them all. When we had dinner, no one remembered to grab a napkin and they always needed something, and I was usually the one to get up and get it.

I was still wearing the ring. I only took it off to shower, and my hand felt cold and naked without it. Hunter hadn't made further mention of the cost, and I had kind of let it go. Or so he thought. I was determined to find out where he got the cash. I knew he wasn't selling drugs or robbing banks or anything like that, but I knew it had something to do with Joe. It just had to.

The same night I made the pumpkin cookies I was cleaning up our bedroom, or at least my side of it, when I saw what looked like a crumpled-up check. Puzzled, I unfolded it.

It was made out to Hunter in the amount of five thousand dollars.

"Holy shit," I said, dropping the check.

"What are you doing?" a voice said behind me. A Hunter voice.

"Cleaning. And stop sneaking up on me."

"What were you holy shitting?"

"Nothing. Nothing." I tried to push the check with my

foot so it would go under a T-shirt I hadn't picked up yet, but he caught me. Boy was too damn observant.

"Then why are you trying to hide it?"

"Hide what?"

"You're not a moron, and you can't play one very well." He reached for the check, but I got there first.

"Then why don't you tell me what the hell this is?" I held it in front of his face and watched as all the color drained. Impressive.

"Give it back." He reached for it, but I'd been to kickboxing that week and my reflexes were on.

"Tell me what it is."

"Give. It. Back," he said through clenched teeth.

I stepped back, putting the check behind my back. He was going to get hold of it, because, let's face it, he was taller and stronger. But at least I might be able to find out what this was all about.

"Tell me what it is. Where did you get this kind of money?"

"Give. Me. The. Check."

I'd never seen Hunter so angry. Never. His blue eyes blazed with it. For the first time, I was scared of him. Didn't mean I was going to give it to him before I found out what the hell it was.

"Tell me," I said softly, backing up until my back hit my bed.

"I swear to God, if you don't give that to me in the next five seconds, I'm going to take it from you and I'm not going to be very nice about it."

I shook my head.

"Fine."

He dived at me, knocking me back so we were on my bed. I fought, but he had weight and momentum on his side.

"Get off me!"

"Not until you give it to me."

"Tell me and I will."

That only seemed to make him madder, and he grabbed my arm, wrenching it around as I fought.

"You're hurting me."

He didn't answer.

We continued to struggle as he finally got hold of it.

"Thank you. Now get the fuck out," he said as he got up. I was panting, but he wasn't. But at least we were both pissed now.

"What?"

"Get the fuck out," he roared.

"Where am I supposed to go?"

"That's not my problem."

"I'm not leaving," I said, crossing my arms.

"Then I'm going to have to remove you."

"I'd like to see you try."

With steel in his eyes, he reached for me. I thrashed, but he threw me over his shoulder and marched out the door, past Renee and Paul, who were having a tickle fight on the couch, and out to the hallway where he dumped me. I tried to get a good kick or punch in, but he was able to avoid them.

"Don't touch my stuff. Ever." He shut the door in my face and clicked the lock.

CHAPTER 20

I sat on the floor in the hallway for a few stunned seconds before I got up and banged on the door. Of course, I didn't have my key, so I banged on it until Renee sheepishly opened it and let me in.

"Thanks for that," I snapped.

"I...I didn't know what to do. I just...I've never seen him like that. He went in your room and locked the door and he won't come out."

Paul was in the process of banging on our bedroom door.

"Here, let me," I said, taking his place at the door. "I'm leaving, you douche bag. I just have one thing to say to you. I. Hate. You. If you don't believe me, whatever. But I'm not moving out permanently. I was here first before you barged your way in. I don't care where you go, but when I come back tomorrow, you'd better be gone. Screw you, Hunter Zaccadelli."

I grabbed my purse and left, calling Megan to ask if she had a free couch for the night.

"Of course, what happened?"

"I'll tell you when I get there."

Sassy roared to life, and I drove as fast as I could away from campus without getting busted by campus security for speeding. I still wasn't crying. Oh no. Tears were the last thing on my mind. I was pissed. Beyond pissed. I was livid.

Megan was waiting with a plate of chocolate cake and a sympathetic shoulder.

"Jake's still at work, and his crusty friends aren't coming over tonight, so the couch is all yours. I already made it up with fresh sheets. Do you need some clothes?"

I'd run out without anything, but I had an emergency stash in my car for moments like this.

As I mowed through two pieces of sticky cake and a glass of milk, I told Megan everything. I hadn't really had a chance to catch up with her in a while, so I filled her in on the ring affair and everything else.

"He's got money, and he's hiding it. If it were from his aunt and uncle, he would have admitted it. I just keep coming back to this Joe guy."

"So he had a meeting with him and he said something about not wanting...something. Maybe it was the money."

"That's the first thing I thought of. I mean, his parents are dead, this weird Joe guy has a meeting with him and then this," I said, holding up the ring. "And then the check for five grand. It's got to be connected. I just don't know why he would lie to me about it."

"I hate to say it, but you're lying to him, too."

"This is different."

"It isn't, and you know it. You can't expect him to be open with you if you aren't open with him. It goes both ways, babe."

"I know it does."

"Just stay the night here and think about it and see how you feel in the morning. This couch is yours as long as you need it. I'd much rather have you here than Jake's gross friends."

"Thanks, Meg. I don't know what I would have done."

"You're a resourceful girl. You would have figured something out."

"Thanks."

"Good night."

"Night."

I slept horribly on the sofa, but I told Megan I'd slept great. Jake tried not to make a lot of noise when he came home at six from his graveyard shift, but he couldn't help it. I got up as soon as I could in the morning. I didn't have any early classes and neither did Megan, so we had pancakes and talked some more.

"Any revelations after a night of sleep?" she said.

"Nope. But my voice mail box is full on my phone, and I have about a million texts that I haven't read."

"Maybe you should talk to him. Work things out."

"I just don't know if we can. There are just too many things in our way."

"Things you put there."

"Exactly. Meg, you know I can't do it. I just can't. Not even for him."

"You know everyone has secrets. Some are bigger than others, but it seems like he's got one equally as big as yours. So why don't you swap and call it even? Why let that stand in the way of something that could be amazing?"

The thing was that I didn't have a good answer. Letting Hunter in on my secret didn't seem so big anymore.

Seeing the look on his face last night had been terrible. It put me in a dark place that I'd thought I'd crawled out of years ago. I just didn't think I was ready.

There was a knock at the door, and Megan went to answer it.

"I'm not going to let you in. It's up to her," she said, moving the door so I could see who it was.

Hunter. With his guitar.

"Please. Just listen. I…I'm so sorry. I've been trying to figure out how I could show you, and this was all I could come up with. You don't have to do anything but listen. Just listen."

Megan looked at me, and I nodded.

"I'll be in the kitchen. Just scream if you need anything and I'll be there with a knife or two."

"Thanks." I turned my attention back to Hunter and his guitar. "You can stay on the porch. Like how you left me on the floor outside our room."

"I didn't know what else to do. You found the check, and I panicked."

"That isn't an excuse."

"I know. And I'm not saying that this is going to make up for it. I'm going to try, really try, to make you trust me again. I want you to trust me. I just…I couldn't sleep last night without you. It was the strangest thing, being in the room alone without you. I couldn't hear you breathing, and your laughter was gone and you were gone, and it was like a part of my life was missing. A big part. I tripped going to the bathroom and banged my head. See?" He pointed to a lovely gash on his forehead. "And then I burned my hand on the toaster oven. And then my car wouldn't start. Again. I've never had such bad luck in my life."

He brought the guitar around and settled it so he could play.

"I've been thinking about this song since I closed the door on you. I was going to come and see you last night, but I wanted to give you space."

I waited.

"So, here is part one of my apology."

He strummed the guitar in a familiar melody and started to sing. It was "Honey, Come Home" by The Head and the Heart. The lyrics were about a married couple where the husband was begging the wife to come back. He'd done the dishes and cleaned the house, and all he wanted was to lie next to her, with the one he loved.

He'd done a new arrangement that was both sad and beautiful. I melted into the music and Hunter's voice and I could see it. I could see us washing the dishes and waking up tangled up in him in the morning. It was so close I could taste it. I could taste his lips on mine.

When he ended the song, he looked at me.

"Can I come in?"

"I don't trust you."

"I know, Missy. But I don't trust you either. You've got a secret, too. You've been pushing me away to keep it. I pushed you away to keep mine."

"You were so angry. I was scared of you."

"I was scared of me, too."

"Are you going to tell me?"

"If that's what it will take to get you to come home. Yes. You might not like it, but if you want to know that badly, then yes."

"Okay then. You can come in."

"Are you okay in there?" Megan said.

"We're good," I called back.

"Okay, I'm going to take a shower. The knives are right here if you need them." Moments later I heard the water clunk to life and Megan humming.

"No wonder you two are friends. She sings in the shower, too," he said, slowly coming in. Instead of the couch, he grabbed a crappy falling-apart chair the guys used when they had game night.

"So, Joe," I said.

"Joe." Hunter took a breath. "Joe is my lawyer. Well, he's really my parents' lawyer. When they died, he was put in charge of managing their money until I came of age. Now that I am, he's still in charge of it."

"Why?"

"Because I don't want any of it."

"How much money?"

"I don't even know. Millions."

I nearly choked on my tongue. "Millions?"

"Yes. My dad was an oil executive in Texas. So he had a lot of money."

"Why don't you want it?" Who wouldn't want millions of dollars? I couldn't think of anyone.

"Because it's blood money."

"How?" Maybe his father had been involved in organized crime. Maybe that was it. That wouldn't surprise me too much.

"Because my father killed my mother and then killed himself."

Time stopped for a second after he said it. I had to have heard him wrong. That couldn't be it.

And then it all made sense. The nightmares, the reluctance to talk about them, his rich aunt and uncle.

"Oh."

"Yeah, there isn't much to say. It is what it is. It happened a long time ago, and I've moved on. At least I thought so."

"What happened?"

"My dad thought my mom was having an affair. She wasn't, but that didn't matter. Things were getting tight at the company, and he was under a lot of scrutiny. He got drunk one night, and they had a huge fight. He shot her." He paused for a moment. "I was in my room and I was trying to plug my ears so I couldn't hear them anymore. Then I heard the pop. I knew what it meant. I ran out and saw her on the floor in a puddle of blood. I tried to save her, but it was too late. Dad just stared at me, at her. And then he put the gun in his mouth and pulled the trigger."

"Oh my God," I said, horrified. It was so much worse than what I'd thought.

"You'd be shocked what happens to a person's face when it's blown off by a gun." He plucked a guitar string. "So there it is. You know everything there is to know. The only other people who know about it are my family and of course that town in Texas where I lived. I was the kid with the dead parents for a long time until Hope and John moved up here and I got to start over. Joe only comes up a few times a year to give me updates on investments and such. He keeps trying to get me to be more involved, to take some of the money for myself, but I don't want it."

Oh. *That* was what he didn't want. The money.

"What does he want you to do with it?"

"Invest it and make more money. Joe's very into that sort of thing. Playing the stock market and all that. He thinks I'm crazy for not wanting it. If he'd let me, I'd give all of it away. I give as much as he'll let me."

"You give it away?"

"Well, yeah. What am I going to do with millions of dollars I don't want? I feel like…" He paused and thought for a second. "I feel like if the money can do some good in this world, then they wouldn't have died for nothing. The money destroyed them. It made Dad crazy and angry and stressed, and he just snapped that day. I know I should blame him and be angry, but I can't. I have too many good memories of him to let that one bad one ruin everything."

Wow.

"So there you have it. My deep, dark secret. Well, one of them at least. A man has to keep some mystery, doesn't he?"

"I...I had no idea."

"No, you didn't. But it's okay. I should have told you. You deserved to know."

No, I really didn't.

"I'm so sorry."

"You know, you're one of the few people I believe when they say that. When your parents die when you're young, especially if they are well-known, all kinds of people tell you they're sorry, but it's mostly bullshit. They have to say that. But I know you feel it."

"I do. I'm so sorry I pushed you."

He put his hand on my shoulder. "It's okay, Taylor. I should have known you'd be so curious you were going to use other ways to find out."

"I spied on you. At your uncle's house. I told Hope I was going to the bathroom, but I went down the hall and listened at the door."

"Of course you did. I didn't expect anything less. What did you hear?" He was completely unfazed. He knew me better than I thought.

"Just you saying that you didn't want something. I know what that was now."

"Ah, so you didn't hear me calling Joe a pushy asshat?"

"You called him an asshat?"

"Yeah, this really cool girl I know uses it, and I decided to steal it."

"She approves."

"Does that mean you forgive me?"

"I want to," I said, being totally honest. "When you… when you looked at me…like that…" I shook my head, remembering. It made me think of that night. "You can't touch me like that ever again, or else I will rip your balls off and hand them to you."

He nodded.

"It reminded me of something I've spent almost eight years trying to forget. I…can tell you about it if you want." I wanted to swallow the words back once I said them.

"Taylor," he said, his voice and eyes soft. Nothing compared to last night. I never wanted to remember that night again. I wanted to erase it from my life. "You don't have to. I can see that it hurts you and it weighs on you, but if you don't want to tell me, you don't have to. Just listening to me tell you about my parents is enough. I'll take you no matter what. I'm so sorry for how I acted. I never want to be that guy again."

"I don't want you to, either." He moved onto the couch. "I just…I don't know if I can tell you. I don't know how." He'd made it look so easy. He'd just sat down and told me. God, he'd watched two deaths. I had nothing on that.

"I want to take you out to dinner. Someplace nice where I can continue to grovel and show you that you can trust me. I want you to trust me. I need it. I need you more than anything. Everything makes sense when you're around. Everything is better. I couldn't even cook dinner last night because you weren't there. I had a nightmare, and there was no one to wake me up from it. It's not your job to save me, but…I want you around."

"Me, too." I didn't tell Megan, but I'd woken up with my face pressed to the pillow and my teeth clenched in a scream.

Luckily, or else she might have thought someone was trying to murder me.

"So how about it? Will you let me take you on a date?"

"Will you help me pick out something to wear?"

"Absolutely." His face turned up into the smile I knew was trouble.

"I'm not wearing lingerie, so you can just get that image out of your head."

"Damn. It was worth a shot."

"I have the right to veto any of your choices."

"I suppose."

"Okay then. We're going on a date."

"Okay then."

I didn't tell him that it was technically my first date. I'd been on group things, but never where a guy picked me up and was expected to pay and pull my chair out and give me a chaste kiss at the end.

Hunter got up from the couch as Megan turned off the shower.

"You still alive out there?"

"Yes," we both called.

"Have you sliced off any limbs?" she asked.

"No. He's intact."

"Well, tell him if he ever hurts you again, he won't be."

"Got it." I turned to Hunter. "She says—"

"I got it. Will you come home now? There's a pot of blacker-than-sin coffee waiting for you."

"I'll meet you there, okay? I just want to thank Megan and get my stuff together."

"Okay, Miss. I'll see you at home."

He left, and I fell back against the couch. Megan emerged from her bedroom with her hair wrapped in a towel.

"Well?"

"He apologized in the most romantic way possible and he's taking me out to dinner."

"You still need to be careful."

"I know." I knew what she was saying.

"He's not Travis."

"No, he's not."

"Still."

"I know, Meg."

"Okay then."

I got up to grab my bag and my clothes from last night. I was still wearing my pj's.

"Thanks for letting me crash," I said, giving her a hug.

"Anytime, girl. You know I'm here for you."

"Thanks."

"Call me. I want to hear all the details. Make him work for it."

"Oh, believe me, I will. He's going to be on dish duty for at least two weeks. I'll see you later."

"Bye."

CHAPTER 21

"I'm excited," Hunter whispered in my ear during Human Sexuality.

"Well, we are talking about STDs, but whatever blows your whistle," I hissed back. It didn't really matter if we talked at normal volume. Most of the class did, so there was a constant hum of conversation that the professor didn't bother to hush.

"About our date. I know just what you should wear."

"Are you sure you're not gay? You have intimate knowledge of my closet."

"No, I just have intimate knowledge of you. I mean, we do sleep in the same room."

It was true. I knew pretty much his entire wardrobe, including his boxers, which I saw way too much of or not enough, depending on the day.

"You look really beautiful today. I mean, you do every day, but I don't say it enough."

"Wow, you are really buttering me up," I said as Marjorie motioned for the TAs to pass around little baskets of condoms.

You could do things like that in colleges. I just hoped she wasn't going to give us a demonstration with a banana.

"Wrap it before you tap it, pass it on," said Carissa, one of the TAs, as she handed me the basket.

"Think you can remember that?" I asked Hunter.

"You'll have to remind me," he said in a way that made shivers crawl up and down my spine.

"I'll give you a banana lesson later," I whispered as Marjorie tried to call us to order so she could talk about chlamydia. *Delightful.*

"Looking forward to it," he said with a wink.

We walked back to the apartment together, and Hunter was strangely quiet.

"Penny for your thoughts?" I said.

"I was just thinking that my mom would have loved you."

"What was she like?"

"Beautiful. I have this black-and-white picture of her I'll have to show you. She spent most of her time doing charity work, but she also had a degree in architecture. She always joked that people thought she was a trophy wife until she opened her mouth and set them straight. Sharp as a whip, Dad used to say. She had a comeback for everything. I don't think that woman ever lost an argument in her life."

"What did she look like?" I pictured dark hair and Hunter's smile.

"I got my blue eyes from her. And some people say my smile. I look more like my dad than I do her. I have a picture of him, too, if you want to see."

I did. I wanted to see where he had come from, since I couldn't meet them. If he wasn't going to let what his father did define how he felt about him, I wasn't going to, either.

"You aren't mad at him? Really?"

"I was, for a while. I did a lot of thinking and talking with my aunt and therapy and so forth. I used to break things and set them on fire. I was in detention more than a few times."

"Imagine that," I said, pretending to be shocked.

"I was a punk for a while."

"Let me guess," I said, turning around and walking backward so I could watch him. "You were a skater boy with a Mohawk, and you may or may not have had a pierced ear. Your pants also probably fell off a lot."

He glared at me. "I was not a skater boy. I was just a boy who rode a skateboard frequently."

"Same thing. So I'm right about everything else?"

"Still have the scar from the earring."

He stopped walking and tipped his head down so I could see the minuscule hole that dotted his left earlobe. I turned my head and realized how close my lips were to his and how much they wanted to be attached to his. *No. Bad lips.*

I turned and started walking again.

"Do I get to do the same thing?"

"Go ahead." He'd never get it right.

"Let's see. I bet you wore torn black fishnets and lots of eyeliner and you were into really deep poetry and studied French."

"Way off," I said, scoffing. He wasn't even close.

"I know. I was just messing with you. I bet you did a little bit of everything. Art, maybe a sport like tennis, and you read a lot and I'm guessing National Honor Society. Oh, and I bet you did dance. You move like you danced at one point in your life. How did I do?"

Holy shit. He'd gotten it exactly.

"Stalker," I said, walking faster. There was no way he could have known that without doing some heavy research.

"Hold up. I swear I didn't stalk you. I told you, I'm just really observant. Think of me as Sherlock Holmes, only without the bad social skills and cocaine use."

"Holmes was into cocaine?"

"How else was he able to stay up all night and solve crimes?"

"True." He moved into stride next to me. "So you didn't stalk me?"

"I may have checked out some of your old Facebook posts, but that's it." I forgot about that. Damn social networking. No one was anonymous anymore.

"I did dance for a few years, but it got too expensive so I had to stop. I also got kicked out."

"You got kicked out of dance?"

"Yeah. I kind of told a girl I was going to rip her throat out."

He started laughing, throwing his head back. "Why?"

I sighed. "Because she said that my dad had been cheating on my mom even before the divorce, and my mom had something on the side as well."

"How old were you?"

"Fourteen. She was just repeating something her mom had said, but she was old enough to know what she was saying."

"God, girls are bitches."

"Tell me about it."

"So anyway, I tried to yank her snotty platinum ponytail out of her head and that was that. I was asked to leave and never come back. Thus ended my career as a dancer."

"Shame. You've still got the moves." I stopped and did a little shimmy. "You could always take classes."

"Maybe I will."

"You should. If you liked it."

"I did."

"Well there you go."

Renee was studying on the couch as Paul was spread out over the dining table with what looked like some sort of math conundrum. Paul was crazy smart and was majoring in both mechanical and chemical engineering. Renee always joked that he was going to get a fancy job as an oil baron or something and then she'd be his trophy nurse. All she wanted was to work in a neonatal intensive care unit, taking care of babies.

"Hey, you made up yet?" Renee said, her eyes not leaving her textbook.

"Sort of," I said.

"Good."

"Hey," Paul said, waving and not looking up from his calculator. Two peas in a pod.

"We're going out tonight and then back to Paul's, FYI, so we won't be here for dinner."

"Got it. We're not going to be here either," I said.

"Oh, really?"

"I am taking Taylor on a date." Hunter smiled as if he'd won the lottery.

"Good. You owe her about a million dinners. I hope you're taking her someplace nice."

"I am."

"Ooh, tell me, tell me," she said.

"No way! If I don't get to know, you don't get to know," I said.

But Hunter leaned over and whispered in Renee's ear.

"Very nice. You have good taste, dude."

"Thank you. Now, if you don't mind, we both need to do some homework before said date."

"Enjoy," Renee said, her eyes drifting back to her book.

Hunter made a snack while I got my homework crap

together. Somehow we were able to function and study without distracting one another. At least, most of the time. Every now and then I'd find him looking at me, or I'd steal a moment to stare at him. I loved watching him concentrate. His face got so calm and beautiful. I couldn't deny the power of his smirk, but I loved watching him study.

I settled on my bed, propping up my pillows to prepare myself for a bunch of reading for medieval European history, and then I had a bunch of notes to review for French on the subjunctive. Gag me. I was going to do the French first since it was the suckiest. Don't get me wrong, I loved the country, but conjugating verbs wasn't my activity of choice.

Hunter came back with my no-fire-required s'mores, which were made with Nutella, Fluff and graham crackers. He also had two glasses of iced tea.

"Here you go, Miss Caldwell. Happy studying."

"Thank you, Mr. Zaccadelli. Same to you."

We retired to our separate beds and got to work. Our desks were crammed so tight under our beds that you couldn't sit comfortably. Bed studying was much more preferable.

The only sound was the turn of a page, the scratch of a pen and our breathing. Every now and then I'd feel Hunter's eyes on me and I'd look up, only to meet those intense blue eyes. I always looked away first.

I finished what I wanted to do for French and got started on reading about medieval clothing. It was fascinating, but not as interesting as watching Hunter study his boring economics books. *Yum*.

"You're staring," he said.

"Not for very long. I'm admiring your sexy brain."

"Go ahead. I don't mind. I do it enough to you."

"Yeah, I'm aware," I said, rolling my eyes.

"If you don't like it, I'll stop. You just say the word about anything and I'll stop."

"You don't have to stop."

"Okay then," he said.

We worked for a little while longer, until my eyes were crossing. The lack of sleep the night before wasn't really helping with my attempt to cram a bunch of information into my brain.

"I'm done," I said, closing my book.

"Me, too. I like economics, but I like you more."

"I should hope so."

"You can shower first. I know it takes your hair longer to dry."

"This is true." His dried in about five seconds.

I grabbed some clothes and hopped in the shower, singing Taylor Swift as loud as I wanted, knowing Hunter could hear me through the door.

I shaved extra carefully, because if we were going someplace fancy, he was going to make me wear a dress. I wiped off the steamy mirror and checked my naked self out, turning from side to side. *Meh.* Nothing special, but nothing hideous either. Hunter didn't seem to care, but he hadn't seen all of me either.

The closest I'd been to naked was a tank top and booty shorts. He'd never seen my stomach, and I was pretty sure he was still unaware of my belly ring. I'd managed to keep that little secret for myself.

I slipped on a robe and padded back to our room, drying my hair with a towel.

"Cruel, that robe is cruel," he said, looking up from the book I'd bought with Megan at our last mall trip.

"Why?"

"Because it covers everything up."

"Exactly. That's what it's supposed to do."

He shook his head and grabbed his shower stuff. I'd never told him, but sometimes when he wasn't around, I'd open the top of his body wash and smell it, which was weird. He wouldn't do anything that creepy.

As I waited for him to come back, I scrunched my hair up so it would dry better and kind of wavy. I'd recently seen this cool twist idea online that I wanted to try. Hunter came back to find me jamming bobby pins in my hair.

"What are you doing?" He only had a towel on. Of course. He stood behind me and reached for my hair.

"What are *you* doing?" I ducked away from his meddling hands. "This took ten minutes to get like this."

"Wear it down. It looks better down."

"I'll wear it however I want."

"Okay," he said, turning away, but stopped and reached out to tug a little piece out so it framed my face. "There. Perfect."

I studied the effect in the mirror and sighed. The updo was pretty, but it wasn't me. It looked like me dressing up as a lawyer for Halloween. I was never going to be able to find all the pins.

"Okay, you win. Give me a hand." Hunter and I spent the next ten minutes rooting though my thick hair to find all the pins. Our hands kept bumping into one another.

"Do you do some special girlie hair treatment?"

"No, why?"

He removed his hands and stepped back. We were still wary around each other after the blowup.

"Because you've got amazing hair."

"Good genes, I guess." I did a mayonnaise treatment every now and then, but I only did it when I knew he wasn't going to be around. I didn't care if he saw me flipping my retainer, but beauty treatments were personal.

"There. I think that's the last one," I said. My hair tumbled around my shoulders. I fluffed it and called it good.

"That's what I like to see. Natural. I'm going to get un-naked, so you might want to stay turned around. Unless you want to give me a hand…"

"No, I'm good. I'm going to go, um, brush my teeth?" It sounded like a question.

"Have fun with that."

I did end up brushing my teeth and came back when I was sure Hunter had enough time to be clothed.

"Wow," I said. He was wearing a black button-up with khakis and even a pair of dress shoes. Where the hell had those come from? I'd never seen them.

"I have my secrets, too, Miss Caldwell."

"You look very nice, Mr. Zaccadelli."

"Yours is waiting on your bed."

He'd picked out a black cocktail dress that I'd bought on sale on a crazy whim because Megan had told me every girl needed a little black dress.

"I thought it would look good on you. You don't have to wear it if you don't want to."

"No, no. I like it. I've just never had a place to wear it."

"Now you do."

"I'm gonna go get ready," I said, and he left.

I locked the door before I slipped the dress on. It was slinky and fell just short of my knees, but came up high on my neck in the front. It reminded me of Audrey Hepburn. I found a necklace of black beads and some matching earrings that I'd borrowed from Tawny and never returned. By the time Hunter came back, I was putting on mascara.

"Don't poke yourself in the eye."

"I think I can handle it."

"Okay, okay." He watched me for a moment and then left, probably to give me some more privacy. Good boy.

I was just about ready when he knocked on the door. "Are you ready, Miss Caldwell?"

"Yes, I am, Mr. Zaccadelli. You may escort me now."

He opened the door and even though he'd seen me before, his eyes still popped. "Gorgeous."

"Thank you."

"Shall we?" He held out his arm. I took it and we left.

"Where's Darah?" I asked.

"She had to work."

"Oh. She didn't say goodbye."

Hunter shrugged. *Huh.*

He did all the things he was supposed to do, the door-opening and the escorting and such. The feminist in me balked at the idea that I couldn't open a door, but it was nice not to have to do those things for one night. Letting Hunter pull out my chair for one night wasn't going to set the women's liberation movement backward. I hoped.

"You're in charge, Missy. I see that look on your face."

"What look?"

"It's not a sin to let me open a door for you. I know you're perfectly capable of doing it yourself."

"Who said it was?"

"Okay then."

The restaurant, the Broadway Public House, was in a brick building in downtown Bangor, a few minutes away from the college. Somehow Hunter found a parking spot for his Pontiac Sunfire right next to the restaurant.

"I'm lucky," he said as he opened the door for me.

The restaurant was in a strip of brick buildings that went all the way down the main street, with an old brick mill on the end. It was all white linen and candlelight and fancy French things on the menu. Thank goodness I knew enough of that to know what was what.

The waiter had an accent, which probably meant his family was French Canadian and had just come over the border. We ordered hors d'oeuvres of French bread and a goat cheese dip and a nicoise salad.

We didn't want to risk the fake IDs, so we both got sparkling water.

When it came time to order, I went with the tomato bisque with a mushroom and swiss quiche, and then it was Hunter's turn.

"Peanut butter and jelly with a side of the asparagus." The waiter gaped at him for a second, but he wrote it down.

"What type of jelly would you like?"

"Strawberry." The waiter wrote that down and left, shaking his head a little.

"We come to this fancy restaurant and you order PB and J?"

He shrugged, unfazed that the waiter was probably telling the entire kitchen about the crazy guy who had ordered peanut butter and jelly.

"I've never eaten here, so I don't know what's good. Peanut butter and jelly is always good. You can't screw that up. Peanut butter and jelly has always been there for me and is one of the constants in my life. Peanut butter and jelly has never done me wrong. It's my favorite." His eyes bored into me as he said it, and I had the feeling we weren't talking about a sandwich.

"Should I leave you two alone when it gets here? Sounds like you don't need me."

"I might be projecting my views of someone else onto the sandwich."

"Just a little."

The waiter had composed himself by the time he brought our dinner out. They'd done what they could in the kitchen to make the sandwich look fancy, but really, it was still a PB and J. It looked silly sitting on the plate with parsley on the side and some sort of drizzle around the edge of the plate.

"I propose a toast," Hunter said, raising his glass. I raised mine as well. "To peanut butter and jelly. My favorite sandwich."

"PB and J," I said, and we clinked our glasses. Some of the other diners gave us weird looks, but I ignored them. They just didn't understand the awesomeness of PB and J.

"You want a bite?" Hunter said, holding up his sandwich. One woman looked absolutely horrified that he'd just held up his sandwich for me to take a bite.

I leaned over and took a bite. *Damn.* That was good. The peanut butter had to be organic, and it had just the right amount of crunch. The jelly was also clearly homemade. *Yum.*

"You want a bite of mine?" I fed him a bite of my amazing quiche.

"Not as good as mine."

"Whatever. Eat your sandwich, Mr. Zaccadelli."

"Yes, Miss Caldwell."

We chewed some more, and I soaked in the quiet ambience of the restaurant. Soft piano music floated from one corner where a professional played, and the clink of china added to the cozy feel. It was definitely a nice place, and I did feel a little out of place.

"So, you want to play a game?" he said.

"What kind of game?" The mind reeled.

"I say something and you say the first thing that comes to your mind. Then you can turn it around on me."

"Okay." He wiped his mouth with his napkin and took a sip of water.

"What was the first thing that came to your mind when you saw me?" he asked.

"Crap."

"As in, 'Oh crap, that is one hot guy'?"

"More like, 'Oh crap, that is not a girl.'"

"Fair enough. What was the second thing you thought when you saw me?"

"Trouble."

He laughed loudly, startling the other diners.

"Is it my turn?" I said.

"Go ahead," he said, leaning back as if to prepare himself.

"First thing you thought when you saw me?"

"I had three simultaneous thoughts. One—" he held one finger up "—stunning, two—" another finger "—this can't be real, and three, that I really, really hoped I was going to get to share a room with you so I could stare at you all the time."

"You were only supposed to use one word."

"Missy, one word can't describe you."

I'd say the same about him.

"Okay, how about this. What's the first thing you think when you wake up?"

"You."

I rolled my eyes.

"What about you?" he said.

"First thing I think is, 'Oh crap, I have to get up.' The second is, 'I hope Hunter's blanket is pulled up.'"

"Liar."

I blushed. Sometimes it was a lie.

"What did you think when you woke up that morning when we were together?" he asked.

"Safe," I said without thinking.

"Me, too. And warm."

"You do get pretty hot when you sleep. Has anyone ever told you that?"

"Missy, I'm always hot," he said, leaning back farther and smiling.

"Whatever. Okay, how about when I punched you?"

"First was, 'Ow, she has quite a right hook,' and second was, 'That's one of the sexiest things I've ever seen.'"

"Really?"

"Missy, nothing is sexier than a woman who can take care of herself. As far as I'm concerned, the 1950s are over. Although, you would look damn cute in a poodle skirt and saddle shoes. But I like you better when you can show your knees and speak without being spoken to. Not that you would have followed those rules anyway."

"Damn right. I would have been a horrible housewife."

"Yeah, I can't see you saying, 'How was your day, dear?' and handing me my pipe and slippers."

"I'd probably chuck them at you."

"Probably."

"And then I'd have to punish you," he said with a wicked smile.

"Would you toss me outside on my ass?" His smile fell.

"I am so sorry about that." He stared down at his empty plate. I still had some food left, but I'd done it on purpose so I could bring some home with me. I never left a restaurant without a doggie bag.

"I know. I just…I'm scared that you're going to be sweet and nice now and everything will be fine and then I'll do something and it will happen again. I've...I've seen how abusive relationships work, and I don't want that."

"I would never, ever want you to be afraid of me. Ever."

"Then make sure it doesn't happen. Because if it does, I'm gone, and you'll probably be missing one or more appendages."

"That's my girl," he said. I put my fork down and the waiter came to ask us if we wanted desert. "Want to share something?"

"Do you have red velvet cake?" I said.

"Of course," the waiter said, as if this was a ridiculous question. How *dare* I assume that they didn't have red velvet cake. The nerve.

"Bring two forks, please," Hunter said. The waiter nodded. "You want to keep playing?"

"Why not?"

"Okay, how about the first thing you thought when you saw me in Human Sex?" A woman who had been eavesdropping from the next table nearly choked on her filet mignon. That was what she got for listening in.

"Honestly? Oh, fuck," I whispered the last part so the woman wouldn't actually choke. I didn't want to be responsible for that. "You?"

"Score."

"Ass."

The cake came, and it was glorious, with tons of cream and chocolate drizzle and it was almost too pretty to eat. Almost.

"Ladies first," Hunter said when we each went at it with our forks. *Damn right.*

I nearly had a cakegasm at the table. My eyes rolled back in my head, and I moaned.

"Sweet Christ." I opened my eyes to find Hunter watching me with the strangest expression on his face. "What? It's really good. You should try some," I said, pushing the plate at him. It was a testament to how embarrassed I was about the cakegasm that I was even sharing at all.

"I swear, if there weren't a table between us, I would be kissing you right now. And none too gently."

I put my fork down and swallowed so I wouldn't choke. "You didn't seem to mind about the recliner," I said.

"True. But there wasn't an audience, and that's a very ugly recliner. This is a very nice table. Also, there is glass and sharp things I wouldn't want hurting you."

"Good point. Please, have some."

"If you're going to make that noise and that face again, I don't know if I can let you have any more."

"I'll be good. I swear."

"You're not good. That's the problem."

"You're right. I'm not," I said, giving him my own smirk. "I do try, though."

"Cruel. That's the word to describe you right now."

"Just have some cake."

He picked up the fork and took a bite. "Damn. That *is* good." He had another bite, and then I had to fight him for the rest of it. I was able to refrain from any further public displays of cake affection.

"I told you."

"That is some mighty fine cake," he said with a southern accent. My jaw may have dropped a little. "What? You know I'm half-Texan. I tried to get rid of it, but it comes out every now and then, especially when I spend time with my family."

"Do you have more family in Texas?"

"My dad's family relocated there from New York when he was a kid. I don't see them much."

The waiter came to take our cake plate, and I sat back in my chair. I was satiated.

"Would you excuse me?" I raised an eyebrow at his overt politeness. "I'm being a gentleman—don't ruin it."

"Yes, you may be excused, Mr. Zaccadelli."

"Thank you, Miss Caldwell. I will return momentarily." He got up and left the restaurant. *What the what?*

"Are you ready for the check?" The waiter was back.

"Um, sure." He looked at Hunter's empty seat with disapproval as if he'd run away and left me.

"He'll be right back," I felt the need to say.

"Of course." He soooo didn't believe me.

I spent the next thirty seconds staring at the door, praying that Hunter would walk through it. He finally did, and he had something with him. His guitar.

What the hell was he up to?

He didn't come back to the table, but went right to the guy who was playing the piano, interrupting him in the middle of a song. Hunter leaned in to speak to piano man, who, to his credit, kept playing. Hunter gestured with his hands like he did when he really wanted to get his point across. Piano man nodded, and then Hunter said something that made him smile.

He finished his song with a flourish and got up. The entire restaurant turned toward that spot. Piano man waved at a waiter and quickly explained the situation. Waiter went and got a stool and moved the mic away from the piano. I could see where this was going.

Hunter sat down on the stool and pulled his guitar out, settling it so he could play. Everyone watched in fascination.

"Hello, everyone. I'm sorry to disturb your dinner. I'll only take a few moments of your time." He adjusted the strap, and I could tell he was nervous. His knee was going a mile a minute. "I just wanted to play a little song for my girl, Taylor, over there. She agreed to come here with me tonight, even after I wasn't very nice to her. This is part of my apology. I hope you like it."

Everyone stared at me, and I felt like I was under a spotlight roughly the luminosity of the sun. I wasn't a big blusher, but I did right then.

He started the song, and I recognized it immediately as "Fix You" by Coldplay. It was an older song, but one that I'd always loved. I'd never told him that I did and I wondered if he'd picked it for that or he'd picked it on his own. It didn't matter.

His voice wrapped around the song, and I could tell he'd sung it a hundred times. I sat back and watched him. He'd started out looking at the guitar, but soon he looked up to find my eyes. The lyrics were perfect for both of us. We were both broken, trying to become unbroken. Maybe we just needed a little help. Not to fix each other, but to help us fix ourselves.

The chatter in the restaurant ceased as Hunter sang about lights guiding you home. The woman who had been eavesdropping wiped at her eyes with her napkin.

He ended the song, and the room was silent for half a second. Then there was a smattering of applause that built until Hunter was required to get up and take a bow.

"I'm sorry, Missy. Thank you for listening," he said into the mic before coming back to our table. He sat down slowly, as if waiting for me to yell at him. "Well?" he said after I didn't respond.

"I don't really know what to say."

"You've never been at a loss for words in your life. Let me have it. You hated it."

"No, I didn't."

I could feel everyone else listening to us.

"Oh, honey, forgive him! My husband would never do something that romantic," the eavesdropper said. Her husband looked sheepish. I waited for someone else to give their opinion, but no one else came forward.

"I'm not one for public displays, but I think I can make an exception for that. How did you know I loved that song?" I said.

"I didn't. Lucky guess."

"The luckiest." I got up from my seat and went to his, giving him a kiss on the cheek. "Thank you. It was perfect."

"It wasn't, but it means the world that you think so. I meant it. I know we're both screwed up, but even screwed up people should be able to be happy."

"I think so, too." I gave him another kiss, lingering for a moment so I could breathe him in. He snaked his arms around my waist, and I put my head on his for a second. There it was, our bubble, sealing around us again.

Eavesdropper sighed happily behind me.

"Shall we go?" he said, putting his guitar back in the case.

"Sure." He took out his card and put it in the book. The waiter came to collect it, looking slightly stunned.

"That was awesome. Really, you're talented. You're welcome back anytime." Hunter tried to hand him the book, but the waiter refused. "Your meal has been taken care of. You have a good night." Hunter tried again, but the waiter stood firm.

"Can I get your name?" Hunter asked.

"It's Will."

"Thank you, Will. You have a good night," Hunter said, shaking his hand. "You ready, Miss?"

I took my doggie bag in one hand and Hunter's with the

other, and he had his guitar case on the outside. Eavesdropper waved to me on our way out.

"You take care of that pretty girl now."

"I will."

CHAPTER 22

I held Hunter's hand on the way back home. It felt like the right thing to do. Like we were on a real date, and we could be a real couple. My mind never strayed far from thinking about my secret. About finally telling him and letting things fall where they may. There it was again. That falling word.

"You look amazing."

"Thank you. You look pretty good." *Understatement.*

"Oh this old thing? Shucks," he said.

"Dork."

"Goddess."

He took my hand and kissed the back of it, taking his eyes off the road for a moment.

"So you're not still mad at me? I mean, it's okay if you are."

"I'm not mad exactly. Well, not anymore. I just…I never thought you had that in you."

"I did," he said. "I've…I've lost control like that before, but not for a long time. I wanted to go after you, but I was so ashamed of what I'd done. I didn't want you to feel threatened by me at all."

"I can take care of myself, Hunter."

"I know."

"Let's just not talk about it anymore. Talking about it isn't going to change it. It happened and that's that," I said.

"It's not, but I can agree to a change in topic. What would you like to discuss?"

"What did you say to the piano player?"

"I just told him that I'd been a jerk and there was a special lady who needed a very special apology."

"Let me guess—I'm the special lady."

He shook his head. "Nope, it was the lady at the next table."

"The eavesdropper? How dare you."

"Are you kidding? Nothing turns a man on like giant gold earrings and an animal-print top. Rawr."

I laughed as we pulled into the student lot. This time I waited for Hunter to come open my door.

"So do you have anything further planned for this lovely evening?" I asked.

"Well, I know how much you like that wedding movie and it always makes you laugh, so I figured we could watch it with some kettle corn. Sound good?"

"Sounds perfect." I could see the whole scene in my head. Me and Hunter in our pj's, with me draped across him on the couch, laughing so much our stomachs hurt.

"You don't have to tell me tonight. One secret is enough for a day, don't you think?"

"Yeah." Part of me wanted to blurt it out, to unburden myself and kill the suspense already. He wanted to know. How could he not? I'd practically pried his secret out of him, like digging a pearl from a clam. But I was glad I knew. I hoped he didn't regret telling me. I hoped I wouldn't regret telling him.

There was a note on the front door as we came up the stairs.

You kids have fun. The place is all yours. Please wipe all surfaces you become amorous on with the wipes in the kitchen. Love you, Darah and Renee

"I wonder who wrote that note."

"Well, I'm guessing Renee wrote it and Darah added the part about the wipes."

"Sounds about right." He took the note down and put his key in the lock.

"So," he said when he'd opened the door and turned the light on. "I guess it's just us."

We'd never been alone together all night before. Daytime was a whole other ball of wax.

Hunter was still holding my hand.

"I'll, um, let you get changed and I'll start the popcorn," he said, dropping it like a burning coal.

A little voice inside me screamed in frustration, but I turned and went to the bedroom anyway. I reached around my back to undo the zipper, but it wouldn't undo. I'd had no problem getting it up, but down was another story. I nearly wrenched my arms out of my sockets trying to get the damn thing to cooperate with me.

"Son of a bitch!"

There was a knock at the door.

"You okay in there?"

"Yes, fine." I tried pulling the hem of the dress up and over my head that way, but it was too formfitting. *Well, shit.*

I tried one last time before I gave up.

"Okay, so can you give me a hand? The stupid zipper is stuck."

"Oh, really?"

"Shut up and just help me, please?" I opened the door and turned my back to him. "Just get it started—"

I stopped talking when I felt his warm hands on my back. Breathing suddenly became very challenging. His fingers took their sweet time brushing across my skin and tucking my hair out of the way of the traitorous zipper.

He pulled gently, and down it zipped.

"There. I didn't seem to have any problem."

"Well that's so nice for you," I snapped, trying to turn back around.

He held my shoulders so I couldn't. Ever so slowly, he pressed his lips on the spot the zipper had revealed. My skin burned with the contact and the rest of me melted into jelly. I wanted to sag against him, but I didn't.

"Hunter," I said. Well, it was more like a whisper.

"Sorry. Couldn't resist. I'm drawn to you. It drives me absolutely insane that I have to be with you all the time and I can't touch you."

I willed my foot to move so I could take a step forward and thus away from him. Finally, my foot complied. I felt the exact same way about him, but I couldn't move forward. There was a giant secret standing in our way.

"I can't."

"I know. I'm sorry. I'll behave." I met his eyes and had to look away. I wanted to tell him not to. To throw everything out of the window and kiss me like he had when we'd nearly broken the recliner.

"I need to change," I said, my voice loud in the quiet room.

"Okay." He turned and left.

I could still feel his lips on my back as I slid a T-shirt over my head and put on some shorts. I should have put on a long-sleeved ensemble so as to leave the least amount of skin visible, but it was a warm night and our apartment had crappy ventilation.

I heard the microwave ding when I came out.

"I think I might need a little help with my zipper, why don't you give me a hand?" Hunter said, turning his back.

"Sorry, my hands are full," I said, grabbing the steaming popcorn bag and the bowl he'd set out and holding them up. "You'll have to do it all by yourself."

"Fine. But you're missing out." Didn't I know it.

He closed the door, and I leaned against the counter. Why, why did the things he said have to start sounding good? Why did I want to walk into that room and say, "Hell yes, I'll help you with that zipper and the rest of your clothes, get them off *now*"?

I felt my forehead. Maybe I had a fever. Maybe it was the red velvet cake that had gotten me all riled up. Or maybe it was the damn song. What girl wasn't a sucker for a guy who could sing? It was why Christine had gone down to the Phantom's creepy underground lair. It was why so many women threw themselves at rock stars, good-looking or not so much.

By the time he came out, I was situated on the couch with the popcorn in a bowl and two sodas complete with coasters. Darah would have a hissy fit if she knew we hadn't used coasters.

"Coasters, good thinking," Hunter said, nodding to our drinks.

"I thought so."

He had boxers and a gray tank on. On anyone else, it would have been boxers and a gray tank. On Hunter, it was...damn sexy.

"Do I have something on my face?" he said, catching me in the act of staring.

"No."

"Then why were you looking at me like that?"

"I wasn't." *Deny, deny, deny.*

"Okay then, you weren't." He sat down next to me and grabbed his drink. "You got the movie in?"

"Yup." I had the remote in my hand, but I didn't want to push Play. Hunter took a sip of his drink as I fought the urge to throw myself at him. I grabbed the popcorn bowl and put it between us as a buffer. Why had Renee and Darah done this to me? I knew they thought they were helping, but this most certainly was not helping.

I hit Play on the movie, hoping against hope that it would serve as a distraction. It worked for about five seconds. Then Hunter's hand and mine collided in the popcorn bowl in one of those movie moments. I snatched mine back, but he stopped me.

"Can I be honest with you right now?" he said.

My mouth was dry as I said, "Sure. When are you not honest with me? With the exception of one time."

"Yes, well," he said, rubbing his tattoo one, two, three times. *Uh-oh.* "I'm going to be brutally honest, okay?"

"Once again, when are you not? But carry on," I said, waving my hand for him to continue. The movie blared in the background, but it might as well have been in Esperanto for all the attention I was paying to it.

He took a breath. "I want you. Right now. If you said yes, I would kiss you. I would kiss you until we both forgot that lips were made for anything other than kissing. I'd take you out of that outfit, as cute as it is. I want to see what you look like with nothing on. I want to make you sigh like you did with the cake. I want to be with you. Right now."

"Right now?" I squeaked.

"Right now. Fuck the movie." He grabbed the remote

and paused the movie. "I just thought you should know how I feel."

I had to close my eyes for a second. He was so close, it was hard to think. My brain just went blank and decided to picture all the things he'd talked about. My skin hummed, ready and waiting.

"I..."

"I'm not asking you to. I know this is hard for you. I just wanted you to know that that was something I wanted to do." I opened my eyes.

"You've been saying stuff like that to me since day one."

"Not like this. Those other girls? That stuff I did with them? That was just sex. I never want to have just sex again. I want to get lucky with you. Only you. Bottom line."

I fumbled for a response. "I'll make a note of it," I said.

"Okay then." He took the remote and turned the movie back on, settling back as if nothing had happened. *What. The. Fuck.*

I turned my head toward the movie, but I was even more distracted. He'd planted the seed of that idea in my head and now that thing was growing as if someone had Miracle-Gro-ed the shit out of it. Mental weed killer wasn't going to work on that sucker.

The next hour was pure torture. Part of me wondered if he'd done it on purpose. To tease me. He'd done things like that before. Our hands didn't collide in the popcorn bowl, and he pretended as if we were two friends watching a movie.

When it was over, and the popcorn was gone, I waited for him to say something.

"You tired?" I asked. I didn't have to be up too early, but I knew he did.

"Yeah, I guess we should go to bed."

It was a very anticlimactic end to our date. He got up and gathered the remnants of our movie snacks and threw them in the sink.

"I'm gonna go brush my teeth," he said, stepping around me.

I went into the bedroom and tried to get myself under control.

Not good, not good, not good.

I had to put a cork in my hormones. I'd never reacted like that to anyone. No guy had ever made me feel like I was on fire. I'd thought all that talk about it was just people being melodramatic. Guess it wasn't.

He came back and, without another look at me, shucked off his shirt and got into bed. Oh that was *it.*

"What the hell, dude?"

"What?" He turned over, as if he had no idea what I was talking about.

"Are you kidding? Seriously? All that talk about the wanting and the kissing and everything and now you're going to just pretend like it didn't happen? What the hell is wrong with you?"

"I just thought that I'd been too forward and I thought that I'd freaked you out. I was just giving you space."

"Oh."

"So how did you feel about what I said?"

I sputtered for a second, unable to use actual words. Just sounds.

"Can I take that as a confirmation that yes, it would be something you would be interested in?" His blue eyes begged me to say yes.

"I don't know. Maybe?"

"There's no maybe about it, Missy. Either yes or no."

"Can I have some time?"

"Sure, Miss. There's no expiration date on my offer. If you come to me in sixty years, I'll be waiting with a bottle of Viagra."

Ew and yuck.

"Thanks for tonight. I had a really good time." How was this supposed to work? I mean, usually a date ended and the guy dropped the girl off and they said good-night. With us, there was no good-night. We'd see each other when we woke up.

"Good. That was the plan." I got into bed, trying not to stare at his chest. "Can I ask one more thing?" he said.

"Uh, sure."

"Can I kiss you good-night?"

"I guess so."

"You seemed to enjoy it the last couple times."

"Shut up." And kiss me, I didn't say.

He got out of bed and walked slowly to mine. I got up and we stared at one another for a breath of time. He leaned down, and I waited this time.

"Good night, Taylor."

He leaned down and pressed the sweetest, briefest kiss in the history of the world. He tried to pull away, but my lips and the rest of me wouldn't let him. I pulled him back for just a second before I slammed the door on my desire and was able to detach myself from him.

"Good night, Hunter." I somehow got myself back into bed. He stood there for a moment before sighing and going to his bed.

"Love me?" he whispered as he tossed his boxers on the floor.

"Nope."

"Hate me?"

"Not as much as conjugating verbs."

"Good."

My body hummed with energy. There was no way I was getting to sleep at this point. It was going to be a long night.

CHAPTER 23

I'd never experienced the "hot and bothered" feeling, but around 3:00 a.m., I had to get up and get out of the room. I could hear Hunter's every breath and movement like never before. I had a brief notion of going to sleep, or trying to, in Darah and Renee's room, but then Hunter would know that I was hot and bothered.

I didn't look at my face in the mirror because I didn't want to see it. Instead I sat on the rim of the tub and twirled my hair with one finger. It was a habit I'd picked up when I was a kid that I hadn't done in a long time. When I'd been young, I'd twirled so much I'd actually pulled some of my hair out. My therapist at the time, Dr. Blood, had given me a stress ball, but that hadn't helped. I was irreparably broken.

I'd accepted the fact that I was messed up a long time ago. It was one of the reasons I'd promised myself to not get involved with anyone. No one should have to deal with my issues other than me. It was easy, because there wasn't anyone that I wanted to be with anyway.

Until now.

Hunter had said that he wanted me, and I couldn't deny it any longer. I wanted him, too. I wanted him so much I could barely stand it. I spent nearly every waking hour with him and I lamented the hours we were apart. Not because I needed him all the time, but I missed him when he wasn't around. There were times when I'd see something, or someone would say something, and I'd think, "Hunter would love that," or "the only other person who would find this funny is Hunter." I missed having his running commentary on everything.

He'd told me I wasn't in love with him yet. Oh, but I was close. If this wasn't almost love, I didn't know what was.

A knock interrupted my thoughts.

"You okay?"

"Yeah. Can I have some freaking privacy?"

"Sorry. You've just been in there for a while. I wanted to make sure you weren't sick or anything. I'm leaving now. Also, I'm naked, so if you open the door right now, you're going to get the full show."

"Pass."

"Suit yourself." I heard him turn and go back to our room and close the door.

I stayed in the bathroom for a few more minutes, deciding I was just as hot and bothered there as in my bed, so I might as well be comfortable.

I didn't say anything as I got back into bed.

"You know if you're uncomfortable with what I said, it's okay. I did kind of spring it on you," he said. "I can take it back if you want."

"The problem isn't that I'm uncomfortable with it. The problem is that I want it!" I yelled. It was official; I'd lost it. Oh well, I wasn't known for having a long fuse. "Are you happy? Jesus. You say something like that and then expect me to just be whatever about it. That's like teasing someone with a giant red velvet cake and then putting it in one of those glass rotating dessert thingies." I wasn't my most eloquent at the moment.

"Does this mean I'm the cake?"

"Shut up. It was a metaphor."

"So you want me?"

So much it hurt. "Yes," I whispered.

"Right now?"

"Yes."

"Oh." Now he was the one who sounded nervous.

"What?"

"It's just...a surprise."

"I told you I would entertain the idea."

"I know. I just didn't think you'd be so enthusiastic so soon."

"Hunter, I'm a virgin. Not a nun."

He didn't talk for a moment.

"That was the sexiest thing you've ever said. God, why do you do this to me?" He rolled over onto his back and stared at the ceiling. I could just make out his naked chest in the dark.

"Ditto."

"I feel both honored and terrified at the same time."

"Why terrified?" I said. Hunter Zaccadelli wasn't afraid of anything, let alone sex.

"That's a lot of pressure. I mean, to ask me to be the first. I just...I don't want to fuck it up. You're too important for that."

"I'm sure you've got plenty of experience." I would be the one messing it up.

"All that doesn't matter. All that stuff I did before was just sex. I told you, I don't want to have sex with you. I want to do more. You deserve so much more. More than me anyway."

"What if I don't want more? What if I just want you?"

All my feelings and frustrations had finally spilled out of my mouth.

"I take it back. *That* was the sexiest thing you've ever said."

"So what now?"

"Well, I know we both have class tomorrow, but I don't really want this date to end."

"Me neither."

"Hooky? I've got somewhere I want to take you." I'd never played hooky in college. High school, plenty of times. I figured I'd paid enough damn money for my college education that I shouldn't waste it. But maybe just this once.

I'd have to call out of work, but I was only scheduled for two hours, so it wasn't that big of a deal. It would probably be the one and only time. I'd only called in sick once to any of the jobs I'd ever had and that was because I had food poisoning and had to be next to a trash can at all times.

"Okay," I said.

"Okay."

We both lay there for a moment.

"I can't sleep," he said.

"Neither can I."

"I have something in mind that we could do."

"I'm sure you do."

"If you want."

"Noted."

"All you'd have to do is come over here. Or I could come to you."

"Okay."

"I've never discussed it this much."

"Sex?"

"Yeah, it usually just happens."

"See, I've never understood that. It can't 'just happen.' You can't go from point A to sex in a moment."

"It depends."

"On what?"

"Usually on how much you've had to drink or how hot the girl is."

"Pig."

"Hey, I told you all that other stuff was in the past. It would be different with you."

"How?"

"You want a play-by-play?"

"I'm just...curious."

"I swear, you are killing me in the slowest most torturous way possible. I think I'm going to need about twenty cold showers after this conversation."

I was going to need more than a few.

"We should go to bed," I said.

"We should." He sighed. "Nope, not going to happen. If you want me, I'll be on the couch." With that, he grabbed his boxers, slid them on, grabbed his pillow and blanket and was out the door before you could say condom.

Thank God.

It was easier to think about other things like French verbs and the subtle expression of misogyny in film when he wasn't in the room. I also thought about other things. I imagined us being...together. It was a nice image, but then it morphed into another image. The image of Travis's face when he... No. I shut the mental replay down and tried to think about something else.

The bottom line was that I couldn't be with Hunter until I'd told him. I'd have to risk big to get a bigger reward. Did I have the guts to do it?

I probably got about three hours tops when I heard Hunter moving around in the kitchen. It was like I had an alarm set to go off if he was doing anything. The sleep I'd gotten hadn't been quality. It seemed I couldn't sleep with him, but I couldn't sleep without him either.

"Hey," I said as I shuffled to the bathroom. I didn't really care what I looked like. If he hadn't seen my morning look and run by now, he wasn't going to.

"Morning, gorgeous."

"Unghn," I said in response.

I felt a little better after Hunter shoved a cup of coffee into my hands and I took a few sips.

"So what are we doing today?" I said.

"No way. I got to surprise you last night and I intend to do the same today."

"Do I get a hint? Maybe one word to describe it?"

He thought for a moment, sipping from his cup.

"Princess."

"Princess?"

"Yup. That's all you get." I glared at him, but he just smiled.

"Tease," I said. He laughed. "You gonna pick out my outfit seeing as how I don't know where we're going?"

"You can wear what you want, just bring a sweatshirt and comfortable shoes."

"So we're going someplace that could potentially be cold," I said, tapping my chin.

"Hmm," Hunter said, joining me.

"I'm going to go get dressed and ponder that. How was the couch?"

"Uncomfortable, but I don't think it had anything to do with the couch."

"Maybe not."

I finished my coffee and went to change. It was a chilly day, but the sun was out, so I picked a rust-colored shirt and jeans, grabbing my UMaine sweatshirt and throwing on some ratty sneakers.

"This work?"

"Perfect. My turn."

I texted Tawny while he changed, telling her that I needed to talk. I really, really needed to talk to Tawny. I texted Megan as well, telling her about my plans. She said she was excited and to call her with all the details.

Renee texted me just as Hunter came out of the room, asking how our night was. I knew what she was asking. I wasn't telling. There wasn't really anything to tell, yet.

"What's the verdict?" He did a turn, and I remembered the break-dancing display I'd seen the first weekend I'd met him.

"Where did you learn how to dance?"

"Mase and I used to mess around when we were kids, so we just kind of taught ourselves. I could show you a few moves. You're a natural dancer. I could show you how to do a chest pop." He demonstrated as I rolled my eyes.

"Yeah, okay."

"What? It's a legitimate move, which you would be excellent at." I didn't have too much of a chest to pop. Just enough to know that I couldn't walk around without a bra comfortably.

"You ready?"

"Yes, Miss Caldwell. Your chariot awaits you."

"You mean your beat-up car?" He ignored me and offered his arm. "Do I get a tiara? Please say I get a tiara."

"I'll work something out," he said as he locked our door.

"The tiara is like, the most important part of princessery. Oh, I need to call work."

"Already taken care of."

"What?"

"I called Tom and said you were in the bathroom puking your guts out."

"But what if someone on campus sees us?"

"Relax. You're not the first student who's ever played hooky. I'm sure he knew I was making it up."

"But I need that job, Hunter—"

He cut me off with a finger to my lips. "Princesses don't stress. They take charge and let other people worry about the details."

"Fine. But if I get fired, I'm blaming you."

"If you get fired, I'll quit."

"Deal."

"Deal."

I let Hunter help me into the car, because princesses couldn't get into cars without assistance or some such crap.

"It's so the paparazzi won't get a shot of your undies."

"I'm not wearing a skirt."

"You can never be too careful," he said seriously.

I made him stop and get me a blueberry muffin and some iced tea. I figured I should really milk this princess thing while it lasted.

"It's not as good as Hope's," I said about the iced tea.

"That's something they know about in the South. I miss it sometimes."

"What do you miss?"

"It feels...I don't know, cozier, for lack of a better term. Not that Maine isn't like that. It's just different."

"I wouldn't know. I've never been down south."

"Well, I'll just have to take you. I don't want your first experience to be with someone else."

"You're talking about traveling, right?"

"Right."

We turned south on I-95, which meant we were headed for the coast.

"We're not leaving the state, are we?"

"Nope. Just going a little ways up the coast."

"So we're going to the coast. Interesting…" I pondered as we drove. "What, no road trip princess mix?"

"I didn't plan that far ahead. Pick a CD." He tossed me a zipped folder that weighed about five pounds. "I still like having them just in case my MP3 dies for some reason. Like having records."

I shuffled through them, and there were quite a few bands I hadn't heard of that I made mental notes to check out. I grabbed the first thing that made me smile. The Head and the Heart.

He smiled too when he heard the first song. I skipped to "Honey, Come Home."

"So you liked that?"

"It should have been totally cheesy, but it wasn't." I placed my hand on top of his as it rested on the shifter.

"I was going for noncheesy. I eliminated a lot of other songs before I picked that one."

"It was perfect."

"Well, I was going to go with 'Love Story,' but I figured that would be cheesy."

"If you'd gone with that, I probably would have had my way with you on the couch while Megan was in the shower."

"Damn. What a wasted opportunity." We both laughed as Hunter hit the gas and passed a gigantic motor home.

"Where are we going?" I whined.

"God, that's a sound I never want to hear again."

"Tell me where we're going and you won't."

"Nice try, Miss."

"I think, as the princess, I have a right to this information. Otherwise, this is a kidnapping."

"I'm sorry, Miss Caldwell. I'm under strict orders not to disclose that information."

"Asshat."

"Yes, Miss Caldwell. Whatever you say."

I gave his shoulder a light punch in response.

He turned off I-95 onto 202 and then onto 1A. Hmm...

"The Coastal Route?" He nodded in response. "There are only so many places you could take me. If we were going to Portland, you would have just stayed on I-95. So we must be going to one of the places along the way." I got out my phone and looked up the names of the towns along the route.

"We just passed Winterport, so it isn't that. Belfast? Lincolnville? Camden?"

"I'm not going to tell you."

"I think I'm getting warmer."

"Can't you just let me surprise you without being curious?" His eyes pleaded in a really sweet way.

"Fine." I put my phone back in my purse and sat back in my seat.

"It's killing you, isn't it?" he said after about two minutes.

"No."

"Liar."

"Kidnapper."

It was kind of fun driving through the various towns, wondering which one he was going to stop at. We went through Belfast and then Lincolnville, going right past the beach. I'd thought of that as a possibility, but it wasn't.

"Camden. I bet it's Camden," I said just as we passed the "You are now leaving Lincolnville" sign.

"Maybe it is and maybe it is."

"Ha! Okay, so what's in Camden…?" I racked my brain, trying to remember. I assembled the clues I already had as we passed inns, hotels and bed-and-breakfasts. Camden had about a million of them. It was a coastal town, but of the hoity-toity variety, with lots of windjammers and fancy shops and such.

Princess, comfortable shoes, a sweatshirt…

"We're not going hiking, are we?" There were two mountains in Camden, Mount Battie and Megunticook. I'd hiked both several times with Tawny when we'd been younger and also on school trips.

"We don't have enough time and I didn't plan far enough ahead for that, but I thought we could go up the auto road and have lunch."

"So what's with the princess part?"

"This," he said, putting on his turn signal. I looked to see where he was turning.

"Norumbega?"

"The only castle in Maine."

My mouth dropped open. When I was little and we'd driven through Camden, I'd always begged my mother to stop there, but we were always on our way somewhere else. The Norumbega Inn seemed like the most magical place to my young eyes. It looked pretty damn magical now.

Hunter pulled in front of the building, and we sat and stared at it. It certainly looked like a castle, built in stone, some of it painted in dark green, giving it an almost Gothic feel. There was even a turret on one side.

"Come on, princess," he said, getting out of the car. I followed before he could open my door.

"What?"

"Let's go in."

I put my hand on his arm to stop him. "We can't."

"Why not?"

"They're not going to just let us wander around."

"Take your ring off."

"What?"

He took my right hand and slipped my ring off, and then took my left hand and put it on my ring finger.

"There. Now we can say we're looking at places to get married. They'll be falling over themselves to show us around."

He took my hand and dragged me up the steps to the front door. He didn't bother knocking, just went in. I caught my breath. Wow. I felt just as out of place here as I had in Hunter's uncle's house. I'd barely gotten to look at the caramel-colored wooden floors and the matching wooden paneling on the walls before a woman in a smart suit spotted us.

"Can I help you?"

"Yes, my fiancée and I are getting married in the spring, and we're checking out potential locations. We were just going for a hike up to Mount Battie and saw this place and couldn't resist coming in. Right, baby?"

He brought our linked hands to his mouth and kissed the top of my hand before winking. *Sweet Christ.*

"Oh, how wonderful. Congratulations. When's the big day?" She beamed at us.

"March twenty-first, the first day of spring," I blurted out. Hunter gave me a look. I'd just pulled it out of my ass.

"How lovely. Well, we have a lot to offer when it comes to weddings. If you'll just follow me," she said, leading us to the left and up to a huge desk. I couldn't stop staring at the ornate wooden latticed ceilings and the gilded mirrors. Some of the walls were covered in dark green wallpaper. It gave a cozy old-time study feel to the place.

"I'm Susan, by the way. It's so nice to meet you."

"Hunter," he said, shaking her hand. "This is Missy."

"Missy. Is that short for Marissa?"

"Yeah," I said, giving him a glare when she turned to grab a brochure.

"This has all our options and lists all of our vendors. If you want to do the complete package, we can provide you with everything. Food, drinks, chairs, the works. Would you like to take a look at a few of the rooms? What size wedding were you thinking?"

"Small. Definitely," I said, beating Hunter to the punch. Neither of us had big families. You know, if we were getting married, which we weren't, because this was just for pretend.

"Less than twenty-five people?"

"Probably. We hadn't really sat down and counted yet," Hunter said. "But it'll be what? Your parents, Tawny, my family, that's eight. Then Darah, Renee, Paul, Megan and Jake, and then Dev and Sean. And a few cousins. Right?" It was like he'd actually thought about it.

"That's right," I said with a sweeter-than-sweet smile.

"Okay, well that would be perfect. I don't think we could accommodate everyone, but definitely the bridal and groom parties. Let's go upstairs and see some of the rooms and then we can go over the grounds."

"Sounds good," I said with another teeth-hurting smile.

"Good job, Missy girl," Hunter said as we walked up the spiral stairs to the rest of the inn.

"Bite me, Mr. Zaccadelli."

"Anytime, Mrs. Zaccadelli." I nearly tripped on the next step. Hearing him call me that made a strange feeling come over me that wasn't entirely unpleasant.

Susan showed us a few rooms that weren't occupied. They

were all quaintly furnished and had great views. My favorite was the library suite. I gasped when we walked down a set of narrow white stairs and came into a room furnished in dark green with red accents. It was a bit like a strawberry gone nuts, but with *books*. There was even a balcony with more rows of bookshelves. I nearly lost it.

"Hey, you're going to squeeze the blood out of my hand," Hunter whispered.

I looked down and saw that I was clenching his hand in excitement. Maybe a bit too hard. "You can take it. Do you *not* see the books?"

"Would you have your way with me right now?"

Surrounded by all that literature? Oh hell yes. Damn Susan. She was still yammering, but I wasn't hearing her. Too many pretty books were calling my name.

"Why do you think Beauty picked the Beast? It was the library."

"I guess I'm the Beast in that situation."

"Unless you want to be the Beauty."

"Nope, that's all you." He pulled me toward him and gave me a kiss on the forehead. I thought I heard Susan sigh.

"Would you like to see the grounds?"

"Sure," I said, taking one last, longing look at the library room.

"Hold on," Hunter said, taking out his phone. "Would you take a picture of us?"

"Absolutely," Susan said, taking the phone.

Hunter pulled me close and put his arm around me.

"Smile, baby." I did, and Susan took a few shots of us.

"Perfect," she said. Hunter grinned at me, and I wanted to slap it off his face and kiss him at the same time.

Susan took us around the back of the inn, which had a huge sloping lawn.

"Now we can do tents, or some couples prefer the gazebo."

"What do you think, babe? Gazebo or tent?" I said.

"Whatever your little heart desires, my love." He was laying it on thick. I hoped Susan couldn't hear the sarcasm. She seemed oblivious.

"I like the gazebo. I've always imagined getting married in a gazebo." Now I was the one laying it on.

Susan gave us the rest of the tour, barely stopping her torrent of words to take a breath. Hunter and I had a little battle, with me elbowing him and him trying to get me back. Susan was oblivious. We took some more pictures of the inn, and Hunter made Susan take some more of us.

"I swear to God, if you post these online, I will strangle you in your sleep," I hissed while she took another shot of us in the gazebo.

"Noted," he hissed back.

Susan gave us a bunch more brochures about all sorts of things and blathered on about catering. I was exhausted by the time we walked outside.

I turned around and looked one more time at it.

"Like your castle, princess?"

I shrugged. "It's okay."

He narrowed his eyes. "I'm sorry it's not up to your standards. Would you like me to call my private jet and take you to England to see a real one?"

"Well, if you insist."

"You're a demanding girl, Missy. You're not going to want swans for our wedding, right?"

"Only a few dozen. And doves. We must release doves."

"Oh, doves are a given. That's why I didn't mention them."
He turned on the car and swung around the circular driveway.

"It is really cool inside. Thanks for bringing me here."

"Anytime, princess."

We went downtown to the Camden Deli to get sandwiches
and then we drove to the top of the mountain. Luckily, since
it was the middle of the week, there weren't that many people
up there. The tourists had mostly left, but the leaf peepers were
already out in full force, and there were always the birders to
contend with. You could always spot them because they had
huge binoculars.

We found a semiflat spot and settled down to watch the
boats come in and out of the small harbor and the bustling
town. Hunter found an old blanket in his car, and we spread
that out. Of course he'd brought his guitar.

"You never know when you might need it. What if our
wallets were stolen and we ran out of gas? Then I'd have my
guitar and I could play so people would take pity on us and
give us gas money. So really, this guitar could save our lives."

"Never insult Hunter's guitar. Note made," I said, tapping
my head. "You didn't have to go veggie for me. I don't care
if you eat meat, as long as you don't shove it in my face or
down my throat."

"I like hummus. I don't know what you're talking about."

"Since when?"

He rolled his eyes. "Since you made me eat it three weeks
ago."

"Exactly."

"You're cute when you're smug."

"Shut up."

"Missy does not take compliments well. Note taken."

It was my turn to roll my eyes and munch on my sandwich

for something to do. We finished and then had double chocolate chip cookies for desert.

"You want to go up to the tower?"

"Sure." The most prominent item on the top of the mountain was a stone tower with a winding staircase that you could climb to the top. I wasn't much for stairs that you could see through, but I wasn't going to tell Hunter that. I went first, and somehow made it to the top without freaking out.

"Can I tell you something?" Hunter said when we were both at the top. I nodded. "Your ass looks amazing from that angle."

"I swear, I will throw you off this tower."

"No you won't," he said with a smile as he picked me up and placed me on the edge of the wall that surrounded the tower. It had little crenellations, and I fit exactly between them.

"No stay still, I want to take a picture. Smile, baby." He was still calling me baby, even though Susan wasn't anywhere to be found.

I did, which was easy to do with him looking at me like I was the best Christmas present he'd ever gotten.

"Gorgeous. Okay, let's get you down." I begrudgingly let him help me down. "Let's do one more. Smile big." He held the camera out with one hand and put his face next to mine. "One, two—" Before he got to three he moved his head and kissed my cheek. I squished up my face in surprise.

"Hey, no ambush kissing." I whacked his chest halfheartedly. He captured my hand and kissed my palm.

"Even if you like it?"

I shook my head. "Nope."

We heard voices on the stairs and in a moment we were joined by a mother, father, two kids and a set of what were probably grandparents. The top of the tower wasn't that wide, so we had to squish in.

"Sorry, there's not a lot of space up here," the mother said as one of the kids begged his father to be held up so they could see over the wall.

"It's okay. I think we're going down soon," I said.

"Oh, would you mind taking a picture of us?" the woman said, trying to gather her son so he wouldn't throw himself down the stairs.

"Sure," I said, taking the camera. They got themselves sorted, and I had to back up nearly to the other end of the tower and zoom all the way out to get them all in.

"Say Mount Battie!"

"Mount Battie!" they all chimed in.

"Thank you so much," the woman said as I showed her the pictures on the camera. "Oh my goodness, what a beautiful ring. When are you getting married?"

"March twenty-first, first day of spring," Hunter said, putting his arm around me.

"Well, congratulations."

"Thank you," I said, trying to grind my heel into Hunter's foot. He avoided me, and we said goodbye to the family and started back down the steps.

"You go first."

"What a buzz kill," he said, but he did go first.

I almost reached out and held on to his shirt as we went down, but I resisted and before we knew it, we were back down. *Phew.*

"You want to walk around a bit?" He didn't let go of my hand, and we walked around the road a bit, making a loop and then back again. "I'd love to come here at night to see what the town looked like all lit up. They close the gates, so you'd have to walk up with flashlights. Still, it would be worth it."

I nodded, looking down at our linked hands.

"So is that how you'd see your wedding? With swans and all that?" he said.

"I never really imagined a wedding."

"I thought that was something all girls did."

"Well, like you said, I'm not a normal girl."

"You know I didn't mean it like that."

"How did you mean it?"

"I meant it that you're not just any other girl. You're you."

"Profound."

"Come on. Don't be like that. All the other girls I've known would have been thrilled and would have showed it to anyone whether they wanted to see it or not. Some would have thought it was a proposal. But you didn't. You were pissed I'd spent money on you."

"I'm still pissed about it, but what am I going to do about it?"

"Exactly."

"What?"

"You're just different. I like that."

"Whatever."

We kept walking silently.

"I like that you're nice to people," I said.

"What?"

I had sort of mumbled it. "You're nice to people when you don't have to be. Like those drunk girls and Susan. You act like you're this big badass, but you're really not."

"Are you saying I'm not a badass? Then all these tattoos were for nothing. What shall I do?" He shook his fist to the sky.

"Aw, did I insult your badassery?"

"I'm wounded," he said, clutching his heart. "You must soothe my wounds."

"How?"

"Gimme some sugar," he said, stopping and pointing to his puckered lips.

"No way, man." I tried to walk, but he wouldn't let me.

"Come on. Give your fiancé a kiss."

"That was your stupid idea."

"Nonetheless. Kiss me, please." If only he hadn't said please.

"Fine," I said through gritted teeth. It wasn't that I didn't want to. It was that I knew if our lips met, I wasn't in control of what happened next. It was like I had an excess of sexual frustration built up after so many years of celibacy. Could that happen?

I pressed my lips together so there was no hope of tongue and gave him a little peck.

He shook his head.

"Nope. Still in pain. Gotta do better than that." I tried again, giving him a little bit longer, but still pulling back as soon as I wanted more.

"Who are you, my grandmother?"

I was about to stomp my foot and say enough when my phone rang.

"Forget about it," he said, leaning in.

"It's my mom's ringtone." It was "Hip to My Heart" by The Band Perry. She loved that song. "I need to take this." I hadn't talked to my mom in a while, and I felt horrible about it.

"Hey, Mom."

"Hey, Kid! I feel like it's been ages since we talked. I got out of work early, so I thought I'd give you a ring. You're not in class, are you?"

"Nope. I wouldn't have answered if I was. Or I'd be whispering."

"Right. So how are you?"

"I'm good. Busy. Classes are nuts."

"That's good. How's the job?"

"That's good, too."

"And the roommate situation?"

"Tell her it's great," Hunter whispered. The volume on the phone was loud enough for him to hear. I turned it down and walked away from him.

"It's sort of been resolved." *So far.* "I'm going to deal with it for the rest of the semester, and then we'll see."

"Oh, good. You sound better. You sound really happy, actually."

"Do I?"

"Yes, you do. What's the cause?" *The boy who is currently trying to wind his arms around my waist and distract me from talking to you.*

"Oh, I don't know. Maybe it's just the new year. My birthday is coming up."

Mom wasn't fooled. "It's a boy, isn't it?"

"Not really."

"Oh. My. God. I thought it would never happen. I want details, Kid." She sounded like Tawny.

"He's just a guy."

"You know that's not true."

"Not really," I said. Hunter was trying to tickle me. "Will you stop that?"

"What?" Mom said. I glared at Hunter, and he gave me a wide-eyed innocent look.

"Nothing, I wasn't talking to you."

"That was him, wasn't it? Is he there with you? If you're

on a date, we can talk later, as long as I get details. Oh, God, you're not in the middle of something, are you?"

"Mom!" My face went scarlet as Hunter laughed quietly.

"I was just asking. You never know. Are you on a date?" The excitement in her voice was palpable, even over the phone.

"We're not on a date."

"Yes, we are," Hunter said, loud enough for her to hear.

I put my hand over the speaker. "Will you shut up?"

"Kid, why don't you call me back? Oh, before you go, I thought I could have you and Tawny over for family dinner on Saturday night. Why don't you bring him? I'd love to meet him."

"You don't even know his name."

"Doesn't matter. If he's gotten through your walls, I know he's something special. Your standards are high."

"Yes, they are," Hunter said in my ear. His warm breath was making it very hard to think. "I'd love to meet your mother."

"Was that him?"

"Yes."

"Tell her I'd love to meet her," he said so loud that I'm sure people from miles around could have heard him. I gave him a death glare.

"Tell him that's great. I'll be sure to make you something special."

"Thanks, Mom."

"Call me later, Kid."

"I will."

"You'd better. Love you."

"Love you, too."

I hung up with Mom and jabbed my fist into Hunter's stomach. He dodged at the last moment and wrapped his arms around me, giving me a bear hug.

"I can't wait to meet your mom. I want to see what you'll look like in twenty-five years."

"Well, since you invited yourself to dinner, I guess there's nothing I can do to stop you."

"Exactly." He dived in and got a good kiss in, smiling against my mouth. I totally let him. "There. Now was that so hard?"

I made a grumpy noise.

"Come on. Let's go have some music sex."

We settled back in our spot, and Hunter serenaded me as the sun sank lower in the sky. Renee and Darah texted me, asking when we were getting back. I messaged them back and said I didn't know. I was at Hunter's mercy. Renee was dying for details. She'd probably be disappointed with my lame details.

"One last song. What'll it be?" he said.

"How about something older? Oooh, how about 'Love Me Tender'?"

"Elvis?"

"What? He's the King."

"Yes, yes, he is."

I put my hands behind my head and stared up at the sky as Hunter's voice lulled me into that safe bubble again. My stupid phone popped it.

I stared at the screen. Tawny. I ignored the call. I'd call her back later. Hunter kept singing, drawing the song out longer than it normally would be.

Immediately, she called back. That raised a red flag. She didn't do that unless there was a reason.

"What's up?" I said, trying to keep the panic out of my voice. Hunter stopped playing.

"Travis is up for parole."

CHAPTER 24

Every bit of oxygen I'd had in my lungs left in one puff of air.

"What?" Hunter looked at me with a question mark on his face. I turned away from him.

"He's up for parole. There's a hearing in a couple of weeks."

"But he has two more years."

"I know, but you know how it works. He got the date almost two months ago, but they forgot to let us know."

"They can't let him out," I whispered.

"They could."

"Can we go?"

"We should be able to since we're both victims. They should have called you, too." I'd had a call earlier, but I'd let it go to voice mail since I didn't know the number. What a moron.

"What's wrong? You're shaking." Hunter put his hands on my shoulders.

"Don't fucking touch me!" I shrieked.

"Taylor! Don't freak out. It will be fine. They're not going to let him out. Where are you?" Tawny said.

"Camden."

"What are you doing there?"

"Not important."

"Okay, well, I want you to go back to your apartment and stay there. Is there someone to stay with you?"

"Uh-huh." Hunter didn't touch me, but started packing up our stuff.

"It's Hunter, isn't it? Have you told him yet?" Tawny said.

"No."

"Let me talk to him."

"*No!*"

"I'm not going to tell him. Just let me talk to him."

"She wants to talk to you." I handed him the phone. Nothing after she'd said the thing about Travis had seemed real.

"Hi, Tawny, what's up?" His voice was clipped. He walked away from me and listened, then responded in a hushed tone. "Okay, we're going."

I didn't move. I wasn't sure if I could.

"We were supposed to have two more years. Then I was going to leave and go where he couldn't find me," I said to whoever would listen.

"Come on. We need to get you home," Hunter said. My legs wouldn't work. "All right, baby, I'm going to pick you up, okay?"

"No, I can do it." I reached out for his hand, and he pulled me to my feet.

"You don't always have to do everything yourself," he said, taking my arm with one hand and carrying his guitar with the other.

I stumbled like I was drunk back to Hunter's car. I didn't want him touching me, but then I knew I wouldn't have gotten back to the car by myself. Hunter didn't ask for details as he drove as fast as he could down the windy road back down the mountain.

"Slow down," I said.

"I'm getting you home."

"Well, I'd like to get there in one piece."

"Fine."

"Did Tawny tell you?"

"No. She said you would. All she told me was that I should get you home and stay there."

"Nothing else?"

"No. I wished she would have."

"So I'm guessing you're waiting on an explanation." My shock was thawing a little having him there.

"I've wanted one ever since I met you. You've got secret written all over you. But I'm one to talk about that. I just wish you'd trust me with it. I know it can't be easy for you to carry."

"It's not." I was not going to cry.

"I'd like to help you. Telling you about my parents made it better, not worse. Outside of family, you're the only one I've ever really told, and it was scary as hell, but it felt good after. The truth will set you free and all that."

"I'm afraid of what you'll say."

"Missy girl, there isn't anything you could tell me that would make you think any different."

Oh, but there was. It had the power to change everything. Especially now.

"I wish I could believe that."

"Then do. Believe it. Believe me."

I wanted to. More than anything.

I sat back in my seat and tried to calm my racing heart. I turned on The Head and the Heart again. I found the folksy, slightly bluegrassy melodies soothing.

"Can you hand me my phone?" he said when we got back to the entrance of the park. He stopped the car but left it running. I handed him his phone, and he hit the speed dial.

"Hey, Mase. I need a favor. Can you take Dare for the night? I need some time with Taylor. Yes. Uh-huh. Thanks, man. Yes, I know I owe you. Thanks. Bye."

He hit dial on another number.

"Hey, Ne. Can you do me a favor? Taylor and I, um, need another night. Yes. No. I will. Don't worry. See you tomorrow. Bye."

He tossed the phone in his cup holder.

"I thought you wouldn't want a bunch of people around bugging you." He knew me far too well. "I'm not going anywhere, okay?"

"Okay." All the fight had gone out of me. My mind was already picturing Travis getting out of jail and then fulfilling the promise he'd made to me that night.

I didn't talk for the next half hour as Hunter drove as fast as he could while still driving safely. I kept hearing him counting under his breath.

One, two, three, four, five.

I listened to him, and it lulled me into a weird sort of waking shock. It was like that feeling when you stare off into space. Only it didn't end. By the time we got back to the apartment, Renee and Darah were already gone. They'd left us a little surprise in the form of a heart made of cupcakes.

"Look at me," Hunter said as we walked in the door. Rationally, I knew that there was no way Travis was there, but my head still went there.

"No one is going to hurt you. You're not a weak girl. You kicked me in the balls within hours of meeting me. You're not afraid of anyone," he said.

I was just afraid of one person.

"I'm fine."

"No, you're not. Go take a shower, and I'll make some dinner."

"I'm not hungry."

"Sorry, but Tawny told me to make you eat." That was something she'd say. She used to force me when we were younger, too.

"Don't tell me what to do."

"Okay."

He went to the fridge and started assembling ingredients.

"I'm going to take a shower."

"Okay then." He smiled and shook his head.

I slowly pushed the door to my bedroom open with my foot. I waited a second before reaching in and turning on the light. I slowly walked in, my heart pounding the whole time. I glanced in every corner before I completely entered the room.

I grabbed my clothes and shower stuff as quickly as I could and rushed to the bathroom. I took a quick shower, jumping at every single noise. I remembered this feeling well. I'd lived years of my life like this, but it had dulled in the last few. Now it was back full force, and I was twelve again and throwing up out of fear every day. I'd almost given myself an ulcer. That was when the therapy had started.

I came out and Hunter was busy with tomato soup and grilled cheese sandwiches.

"I made the margherita ones you like, along with the avocado," he said.

"I'm not hungry."

"You're going to eat a damn sandwich and a bowl of soup even if I have to kiss you into submission. Got it?"

"Please don't touch me."

"Then eat."

"I hate you."

"Nice try. I'm not going anywhere." He put a sandwich on a plate, cutting it crossways so I could see the mozzarella cheese oozing out. Normally I would have devoured the thing and burned my mouth, but I didn't want to eat ever again.

He poured a bowl of soup. He'd even added milk to make it creamy.

"Why don't we have a tray? We need to get a tray," he muttered.

I had no idea what he was talking about. I finger-combed my hair and waited for him to be done.

"Go sit on the couch."

"Don't tell me what to do." I didn't want him treating me like an invalid. Worse, I didn't want him treating me like he had to take care of me. That I was some sort of burden. A person he was obligated to take care of.

I went and sat on the recliner instead of the couch and turned the television on, flipping from one channel to the next, not even noticing what was on before I changed it.

"Here we go." He set a plate and bowl down on the table, pulling it close to the recliner. He handed me a spoon and a napkin.

"I would suggest you eat, but I'm not telling you what to do. Because you don't want me to," he said.

"That's right."

He got his dinner and sat down on the opposite end of the couch, as far away from me as he could get and still be sitting in the living room.

I found a marathon of romantic comedies, starting with *Pretty Woman*. *Score.*

"She has way too many teeth. And no hooker has ever

looked like that—I can guarantee you," Hunter said, sitting back and munching his sandwich.

I ignored him and tried to watch the movie, but I kept jumping at every little sound. My brain had convinced itself that Travis was going to burst through the door at any moment. I kind of wished I had a sharp object, but I'd have to settle for my spoon or the remote. Or Hunter. He'd probably do as a weapon in a pinch.

"Can I get you something?" he said. *How about a gun?* I'd feel a lot better if I had one. Why, oh why hadn't I gone to the shooting range yet? "Taylor?"

"What?"

"Can I get you anything?" he repeated.

"No."

"Are you sure?"

"Why don't you just leave me alone?" I snapped.

"Maybe if you would tell me what has got you like this, I will. Until then, I'm watching you like a hawk." I didn't like his intense watching, but I also didn't want to be alone. So I was fifty-fifty on having him there.

"I'm fine."

"Sure." He got up to take my bowl, and I flinched away from him.

"Aw, Miss. I wish you'd tell me."

I shook my head, clamping my lips shut.

"You stubborn, stubborn girl." He took our dishes to the sink and started washing them, humming the dishes song he'd written. I tried to keep my eyes glued to the movie.

I had a habit of getting really cold when I was freaking out, and I started shivering uncontrollably, my teeth chattering. I wrapped my arms around myself, trying to keep myself from flying into a million pieces. I'd thought this was over. I never saw the day that he would get out actually coming, but maybe they wouldn't let him out. Maybe they'd send him back to prison to serve the rest of his time.

But I'd still have to see him. That was what scared me more than anything. That was the thing that I didn't want to tell anyone. For all my anger and confidence, I was really just a scared twelve-year-old girl inside.

"Here," Hunter said, coming behind me and putting a blanket over me.

"Don't touch me."

"I'm just tucking a blanket in. Get a grip."

"I said, don't touch me."

He came around front, ignoring me and trying to get the blanket all around me.

"Stop it!" I thrashed, but he wouldn't let go of me. He tried to pick me up, but I was ready for him, landing punches and kicks right and left. His face was blank. Somehow he got me to my feet, and the blanket fell away. It was like I'd unleashed something dark and violent that had been stirring inside me since that night eight years ago.

"Stop it! Stop it! Stop it!" I pounded on his chest. I slapped his face and I kicked him. I kept going until my lungs were heaving and my arms were sore and a strangled sob had escaped my mouth.

He stood with his arms at his sides. His face was red from me slapping him.

My knees caved, and he caught me before I went down, picking me up and putting me on the couch.

"Don't touch me."

He didn't answer, but wrapped his arms around me as I started sobbing. I never cried, but there I was, salty tears streaming down my face, being held by Hunter, the guy

I'd just beat the shit out of. He rocked me, his strong arms encircling me tightly. He started humming, but I was too wrecked to recognize the tune. My throat hurt from crying, and my tears were dripping everywhere, but I didn't care.

I started hyperventilating, and Hunter had to tell me to breathe slowly so I wouldn't pass out. That had happened before, but he didn't know that. I'd had episodes like this before, only those times it was Mom and Tawny taking care of me.

Hunter waited until I had mostly cried myself out and was just sniffing. Luckily, he had a spare napkin and I blew my nose.

"Are you okay?" I said.

"That's my line."

"I'm sorry for beating you up."

"It's okay. You needed to get it out."

"I haven't done that in a long time." I felt his lips on my temple.

"You scared me," he said.

"Sorry."

"You don't have to apologize. I'll be fine."

"But I won't."

He inhaled slowly. "When my parents died, I used to have these freak-outs were I'd go nuts and break everything I could. My mother had this collection of crystal animals that was worth thousands of dollars. I smashed every single one. Joe was furious, but what could he do? They ended up taking everything breakable out of the house and moving me to Hope and John's as soon as possible. They Hunter-proofed the house, but I still found things to break."

It was my turn.

"They used to have to restrain me so I wouldn't hurt myself.

My mom didn't have a straitjacket, but she and Tawny used to hold me down," I said. There was a pause, and he started stroking my hair. I settled against his chest. His arms were like cables, holding me in one place. I wasn't shivering anymore.

I took a deep breath.

"Tawny was supposed to be babysitting. That was before my parents split up, so they were out on a date night. I was twelve, but they didn't want me staying alone at night for some reason. I can't remember why. The rule was that she wasn't supposed to have anyone over, but she invited her boyfriend, Travis, to hang out." Saying his name was like running razor blades over my tongue, but I had to do this.

"She'd only been dating him for a few weeks, and my parents didn't like him. It wasn't that he had a motorcycle or he got in trouble or any of that. He just rubbed them the wrong way, especially my mom. He was older and he had a temper, but he kept it in check most of the time. He was pissed about something that night. Once again, I don't remember what. Tawny was different around him. When it was just us, we'd do movies and have fun, but when Travis was over, she'd make me go to bed so they could make out on the couch. I got mad at her that night about sending me to bed early, but she yelled at me and Travis backed her up, so I had no choice."

I took another deep breath. Hunter kept stroking my hair.

"As I was walking back to my bedroom, I saw something sparkly on the floor. It was one of my mother's peacock earrings. Tawny had borrowed them without asking, and I knew she was wearing one. The other must have fallen out. I was jealous, because I'd never been allowed to wear them, so I went to my room and put it on. I stayed up reading for a while, but then I heard a noise. I got up and I heard it again. Then there was a scream."

Hunter's arms tightened around me, and I gripped on to his shirt.

"I went back to Tawny's bedroom, and she was screaming while I heard a slapping noise and Travis telling her to shut up. She screamed some more, and then I heard him punch her. She was pleading with him. I didn't know what to do. The door was cracked just a little, and I looked in. He was on top of her and her shirt was torn. He was unzipping his pants and telling her that he'd waited long enough. She was crying and struggling to get out from under him. He slapped her again, and her head flew to the side. We locked eyes, and she whispered something. Travis saw her looking, and I couldn't close the door fast enough."

I started shaking again, but Hunter wasn't going to let me go.

"He chased me down the hall and grabbed me. He screamed at me for interrupting them and then said that maybe I wanted some, too. He started ripping at my pants, and I couldn't breathe because he was so heavy and he was on top of me and I thought I was going to die. He ripped at my shirt and scratched my chest. I was only wearing leggings, so he tore those and my underwear and went for his pants again, telling me if I ever told anyone about any of it, he'd come and find me and kill me. I prayed for someone to save me, and that was when Tawny hit him as hard as she could with her softball bat that she kept under her bed. He collapsed on me, and Tawny had to roll him off. We tied him up with a couple of my jump ropes and some tape and called the police. There was a trial. He was convicted and got ten years. He's supposed to be in for two more, but Tawny called and said he's up for parole."

I sniffed again, and he handed me the napkin.

"So there. Now you know. The only other person I've

ever told was Megan. Everyone in my town knew about it. I got labeled a whore in school, and when I started getting angry and fighting, no one wanted anything to do with me. I made a pact with myself that I would never date, never have a boyfriend. I'd be alone, because the only person I can trust is me. Everyone will let you down. I'd never told Tawny that, but she apologized for years. I think she's still apologizing, even though she was a victim, too. My parents felt so guilty about leaving that they broke up. I mean, that wasn't the entire reason, but it had a lot to do with it. Everything just kind of fell apart after that one night. And now you know why I have the peacock obsession. Tawny was wearing one earring, and I was wearing the other. Those earrings saved our lives."

Hunter thought for a moment, and I could almost hear him trying to pick the right words. "I wish I could kill him in the most slow, painful way possible," he said.

"Me, too." I'd imagined it more times than I would ever admit.

"Thank you for telling me."

"Now you know why I'm so fucked up."

"You're not, that's the thing. You've been through something most people can't imagine. Don't be ashamed of the way that you cope with it."

"I'm not coping with it, according to my therapists. There have been many."

"Fuck them. If breaking things and punching people every now and then helps you, I'll be your punching bag and we can get you some stuff to throw off the roof. Deal?"

"Okay."

"So he's up for parole?"

"Yeah, there's a hearing. My lawyer called."

"But you get to go to it, right? Make a statement?"

"Yeah."

"Okay then. We'll just have to get you ready to make a really good statement."

"I can't."

"Why?"

"I can't face him again." Harder even than telling him the story was telling him that. That I was a coward.

"Yes, you can. You just don't think you can. There's a difference."

"But I couldn't face him then. He was raping my sister, and I did *nothing*. I could have gotten the phone. I could have run in and hit him with something. I could have done something," I said.

"You were a child."

I tried to shake my head, but he wouldn't let me. "I should have done something."

"I let my father shoot my mother and then himself. If anyone should have done something, it's me."

"He had a gun."

"He had your sister."

"It's not the same."

He sighed. "Taylor, we can what-if ourselves to death, but it won't do anything. The only thing we can do is keep moving, even when it feels like you're walking through a pit of cement."

"With cinder blocks on your shoulders."

"Exactly."

"The only difference is that your demon has a human form." His hand traveled up and down my arm in a soothing motion.

"I'm still sorry I beat you," I said, touching his perfect face.

"How's my face looking?"

I glanced up. He was going to look quite pretty tomorrow. "A little battered."

"That's okay. I'll just tell everyone I was in a bar fight."

"What, you're ashamed to say you were hit by a girl?"

"No, but I'm worried you'll get hauled in for domestic violence," he said with a smile.

"Okay, fine."

"Feel better?"

"I guess. I'll let you know."

"It's okay to be scared."

"I hate being scared."

"I know. But you don't have to be scared of him. He's locked up right now, and you're not alone. I want you to remember that. You. Are. Not. Alone."

"I've always been alone. Old habits die hard."

"Yes, they do." He laughed a little. "Are you tired?"

"Not really."

"Then do you mind if I just hold you like this? It's very nice."

"Yes, it is." I shifted so I could wrap my legs with his, like we had that night we'd spent together.

"Well, that's even nicer."

"Hunter."

"Sorry, Miss."

"Every time I think about being physical with someone, all I can remember are his hands and his face above mine and not being able to breathe. I know I shouldn't associate those things, but I do and I can't seem to change it. Every time I think about sex, that's what I think about. That's why I've never been with anyone. Well, part of the reason. I just never met anyone who I wanted to even attempt it with."

"Until me? Please say until me."

"Until you." I reached up and touched a spot that was starting to turn purple on his cheek. "But I'm a freak. You wouldn't want me."

"I don't want anyone *but* you."

"You're just going to have to be patient with me," I said, tracing his face with one finger. He grabbed my hand and kissed it.

"I'll do my best. Not making any promises."

"How about this?" I said, having an idea. "We have a word that I can say if I start freaking out."

"Like a safe word? Baby, you've been reading too many sketchy romance novels, haven't you? I saw them on your e-reader."

"Whatever. Okay, so what should my safe word be?"

"How about stop?"

"Boring." I went through a bunch of words.

"Mistake," Hunter said, smiling.

"Perfect." He held my hand in front of his face, turning it back and forth, as if he was fascinated.

"You have such tiny hands," he said.

"Uh, thank you?"

"They're cute and feminine. I like them."

"I think I'll keep them. I don't have my receipt for the hand store, so I can't trade them in."

He laughed, his chest moving under me in a wonderful way. He stared down at me and smiled, bringing my hand to his lips. He kissed each of my fingers and then the back of my hand. He turned my palm over and kissed that. He took his time, as if waiting for me to say the safe word. I didn't.

Hunter kissed down my arm, all the way into the inside of my elbow, which was surprisingly sensitive. He waited before putting one hand under my chin and tipping my face up. He moved so close our noses touched before he tentatively kissed my lips. Pulling back, he waited for me to tell him to stop. I didn't.

He reached for my lips again, this time lingering. I kissed him back, moving my mouth so it fit against his. How was it we fit so well together? Hunter pulled back again, and I opened my eyes.

"I'm going to kiss you now, and I'm not going to stop."

"I don't want you to."

"Okay then." He brought my face toward his again and opened his mouth as I opened mine to deepen the kiss. At that moment, I wanted to crawl inside him and hide. His tongue entered my mouth, and I let him. I couldn't really use the safe word because my mouth was occupied. I didn't want to use it anyway.

Hunter pulled me closer, twisting our fingers together as he nipped at my bottom lip.

For a moment, he pulled away so we could both breathe.

"Want me to stop?" he said.

"Nope."

"Then I suggest we move this to our bedroom. Your bed or mine?"

"Mine," I said.

He wiggled out from under me and picked me up, kissing my lips as he did so.

"No kissing and walking. I don't want to hurt you," he said while he carried me back to our room. He nearly tripped on a few T-shirts, but he got me on the bed and then his lips were back on mine. I moved over so he could climb on. Damn those tiny beds.

Before he continued, he held my face in his hands.

"Are you sure?"

"Right now, yes." I didn't know if I'd change my mind. Kissing was nice and well and good, but once clothes started coming off, and other areas started getting explored, I wasn't sure if the ugly shadow of that horrible night would swallow me up again.

In response, he kissed me again and then sat up, pulling at the hem of his shirt.

"I want to do it," I said, propping myself on my elbows.

"Your wish is my command, princess."

I'd never taken a shirt off a guy before, but guy's shirts weren't that different from girl's shirts, right? They had armholes and were made of cotton and all that. How hard could it be? I started pulling up, and he put his arms up. I got it kind of stuck on his nose, but he moved it so he could get his head through before he chucked it onto the floor.

"We'll have to practice that one," he said, coming back for another kiss. He moved down to my ear, which made me giggle, and then down to my neck, which made me sigh. I ran my hands up and down his chest, tracing his tattoos. I wondered what they tasted like.

"I want to see you," he said into my neck. "Roll with me." He got his arms around me and we rolled, somehow not coming off the bed, so I was on top of him. He reached for the hem of my shirt, never taking his eyes off mine and waiting for me to say the word. I put my arms up.

He got the shirt off with more grace than I had, but he'd had practice.

"Show-off," I said as he stared at me. I only had a bra on, and it wasn't a very sexy one.

"A belly ring? Christ, you are trying to kill me. How did I not know about that?" His finger dipped into my belly button, and I had to bite my lip.

"It's my little secret."

He stared at me for a few more seconds before he reached for me so we could roll back the other way.

"You're so pretty it hurts." He ran his hands over my royal blue bra. At least it had a little lace on it, but it had seen better days.

He moved his head down and kissed his way across my chest, my skin shivering in anticipation. When he got to my belly button he kissed that, too, and I moaned a little. I wasn't thinking about anything else but me and him. We were in our bubble again.

His hands were all over me, covering every inch of my skin with a light touch, setting my skin aflame. I touched him as well, and he made a sound in response.

"Too fast?" he said, stopping.

"No."

I kissed him again; this time his hands roamed the rest of me, going lower and setting a fire there as well. I ran my hands across his back and grabbed his ass. I'd wanted to touch it for a very long time.

It was well worth the wait.

"I need to get something. Damn, I should have thought of this ahead of time." He glanced over to his dresser, which was several feet away. "You're coming with me." He got up and picked me up again, walking with me to the dresser, where he grabbed a foil packet from his sock drawer. My chest was pressed to his, and I only wanted to be closer, closer, closer.

"Wrap it before you tap it," he said, holding the package in his fist before taking us back to my bed. I laughed.

It was happening. It was really happening.

Hunter set me back down and made sure the packet was in easy reach for when he needed it.

"Not yet," he said.

"Not yet," I agreed.

We kissed some more, and he ran his hands all over me. I decided that clothes were highly overrated. They were between me and him, and I did not like them at the moment. I started tugging at his boxers, mad at them for separating us.

"No way. You first," he said.

It wasn't really fair that he would be completely naked, and me not so much at all, so I leaned up so he could undo the clasp of my bra. Of course he got it with one hand.

"I've had practice," he said as he slid the straps down my arms and removed it. Well, there I was.

He smiled and kissed my lips before moving his mouth lower and kissing my nipples. My breath hissed out from between my teeth, and my back arched. Hunter laughed, which tickled in the best way, making things even worse.

"My turn," I said, trying to push him so I could kiss his chest. He settled for lying on his side while I was on mine. I kissed his tattoos, one by one. His eyes closed, and he made a contented sound. That made me smile. I kissed my way across his chest as he moved his hands through my hair and all over my back.

We moved our lips back together, and he rolled back above me. I moved my hands down to his boxers, insistent again.

"Taylor, if you touch me there, I'm not going to be able to make it. Just warning you."

"Okay," I said, moving my hands away from that particular area. He pushed against me, and I could feel that he was ready. Was I?

"I want to touch you," he said.

"You are."

"Everywhere."

I didn't hesitate. "Okay."

"Okay?"

"Yes." Oh, it was more than okay.

His hands made their way down my stomach and into my shorts. *Holy crappity fuck.* I'd never felt *that* before. Doing it yourself was one thing, but having a man with slightly calloused hands touch you there was something else entirely. It was like he'd taken a class and gotten an A.

I'd had orgasms before. I mean, who hadn't? Renee had dragged me to a sex toy party last year, and I'd bought a few things, but nothing worked better than Hunter Zaccadelli's hands.

My back arched and I bit my lip so I wouldn't be too loud.

"We're alone. You be as loud as you want, Missy. I plan for this to be a regular thing," he said, kissing me. His hand continued to work, torturing me again.

I wasn't sure how much more I could take. On my own my record was three. I was coming up on number two in a very short span of time.

"I want you so bad right now."

"Okay," I said as another one hit me. That time I made a lot of noise. Hunter kissed me again and decided that he'd had enough of clothes, too.

The next thing I knew we were both naked, and his entire body was pressed on mine.

"This is going to hurt. If you want me to stop, just say the word and I will. There are plenty of other things we can do," he said with a smirk. "But I don't want this to be a bad memory. I want this to be a good one."

He kissed me again, and I reveled in the feeling of his warm skin against mine. Hunter pulled away to rip open the wrapper and roll the condom on.

"Are you ready?"

"Yes." I was. This was *my* choice. *My* body. *My* Hunter.

He pushed into me, and I tried not to cry out in pain. It hurt.

"Aw, baby, I'm sorry." He kissed me, and I held on to him until he was all the way in. "Are you okay?"

"Yeah." He stayed still for a few seconds, and my body started to adjust. It was a strange sensation, but I didn't want it to stop.

"Taylor?" Hunter said, brushing my hair back from my face. "I love you."

"I love you," I said without even hesitating. In that moment, as we were joined together as one person, I did. He pulled out and thrust in again. It hurt again, but not as bad.

"Again?" he asked, his muscles trembling.

"Again."

He started going faster, and the pleasure started overwhelming the pain. I moved my hips up to meet him, and he kissed me hard. He groaned a little while later, and I felt him come. He fell against me, exhausted. Hunter tried to pull out, but I wrapped my legs around him so he wouldn't.

"Not yet," I said. I wanted to keep this moment for as long as I could.

"I love you," he said, kissing me as he rolled us both onto our sides. We were both sweaty and still a little out of breath, but it didn't matter. "More than the stars."

"I love you, too," I said, holding him close.

"I believe you."

We stayed connected as long as we could, but then he had to pull out and toss the condom. When he came back we lay naked for a while, touching each other softly and trying to figure out what we could say that would make sense.

"Did I hurt you?" he said.

"Yes, but it doesn't matter."

"I wish I hadn't."

"Don't unwish it. It was perfect."

"Perfectly imperfect."

"Like us," I said.

"Just like us." He kissed my nose. "More?"

"More what?"

"I have a whole repertoire that I want to use on you. It's one of my many talents. It's my goal to satisfy."

"And I appreciate that. Must be those fingers," I said, bringing them to my mouth and kissing them. I rubbed them across my lips.

"Must be."

I wasn't a virgin anymore.

"I know I should be freaking out right now, but I'm not," I said.

"Good." He ran his finger between my breasts and flicked my belly ring. "I have to say that I enjoy that, very much."

"I didn't get it with you in mind."

"Why did you get it?"

I propped my head on my hand. "I always thought they looked pretty, and it seemed daring."

"I like it on you." He leaned forward and kissed my belly. I sighed again. God, that felt so good. He felt good.

"Shit," he said, pointing to my comforter. I'd sort of forgotten about the bleeding part in the heat of the moment.

"Aw, crap. Guess I'm due for a new one." My face went red, and I stuffed my face into my pillow.

"It's okay. We'll just stay in mine tonight."

"I should get cleaned up."

He raised one eyebrow. "Can I help?" I was about to say

hell no, but then I thought of all the times I'd thought about bathing with Hunter. They were too numerous to count.

"To the shower," I said, raising my arm. He took the opportunity to tickle me under my armpit as he climbed over me so he could pick me up.

"We can soak that in the tub later," he said about my comforter.

There was something absolutely weird about being completely naked with another person and not caring.

He turned the shower on and made sure it was the right temperature before he let me get in. We spent most of the time kissing, with me trying not to drown under the water and him laughing at me. My hair kept getting in the way. I had way too much of it. We soaped each other up and had a little too much fun washing special parts. He made me come a few more times, and I had to hold on to him because my legs wouldn't support me.

"You are really good at that," I said after another one.

"You're easy." I smacked his chest with a wet slap. "You know what I mean. All those years of not doing anything and you're all pent up. All I have to do is push the button." He pushed said button and I cried out, falling against him.

"I told you I was a virgin, not a nun. I know how to make it happen. It's just better when you do it."

"I *knew* girls did that. Most of the ones I've been with denied it."

"Not as much as boys, but we have needs, too."

"Needy, needy girl." He kissed my mouth and moved me so the water pounded on my back. He lifted me up, and I wrapped my legs around him.

I loved him.

CHAPTER 25

Neither of us wanted to put clothes on, so we didn't. We spent the rest of the night in Hunter's bed, talking and kissing and touching. It was sweet and nice and glorious.

He told me more about his parents and different stories about growing up. I told him about my childhood, about the good times before my dad became a douche.

"So are we going to talk about what happened?" he said.

"You mean the sex?"

"I mean the love part that happened during the sex. There should really be a better word for it. Sex sounds so clinical."

"Canoodling?" I suggested.

"Making whoopee."

"Rolling in the hay."

"Making love."

We both laughed. He ran his hands across my breasts and up to my face.

"So, the love part," I said.

"Yeah. That happened, didn't it?"

"Yes, it did. You're not the only one who said it."

"I realize that. So what are we going to do about it?"

"Pretend it was a fluke during the heat of the moment?"

He thought about that, making a circle around my navel. "Nope, still love you." He kissed the spot right where my heart beat.

I thought about it, running my hands over his short hair. It prickled against my palm. "Yeah, still love you."

He looked up with the biggest smile on his face. He rolled over until he was on top of me again and rested his chin on my stomach. "When I used to say I loved my mom, she'd always tell me she loved me more than the stars. I love you more than the stars, Taylor Caldwell."

I didn't have a good enough response to that, so I just kept tracing hearts across his back.

He kissed my stomach. "Guess that means I'm moving out."

"Guess so," I said, shrugging.

"I'm going now." He didn't make a move. I ran my fingers over his head, enjoying the feel of him. "I swear, I'm going to get up and pack my stuff."

"Okay."

"You're supposed to wail and clutch at me and beg me not to go."

"I don't beg."

"I could make you," he said moving his hand lower.

"No," I said, grabbing his wrist. My poor, destroyed body couldn't take it again.

"So here I go." He moved just a little, and I grabbed him. "That's what I thought."

"You said you wouldn't leave me." If I'd been terrified of him leaving me before, I was even more terrified now.

"Aw, Missy, I wouldn't leave you right now. I'm gonna be stuck to you. Just like this."

"It's going to be hard for me to go to class."

"Just throw a towel over me, no one will notice." I rubbed my thumb over his bottom lip, and he flicked his tongue out and licked it.

It was official. I was in love with Hunter Zaccadelli.

"I love you. Even when you're an ass."

"I love you, even when you're kicking me in the balls."

"How romantic," I said, rolling my eyes.

"Hey, I could sing to you. All you have to do is ask."

"'Honey Come Home,'" I said.

He started the song, singing it a cappella. He slowed it down and kissed me during the pauses. He finished pretending to play chords on my belly. It tickled.

"My personal rock star," I said.

"Only yours, baby."

"What's up with that? You abandoned Missy as my official nickname?"

"Baby sounds more girlfriendy."

"Is that what I am?"

"Well, I assumed, given the love exchange and the hay rolling."

"Yeah, I guess that's what it means." *Huh.*

"Don't look so excited about it."

"It's not that. I just never thought it would be a thing I'd be into."

"You're not alone in the no-commitment zone. I've never really done it either. That's one of the things I love about you. Everything is new."

"Yay for virginity."

"I'd give it a round of applause."

I rolled my eyes again. "Yeah, it's great. I have no idea what the hell I'm doing."

He shook his head, running his lips over my skin. "Doesn't matter. You can learn."

"You gonna teach me?"

"Oh, I'd like to see what you can pick up on your own, Missy girl."

"You're not into anything weird, are you?"

"What would you call weird?"

"I don't know. Like bondage and leather and crap like that."

He laughed. "Sometimes I have no idea where your mind is going. When it comes to sex, it's always different. Most of the girls I've been with have been a quick fuck just for the hell of it. I never wanted to stay around them long enough to do other stuff."

"The feminist in me is really offended right now."

"They knew what they were getting into. Two consenting adults having a sexual experience. I told you, you're different."

"So you don't want me to wear a cat costume or kiss your boots or call you sir or anything?"

He laughed even harder, burying his face in my navel.

"Stop it—that tickles!" I squealed.

"God, I love you. I know I've said it a ton of times today, but I can't stop."

"I'm waiting…" I said, tapping his head.

"We'll do whatever you want to do. If you want to hang me upside down by my toes, I'm all for it. I would like to try a few different positions to find which one you like. It'll come in time. Let's just get the basics down first."

"Have you always been this open about sex?"

He shrugged one shoulder. "Why be closed? Sooner or later, most people in this world will have sex. It's nothing to be ashamed of. Being ashamed of it only leads to people doing dumb things."

"So, you think you want to do it again?" I managed to keep my voice at a normal volume.

"I'd say that's a yes."

"Good...So it was good for you?" I said, voicing one of my anxieties.

"Baby, it was more than good. That blew good up. I would never use good to describe being with you." He grinned at me, and I smiled back.

"What time is it?"

"Um." Hunter squinted at my clock across the room. "Midnight."

"Jesus. I had no idea."

"Can you believe we have to go to class tomorrow?" he said.

"Not really. Can't we just do this for the rest of our lives?"

"I'd be content, but we need food and I think after a few days our roommates and my cousin would wonder where we were."

"Then let's move to a private island and live out our days there."

"Can we bring Harper? I'd miss that kid like crazy."

"Only if she doesn't interrupt us during lovemaking," I said. My stomach growled, and we both heard it.

"Hungry?"

"If I say no, you'll know I'm lying."

"Here," he said, reaching over me to grab one of his shirts. "It's only so you don't get grease from the stove on your pretty skin."

I put the shirt on, and he donned his boxers. I grabbed his ass as we trooped to the kitchen.

"Hey!" he yelled.

"Now you know how it feels."

We made chocolate chip pancakes, with the dark chocolate

chips Hunter had bought last week. It was messy, and we both ended up needing another shower, but we just kissed most of the pancake batter and melted chocolate off. I never knew how much *fun* it could be, being with Hunter. He chased me around with the spatula and tickled me into submission.

I hadn't thought about Travis, or him coming after me, for hours. I shoved it aside. I wasn't going to let it invade our sexy little bubble.

Hunter and I got naked again and finally fell asleep with bellies full of pancakes. He hummed little tunes, and I pulled myself as close as I could get. It wasn't enough. I wanted every night to be like this. Forever.

I woke up in the morning to lips kissing mine and a male body pressed against me. Warmth swirled through my body, settling several key places.

"Good morning," he said, kissing my nose.

"Good morning to you, too, and to your little friend." I reached my hand down and gave him a little squeeze.

"Hey, hey. Careful with that." He kissed me again and snuffled in my neck. "How are you feeling?"

I tested my body.

"Sore. Nothing worse than bad PMS. I'll live." I took my retainer out and put it back in the little case.

"Good, because I'd like to do that again in the not-so-distant future. Just tell me when you're ready."

My alarm clanged, reminding us that the real world was calling.

"Nooooo…" I said, hiding my head in Hunter's shoulder.

"Come on, Miss. We've got human sexuality to learn."

"Ha-ha."

We got up and had toast, with him sitting in his recliner,

me in his lap, feeding each other bites. I had about a million messages and voice mails and so forth, but I ignored them. I'd deal with them later. I did message Tawny and my mother back, saying that I was fine. I listened to the voice mail from the assistant district attorney, but I couldn't absorb the details. Maybe I'd get Hunter to do it for me.

He had class first, so I walked him down and decided to hang out in the Union for a while until my class. He took my hand, and we walked like a regular couple.

"Another date tonight?"

"Maybe. We should probably, you know, do homework and socialize with other people though."

"Other people are overrated."

"Aw, they're not that bad. We'll have all the time we need tonight when we're alone. I'll tell Renee to wear her earplugs."

He shook his head slowly.

"Cruel, cruel woman. I'll be thinking about the possibilities all day."

"Then I won't tell you what color my underwear is."

"White, with little pink polka dots."

"Damn." We'd watched each other get dressed this morning. "The mystery is gone."

"Why don't you go back to the room, change and then it will be a surprise."

"Maybe I'll do that." We stopped in front of his building, and I gave him a long, steamy kiss. "Just something to remember me by."

"See you later, Miss."

"Bye, Hunter."

We walked until we couldn't hold hands anymore, and I watched him walk inside. *Damn.* How had I not noticed how effing sexy he was, even when he was opening a door?

I stumbled to the Union and called Megan.

"Hey, where are you?" I said.

"Union. Why?"

I glanced around and found her flaming hair. "Oh, never mind. I see you." I hung up and walked toward her, wondering if she would notice, if anyone would notice, that I looked different.

"Hey, how are you? I texted you a bunch of times yesterday. Where were you—" She saw my face and the stupid grin that was plastered all over it. "Oh my God. What happened?"

"Um, well. Hunter and I are...um...together."

"Holy crap," she said, grabbing at my hand. "You did *not* get engaged."

"Of course not. Oh, I switched it to the other finger yesterday. Long story."

"We have some time before class. Get to the good stuff!"

I sat down, leaning forward so no one would overhear. "I turned in my V card."

Megan gaped. "So you really, *really* forgave him."

"Yeah. He's one of the good ones. I told him about Travis. He's up for parole, by the way."

She gasped, covering her mouth with her hand. "You're kidding."

"I wish I was."

"So what are you going to do?"

I grabbed a fry from her plate and dipped it in ketchup. "I don't know right now. I have to meet with the ADA, which should be a great time. I'll have to get up and speak at the hearing, which I'm not looking forward to." Understatement of the year.

"Can anyone else go with you?"

"It think it's just me and Tawny and immediate family." I

took another fry. "But I don't want to think about that. I've obsessed about Travis for way too many years of my life. I just want to be happy."

"Does Hunter make you happy?"

"Happier than I knew was possible."

"So hold on to that."

"I will."

"So, um, I have some news."

"What?"

In answer she held up her left hand, which had a thin gold band with one square-cut diamond on it.

"Oh my God!" We both squealed, and everyone stared.

"He finally popped the question. It's not going to be for a while, but at least I have a ring on my finger."

"It's about time!" I gave her a huge hug. "Does this mean you're moving out of your craptastic apartment?"

"I've been looking for nicer places, and I think I found one. I'll have to take on another job, but I think we can swing it."

"Good for you, being all adultlike."

"Maybe you'll be next. They say one wedding brings on another. Maybe one engagement brings on another, too."

"I don't think so. Marriage isn't really our thing."

"Whatever," she said, rolling her eyes.

We chatted about my night with Hunter, with me giving her a few details about our night.

"So it was good?"

"I can't really imagine it getting better."

"Oh, it will. Top is the best. Trust me."

"I'll put that on the list of things to try."

"You have a list?" she asked.

"No, but I'm sure Hunter does."

We both laughed.

"Boys. They always have that on the brain."

We giggled some more as she finished her fries and we went to our class. I gave her a few whispered details, and she told me more about her wedding plans while a movie rolled and we pretended to take notes. I had a hard time focusing. All I could think about was being naked with Hunter, and how I wanted to be naked with him again.

I beat him to Human Sex, so I got out my e-reader and pretended to be engrossed in whatever I was trying to read. I didn't even know what it was.

"Miss Caldwell," a voice said next to me, making me grin uncontrollably. I stifled it.

"Mr. Zaccadelli. How wonderful to see you again."

"What brings you here on this lovely day?" He moved past me and sat down, giving me a kiss on the cheek. My lips wanted more, but I didn't want to look like a slut.

"I am here to study the sexual practices of humans. How about you?"

"The same. What a coincidence."

"Isn't it?" He kissed my cheek again.

"Hey, baby."

"Hey."

"I missed you."

"I missed you, too."

He twisted our fingers together as Marjorie walked in and started class. If I'd thought I'd had a hard time focusing without Hunter in a class, it was even worse when he was there. He kept whispering to me, touching me and making me remember the night before.

"Will you stop it?" I hissed as I tried to take notes, and he stuck his tongue in my ear.

"Why, does this bother you?"

"You are interfering with my learning, Mr. Zaccadelli."

"That's the point, Miss Caldwell."

"I'm going to have to report you to Marjorie."

"Go ahead. I'm sure she would approve of us having a healthy sex life."

I gave him a good pinch on his leg. "Next time, I'm pinching something else."

"Maybe I'm into that."

I ended it there and went back to my note taking. "You are a bad influence, Mr. Zaccadelli," I said when class ended.

He nodded. "I try to be, Miss Caldwell." He dived toward me and gave me a huge kiss. I heard someone make a noise of disgust behind us. "Ready to go?" he said.

"Sure."

I walked him to the library, where he had his shift, and then I went back to the apartment.

"Sweet Jesus, is she alive?" Renee said as I walked through the door.

"Barely." Through the day, I'd become more sore, especially with sitting down so often. I'd taken some pain medication, but I still had a twinge every time I moved.

"Details now," she said, pointing to the one end of the couch that wasn't covered in notebooks and textbooks.

"Where's Paul?"

"He had a geology seminar, and don't change the subject."

"Dare?"

"At work." I sat down with a minimum amount of pain. "Little sore, are we?"

I blushed and nodded.

"Good for you. Means you did it right. I cried after my first time, but that's probably because I was fifteen and we had no idea what the hell we were doing." I couldn't imagine. "You were smart to wait."

"How did you know—?"

"Sweetie, I'm not a moron. You had virgin written all over you." I'd never actually come out and told them, but I guessed it must have been obvious. "So, how was it?"

"Good," I said, smiling. Hunter would have been mad at me. *Good* really wasn't the word to describe it, but I didn't want to share our special moment with anyone.

"Oh, it had to be more than good."

"Maybe it was."

"As I said, just let me know when I need earplugs. This is your place, too."

"Will do."

"Great." She shut her book with a slam. "I'm so happy for you."

"Thanks, Nene."

"God, that nickname is never going to die."

"I'm 'baby' now, so I know how you feel."

"Ooohh, baby. That's so cute."

"'Nobody puts Baby in a corner.'"

"Just Hunter."

"Not even him."

"Good girl. You wear the pants."

"I do."

"Have you seen your doctor yet?"

"Uh, no."

"But you're on the pill, right?"

"Yeah." I'd had horrible PMS since I was much younger, so as soon as I could I got on the pill to regulate my hormones. I'd been taking it for so long that it was second nature.

"Well, just be careful. Urinary tract infections are not fun."

"Ew."

"Cranberry juice is in the fridge. Go see your gyno. That's all you have to do. I'm just looking out for your vaginal welfare." That made me blush.

"Thanks."

"Anytime, girl."

She nodded and went back to homework, as if we hadn't just been talking about my vaginal welfare. I made a note to call my doctor to set up an appointment. You could never be too safe.

I figured homework was a good idea for me as well, so I got a bunch of mine done while Hunter was gone. My comforter was still damp, so I went and threw it in the wash downstairs. I was still going to buy another, because the blood hadn't completely come out.

By the time he got back from work, it was dinnertime and Paul was over. Mase had decided to join us before he picked Darah up from work.

"So, we have an announcement to make," Hunter said, grabbing my hand and holding it up for the world to see. "We are together. Aren't we, baby?"

"As long as you stop calling me baby."

"You know you love it."

"Not really."

"Okay, okay, enough with the cute, we get it," Renee said.

"Aw, come on, Ne. Be nice," Paul said.

"I think it's great. Welcome to the family, Tay." Mase gave me a huge hug. "Not that you weren't already a part of it, but I know Hope will be thrilled and Harper will be over the moon."

"Thanks."

Hunter pulled me to his chest, rocking me back and forth

and giving me another kiss. It was like we couldn't get enough of each other.

"Okay, dinner. I've got rice and veggies and teriyaki sauce. So it looks like stir-fry. Anyone have objections?" Hunter said.

We all shook our heads.

"Stir-fry it is."

Hunter divvied up the tasks, giving me the task of chopping peppers. I was really good at it, apparently. We all bustled around the kitchen, knocking into one another and laughing and generally making a mess. When we finally sat down, it was pretty late for dinner. Hunter claimed the recliner, and I claimed his lap. Hey, it was the best seat in the house.

My phone buzzed with a text from Tawny. I read it, but it wasn't anything major.

"You okay?" Hunter hadn't seen the text.

"Yeah, fine. I just have to call her later."

"What are you whispering about over there?" Renee said, pointing her fork at us.

"Your mom," I said.

"Hey, don't you dare insult my mother."

"Oh, but it's fine for you to?" I said.

"You didn't have to spend eighteen years of your life with her."

"True story," I said.

I missed Hunter in the shower, but I just didn't feel comfortable doing that when Renee and Paul were in the living room studying. Hunter also had a lot of work for econ that he'd been putting off. We had another of our study sessions after my shower.

"You know, if I copied my notes onto your skin, I bet I would learn them a *whole* lot better," he said.

"You'd have to write really, really small. There's not a lot of me to write on."

"Oh, I'm sure I'd find room."

"I'm going to go back to studying now."

"Me, too."

Somehow, we both went back and got some more work done. Darah ducked her head in, saying hello and that she was happy for us. She was exhausted and Mase decided to stay the night with her, and Paul was taking Renee back to his place.

"We need to get our own place," Hunter said.

"What?"

"Well, I did lose the bet, so I should have moved out. I just want to take you with me. I have plenty of money for one."

I slammed my book shut. "No way. First of all, I'm not letting you pay for an apartment for me. Second, I'm not letting you pay for an apartment for me. Third, you're giving that money to someone who needs it."

"It would be *our* apartment. Big difference."

"I already paid to live here. And what happened to the guy who didn't want the money?"

He shrugged.

"You made me realize that it was just money. It doesn't represent that night and what happened. My dad worked hard for that money, and he left it to me. I should do something with it."

"Well, you should. Give it to a domestic violence shelter."

He snapped his fingers. "That's a good idea. But I still have plenty to pay for a crappy apartment for the two of us."

"It's not happening."

"We'll see when I meet your mom this weekend."

"Don't you dare mention this to her. Or Tawny."

"No promises, baby."

"Stop calling me that."

"No promises, Missy."

I sighed heavily and shut the rest of my books. I guessed I was done with work. That made me think of other things we could do with our time.

"I have something for you," he said, getting up and grabbing his car keys. "I was waiting until no one else was around. Just stay here. I'll be right back."

A few minutes later he came in with a brand-new comforter and set of sheets.

"They didn't have the peacock one, but I found it online, so I ordered one. Until it comes, I got this. I figured the colors were close." The comforter was turquoise and the sheets were in green and dark blue.

"You didn't have to do that."

"I was responsible for ruining the last set, so I figured it was the least I could do."

"You have to stop buying me things."

"No, I won't. Come on. I'll help you put them on."

My bed was already bare, so it only took us a little bit of effort to get it made up again.

"Thank you," I said, giving him a hug.

"Anything for you."

"I should probably call Tawny."

"Do you want some privacy? I need to take a shower anyway."

"Thanks."

I sat on my newly made bed to call Tawny.

"Hey, what's up?"

"Nothing except I've been calling and calling you and you didn't call me back."

"I texted you."

"I know, but I needed to hear your voice, Kid."

"I'm sorry, Tawn."

She sighed. "It's okay. I just wanted to tell you that I talked with Mr. Woodward today. The hearing is in two weeks, and we're both going to be able to make a statement to the parole board. We're only allowed to have immediate family, so it will be just us and Mom and Mr. Woodward."

"Okay. Travis will be there, though, right?"

"Yeah, he'll be there."

"I don't know if I can do it."

"Yes, you can. You faced him that night, and you can again. He can't hurt you anymore. He can't hurt either of us anymore. You know I've got a gun just in case. I was going to get you those shooting lessons for Christmas, but you might need them sooner. Maybe Hunter can take you."

"What a romantic date." I tried to laugh it off, but something told me Hunter wouldn't be up for that kind of date.

"Hey, the couple that shoots together, stays together." Her words sent a chill down my spine and made me think about Hunter's parents.

"I guess. I don't know, I think I'm all set." I groped for a subject change.

"You found anybody that meets your standards yet?"

"Well, there is this new guy at the firm. He's another paralegal, so it's completely against the rules for me to even entertain the idea of dating him, but he's cute."

"How old?"

"He's younger than me, but he doesn't act it. He bought me lunch the other day out of the blue."

"Must be love."

"Must be." There was a pause as I heard the shower turn

off. "Hey, it will be okay. I wasn't there for you on that night, but I'm not going to do that ever again."

"You were there for me. If you hadn't hit him with the bat, he would have—" I couldn't say the rest.

"I shouldn't have had him over."

"Look, Tawn, I don't want to argue with you now. It's useless. What's done is done and all we can do is move forward."

"Wow, who are you and what have you done with my sister?"

"I just have a new perspective on life."

"You totally got laid."

"Why does everyone think everything is about sex?"

"Sometimes, Kid, it is."

"Whatever."

"Listen, we have to meet with Mr. Woodward in two weeks. Do you think you can come down?"

"I'll have to miss class."

"You don't really have a choice. I can get him to excuse you."

"Okay. Let me know what time."

"Will do."

We hung up just as Hunter came back. I had to stop myself from grabbing his wet and sexy body.

"You look like you want me," he said.

"I do."

"I thought you were still sore."

"I am, but you said there were other things. Maybe we could try some other things?"

"If you want to. I didn't think you'd be ready for that yet, but if you want to, I'm not going to say no."

"Unless you think we should go to bed, because we could do that."

"Are you kidding?" He dived forward and grabbed me, throwing me on his bed and kissing the daylights out of me.

"It could be like this all the time, you know? Just you and me."

"You're not getting us an apartment."

"What if I make you orgasm five times a day, every day?"

"I wouldn't be able to walk, that's for sure."

"But would you let me rent us an apartment?"

"No."

"Fine. Enough talking. I want more loving."

"Me, too," I said against his lips.

We went slower this time, kissing more and taking our time.

"What do you want?" he said as he peeled my shirt off.

"You."

"I'm all yours. Tell me what you want."

I kissed him hard, nearly biting his lip.

"Easy, girl," he said, undoing my bra. I'd decided to wear a sexier one in black lace that hadn't been through the wash too many times.

"How about this?" He slid his hand down my stomach and under my shorts.

"That's good," I said, and my body responded.

"Good? Okay, I want to try something else. Something I think you're really, really going to like."

He worked his way down my body, kissing and sucking until I was a quivering mess. He went lower and started to pull off my shorts.

"You changed," he said, staring down at the matching black lace panties I'd put on earlier.

"Surprise," I said. I wasn't up to speaking more than one word at a time. Not enough blood in my brain.

He kissed me there, and I started freaking out a little, grabbing on to his ears.

"Hey, it's okay. I promise," he said, looking up.

"Are you sure?"

"Yes."

A few moments later when he removed my underwear, I was pretty damn sure.

"Christ." He laughed, which made it even better. All I could do was hold on and hope I didn't break apart into a million pieces. I certainly felt like I had. Several times.

"Satisfied?" he said a little while later.

"Where the hell did you learn how to do that?"

"Camp."

"Shut up." My body was still quaking with aftershocks. If the apartment caught fire right then, I wouldn't have been able to move.

"Practice. You like?"

"Too much."

He crawled back up my body and tried to kiss me, but I was a little weirded out by that.

"One step at a time." He kissed my forehead instead. He moved to my cheeks and then down my neck and my ears and finally, my lips got lonely, so I moved my head so he could kiss me.

Not as weird as I'd thought.

"You never know until you try," he said against my mouth, smiling. Despite the fact that kissing Hunter was explosive, my eyelids started getting heavy.

"Did I wear you out?"

"A little. I feel like I should reciprocate."

"Tomorrow."

"Okay."

"Sleep now." He kissed my eyelids and pulled his comforter over us. I'd never seen the advantages of sleeping naked, but I did now.

"Good night, baby."

"Good night, Hunter. I owe you a blow job," I said through a yawn.

"Then I hope I live until the morning."

I snuggled into his chest and thought about how quickly life could change, and how good it could be.

CHAPTER 26

Hunter got his promised reward, which I somehow muddled my way through to his satisfaction. We continued our love-making education every chance we got until all he had to do was breathe on me and I'd be thinking of ripping his clothes off and having my way with him.

Every day he mentioned the apartment, and every day I said no. He tried every which way to convince me, but I refused. He always asked at the most inopportune times, usually when my mind and body were busy with something else that I had the feeling he was doing it on purpose. Ambush me in a moment when I was otherwise occupied and spring it on me, hoping I'd be too distracted to say no. Nice try, dude.

Mom kept calling me with little questions, asking what Hunter would like to eat, if we wanted to stay over, etc. I took her up on her offer to have us stay over because it would be kind of fun to show him around Waterville and my old haunts, especially the library.

Saturday morning we got up late, both of us a little sore

after we'd tried something slightly ridiculous in the bedroom department that had led to more giggling than anything else.

"I think we can cross that off our list," Hunter said, getting slowly out of bed.

"You have a list?"

"Well, there is a Periodic Table of Sex. And there's always the *Kama Sutra*."

"You'd have to have no spine to do most of those things," I said, stretching my arms up as he tickled my stomach.

"You never know until you try."

"True."

"Breakfast?"

"I heard Paul out there rustling around. Maybe he made something?"

"I hope so."

Paul had made French toast, and, luckily, he'd made enough for all of us.

"Morning," he said, wearing just a set of pj pants and a rumpled hairdo. I grinned at Renee, knowing what caused it. She winked and gave me a huge smile. I gave it back to her.

"So you're meeting the parents today. You ready?" Paul asked Hunter.

"I'm hoping the apple didn't fall far from the tree in this case," Hunter said, passing me the syrup.

"My mom isn't as angry as I am. She's much nicer."

"How could anyone be nicer than you?"

"I'm thinking of two words to describe you, and they are *ass* and *kisser*."

"I *love* kissing your ass." This was true. He'd done it the night before.

"Ugh, I'm eating here," Renee said. I wrinkled my nose at

her. "I think I liked you two better when you weren't having sex."

"But we weren't as much fun," I said.

"You mean you weren't *having* as much fun."

"What do you think? More fun now?" Hunter asked me, putting his arms around me and rocking side to side.

"Definitely."

We finished breakfast. It was Renee's turn for the dishes, so Paul did most of them.

"Okay, what to wear?" Hunter said as we were getting dressed.

"You never have a wardrobe crisis. That's all me."

"It's not every day that you meet the mother of the girl you adore."

"True. What are your options?"

He had a dark blue shirt and khaki combo, a black T-shirt and jeans combo and a white button-up with brown pants.

"This one says, 'I'm a nice boy who would never hurt your daughter,'" I said, pointing to the first. "This says, 'I'm casual and probably own a motorcycle that I drive too fast.'" I pointed to the second. "And this says, 'Hey, I look amazing in this shirt and I'm reliable.' So it all depends on what you want to go for."

"Reliable it is," he said, taking the white shirt and putting it on over his white tank.

"Let me," I said, reaching for his buttons. Dressing him wasn't nearly as fun as undressing, but I still liked treating him like a human Ken doll every now and then.

"What are you wearing?"

"That," I said, pointing to my bed. I'd chosen a plum sweater and dark brown skirt along with black boots.

"It says, 'I'm a nice girl who would never, ever do anything bad.'"

"It does?"

"I hope it does. Your mom isn't going threaten to beat me up like her daughter does, is she?"

"Ah, no. That would be a negative."

"Good."

"Don't worry, baby. I'll protect you," I said.

"I'm not scared."

"Liar."

"Sex goddess."

"Wuss."

"Beautiful."

I sighed. "You're going to make my head gigantic."

"I'd love you even with a giant head." He kissed the top of my head as I pulled my skirt on.

"So sweet."

"Don't tell anyone. I didn't get these tattoos for people to think I was sweet. Speaking of that, your mom isn't one of those people who thinks guys with tattoos are thugs, is she? I can cover up most of them and just keep my hand on this side of my head," he said, putting his hand over his ear to cover the tattoo behind it.

"I don't really know. This is going to be another first."

"Did *he* have tattoos?"

I knew who *he* was. Travis. Hunter was sensitive about saying his name.

"Nope."

"Good. The more different I am from him, the better."

"You don't have to worry about that. She's really excited to meet you. I think her hope for grandchildren has been rekindled. She'll probably try to talk you into proposing."

"I wouldn't need much convincing."

"Yeah, right." I went to the mirror and started brushing my hair. He put his hands on my shoulders.

"I'm serious," he said.

"I thought you weren't the marrying kind."

"Yeah, well, I've never told a girl I loved her either."

My eyes met his in the mirror. "Never?"

"No. I never loved anyone before you."

"Ditto."

"I can't imagine *not* wanting to marry you."

"Even though I make a mess?"

"The mess is part of you. I get you—I get the mess. We can hire people to clean."

"No way. No one is cleaning up after me. That's just way too weird."

"Okay, I'll be the maid. As long as I get you."

"What if you get sick of me? What if we have a huge fight?"

"Missy, we fight all the time."

"Not like that."

"We'll get through it. We've already gotten through more than most couples our age."

"We're too young."

"Age is just a number."

"We'll change our minds."

"Not a chance."

"It's crazy."

"Not any crazier than me tattooing good luck charms all over my body. Those are permanent. I want you to be permanent."

God, he was stubborn.

"I'm not marrying you."

"Maybe not right now."

"I'm not doing this with you, okay?" I pulled my hair into a loose bun so it would be out of my way.

"Missy," he said, drawing it out so it somehow turned into two words. "Forget I said it. I want this to be a good day, okay?" He kissed my shoulder and tugged a lock of my hair.

"Fine." He was too irresistible. I turned and handed him my keys. "We are not taking your car, and I know you won't let me drive, so here you go. Be careful with her, and I will be careful with you." I gave a certain part of his body a little squeeze so he'd understand.

"Got it."

It was the strangest sensation to sit in the passenger seat of my own car. It did mean I got to pick the music, and I settled on a mixed CD I'd made last summer.

"Since you didn't tell me much about your family, I'll be nice and tell you about mine. You already know Tawny, which is good. Other than Mom and one sister and a few cousins, that's it. Grandparents are already long gone. Lots of heart attacks and cancer and stuff. So, my house isn't even half the size of Hope and John's. There are only three bedrooms, and we're going to be bunking on a twin that I think is made up with Disney princess sheets right now because I brought all the ones I used with me to school. Um, what else? Oh, Mom's really into family photos. She'll probably make us pose for a few while you're here, so get your picture smile ready."

"How's this?" He turned his head and gave me a huge fake grin that did nothing but make me laugh.

"Tone it down, dude."

"Anything else?"

"I hope you like potato salad."

"Maybe I do, and maybe I do."

He started humming along with the CD, and I sat back and watched the highway blur by.

I got more nervous the closer we got to my house. When we got off at the Waterville exit, it all sort of crashed down on me. Hunter and I were together. He was meeting my mother. I'd met his family. We'd talked about marriage. This was really happening.

"Turn here," I said, pointing to our street, Blackbird Lane. "And here," I said, pointing to our driveway.

He stopped the car and looked around. Tawny wasn't there yet.

"This is nice. From the way you were talking I thought it was going to be a shack in the middle of nowhere. Not that I would have had a problem with that, but this isn't as bad as you were describing."

"We don't have a chandelier," I said.

"Not many people do."

"Did your parents?"

"Several," he said, getting out and grabbing his overnight bag from the back. "They paid people to clean them," he said as he opened my door and took my hand. I got my bag, and we walked across the porch and to the front door.

"Ready?"

"As I'll ever be," he said, adjusting his bag. He'd also brought his guitar but had left it in the car.

"Mom?"

"Hey, Kid!" She flew out from the kitchen and pulled me into a hug. "It's been way too long since you were home. But I see you've been occupied. Hello, I'm Blaire Caldwell." My mom and I were the same height and shared our brown hair. Her face was more oval than mine, and she looked much more sophisticated than I could ever hope to, but that was mostly due to her job.

"Nice to meet you, Mrs. Caldwell."

"I'm divorced, so that title no longer applies. I will, however, let you call me Blaire."

Hunter grinned. "Nice to meet you, Blaire." He shook her hand, and she gave him the once-over. I remembered how I'd felt when Hope had done the same thing.

"Come on in. You can go put your things in Taylor's room. I'm going to pretend like you're going to sleep on the floor like a gentleman while Taylor takes the bed, but I'm not naive."

"Yes, ma'am." All of a sudden the Texas accent and manners had come out. He should have tipped his hat as he left the room to take our stuff away.

"He's cute, Taylor. Well done." She put her arm around me and led me to the kitchen. "We need to have a little chat, you and I, but not right now."

"Okay," I said. There was probably a look of horror on my face, which made her laugh.

"It's not a sex talk, I swear. It is just surprising, that's all. Seeing you with a boy."

"He's not just a boy."

"I can tell already. You wouldn't take up with just anyone. I hope he's worthy of you," she said, patting my cheek.

"He is."

"I hope so."

Hunter made sure he walked noisily enough that we knew he was coming back into the room.

"Well, Hunter. Tell me about yourself. I've heard next to nothing from my daughter."

There was a *bang* from the porch and seconds later Tawny barged in. She never entered a room quietly.

"Hey, Kid! Boyfriend. Mom!" She hugged me and Mom and held her fist up for a fist bump from Hunter. He reciprocated.

"So, what's new in W town?" Tawny said.

"They're repaving the road next week. I'm going to have to add a ton of time on to my commute," Mom said.

"Wow, big doings," Tawny said, rolling her eyes. "I'm starved. Is there anything ready?"

"There's fruit salad and potato salad and chips. I wasn't sure what you'd like, Hunter."

"That all sounds wonderful."

"Good. Why don't we go sit down?"

It was a mirror image of meeting Hunter's family, only it was a shorter walk to the living room and the furniture wasn't as nice. We also had lemonade instead of iced tea, but at least this time Hunter was under the microscope. I had to put my hand on his knee and hold his hand in an iron grip so he wouldn't fidget too much. Pretty soon his eye was going to start twitching.

Hunter talked about his major, his family and so forth. The normal stuff. So far, so good, except for calling her ma'am. It was kind of adorable.

"So you're going to be a lawyer?"

"Yes, ma'am. I plan on having my own practice and working on family cases. Specifically with children."

"That's a very good goal for someone your age. What made you choose that?"

I had to clamp my teeth down on my tongue so I wouldn't answer for him and tell her that he was awesome and I loved him and he was awesome.

"Because I think anyone who hurts a child should be brought to justice. Someone has to do it. Why not me?" His voice rang with so much sincerity and passion, I wanted to make out with him right there on the sofa.

"Up top," Tawny said, holding her hand up for a high five. He slapped her hand and then looked at Mom, to make sure she didn't think it was weird. She was studying him. *Uh-oh.* I'd had that look before.

"You're a very interesting young man."

"Thank you, ma'am."

I pinched him so he'd stop calling her ma'am. She *hated* it. I should have mentioned that in the car.

"Well, are you ready to eat?" Mom said.

"Sure."

"Taylor, can you and Tawny get the plates?" She purposefully left Hunter out. Damn, she was testing him to see if he'd take the plates from me.

"I'll do that," Hunter said, slipping in front of me and going to the cabinet. "Which ones?"

"The ones with the blue flowers." They were my grandmother's, and we only used them for special occasions. The real plates we used didn't match and were mostly from yard sales. Tawny made sure to grab the good cups and not the Disney Collector's Edition glasses.

Hunter set our small dining table, which was covered with a tablecloth I was sure Mom had bought yesterday, since it still had creases from being folded in the package.

"Good call on the plates," I said.

"I figured that was an opening for me to be a gentleman."

"Exactly. Just a little note, don't call her ma'am. She hates it."

"Was I?" He seemed to genuinely not know.

I laughed and put my arm around his waist. "Yes, Mr.

Zaccadelli. Just keep the Texas in check, okay? You're in Yankee country."

"I'll try."

I touched his arm. "Hey, you're doing great."

"If you say so." He put a plate down and it clanged a little. God, he was nervous.

"Be careful, that's my gram's china."

"I'll try."

He set the places more carefully, and I followed behind him with the silverware and napkins. Tawny and Mom brought in the meal, which consisted of a spinach, walnut and strawberry salad for me, grilled chicken for everyone else, potato salad and fruit salad and a cheesecake for dessert.

Hunter loaded up on the nonmeat things, which Mom noticed.

"Are you a vegetarian?"

"Not really, but I've been cutting back on meat since I met Taylor."

I passed him the balsamic dressing, and he poured it over his salad. He always used way too much dressing.

"You're not just doing that to impress her, are you?"

"Everything I do is to impress her. It's my mission in life," he said with a completely serious face, while he squeezed my knee under the table.

Mom burst out laughing. "I like him," she said.

"Me, too. I think I'll keep him," I said, taking his hand and twisting my fingers with his.

"Good," he said, giving my hand a squeeze.

The tension eased a little as we sat in the living room making small talk. Hunter seemed a lot more comfortable and stopped twitching so much. He even laughed, albeit nervously.

Tawny was being so mean to him, and I had to keep shooting her dirty looks.

I thought Hunter was going to die when Mom grilled him about the ring, which I'd forgotten to take off. My hand didn't look like my hand without it anymore.

"What did you do, rob a bank?" Tawny said as she gaped at it.

"It was my mother's. I inherited it and I thought, what better place to keep it safe?" Okay, so he didn't inherit the ring, but he inherited the money for it, so I figured it was close enough.

"Your mother had really good taste," Mom said, holding my hand so she could get a better look at it.

"She did."

"You're awfully young to have lost both parents."

"I was eleven when they died, but my mother's sister and husband took me in."

"I'm sorry about your family."

"Thank you."

"Mom? I think I'm going to show Hunter around town."

"Be sure you show him the telephone pole you crashed into during your driving test."

"What?" Hunter said, looking at me.

"We're leaving now," I said, getting up and yanking Hunter to his feet. Any moment the naked baby pictures were going to come out, and there were a lot. I'd had a no-clothes phase for several months, and there was plenty of evidence. Not that Hunter hadn't seen everything there was to see, but still.

"You crashed into a telephone pole? Missy, why don't you let me drive?" Hunter said.

"Shut up," I said as I got in the driver's side. "You don't know this town like I do. So I'm in charge."

"Yes, ma'am," he said, tipping an imaginary hat.

"Do you own a cowboy hat?"

"I have one in my closet at Hope and John's. Why?"

"Oh, no reason." I turned on the car, picturing Hunter in a cowboy hat and nothing else. *Yum.*

"So, where to?"

"The library. Duh."

"Of course." He turned on my CD, skipping to a song he liked. "By the way, you need to bring that little red dress back to school with you."

"Was that what took you so long in my room?"

"I was just checking things out," he said.

"Sure you were. You were looking for skeletons. Or at least embarrassing photos of me with braces."

"I bet you were cute with braces."

"Yeah, cute was the word for it."

We drove around Waterville, and I showed Hunter my school, the library and all the places I used to go when I was younger and needed a place to go other than home.

"I didn't have a lot of friends, if you can believe that. I did my own thing a lot."

"Nothing wrong with that. Most girls that age are bitches."

"Ain't that the truth? I didn't really make any until college."

"So do you want to come back here?"

"Ah, hell no. This isn't where I want to be."

"Where do you want to be?"

"Anywhere else. When Travis gets out, I don't want to be where he can find me."

"What made you stay in Maine? You could have gone overseas to school."

I sighed as I drove past the elementary school. I had a silly idea and pulled into the parking lot. I hopped out, and Hunter followed me. I stopped walking until he was right beside me.

"Tag!" I screamed, slapping his chest and running as fast as I could before he could realize what I'd done.

"I don't think so, Missy," he said, growling and chasing me toward the playground. He caught me, mostly due to the fact that his legs were much longer. He scooped me into his arms and ran with me onto the grass, throwing me down and tickling me without mercy. I was laughing so hard I couldn't breathe. When I couldn't take anymore, he kissed me and we rolled on the grass.

"You little cheater," he said, giving my shoulder a little love bite. "You also deflected my question. Quite effectively, I might add."

I rolled onto my back and stared at the semicloudy sky. "Because I got a better scholarship. I got into other schools, but they were too expensive. They were also too far away. I know that doesn't make sense, but I feel safer here because Tawny and my mom are here. I couldn't leave them."

"You should do what you want and not be obligated to stay here for them."

"Why didn't you go somewhere else? I'm sure you could have gotten into any school you wanted with John's help."

"Because I didn't want a handout. I also got a better financial aid package here and I figured, why not? My dad was always harping on me about the evils of state colleges. He wanted me to go to Yale."

"Did you get in?"

"It doesn't matter." He took my hand and kissed it.

"Shit, you totally got in to Yale. Damn, I'm in love with a genius." *Who knew?*

"Joe wrote a letter of recommendation that probably helped a little."

"When do I get to meet Joe?"

"He's not coming up until Christmas, but you'll meet him then. Hope is as nuts about Christmas as she is about pie. So, be prepared. You're part of the family now, so you're invited."

"God, I can't imagine how that house looks decorated for Christmas."

"It's pretty epic."

"I bet."

"Race you to the swings?"

We both got up and ran as fast as we could. He totally let me win. We played on the swings and chased each other down the slide until the sky opened up and it started raining.

"We should get back. Your mother probably thinks we've driven somewhere and parked by now."

"Because I'm totally that kind of girl."

"Don't knock quickies in cars. If we didn't have to go back and see your mom, I would totally be up for that."

"It sounds uncomfortable."

"It's an art."

"Which I'm sure you've mastered."

He shrugged and mussed my hair. "Told you, Miss. Everything before you doesn't matter."

CHAPTER 27

Not fooling around with Hunter in my mom's house wasn't as hard as I'd thought it would be. Her room was right down the hall, and Tawny's across the hall, and my bed was old and creaky.

"Not even a little?" Hunter whispered as we climbed under my Disney princess sheets.

"It's too weird. I can't have sex on a princess's face with my mom down the hall sleeping. I just have to draw the line."

"Okay, okay. Can I still sleep naked?"

"You can. I'm keeping my clothes on."

"Why?"

"In case there's a fire in the middle of the night and we have to leave the house in a hurry."

"You think of everything," he said, keeping his boxers on but removing his shirt. "Fine, fine." If I didn't know better, I would have said he was pouting.

"You're not upset, are you?"

"About the hay rolling? It would be nice, but I'd settle for just being naked with you. That's the best. Nothing between us. Just you and me."

"Tomorrow night, I swear."

"And then I'm out of luck starting Tuesday."

"Why, what's happening on Tuesday?"

"You start your period," he said, completely matter-of-factly.

"I hate that you know that."

"What? I've known that for a while."

I buried my head in the pillow.

"I thought I was the one who was supposed to be embarrassed about that," he said.

"You're not embarrassed about anything."

He moved the pillow away from my face. "Not really. Until tomorrow, good night, princess." He kissed my nose, and I popped in my retainer and snuggled into him.

"Missy?"

"Yeah?"

"Your mom is kind of awesome, but she looks like she wants to hurt me most of the time."

"Don't worry, I've been on the receiving end of that look more than once."

"So it's not just me?"

"Nope."

"Good to know. I thought she was going to be all sweetness and light from the way you were talking."

"She is sweet. Sweeter than I am anyway."

"How could anyone be sweeter than you?"

"Oh, it's possible."

"No way," he said with a yawn.

I yawned and didn't argue. Too tired.

★ ★ ★

Hunter and I didn't beat Mom to the kitchen the next morning, because the coffee was already on when we got up after a night of platonic cuddling.

"I didn't hear anything I didn't want to hear, so I'm going to assume I don't need to have a chat with anyone."

"Mom!" *Seriously?*

"She's not trying to give you a sex talk, is she?" Tawny said, scrubbing her face with her hands and stumbling toward the coffee.

"Ugh, can we not do this right now? I just woke up."

"Eggs, anyone?" Mom said, holding up a frying pan. She'd mixed the eggs with cream cheese, just like she had when I was younger.

"Plates?" Hunter said, going for the cabinet.

"Top shelf," I said, grabbing silverware out of the dishwasher.

Tawny shuffled to the table, crashing into her seat. Tawny didn't do mornings well.

We had breakfast, and after Tawny had consumed three cups of coffee, she grabbed Hunter and made him show her how to play the guitar as a ruse so Mom could grill me.

"Are you being safe?" was the first thing she asked.

"God, Mom. Yes. You know I'm on the pill."

"But that doesn't protect you from everything."

"Mom, just trust me. I'm not a moron." I was helping her do the dishes and contemplating trying to drown myself in the soapy water to avoid the rest of this conversation.

"It's just unexpected, that's all. You've never expressed an interest in anyone, so it was shocking to hear that you had."

"He's different."

"I saw the tattoos. How many does he have?"

"Um," I said, both stalling and counting. "Five."

She held on to the sink. "Dear Lord. Please don't tell me he has a motorcycle."

"He doesn't."

"Well, that's good to know."

"Why? What difference would it make if he had a motor-cycle?"

"Kid, when you're a mother with daughters, you'll under-stand."

"Is the interrogation over?" I asked.

"Taylor, I'm just kind of in shock. He's not the kind of guy I would have picked for you."

I closed my eyes and told myself that she wasn't saying anything bad about him. It was true. He wasn't the kind of guy I would have seen myself with.

"After everything that…happened, and when you couldn't seem to get over it, I just thought you were never going to take the plunge. I'm not saying that it's a bad thing. I'm just saying be careful."

"I will."

"Okay. I can see that he makes you happy."

We both smiled.

"He does. Happier than I knew was possible."

"That's great, Kid. Really great." She gave me a soapy hug that made the back of my shirt damp, but I didn't mind.

"Speaking of love lives. Anything new to report?"

"No, and that is none of your business, young lady."

"Have you talked to Dad?"

"Last week. He's seeing someone new."

"What happened to Michelle?"

"No idea. We didn't talk long. He asked about you, and I said you had a boyfriend. He wasn't very happy."

"He doesn't get a say in my life."

"Kid, he is your father, even if he isn't in your life. You should call him. He'd want to know about the hearing." We'd managed to make it this far into the weekend without talking about it. I'd been hoping we'd make it all the way, but we hadn't.

"I don't want to talk about that."

"You're going to have to deal with it. He's not this monster you've built him up to be in your mind. Granted, he's one sick fuck, but he's just human." Mom didn't swear often, and when she did, I paid attention.

"I know, I know."

"You need to take care of your past before you can move on to your future. If you want a future with Hunter, you're going to have to deal with your past."

"Well, nearly eight years of therapy hasn't helped, so I'm not sure there's much hope," I said, snapping a little.

"Well, when therapy fails, there's love. You love him, don't you?"

"Yeah."

"Love heals all wounds."

"When did you get so philosophical?"

"I just started taking a poetry class at the library."

"Really?"

Mom wasn't one to try new things, so that was huge. We talked about that while Hunter and Tawny sang drinking songs. Apparently, he knew a lot of them.

"I have many talents you are not even aware of, Missy girl," he said.

"What is with the nickname? I've been meaning to ask," Mom said.

"Oh, it's not a very interesting story," I said. For some reason, I didn't want him to tell it.

"That means that it is. Spill, Hunter," Tawny said.

"It's nothing special. Just a little mistake I made when we first met."

"Lame," Tawny said.

"Your father used to call me Sharon," Mom said.

"What?" Tawny and I said at the same time.

"It's an equally dumb story. We met at a party and for some reason he was convinced my name was Sharon. It wasn't until our third date when I set him straight."

Tawny and I laughed after a stunned silence.

"What? I was nervous. He was my first boyfriend."

I looked at Hunter. You just never knew.

Mom made us take a few pictures, mostly of Hunter pretending to teach me to play guitar. She liked action shots. None of those lame posed things where people smiled like they were in pain. Hunter kept whispering innuendos in my ear, so every smile and laugh was genuine.

"Okay, well, we have to get back. We both have tests to study for," I said after the millionth flash. I'd been slacking lately, because canoodling was much more fun than anything my textbooks had to offer. I needed to get my ass in gear if I wanted to keep my GPA high enough to get into Phi Beta Kappa.

"I should probably shove off, too," Tawny said, getting up to give Mom a hug.

"It was so nice of you to have me, Blaire," Hunter said.

"I hope to see you again, Hunter. Please be careful with my baby girl," she said as I hugged her. *Ugh.*

"I will treasure her."

"You'd better," Mom said, sort of puffing herself up. She

didn't mess around. Hunter leaned forward and kissed her on the cheek.

"Yes, ma'am."

On Wednesday, it was my turn to be nervous and jittery. It seemed that whenever Hunter and I were together, at least one of us was trying to help the other not freak out. At least we were balanced that way.

I had a nightmare the night before the scheduled meeting with Mr. Woodward, the assistant district attorney. I woke to find myself biting Hunter's shoulder and him trying to get me to let go. Luckily, I hadn't broken the skin.

"It's okay, Miss. I'm a big boy. I can handle it. I wish I could be there with you."

"I have to do this on my own."

"I know. I'm not trying to say that you can't. I just want to be there." He rubbed my shoulders, and I could almost hear him counting to five. "I got you a little something. No, it didn't cost me a lot. I kind of made it." He handed me a paper bag with another little box in it.

"More jewelry?"

"Just one little thing."

I opened the little cardboard box to find a necklace with several charms on it, all in silver. A number seven, a four-leaf clover, a scarab beetle, a horseshoe and a star.

"I just wanted you to have some luck with you. Some of my luck." The necklace was so long I was able to put it over my head without undoing the clasp. I looked at it in the mirror, fingering the charms.

"Thanks, baby. I love it," I said.

"You do?"

"I do. Did you say that you made it?"

"I had to go to that bead store in downtown Bangor and have the woman help me find the charms. There were fifty million of them, by the way. But you're worth it."

"Thanks."

He held me for a moment and I breathed him in, twisting the necklace around my finger. I wasn't ready, not even for the meeting. I associated Mr. Woodward with a really bad and dark time in my life that I wished I could bury far behind me. I wanted to move forward with Hunter, not go backward.

He kissed my forehead and left, giving me a moment to myself. I stared in the mirror, watching the necklace sparkle. Such a thoughtful boy. I smoothed my hair back and took a breath. I wasn't ready, but I'd have to be. Hunter had wanted to come with me, but I insisted on going alone. It was stupid for him to skip class just to be my bodyguard.

I had to leave soon or else I'd be late. With one last look, I grabbed my purse and keys and walked into the living room to find Hunter and Renee deep in conversation. Probably about me.

"I'm going," I said.

"Good luck," Renee said.

"I've got some," I said, showing her the necklace.

"Dude, I've got to get you to influence Paul. I can't remember the last sparkly thing he bought me."

"I'll do my best," Hunter said, taking my hand to walk me to my car.

"Call me when you're done. I'll have my phone on, just in case. I wish you would let me come with you."

"I can't lean on you for everything."

"You kept yourself propped up for nearly twenty years, so I think you can handle it."

"I hope so."

He gave me a soft kiss and flicked at my necklace.

"Good luck, Miss."

"Love you."

"Love you, too. More than the stars."

"Same here."

I got one more kiss, and then I was alone. I watched him walk away and wave before I started the car. The drive to Mr. Woodward's office in Waterville felt both too long and too short. I pulled in front of his office and I had a flashback of coming here with my mother and Tawny. Not good.

I wrapped Hunter's necklace around my hand and saw that Tawny's car was already there. I sent her a quick text saying that I was as well and went through the front door. Mr. Woodward's office used to be a house, but it had been split into offices. It was pretty swanky, with lush burgundy carpeting and gorgeous lighting that looked like old-time lanterns. Still, the memory of that office made my stomach twist.

His office was on the second floor, so I climbed the oak stairs and saw that his door was open and that Tawny was already inside. I forced my feet to walk forward, one step at a time, until I was inside the office.

"Taylor, it's nice to see you again. How have you been? Your sister has just been filling me in on your doings."

It was a good thing Mr. Woodward looked like a sweet grandpa and liked to chatter to fill awkward silence. I'd had a lot of those with him all those years ago.

"I'm good." He waited for more, but that was all he was going to get. It was all I could do to sit in the chair he offered me and not run away and call Hunter and tell him to come get me.

"Okay, well, I'm sure you know by now that Travis Moore is up for parole. There will be a hearing next Thursday, and you are both welcome to be there to give a statement. I'm so sorry we didn't notify you sooner. It was a clerical oversight that has since been remedied." *Bullshit, bullshit, bullshit.*

"What about other people coming with us to be in the courtroom?" Tawny said. I reached for her hand and gave it a little squeeze. She had been our microphone back then as well.

"Just immediate family. Your mother, your father. Of course, I'll be there."

"What about her fiancé?" Tawny said.

"You're engaged?"

I just nodded and switched my ring from right to left hand, hoping he didn't notice. I held my hand up as soon as the ring was safely on my finger.

"Well, congratulations! That's wonderful. Who is the lucky fellow?"

I cleared my throat to steer him back toward our question. "Can he be with me?"

"Oh, I'm so sorry. Immediate family only."

Fuck. So much for the fake engagement.

"So I just wanted to go over a few things about the hearing and start you getting prepared to speak."

With that, I tuned him out. Tawny stayed aware, sitting forward and nodding, engaging and asking questions. He gave us packets of information that I hoped I'd be able to read. I looked out the window at the tree outside. It was a lot taller than it had been when I'd been in this office last. Tawny had to pinch me to tell me it was time to go.

"If you have any questions, please call me. And just remember, even if he's released early, he will still be on the Sex Offender Registry for the rest of his life. That means he'll be under extreme scrutiny, so there is nothing for you to worry about, okay?" Easy for him to say.

"If that's all, I'll see you next Thursday. Have a good afternoon, ladies."

We both shook his hand and exited, Tawny keeping her hand on my back.

"Stairs," she said, as if I needed reminding.

"I've got it."

"I know."

We walked out of the office, and I finally felt like I could breathe.

"You okay? I thought I lost you again."

"I zoned."

"I noticed."

"Did you get everything?"

"More or less. I'll call you when you're not in zombie mode and we'll discuss. Okay?"

"Works for me." She handed me my half of the packet, which included a breakdown of court proceedings and victims' rights.

We walked back to our separate cars, and I found that someone was leaning against mine.

"What the hell are you doing here?" Hunter looked up, my e-reader in his hand.

"Took a cab. I knew you wouldn't let me come, so I decided to do it without telling you. How are you doing?"

Well, I was vertical and I hadn't thrown up or passed out. That was something. I shrugged one shoulder.

"Thanks for coming," Tawny said, giving him a one-armed hug. He didn't go for me right away, as if sensing I didn't want to be touched at the moment.

"Anytime. Gotta do right by my girl. Hey, do you have my number? You know, just in case Taylor forgets to tell me about things like this?"

"Hello? Standing right here," I said.

"Sure."

They exchanged numbers, and Tawny gave me a hug before hopping in her car and saying she'd see me next week. *Joy.*

"Are you happy to see me?" he said.

"Yes and no. I'm mad at you for missing class, but not mad because it was a very sweet thing to do."

"I can settle for that. Can I touch you?"

I nodded and he gave me a gentle hug, but he refrained from kissing me.

"How was it?"

"It wasn't as bad as I thought it would be. I checked out for most of it. Tawny took notes."

"I'm sure she did. You ready to go home?"

"Yeah." I let him drive because my brain was too tired to drive and think at the same time.

"You hungry?"

"Not really."

"You haven't eaten much today. Why don't we stop somewhere?"

"There's a diner one exit up that has PB and J on the adult menu," I said.

"This is a place we need to visit."

So we did.

I ordered a PB and J with strawberries, and he got banana in his. Hunter turned out to be a master of talking about things that weren't important but interesting enough to keep my mind occupied. He probably learned it from Hope, or his mother, or both.

We shared a dark chocolate shake, with two straws and everything.

"I feel like I should be saying you look swell," he said.

I batted my eyelashes. "Golly gee, Hunter. That sure is sweet of you."

"*Swell* is a cool word. We need to bring it back."

"We should. Let's do it."

"I shall put it in a song."

"And I will applaud that song."

"You are very good at applauding."

I nodded seriously. "It's one of my talents."

I put the meeting with Mr. Woodward to the back of my mind, along with all the other scary things. No doubt they were going to get me in the middle of the night anyway. I didn't want that infringing on my Hunter time.

We drove back to campus, and I fell asleep in the car. When I woke, I was in my bed with Hunter, pj's on, with him lying next to me, lamp on, e-reader in hand.

"What are you so enthralled with?" I said.

"I have to see who she's going to end up with."

"There are still more books."

"There are? Damn. I was hoping we could put this baby to bed."

"You are so weird."

"Swell. I'm swell."

"Oh, right."

He put down my e-reader, making sure it was safe back in the case.

"May I kiss you now? My swell lips have been very lonely." He pouted, making me laugh.

"I think so." I puckered, and we shared a fish-faced kiss.

We switched to regular kissing, and Hunter ran his hands under my shirt. I wasn't wearing a bra.

"Bad boy."

"Why would I let something get in my way of these?" He gave one a little squeeze. I gasped and smacked his hand.

"Two more days." He buried his face into my chest.

"Okay, okay."

I rubbed his head, massaging my fingers in circles. His eyes closed and he hummed. It sounded like "Home" by Phillip Phillips, only a slow and sexy version. I glanced at the clock and saw that it was only nine-thirty.

"The girls gave us another night alone."

"They're so sweet."

"I know. I'm going to miss them when we move out," he said.

"We're not moving out."

"Not this second. But soon."

"I'm not doing this with you now." I took my hands away from his head. He made a grumpy noise in protest.

"That wasn't very swell of me to do, considering the day you had. I'm sorry."

"No, I am, too. I just freak out whenever money is mentioned. It's some sort of weird reflex."

"Why don't you want me to rent us an apartment?"

"Because I think things should be as fair as we can make them. You renting us an apartment makes me feel like a mooch. Like I need you to take care of me."

He seemed to think about that for a moment. "You don't need me to take care of you, but I like spending money on you. The apartment would be a gift. Something for us to share. You give me more than money could ever buy. You love me. Fucked up, tattooed, badass, swell me."

"I wish it were that easy."

"Let's shelve that discussion for another time, shall we?"

"Sure."

We shelved talking, too, and resorted to lots of kissing. I could never get tired of kissing Hunter. He was very good with his mouth.

We stayed up late talking about the pros and cons of dating a vampire and other words that had lost their popularity since 1952.

I somehow slept through the night sans nightmares.

"Thanks," I said as I got out of bed.

"You're welcome?"

"I didn't have any nightmares."

"No, you didn't. Neither did I."

"You haven't had one for a while."

"It's because I have my good luck charm with me all the time." I looked down at the necklace he'd given me the day before. It was all twisted up in my hair. Then I noticed the shirt I was wearing. It was one of his, which I knew last night, but it had a caption on it.

"Does this shirt seriously say, 'Everything's Bigger in Texas'?"

"Why yes it does." I shook my head as I headed for the coffeepot.

I somehow got through a round of early semester tests, even with Hunter distracting me and the whole parole hearing drama.

Tawny and I had nightly chats, reading what we were preparing to say to each other and changing and modifying. I had to take a lot of cursing out of mine. Hunter was all for me leaving it in. Or replacing every curse word with *swell*.

Hunter was there for me every step of the way, but he'd been acting strange. I kept catching him on the phone, and he'd quickly hang up when I came into the room. I'd also caught him having several powwows with the roommates and their men. I'd even caught him having a little chat with Megan when I'd had her over for a girl's spa night, where we'd spent more time online looking at wedding stuff and cheap apartment furniture than doing our nails or deep conditioning our hair.

Then there were the times when he said he was getting extra hours at the library, but I knew for a fact that he wasn't there. I'd become friends with one of the other workers, Ashley, and when he said he was there, I'd text her and she'd confirm or deny since she worked so many hours. He was never there when he said he was.

Something was up with him, and I was determined to find out what it was. Naturally, I pretended that I didn't notice anything and tried to eavesdrop as much as I could. He seemed to be on to me, because I got next to nothing.

I wasn't in top eavesdropping form anyway. I figured after the hearing I'd have plenty of chances. I didn't think about what was going to happen if he got parole. That wasn't an option.

"You don't have to be scared of him anymore," Hunter said.

"I can't help it. I just feel so vulnerable." He tightened his arms around me. "You know, Tawny was going to get me shooting lessons for Christmas. That was before I knew about…about your family."

"I have no problem with people owning guns," he said, propping his chin on my shoulder. "I mean, just about everyone in Texas has one. If it would help you feel safer, I'd be okay with it. As long as you learned to use it properly."

"Are you sure?"

"Baby, I want you to feel safe. That's my top priority. If you want a tank, I'll find a cheap one on the internet for you."

"Can we paint it?"

"We'll paint it whatever color you want." He kissed my nose. "Do you think you could eat a little?"

We'd had pasta for dinner, but I couldn't stomach any of it. I shook my head.

"Maybe tomorrow. I kind of wish I could just get wasted right now so I wouldn't have to think about it."

"Then don't think about it."

"Easy for you to say." I'd been increasingly snappy with him, but he didn't seem to care.

"I could help you forget." There was that cocky smile.

"I'm not feeling very sexy right now."

He got off his bed and put his hand on the chair to stop it spinning. "You're always sexy. And swell."

"I don't feel swell, either. How am I going to do this?"

"You will. Easy as that." He gave me a quick kiss.

"I wish you could be there with me."

"If you'd let me take you to the town courthouse, we could have been married by now."

When Hunter had heard that only direct family could be in the courtroom, he'd immediately asked if I wanted to hop down to the courthouse and get a marriage license. I'd thought he'd lost his mind or he was joking.

"You were not serious about that."

"Maybe I was."

"We're not getting married. My mother would have a coronary."

"Hope probably would, too. You know she's already planning our wedding, right?"

"What?"

"It's this thing she does. She likes to plan. Almost as much as Christmas and pie."

"How about a Christmas wedding with pie as the wedding cake?"

"That would blow her mind."

"Hunter."

"Yes, baby?"

"I can't do it."

"Yes, you can. Just count to five."

"Like you do when you're nervous?"

"Just like that. It's a technique my therapist taught me."

"How come you got all the good ones?" I said.

He shrugged. "Who needs therapy when you've got me?" That made me smile, and he pulled me into his arms, humming and rocking us back and forth. "You ready for bed?"

"Dude, it's only ten," I said.

"I know, but you need your sleep."

"I'm not tired."

"Take off your shirt."

"Uh, no. I don't think that's going to help."

"I don't want to make whoopee with you. I'm just going to give you a massage."

Well, that sounded lovely. He certainly had talented hands. Thinking about them rubbing all over my bare back gave me goose bumps.

I flopped onto my stomach and pulled my shirt over my head. He grabbed my favorite cinnamon lotion (because it smelled like him) and gave me a mind-blowing massage. My body turned into putty in his hands, and I made some sounds that I normally only made when we were doing other kinds of intimate things.

"Why are you good at everything?" I mumbled.

"Not everything. I'm terrible at crossword puzzles. And I have never been able to keep a goldfish alive to save my life.

And...um...Oh! I had a speech problem until I was seven. I couldn't say the letter *L*."

"I don't think we can be together anymore. You're a loser."

"I'd rather be your loser than some other girl's winner."

"You know I was being sarcastic."

"Yes, I do." He gave my shoulder a kiss.

"Now, now."

"I know. But your skin is just so irresistible. My lips are drawn to it. Do you want to go over your letter again?" He knew what the answer to that was.

"No. Just keep massaging."

"Yes, ma'am."

He kept going until my muscles let go of their tension and my eyes closed. I drifted off and only awoke when Hunter climbed in beside me and pulled me in to his bare chest.

CHAPTER 28

I woke abruptly the next morning at five. Hunter was sacked out beside me and grumbled in his sleep when I moved. I had a moment of not being able to breathe, like something was pressing against me.

I'd expected a panic attack. I'd had more than I could count in my lifetime. I knew I had some antianxiety meds somewhere, but they weren't going to do any good at this point, since they took a while to build up in your system. Anything else I could have taken would have made me looped out. So I just stayed where I was, focusing on Hunter's arms and the fact that no, I was not, in fact, dying.

I stared at Hunter. His eyes jumped behind his eyelids. For a guy, he had really thick eyelashes. He looked so sweet when he slept, as long as he wasn't having a nightmare. Every now and then, if he was sleeping really deeply, he'd snore a little.

My love for him settled over me like a blanket fresh from the dryer on a chilly winter night. The tight feeling went away as I stepped into our bubble. It was harder this time, but I somehow got there. Hunter frowned in his sleep and muttered something.

I kissed his nose and lay back down, turning my head so I could look at him. He was pretty damn swell.

I started freaking out again when Hunter tried to make me eat some dry toast and ginger ale.

"I'm not going to force you, but you're going to regret it if you don't." I'd never seen him so stern, so I munched a few bites of toast and drank some of the ginger ale. Darah, Mase and Renee all hugged me and wished me well as they went off to their classes and such for the day. I'd caved and with Hunter's help had told them an abbreviated version of the story. Paul had a cold, so he'd stayed at his place for the night, but he texted me and so did Megan.

If I wouldn't have been so stressed, my heart would have warmed at all the people who were supporting me.

I'd lost the battle to drive, so Hunter was also skipping classes to drive me. I hadn't fought hard on that one. The parole board might make their decision right after the hearing, so I probably wouldn't be in any shape to drive back to campus in any case.

The hearing was scheduled for ten, but I was ready to go at eight-thirty. Hunter got out his guitar and let me make requests, switching from one song to the other, even in the middle. It was a weird mash-up, kind of like flipping radio stations. It amused me for some of the time, but when my legs started twitching so much I couldn't sit down, Hunter grabbed our coats and pushed me outside for a walk across campus. He'd also suggested doing some more blow paintings, but I couldn't sit still long enough to even get the stuff set up. I'd probably just end up using all black and making a huge mess anyway.

The leaves were starting to blush from green to orange and red and yellow. I loved campus in the fall. Even the air tasted better in the fall. We walked slowly, and he kept kicking pinecones in my way so I could crunch them under my feet.

Hunter was uncharacteristically silent during our walk, which was both helpful and not helpful. On the one hand, he wasn't chattering at me like some people would have, trying to fill my head with crap so I wouldn't think about other crap, but, on the other, I could only focus on the bad crap without his voice distracting me.

We passed other students on their way to and from class and dorms and work and sports practices. Their lives seemed so simple. Not for the first time, I wished I could jump into someone else's life. Or maybe at least I could have multiple personalities, so at least I could pretend I was having another life.

"What are you thinking about?" I asked Hunter.

"You."

"What about me?"

"Specifically? That look on your face when you wake up in the morning and see that I'm next to you. It's my second favorite after that look when I make you come."

"Hunter!" I smacked him and glanced around to make sure no one had overheard.

"Baby, no one is paying attention to anyone but themselves. I could throw you down right here right now and most people would just walk right by. You wanna give it a shot? I can prove it to you." He gave me that smirk that I hadn't seen in several hours. It made me feel warm inside.

"I don't want to get arrested for public fornication, thank

you very much. I've had enough time in a courtroom to last me a lifetime."

"I'm sorry. I was trying to avoid making you think about that."

"Hunter, everything makes me think about that."

"You wouldn't be thinking about it if we were hay rolling, I bet."

"Probably not. I don't really think about much of anything when we're doing that."

"That is my goal."

"You're very good at it."

"Why, thank you, Missy."

We walked some more until we had to turn back.

"Do you have everything?" Hunter said as I packed my purse. I had my statement, along with at least five copies stashed in various pockets so I'd have a backup. Hunter also had several copies stashed in his pockets. He'd picked out the pencil skirt and cappuccino-colored sweater and boots I was wearing. He'd dressed nice as well—a show of solidarity.

"Here," he said, handing me his iPod when we got into his car. "Go to Missy's playlist." I plugged the player into his speakers and hit play.

"Honey, Come Home" filled the car, but it wasn't The Head and the Heart singing. It was Hunter. The sound quality wasn't great, but I didn't care. I sat still and silent as I heard his voice cradle the song. When it ended, he paused the playlist.

"Is that what you've been doing when you're supposed to be working?"

"Partly. There's a recording studio in Bangor that rents out by the hour. It's something I've wanted to do for a while, but I finally found a reason to do it."

I reached for his hand and kissed the back of it. Words couldn't really express how I felt.

"So you want to hear more?"

"How much more is there?"

"Plenty. I picked songs that made me think of you."

"Uh-oh." I imagined all the possibilities, shuddering.

"Hit Play and find out," he said, his voice daring me. I accepted that challenge.

The second song was "I Won't Give Up" by Jason Mraz, followed by "She's So Mean" by Matchbox Twenty. That one made me laugh. The rest of the songs were an eclectic mix: some pop, some country, some folk. From Rihanna's "Umbrella" to "Tip of My Tongue" by The Civil Wars to "Ours" by Taylor Swift.

"This is the last song," he said as he turned onto the Waterville exit.

It was the song he'd written for me. He'd slowed it down and changed some of the lyrics so they were sweeter. The song ended as he pulled into the courthouse parking lot. What timing. The playlist didn't end, and Hunter's voice came on, minus the guitar.

"I love you, Missy girl. Even if I can't be with you, know that I'm here. So, that's it. More than the stars, Taylor. More than the stars."

"More than the stars," I said, leaning over and giving him a kiss.

It was time to face the darkness.

CHAPTER 29

We beat Tawny to the hearing, but my mom was there. She grabbed me and pulled me into a hug before I could even say anything.

"Thank you for coming, Hunter. You don't know how good it makes me feel to know that she has someone to support her when I can't be there."

"Thank you, Blaire."

Mom checked her watch. "I swear, your sister would be late to her own funeral." Two seconds later, Tawny came dashing in, hopping on one foot so she could adjust her heel that had slipped off.

"I'm here, I'm here. You all know I'm always late."

"We do," Mom and I said.

There were other people milling around, and I saw Mr. Woodward. There was a man talking with him, and I clutched Hunter's hand tighter.

"Mom? Did you invite him?"

"Your father has every right to be here, Kid."

Dad looked up and met my eyes. I hadn't seen him in almost

a year. He looked older, wearier. I found my features in his face, and it was shocking how much I looked like him. I'd never noticed how much.

"That's your dad?" Hunter whispered in my ear.

"Yeah."

"You have his nose."

"I'm aware."

Dad walked over slowly, as if he couldn't believe I was here. He was all dressed up in a snappy suit. I hadn't seen him in a suit in years and years.

"Hey, Kid."

"Hey, Dad." He was the first one in our family to start calling me that. Hunter tried to let go of my hand, but I wouldn't let him.

"You look so grown up."

"Yeah, that's bound to happen."

"How are you? I've tried calling, but—" He shrugged.

"I've been busy with school and stuff."

"Hey, Dad," Tawny said, coming and giving him a hug. They had a much closer relationship and talked on a regular basis.

"Hey, Tawn. You doing okay?"

"I just want to get this over with."

"You're going to do great. Both of you." He looked back at me, and I saw his eyes flick over Hunter. Damn, I was going to have to introduce them.

"Dad, this is Hunter. Hunter, Dad."

They shook hands and exchanged the normal dad-meets-boyfriend stuff. It was about to get awkward when Mr. Woodward said they were going to seat us.

"More than the stars," Hunter said, giving me a kiss on the forehead. "I'll be waiting. Give him hell."

"I will."

Our hands parted and I had to turn to walk away from him. I took one last look over my shoulder, holding up the necklace he'd given me to show him that he was coming with me, even if he couldn't physically be there.

Walking into the courthouse was like stepping through the looking glass into another space and time. I felt twelve again, only that time I'd been holding my mother's hand in one of mine and my father's in the other.

Tawny walked behind me this time, Mom in front and Dad bringing up the rear.

The wooden benches were the same; the long, tall frosted windows were the same. The creak in the ancient floor was the same.

I saw Travis's mother, brother and stepfather already seated on his side of the courtroom, along with a girl I didn't recognize. His lawyer was there, but not Travis. Five people were seated in the jury box, so that must be the parole board.

There were other people there, and I assumed they were also part of the proceedings. A gentle hum of talking filled the room, but it might as well have been yelling. Tawny had to poke at me to get me to keep walking. I sat down on the wooden bench that had probably supported thousands of butts in its lifetime. I tried to think, but my head was blank. Tawny sat next to me and took my hand, digging her nail into my palm.

"Hey," she said.

"I'm here."

"Good. He's nothing. He can't hurt you or me. He's never going to hurt anyone again, understand? You just have to tell them our story."

"Okay."

A side door opened, and Travis came in. I heard a sharp intake of breath from Tawny. Or maybe it was me. The man who walked into the courtroom wasn't the same teenage boy who had nearly raped me and my sister. This man was older, thinner, and had a hollow, unhealthy look to him. He looked much dirtier, too. Travis had always been well-manscaped back then.

The warden announced that the hearing was about to start, and I braced myself. I knew it was going to be a long time before we were allowed to speak. Part of me wished they had let us sit outside, brought us in to speak and then took us out again.

Travis turned his head and looked at me. I met his eyes and held them. Well, one thing hadn't changed. There was still nothing behind them. Just emptiness. The same emptiness I'd seen that night that felt like yesterday and thousands of years ago at once.

With that, I checked out of the courtroom. There were interviews with Travis's family, with them talking about how he was sorry for what he had done and he had a plan for his life and so forth. The strange girl turned out to be his girlfriend, who cried and carried on about God knows what. His lawyer spoke, and the superintendent of the prison spoke, and it was all talking, talking, talking.

I heard none of it.

I was thinking about waking up in Hunter's arms. I was thinking about making wedding plans with Megan. I was thinking about dancing the night away with Darah and Renee. I was thinking about shopping with Tawny. I filled my head with beautiful things so the ugly things were pushed aside.

And then, it was time for us to speak. Tawny went first, and I tuned back in to listen.

"I don't have much to say, so I'm going to keep this short but not sweet. I don't do sweet. I haven't done sweet since this...animal, tried to have his way with me, and then when my baby sister saw us and tried to help me, he went after her. This person—I don't call him a man, because no man would ever do that to a woman—tried to rape me and then my baby sister. My *baby* sister. Think about that. He tried to rape a *child*. He doesn't deserve to get out early, no matter what he tells you. He's a proven liar and hasn't taken responsibility for his actions. Travis," she said, turning to stare directly at him, "from this day forward, for the rest of my life, I will never think of you again. You don't deserve space in my mind. I'm going to forget you, because you deserve to be forgotten. What was your name again? Thank you." She sat back down, and I could feel her shaking. I grabbed her hand, and she gave me a little hug.

"Your turn, Kid. Knock 'em dead."

I got to my feet and nearly stumbled trying to make my way around everyone's feet to get to the podium. Or was it a lectern? *Stop it, brain.* I unfolded my paper and cleared my throat. The words swam in front of me, and suddenly I couldn't read. I reached down and took hold of Hunter's necklace. I stared at each person on the parole board. Three women, two men. I had to make them understand.

More than the stars.

"When I was twelve, I was nearly raped by that man, Travis Moore. He told me he would kill me if I ever told. Well, I'm still alive and I'm telling you now. Travis Moore tried to rape me and my sister. While rape may not seem as serious a crime as murder, in a way he is a murderer. He killed the happy girl I once was." I paused and pulled out a photograph of me, taken when I was twelve. I had a huge grin on my face as my dad tickled me. Mom had snapped it only a few months before it had happened.

"Do you see this girl? She's gone. Travis killed her. When that girl died, a new one was born. An angry, bitter person who was afraid of every single man she ever saw. Afraid that around every corner an attacker lurked. Afraid to give my heart to anyone for fear that they would hurt me. I have spent countless hours in therapy and broken probably thousands of dollars of china, furniture and a computer because of that thing there. But you know what? I'm not afraid of you anymore. You don't haunt my dreams." I was shaking, but I turned to face Travis, just like Tawny.

"I've found someone to love me, despite becoming that angry, bitter girl. He reminds me that I am the girl I once was, and together, he's helping me heal what you broke on that night. Like Tawny, from this day forward, I will not think your name, I will not picture your face and I will erase you from my life. You no longer have any power over me. You no longer have any power over my ability to love. You know what? Love is so much more powerful than hate. I used to hate you, but it's so much easier to love. And that's something you will never understand." His empty eyes stared into me, but I didn't care. A strange sort of power had taken over me, and I nearly smiled at him.

"I hope that by sharing my story, I can give you a window into what this person is really like. Would you let someone free who had done this to your daughters? Your sisters? Your nieces? Consider if I were your daughter. What would you do? I ask you to consider this as you make your decision. Thank you."

The room was silent, except for a cough and an "excuse me" from Travis's lawyer.

"You rocked it hard, Kid," Tawny said.

I floated on a cloud of victory for the rest of the hearing. I even glanced at him a few times, but he didn't meet my eyes again. *Suck on that.*

The board went out to deliberate, but they didn't call it that. We were all excused, and I went for the door as fast as I could. I wanted to see Hunter. What met me wasn't just Hunter. It was Hunter and Megan and Darah and Renee and Paul and Mase.

"What are you doing here?" I said, stopping in my tracks.

"We're here to support you, Missy. Why else would we be here?" Hunter held his arms open, and I flung myself into them.

"I freaking love you, Hunter Aaron Zaccadelli."

"I love you, too, Taylor Elizabeth Caldwell."

I breathed him in and never wanted to let him go. I finally pulled away but kept both of his hands in mine. "I can't believe you're here."

"You're writing me a note so I can get out of lab, by the way," Renee said. "I'm missing castrating a rat for this." She sounded upset.

"You're welcome?"

"Be nice, Ne," Paul said, his voice all full of mucus. He looked like shit and probably felt worse, but he was here.

"What? I was looking forward to that lab. But you're more important, Tay," Renee said.

"Don't mind her," Darah said.

"I don't normally."

"Some of your friends, Taylor?" Mom said.

"Yeah, you met Hunter, and this is Darah and Renee and Paul and Hunter's cousin, Mase. And you already know Megan." They'd met when I'd brought her home to hang out one weekend so I could get off campus and she could get away from the dudes in her apartment.

"Hey, Blaire," Megan said, giving her a hug. "Jake would have been here, but he had an exam he couldn't get out of. He tried really hard."

"That's okay. It's more than enough that you're here," I said.

"Nice to see you again. It's been a while," Mom said.

I wanted to tell Mom about Meg's engagement, but I didn't have the proper venue. Hunter put his arms around me from behind and his chin on my head.

"So are you done?" Renee said.

"Yes. I got up and talked and I didn't pass out. I just hope they believe me."

"She was awesome," Tawny said.

"So were you," I said.

Hunter let go of me so I could give her a hug, which turned into me hugging everyone and then us all having a huge group hug that made us all laugh. I really wanted to cry instead. They were all here for me and my family. I hadn't even asked them, and they'd come running. Somehow, even though I was bitter and angry, these people had decided I was worthy of their love. Either they were willing to look past all that, or maybe I wasn't as fucked up as I thought.

Or maybe it was a bit of both.

"So how long are they going to take to decide?" Paul said.

"No idea. I guess we just wait and see," I said.

"Why don't we go down the hall? There's a waiting room if you all want to make yourselves comfortable," Mr. Woodward said, subtly telling us to get the hell out of the hallway.

We all went to the waiting room, and it was like the day had somehow turned into a party. I had to introduce Dad to everyone, and I even let him give me a hug and kiss on the cheek.

"I'm so proud of you," he said.

"Thanks, Dad."

"You should come down and see me on your break. I've got a great little nook that would be great to read in. You could bring Hunter, if you wanted." I looked up to tell him that I was busy, and that I'd consider it, but his face was so hopeful that I couldn't.

"Sure, Dad. It's a plan."

"I love you, Kid."

"Love you, too." I hadn't said those words to my father in at least five years. They felt right.

We spent the next two hours waiting and talking. We were all starving but didn't think it would be appropriate to bring in food. We did agree that afterward we were all going to that diner I'd been to with Hunter and pancakes were in order. No matter what happened.

In all honesty, when I really thought about it, I didn't care if they let him out. He couldn't hurt me anymore. It was a revelation that had taken so many years but only a moment to come to. I'd made my secret and *him* into this big impossible thing I could never conquer.

But I'd conquered it. I was done being a victim. It was time for me to take charge and live my life instead of letting something that had happened to me lead it for me. So many people had told me the same thing, hundreds of times. It was something I had to learn for myself.

A clerk finally came and told us that they were ready.

When we walked back into the courtroom for the decision, I held my head high and kept a smile on my face. Outside that room was a whole wonderful world I couldn't wait to be a part of again. And pancakes. I really wanted some pancakes.

I held Tawny's hand as we waited for the board to announce its decision. One of the board members, a woman with sleek black hair and a stern set of glasses, got up and I held my breath.

CHAPTER 30

"Parole is denied until your sentence expiration date." The words rang loudly in the big room. I let out an involuntary noise of joy, and I wasn't the only one. I heard noises of despair from his family, and a wail from the girlfriend. I watched his shoulders slump just a little as his lawyer whispered in his ear. He nodded.

The board member handed a piece of paper to the warden and he passed it to his lawyer. There was more talk about appeals and so forth, but I didn't care. He was going to be in jail for two more years. I took one last look at Travis as we filed out of the courtroom. He didn't turn, and I knew that would be the last time I ever saw him.

My family cleared out as quickly as we could, thanking Mr. Woodward. He said he'd be in touch if there were any changes.

"I don't think you have anything to worry about," Mr. Woodward said as we walked back to the waiting room. "Both of you were the difference. He could say he'd found Jesus all he wanted, but it was you who showed who he really was."

"What?" I didn't know what he was talking about.

"Oh, did you tune out for that part?" Tawny said. "He said he'd found the Lord and become a Christian. Sick bastard."

"I don't think God can help him," Mr. Woodward said.

"I should hope not," she said.

We shook Mr. Woodward's hand and went to give the crew the good news.

"Parole denied," Tawny and I said at the same time to a round of cheers. Hunter swept me up in his arms and spun me around. It seemed like a strange thing to cheer, but we didn't care. It was like UMaine had won a hockey game against the University of New Hampshire.

"I'm so glad that's over," I said to Hunter.

"Me, too. Now we can start our life."

"We haven't started yet? What have we been doing all this time?"

"Just rolling in the hay."

"Bales and bales of it."

Life was both the same and different after the hearing. It was the same because I spent every night with Hunter, and I went to class and hung out with the girls and did more blow paintings and read more vampire smut. It was different because it was easier to laugh. Easier to smile. Easier to sleep. Everything was easier. I didn't have to try to get into that safe bubble anymore. I was there all the time.

"Hey, you want to go somewhere with me?" Hunter said on the second Saturday morning after the hearing.

"Why not? As long as you're not taking me to a place to hook up, I'm in."

"You're such a liar."

"Takes one to know one, Mr. Secret. I know you've been up to something."

"I know you know. Come on."

He pulled me to my feet. We'd been cuddling on the couch and watching mindless reality TV. Everyone else was MIA, which was unusual for a Saturday morning.

I didn't bother asking where we were going. I was getting used to surprises, or I was getting less curious about them. Hunter drove away from campus and headed toward Bangor, toward downtown. He turned onto a side street full of beautiful houses and pulled up in front of one that wasn't as impressive as the others but was cute. Yellow, with white trim and a little porch. It was adorable. There was another car in the driveway, a BMW that I recognized.

"Is that Joe's car?"

"I thought you should meet him."

"Why are we meeting him here?"

"You'll see." We got out of the car and walked up to the house. "We can go in. We're expected." He pushed the front door open, and I was bombarded with, "Surprise!"

"What the hell?" They were all here: Darah, Mase, Renee, Paul, Dev, Sean, Megan and Jake. And someone else I didn't recognize but who had to be Joe.

"It's not my birthday," I said. It wasn't for another few weeks.

"Not yet," Hunter said. "Taylor, this is Joe. Joe, this is Taylor."

Joe was a towering presence, with dark chocolate skin and a suit that was probably made by an Italian designer, and a stern face to match. He looked every bit a lawyer.

"It's nice to meet you, Miss Caldwell."

"He's going to call you that, just so you know. Joe's very formal that way, which is ironic considering he forces me to call him Joe," Hunter said. Joe cleared his throat as a response.

"Okay, so someone's got to tell me what we're doing here," I said.

Everyone looked at each other, and it hit me like three million lightbulbs all going on at once.

"I swear to God, Hunter if you bought me a house, I am going to kill you. Slowly and unpleasantly. We're doing a torture segment in History 226, and I know several ways this can happen."

"Missy, I didn't *buy* you a house for that exact reason."

Joe cleared his throat again.

"It's a rent to own. Hunter made a down payment and the first month's rent. I have the lease papers here for you to sign, as well as signature cards for a new joint checking account," Joe said, whipping out a stack of papers that he shoved in my face.

"Wait, what?"

"We're renting it. To own. Also, guess who else is renting it with us?" Hunter said.

"I give up," I said, on the verge of freaking out.

"We are!" Renee said, throwing some confetti on me. "All of us are moving in together!"

"You've got to be fucking kidding me," I said, looking around and waiting for someone to tell me they were just screwing with me.

"Nope. We worked it all out this week," Hunter said.

I opened my mouth to yell at him. To tell him that it was crazy. It would never work. Who *did* stuff like that? A mother. Fucking. House.

"I'll let you pay every other month's rent," Hunter said, as I tried to assemble my thoughts into coherent words. "All you have to do is sign."

"How much money is in that joint account?"

"Only two hundred dollars. So far. I'd put it all in there, but I knew you wouldn't let me."

"Hunter..."

"It's not a handout. It's building our foundation."

I looked around at all the faces. God, I loved them. So much it hurt to think about.

"Can I at least see it before I sign?"

Everyone breathed a sigh of relief, and Hunter took us on a tour, with Joe pointing out the best features like a real estate agent. Joe was exactly how I'd pictured. Calm, cool, all business. I made it my goal to get him to smile.

I fell in love with the house as soon as I saw the adorable kitchen with a little breakfast nook. There was a big living room where we could fit a gigantic couch and that already had the infamous recliner in it.

"We thought about moving all your stuff without telling you, but we figured you'd get pissed. Getting the recliner here was bad enough," Mase said. Oh, they knew me so well.

On the second floor there were two large bedrooms, each with its own small bathroom, and then on the third floor there was a master room with bath attached.

"This is ours," Hunter said, waving his arm around. The room was big and open and filled with light. There was only one thing in the room. It was a picture of Hunter and I that Mom had snapped the previous weekend, in a peacock-painted frame. It was in black-and-white. His head was bent over my shoulder and he was placing my fingers on the guitar strings and I was laughing at something he'd said.

I picked it up and looked at our happy faces.

"So what do you think?" Hunter said, standing in the bathroom doorway and watching me, his hand tapping a steady rhythm on his leg. *One, two, three, four, five.* "By the way, Stephen King lives down the street. If that helps my cause any."

My mouth dropped. "You're shitting me."

"Did you see the house with the cool iron fence? The huge reddish one?"

"Yeah."

"That's his."

I could live down the street from Stephen King. *Holy crappity fuck.*

"I also changed my major."

"You did?"

"Yep. We're now liberal arts students together. I'm now a proud member of the College of Education. Music, to be exact."

"You changed your major?"

"I decided that it was finally time to do what I wanted to do. Not what I thought I should do." My mind was already overflowing with everything that was happening all at once. I couldn't comprehend it all.

"I thought we could frame our blow paintings and put them here," he said, gesturing to one of the walls. "And a big bed, right here." He went around the rest of the room, and I imagined it. I imagined saying yes and moving in with Hunter next semester. I imagined it, and I decided that I wanted it to be real.

"Okay."

Hunter stopped talking about potential paint colors and stared at me.

"Okay?"

"Okay. But whatever money you put in that joint account, I'm putting in as much. Fifty-fifty. You're not going to be making much as a music teacher."

"You're right. Fifty-fifty," he agreed, coming and putting his arms around me.

"So, Mr. Zaccadelli."

"Yes, Miss Caldwell?"

"I guess I win the bet."

"I guess you do, Missy. I said I would leave the dorm. I

never said anything about you coming with me. So, the way I see it. I won."

"Loving you was the best mistake I ever made," I said.

He shook his head.

"Getting assigned to be your roommate was the luckiest thing that ever happened to me. I don't think I'll ever get so lucky again."

"Wanna bet?"

"No way."

★ ★ ★ ★ ★

ACKNOWLEDGMENTS

From the start, I knew this book was something different, but I had no idea the journey it would take me on.

First, to everyone who helped get the self-published edition of this book off the ground, including my parents, friends (Caroline, Colleen, Liz and Rachel), my former co-workers (my bank girls), my editor (Dani), my betas (Laura and Magan), the awesome book bloggers who took the time to review and rave about the book (too many of you to mention) and all the readers who were so passionate about the book from the beginning, THANK YOU. This book would be nothing without your passion for Hunter and Taylor's story. I love, love, love all of you, and when the zombie apocalypse happens, you are totally on my survival team.

Second, to the team who helped make this particular edition of the book possible. My agent, Kim, for taking a chance on me, and my editor from Harlequin HQN, Margo, for being so passionate about this book. To the rest of the team at HQN, including the copy editors (Robin, especially), the art team and everyone else who has worked hard to make this book the best it can be. You all are also on my zombie apocalypse survival team. How good are you with crossbows?

Third, to my musical inspirations, who will probably never know how much of an impact they've had on me, including The Head and the Heart, The Civil Wars and Taylor Swift, thanks for giving me music to write by.

Fourth, to YOU who are reading this. If you're just picking this book up for the first time, or if you've followed it from the original edition to now, I can't express how happy it makes me to be able to get up every day and do what I love.

~*More than the stars*~